SPL

TANYA ANNE CROSBY

PUBLISHER'S NOTE: This is a work of fiction. Names, characters, places, and incidents either are the product of the author's imagination or are used fictitiously. Any resemblance to actual persons, living or dead, business establishments, events, or locales is entirely coincidental.

© Cover Art by Cora Graphics

0 9 8 7 6 5 4 3 2 1

PRAISE FOR SPEAK NO EVIL & TELL NO LIES

[Speak No Evil is] dangerously addicting.

— SHERRILYN KENYON #1 NEW YORK TIMES BESTSELLING AUTHOR

Crosby serves up suspense, secrets and Southern scandal like no one else!

— HARLAN COBEN #1 NEW YORK TIMES BESTSELLING AUTHOR

Well written, almost Southern Gothic type, romantic suspense with nonstop thrills, chills, and mystery.

— READER

Crosby easily paints an eerie setting that on the outside seems beautiful, but lurking beneath the shadows is something sinister. Reminiscent of an old Hitchcock film, Crosby is able to give the reader the shadowy figure in the background, always close, but unseen by the hero and heroine.

— READER

SERIES BIBLIOGRAPHY

Speak No Evil

Tell No Lies

Leave No Trace

For my husband, Scott, who believes in me.

"When we try to pick out anything by itself, we find it hitched to everything else in the Universe."

— JOHN MUIR

PROLOGUE

Everything hinges on a moment.

Make a split-second decision or submit to a whim . . . and like tumbling dominoes, events will follow, good and bad. In a perfect world, if you make a decision with the best of intentions, only the best of results may come. But sometimes, bad people do the right thing. Sometimes good people do the wrong thing.

You could say a pen led to my death...

Just a simple pen, it sat, not on my desk, but on the kitchen counter, where I abandoned it after scribbling the word "tomatoes" on my grocery list. Sometime before making its way to that spot, it lay on my nightstand, where I set it down after devising a plan to reunite my three daughters. From there, it traveled to my office, where I penned a last codicil to my will. The guilty ruminations of an old woman, mostly. But then, I forgot . . . until I saw the pen and set in motion the chain of dominoes that brought me to this moment. . .

Only now, one breath shy of my last, do I understand that maybe this began long ago . . . in another moment . . . on a beach north of Folly. . . .

1

"I bet my share Sadie gets the house."

As bets went, it was nuts, of course, but Caroline knew Augusta's challenge had nothing to do with any anxiety over preserving "the house" for Aldridge posterity. Like Rhett Butler, Augusta didn't give a damn—at least not about the house.

"Why would Mother do that?" their youngest sister, Savannah, asked.

Augusta shrugged. "Why would Mother do anything?"

Up to this point, Savannah had spent her entire life defending their mother, and Augusta was bound to spend the rest of hers accusing. Caroline was tired of being in the middle. She tuned them out, peering through the window as the limo passed the torched remains of the house's Georgian predecessor. Destroyed during a kitchen fire the year after the "War of Northern Aggression" ended, the original house had escaped Sherman's wrath and one of the South's most pivotal battles only to meet its fate at the hands of a common grease fire. Construction on the "new big house" began the following year. Oyster Point Plantation was her family's legacy . . . along with a lifetime of dysfunction.

Why would Mother do anything?

The answers were buried this morning, along with their mother . . . all that remained now was the mythos: To the rest of the world, Florence Willodean Aldridge was a media darling, heir to one of city's oldest surviving newspapers. To Caroline and her sisters, she was . . .

Like the house.

There was the face people saw through the eye of a camera lens—the lovely Southern plantation that graced the covers of magazines like *Southern Living* and *House Beautiful* . . . where Spanish moss clung to stately trees like hoary curtains . . . and then there was the face that existed behind the red door, where the slow decay of the soul seeped into the fiber of the structure . . . sank down deep into the soil and surrounding marshlands, festered, and stank.

That was how Caroline perceived the smell of the marsh—that unmistakable sulfurous odor that heightened the closer they came to the house . . . that smell her mother never acknowledged though she compulsively planted and obsessed over sickly sweet magnolias and azaleas to mask the scent.

It was funny, Caroline thought, how you could look straight at the house, with its storybook gables, and actually smell the decay, and still your brain believed the beautiful lie. Even now, as the car wound its way up the private drive, through the swooning oaks and shawled magnolia trees, old wounds seemed to reopen and fester . . . as though in the presence of the house, only the memories that were born here had any real vitality.

Caroline thought she had braced herself, but she

wasn't quite prepared for the rush of emotion that assaulted her as the house's steeply pitched gabled roof and perfectly spaced dormers soared into view. Like the body lying inside the coffin they'd just abandoned, the old Victorian seemed to have aged on fast-forward —obvious even through the last thick coat of white paint. And yet there it stood . . . defying the years, a Southern matriarch in its own right, a polite hostess, entertaining callers. The two-story piazza, with more than two thousand square feet of wraparound porch —like the cemetery—was standing room only, leaving no doubt their mother was adored. People milled about, standing in the driveway, marveling over Flo's azaleas.

Caroline desperately wanted to feel what they felt, but instead of grief, all she could muster from the depths of her soul was something like regret.

The limo rolled to a crunchy halt over the gravel drive and Savannah reached over to give her hand a gentle squeeze. "Ready?"

The answer was no, but Caroline nodded anyway.

Savannah was the first to slide out of the car, brushing imaginary specks from her simple black dress while she stood waiting for Caroline. Augusta took the path of least resistance and scooted out of Savannah's door, her pink dress standing out like a sore thumb as she bolted up the front stairs and disappeared into a sea of black dresses and suits.

For a moment, Caroline lingered in the limo, envying Augusta's lack of regard for duty. She didn't have the same option. No matter how she'd felt about Flo, today she was the eldest surviving Aldridge and, fortified by centuries of Southern social graces, propriety ruled.

It was May. The azaleas were in full bloom. Red,

like the door, the shade reminded Caroline of her mother's lipstick, and for an instant, she almost expected Flo to appear on the doorstep with her Jackie o–inspired hairdo, wearing a perfectly ironed A-line dress that made her look like a charming anachronism.

But that was never going to happen again.

She set her poker face and took a deep breath, opening her car door.

Together she and Savannah made their way inside, as one by one, neighbors Caroline hadn't seen in a decade brought sympathy along with their best casseroles. Thanking each for both, she set the food out in the dining room, noting that there was more than enough to feed an army for a year. Maybe they could donate some? She didn't want it to go to waste and didn't intend to remain in Charleston beyond the reading of the will. She was pretty sure her sisters had the same idea. Any arrangements that would need to be made could be handled over the phone, via e-mail and fax. That was the beauty of technology.

"My dear," someone said sympathetically, tapping Caroline's shoulder as she set a third dish of ambrosia salad on the buffet. Unbelievably, there was no more space on the antique Georgian table, even with its six feet of extensions.

"Well, hello, Miss Rose!" Caroline exclaimed. "How lovely to see you!" There was no pretense in the greeting. Rose Simmons's wrinkled face brought back memories of Caroline's earliest years in this old house, the only good ones she could recall.

"Gracious! I wouldn't have missed it," Miss Rose said. "Your mother was a wonderful woman. Such a lovely funeral!" she added with unreserved approval.

"I hope my children will pay their respects so beautifully!"

A prick of guilt jabbed Caroline. Everything had been prearranged. It was the one thing she could thank her mother for: Flo wasn't the sort to leave unfinished business. She skirted the compliment. "Well, I'm glad you could make it," she offered with a smile, and then caught a glimpse of the figure standing in the entrance to the dining room and all thoughts flew out of her head at once.

"Oh, before I forget, I brought the greens!" Miss Rose declared.

Caroline blinked, her gaze fixed on the man she had nearly married ten years before. "Greens?"

His eyes were as vivid a blue as she recalled, with points of light that dimmed or brightened based on the intensity of his smile. Right now, they were practically electric and Caroline could barely focus. "I don't know the Greens, Miss Rose. . . . "

Miss Rose chuckled, gently cuffing Caroline's forearm. "Well, of course you do! You always asked after them and I remembered and brought them!"

Caroline gave the old woman a confused smile, and noticed Jack was smirking, those lights in his eyes dancing impishly. The familiar, playful grin annoyed her far more than it should have.

Miss Rose clasped a hand to her breast. "Poor sweet dear! It must be the shock," she declared. "That's quite understandable." She patted Caroline's arm consolingly. "Flo's death was so unexpected!" She shook her head. "Your mother will be sorely missed, but it should cheer you to know they are talking about planting a garden in Waterfront Park in her honor. I hope they do!

"The Florence Willodean Aldridge Memorial Garden," Rose continued, but Caroline was no longer listening. The old woman peered over her shoulder to see what had captured Caroline's attention and a sudden look of comprehension crossed her features. She smiled knowingly. "Well, goodness! I understand. I shall leave you to your guests, my dear girl. Just make sure you put some of them greens aside for later. I cooked them up just the way you like them, with a nice big ham hock!"

It dawned on Caroline suddenly that the "greens" were not people. Miss Rose had brought mustard greens. And truthfully, she hated them intensely but vaguely recalled being five at Miss Rose's daughter's baptism celebration and feeling incredibly guilty about wanting to spit them out. With a quelling look from her mother, she had reluctantly swallowed them and complimented Miss Rose's greens emphatically— obviously, much too emphatically.

Miss Rose clucked at her, shaking an admonishing finger. "You always were too thin!"

Caroline's cheeks heated as her mother's neighbor ambled away, leaving her completely at Jack's mercy.

The old woman gave Jack a nod on her way out of the dining room and said pleasantly, "Afternoon, Jack."

Jack greeted her with a smile and a nod. "Afternoon, Miss Rose. You look lovely as ever."

Miss Rose ducked her head shyly and giggled like a schoolgirl. The instant she was out of earshot, Jack turned the full impact of his roguish smile on Caroline. "Just make sure you put some of them greens aside for later," he teased, stirring from the doorframe and strolling into the room with a languor that was both infuriating and reassuring in its familiarity.

"I guess your mother never taught you not to

eavesdrop," Caroline said, hating herself for giving in to feelings of resentment.

The twinkles in his eyes vanished. "We both know my *mother* didn't teach me much of anything, Caroline."

He said it calmly, congenially, but Caroline knew she'd hit a nerve. For a long awkward moment, they stood facing one another, neither quite certain what to say. The scent of wilting magnolias drifted between them. Ten years ago, her mother had ordered the flowers as centerpieces for the tables at their wedding. Now, they adorned every corner of the house and Caroline would forever associate the scent with death and sorrow.

Fitting, somehow.

Jack had the decency to look uncomfortable. Hands in his pockets, he peered down at the floor. "We still need to talk to Sadie," he offered, "Finalize the report."

"Well, I'm sure you'll find her in the kitchen."

It was Sadie, their mother's housekeeper, who had discovered Flo sprawled at the foot of the stairs. Doped out on clonazepam, Flo had apparently tripped over a loose board at the top of the stairs.

"It's just a formality," he assured. "It can wait."

She'd rather believe he was here because he was doing his duty for work, not because of some misplaced sense of obligation to their past. "So you're working?"

"I came to pay my respects, not upset you. Sorry, Caroline."

At one time, Caroline couldn't have imagined anyone else she'd rather be comforted by. Now she didn't even know how to talk to him. "Thanks for coming, Jack."

He took a step backward. "You're more like her than you realize," he said quietly, removing his hands from his pockets. He hesitated, clearly wanting to say more. Instead, he turned and left.

Ignoring the surreptitious glances from their guests, Caroline turned her back on him. Trying hard to be casual, she stabbed a silver spoon into a dish before following Jack out into the hall to watch his retreat.

He edged his way through the crowd, somehow avoiding human contact despite the breadth of his shoulders. He never once looked back. Without a word, he opened the front door, stepped out into the afternoon light and closed it quietly behind him.

Caroline choked on a wave of emotion. "Shit," she said softly.

Savannah appeared behind her. "That bad?"

Caroline blinked away tears. "He said he was looking for Sadie."

Savannah lifted a brow. "Well, I doubt that's why he came by here today."

"The past doesn't change just because he wants it to!" Caroline said emphatically and Savannah nodded, wisely recognizing the end of her patience on the subject of Jack Shaw.

2

The Dive Inn was the last refuge before the solitude of home.

During the peak of summer, it was as much a tourist trap as the rest of Folly's Center Street establishments, but today there were plenty of parking spaces around more obvious watering holes and those sitting before the nondescript building were vacant. Jack made a last-minute veer into the unpaved parking lot and went inside, finding the place uninhabited, except for the owner-bartender and an older couple at one of the tables in the back.

"Yo, Jack! Where ya been?"

"Work," Jack offered as an explanation, but the truth was that he came here mostly when he was avoiding Kelly—which he supposed he was doing right now.

"Keeping you busy?"

"Busy enough," Jack replied. "How about a Guinness, Kyle."

"Sure," the bartender said, and reached into a freezer, grabbed a cold mug and proceeded to pour Jack's pint from a shiny silver tap that had been lovingly polished. The wooden counter might have years of character dents and scratches but the draft lines were pristine. Kyle slid the glass over the bar to him. "You hear about the Hutto girl?" he asked, making conversation.

Jack shook his head, taking a chug of his Guinness, glad he hadn't brought up Charleston's biggest news story—the death of Florence W. Aldridge.

Despite that he hated the habit, he reached for a cigarette, but the image of Caroline's face stopped him cold. She used to hate it when he smoked, but these days he only did it when he drank. Tapping his pocket, as though to keep the cancer sticks in check, he wondered why he felt compelled to do anything just because Caroline did or didn't like it. Clearly, she didn't want anything to do with him.

Apparently, forgiveness wasn't an Aldridge virtue.

"Thought maybe you had," Kyle persisted. "They live just a few doors down from you."

"What about her?"

"Apparently she disappeared off the beach a few weeks ago. Hasn't been much in the news on account of that newspaper lady dying, but someone came in earlier and posted that—" He hitched his chin toward a homemade poster with the grainy color image of a pretty little blond girl on it.

"Do they think she drowned?"

Kyle shrugged. "Who knows? Seems someone's always doing something stupid in that ocean out there. Thing is, they aren't tourists. You'd think they'd know better."

Jack tried to recall who the Huttos were, but couldn't place them. Folly Beach was a small, intimate community, but he mostly kept to himself. Things worked out better that way. In fact, it was part of the reason he'd moved to Folly to begin with. He hated lawn work and didn't enjoy chatting over hedges with neighbors. In fact, he hadn't worked on his bike for more than a month because he was sick of the old woman across the street coming over to ask if he was still single. He took another swig of his Guinness and reached into his pocket to grab his cell phone. Three missed calls from Kelly. Zero from Caroline.

Then, again, he hadn't expected Caroline to call. She was as prideful as her mother—damn her! Even ten years later, she wasn't about to forget a stupid mistake. He set the phone down on the counter and drained his glass, eyeing the cell with some malice.

The bartender eyed him curiously. "Bad day?"

Jack shrugged. "Buried a friend," he said.

And fought with the woman who somehow still managed to consume his thoughts even after all these years, but he didn't offer up that part. It was nobody's business.

Caroline was the sole reason he couldn't settle down with Kelly, he realized. Every time he'd considered it, Caroline's face popped into his head—like one of those annoying carnival games. He didn't think that was the way it was supposed to be—married to one girl, obsessed with another.

There was nothing wrong with Kelly.

She just wasn't Caroline.

"I'll take another."

Kyle nodded and complied.

Okay, so maybe as a description of the past twelve years, "obsessed" was a bit of an overstatement, because he had pretty much managed to put Caroline out of his head—except whenever life-changing decisions were about to be made. This minute, however, it *was* a full-on obsession, complete with phantom touches that were hijacking his body. Just seeing her had done that to him. It left him with a sense of longing that was acutely disagreeable, and he couldn't shake it.

Eyeing the phone again, he considered calling her —just so he could stop thinking about her—and it dawned on him that she was probably the reason he had never changed his number. That thought had never even entered his brain before this moment, but he was pretty sure it was true. He wasn't over her. Worse, he was afraid he was never going to be over her, and the thought of living his life in limbo made him feel like chain-smoking half a dozen packs of cigarettes right in front of her.

His cell phone rang and his heart thumped hard. Then he saw the number and felt the letdown: Kelly.

He couldn't avoid her forever.

Draining his glass once more, he took out his wallet, paid the tab, grabbed his cell, and almost as an afterthought, reached into his pocket, digging out his last pack of cigarettes, still half full, and tossed them on the bar, then walked out. The phone stopped ringing, but he would call her back. Now that it was all clear in his head, he realized holding on wasn't fair.

It was time to let go.

WITH THE LAST of the guests gone, Caroline joined Savannah and Sadie's son Josh out on the back porch while Augusta remained upstairs, packing for the flight she'd arranged the moment she'd confirmed a reschedule for the reading of the will. Now the reading was set for ten A.M. Monday morning. Augusta's flight was at three. Somehow, that fact left Caroline feeling gloomier than watching her mother's casket being lowered into the ground this morning.

Once the three of them left . . . once the house was sold, the last "t" was crossed and the last "i" dotted . . . where would home be then?

Enjoy the moment, Caroline.

The moment was all they really had. That was a bitter lesson she had learned after Sammy. The last words Caroline recalled him saying were, *"Yo ho, yo ho —look at me, Cici! I'm a pirate—just like Blackbeard!"*

Indeed, he was.

Just like Blackbeard.

Nothing left but a ghost.

That afternoon, Flo had been sunning further up the beach with a margarita in hand. Flo never heard him, and all three girls had continued drawing pictures in the sand, oblivious to the danger their brother was in. As it turned out, Caroline was the last to see him alive—something neither Caroline nor Flo had ever learned to forgive.

They surmised Sam had floated out into the channel in his little inflatable boat, and from there, there was no telling what might have befallen him . . . a fishing boat that didn't see him in time, a speedboat with a beer-drinking weekend warrior behind the helm, a hole in his raft . . . it could have been anything. The currents could have carried him out to sea.

Once he was gone, nothing was the same.

And no one ever called her Cici again.

On the horizon, a thin ribbon of pink held the descending darkness up high. As it lowered, the creek lost some of its glimmer, fading to black.

She had forgotten how beautiful summer could be on the Island.

Oyster Point Plantation sat on the southwest end

of a finger of land that crooked toward Clark Sound and the sea. The house itself was built so it offered a view of the salt marsh from the front and back verandas. Already, the marsh grasses were tall and verdant, permitting little more than glimpses of the water that glittered like diamonds beneath a mantle of green. A quick breeze bent the spartina grass . . . like rows of bowing performers. At the end of the dock, the last rays of sun glinted off the tin steeple of the boathouse roof. Caroline inhaled the familiar scent of the salt marsh into her lungs, filing it all away for later.

Savannah sighed. "I can't believe she's leaving on her birthday."

It was impossible to control Augusta. Caroline accepted that. "Maybe she has other plans?"

"This is a time to be with family," Savannah argued, "even if you're just going through the motions. But if you ask me, I think she needs us more than we need her."

That was probably true, but Caroline was pretty sure this was Augusta's way of showing the world how little life and death affected her. She made it a point often to say how lucky they were when so many others were not—that any second spent breathing should never be wasted wallowing in sorrow. Considering how abruptly their mother's life had ended, Caroline thought Augusta had a point.

"How can we make her stay?" Savannah persisted.

Josh actually laughed at the question. "Might as well forget that!" He took the fork out of his mouth long enough to wave it at her. "If Augie's set on leaving, she's leaving. That's all there is to it."

For all intents and purposes, Sadie's only son was like a brother to them, but he was much closer to Augusta than he was to Caroline or Savannah. Only months apart in age, as children, the two had spent pretty much every waking moment together.

Augusta was eleven months younger than Caroline and Savannah was nearly two years younger than Augusta. Their parents' relationship had already begun its toxic decline by the time Augusta was born and by the time their baby brother had come along, their parents had barely spoken to one another—even less to their bewildered brood. It was a mystery to all how Sammy was even conceived

This trip, however, Augusta had barely spoken to Josh—to any of them for that matter.

Savannah's brow furrowed. "Why does she have to be so damned contrary?"

Josh shook his head. "After all this time, you two still haven't learned to deal with that girl. You can't tell Augie what to do, and you can't give her ultimatums." His blue eyes gleamed. "You sure as hell can't make plans for her." His tawny skin was flawless—like his mother's, except that Sadie's was at least ten shades darker. Caroline had long suspected he had a mixed heritage, but Sadie had never been very forthcoming about her son's paternity and Caroline was sure Josh just didn't know. It didn't seem to bother Josh. Nothing did. In all her life she didn't recall Josh ever having shed a single tear—not that she could say she was much different. Emotions didn't come easily for Caroline either.

"Who wants ice-cold peach tea?" Sadie called out. With her hip on the door, balancing a tray laden with sweating glasses, she pushed the screen open. Before anyone could stand to help her, she carried the tray over and set it down on the table next to the rocking chair where Josh was seated. She picked a glass up, handing it to Savannah.

Caroline frowned at her. "You don't have to serve us anymore, Sadie."

Sadie turned those soulful black eyes on Caroline. "Enough of that, eah me!" she demanded, shoving a glass of iced tea at Caroline's face. "First of all, your mama took good care of me, but if you think I am doing this because it's my job, you are mistaken, young lady!"

Josh laughed nervously. "Better take it . . . or you're going to wear it."

Caroline reached out to take the glass. She hadn't meant to hurt Sadie's feelings. She was simply aware that Sadie was mourning, too. "At least sit with us," she appealed to their longtime housemaid, surrogate mother and friend.

Sadie grabbed a glass, leaving one remaining on the tray, and seated herself in the rocking chair facing Josh. "I intend to," she proclaimed and began to rock gently as she sipped her peach tea.

Silence punctuated their conversation.

Crickets chirped mournfully and Caroline sighed, giving in to a moment of self-pity for the relationship she no longer had any chance to repair. Flo was gone forever.

Like Sam.

Augie suddenly appeared behind the screen door, pressing her face into the mesh.

Caroline was careful not to betray her disappointment. "All packed?"

"All done."

Sadie raised her glass. "Good. Come on out and grab yourself a cold glass of tea, eah me."

"I'm fine," Augusta replied. She slid her tongue out, smashing it against the dingy screen and rolling her eyes. Savannah laughed at the faces she made.

Josh reached back and tapped the screen door where Augusta's tongue was propped. "Get out here, Augie!"

"Blech! Disgusting!"

"You realize how many mosquito eggs have been laid in that screen?" he countered. "That's what's disgusting!"

Augie pushed the door open, swiping at her tongue. "Point made. Where's the tea?" Spotting the remaining glass, she reached for it and took a hearty swig, then exhaled a self-satisfied sigh.

"Now take a seat," Sadie demanded.

Without further protest, Augie did as she was told. She sat on the floor next to Josh's rocking chair, drawing up her knees. "Sorry to disappear on you guys earlier. I'm not so good with the chit-chat, you know."

Savannah snorted. "That's an understatement!"

Augusta slid their youngest sister a dark look. "We can't all be quite so agreeable, now can we?" There was an edge to the compliment only the deaf would have missed.

Savannah averted her gaze, staring out at the marsh and Caroline was conscious of Savannah's darkening mood. It was evident in the slump of her shoulders, and she wondered why Augusta couldn't see it and give her sister a break.

Just once, she wished they could come together and be a normal family.

"So now that we're all together," Sadie ventured, steering the conversation. "Maybe you girls will humor me with a teensy favor?"

There wasn't much any of them would deny Sadie, but with a preface like that, Caroline had a feeling her favor wasn't all that teensy.

Only the sound of wooden chairs rocking on the uneven deck breached the answering silence.

"Good gracious!" Sadie exclaimed. "It's not like I am gonna ask you for a liver!"

Caroline laughed nervously.

"It's just a tiny exercise," Sadie cajoled. "I want y'all to come up with one happy story about your mama—just one. Let's take a minute to remember something nice about Flo!"

"The liver would be easier," Augie declared. She raised her hand with a bit of a smirk. "Want mine?"

Caroline, Savannah and Josh all chuckled. Sadie did not. "Augusta Marie, you are still a hopeless, pain-in-the-behind little girl, eah me!"

Augie persisted. "I guess that means you won't be wantin' my liver?"

Sadie glared at her with an expression of righteous indignation. It was a look Caroline knew only too well. It was the you're-in-trouble-now glower she gave them all without discrimination.

"I'll start, Mama," Josh offered, giving Augie a chastising glance as he leaned forward, joining his hands as though to concentrate.

Augie snickered. "Think real hard."

Caroline lifted her hand to her mouth to stifle a smile.

Peering down defiantly at Augie, Josh lifted a brow. "When I was seven," he began, nodding in the direction of the pier, "I was out there skipping stones at high tide and Flo came out with two fishing poles, a bucket and a bag of stinkin' shrimp. She handed me a pole and said, 'No man under my roof is gonna grow up not knowin' how to catch trout!'"

Sadie's black eyes glinted. "That was nice. I can eah her now."

Caroline could picture her mother clearly, her tall, willowy figure marching out onto the pier, fishing poles and bucket in hand, bossy as ever, even when she was trying to be nice.

"Yeah . . . she showed me how to bait the hook and then sat for hours, slappin' at mosquitoes." He laughed and shook his head at the memory. "She was happier than I was when I caught the first damned fish."

"What was it?" Sadie asked.

"Redfish, I think."

Caroline remembered that day. It wasn't long before Sammy had disappeared and their lives changed forever. "She made you clean them, too, didn't she?"

Josh nodded and made a disgusted face.

"Of course," Sadie said. "If you're gonna catch 'em, you gotta eat 'em, and you are sure as hell not going to eat 'em unless you clean 'em! You just can't go 'round killing God's creatures for nothing, eah!"

The porch lapsed into silence again—an awkward, uncomfortable stretch that made even Sadie stop rocking. Still nobody made any attempt to leave. Like Caroline, they were probably hell-bent on holding on to what was left of the moment and what was likely the last twilight they'd ever spend on this porch together as a family.

When no one else stepped up, Caroline relented. "Okay, my turn."

"That's my girl!" Sadie said, and began rocking again, smiling.

"Let's see . . . I must've been seven, too—mother had the flu. You—" She pointed at Augie, trying to lighten the mood. "And you—" She pointed at Josh. "We were making breakfast to serve her in bed and between the three of us, we demolished it. Sav was in charge of the toast and it was the only thing we didn't burn." Caroline smiled at the memory. "Augie poured the entire saltshaker over the eggs I mangled. Then we took it up to her. I knew we'd made a mess of it all and I waited for her to hate it." Caroline's eyes stung, but just for an instant. "I'll be damned if she didn't eat it with a smile." For a moment, she basked privately in the memory, and then added for everyone else's benefit, "She told us all how proud she was."

In fact, it was the only time she'd ever said those words to Caroline.

Ever.

"I don't remember that," Savannah said plaintively.

Inexplicably, instead of joy or warmth, the memory's aftermath left Caroline with an empty pit in her soul. Sadness filled it with each passing second.

In the distance, the ocean lay like a black velvet blanket creeping up the banks . . . as though God himself were tucking in the earth for the night.

She didn't know how long they remained lost in that particular reverie as the twilight sky darkened to night. Not a single star shone through the gloom that descended.

While she sat there, the same thought that had been skirting through her consciousness all day returned like a shout in her brain: there would be no more chances to build relationships with her mother. That opportunity was gone forever, stolen by a stupid, untimely slip down the stairs. Regret, like the endless chirping of crickets, was thick in the air.

"Screw this!" Augie declared suddenly, slamming her glass down on the porch. "I'm not gonna sit here and pretend she was something she wasn't!"

Avoiding eye contact with everyone, including Josh, Augie stood and left the porch, slamming the screen door on her way into the house. The sound of it echoed into the marsh.

DEEP IN THE SALT MARSH, *beyond the point where the tall grass parted, a boat hull protruded from the pluff mud, half turned, its sunken mass decomposing into the dark and oozing mud. The remains of innumerable boats littered Folly's wetlands, oftentimes marooned by the fleeing tide. The wooden skeleton barely drew attention. It sat, decaying and feeding the soil surrounding it, nothing more than a reminder that "this far men should never tread."*

Only creatures that couldn't wonder about what lay beneath wandered here.

Occasionally, seabirds swooped in to salvage a forgotten scrap, a mud-stained ribbon, a button, or a bit of tattered lace.

Today, a shiny mud-encrusted zipper tab peeked above the muck, teasing the beaks of swooping birds. It wouldn't budge.

And then the tide rushed in, bringing with it new layers of sediment, swelling the soil with brackish water. Heavy with its burden, the backpack submerged into the mired ground.

Out of sight.

Out of mind.

3

The scent of bacon teased Caroline into consciousness. She opened one eye to peek at her mother's alarm clock: seven thirty A.M. The reading of the will was at ten.

Time to time to get up and get dressed.

She supposed the bacon was Sadie's gentle way of rousing them, and just for a moment, she waxed nostalgic over the memories the scent brought to mind. One thing was certain: mornings in the Aldridge house could be bonding. After Mother had gone to work. Before school. Sundays before church. Lazy summer days. They all began in the kitchen. They had Sadie to thank for that.

Selling the house would be a little like ripping up roots, but that was the inevitable end to it all.

Forcing herself up and out of bed, Caroline found the shorts she'd worn the night before, yanked them on temporarily and grabbed a new T-shirt out of the suitcase she hadn't bothered unpacking. Sadie had placed her in her mother's room, but she tried not to attach any symbolism to that fact. She was the eldest and the first to arrive. That's all. Nor did she intend to brood over what would be lost after today, because, in fact, they didn't need a house to bring them together.

If it really mattered to them, they would find a way.

Her mother's photos—all lined up on the dresser —remained a blur as Caroline passed by, opening the bedroom door to find Tango, her mom's black Lab, lying outside, nose burrowed into the gap beneath the door. "Poor baby!" she exclaimed and stooped to pet him behind the ears. "Miss Mommy?"

In answer, Tango whined, slapping his thick ebony tail against the wooden floor, looking, if possible, even more forlorn. His face showed hints of a white beard and his eyes seemed far too knowing for a dog. They reminded Caroline of a sad old man. "Come on, boy," she coaxed, standing and patting her leg. "No more pining. Let's go get bacon!"

Tango dragged himself up, tail wagging, and followed her down the hall. At the top of the stairs, Caroline stopped for a moment, tapping down a loose board with her toe. The oak slat was slightly warped, peeking up from its groove just enough to catch a toe. Flo had probably been medicated, or drunk, or groggy —maybe all three. Slain by a warped floorboard. How unfortunate was that?

She glanced up to study the ceiling. It was slightly discolored, but otherwise undamaged, and she made a mental note to call someone to check the roof for leaks and then headed downstairs into the kitchen. If they were going to sell the house, they would have to make all the necessary repairs—probably lots of them, since apparently, Flo's attention to detail had deteriorated where the house was concerned.

Really, why should she have cared? In the end, no one had ever bothered to come home. She'd died alone. Caroline only hoped it had happened instantly and her mother hadn't wakened to feel the yawning emptiness surrounding her. The thought of that brought a lump to her throat.

As expected, everyone was already in the kitchen —the one room in the house that didn't seem to fit in the old Victorian. For Sadie, Flo had spared no modern convenience and the stainless-steel industrial kitchen was a chef's dream.

Sadie stood at her commercial-grade, eight-burner stove, frying eggs while Augie sat at the island, doodling with pen and paper. Savannah sat next to her, leaning on one hand with the toaster positioned in front of her. Already on the island sat a heaping plate of bacon and another piled high with thick buttered toast, but it wasn't clear from the position of the butter and knife who exactly was doing the buttering— maybe Augusta, except that she seemed too engrossed in her doodles.

Augie peered up when she came in. "Morning, Sleeping Beauty," she said and went back to scribbling.

"Morning."

"Sleep okay?" Savannah inquired.

"Fine," Caroline replied.

Tango settled at Caroline's feet, peering up at her expectantly, and Caroline wondered if her mother had made plans for the dog. "Sadie, how old is Tango?"

Sadie turned after flipping an egg. "Maybe seven?" She went back to frying up breakfast.

"He misses Mom."

"Life's a bitch!" Augie remarked without looking up.

Sadie turned and waved the spatula at her. "Stop it, Augusta, eah! You don't mean that."

"Of course not," Augusta replied, but kept on doodling without looking up, although maybe with a little more urgency.

They all had demons to exorcise, Caroline realized. If the rest of them were feeling even half the ambivalence she was feeling, it was bound to be messing with their heads. She let her sister's mood go without comment and walked over to kiss Sadie on the cheek. "Thank you, Sadie. You really didn't have to do any of this."

Sadie turned her dark-eyed glare on Caroline. "You, too, missy! If you don't stop it, I'm going to take this spatula to both y'all's skinny rears, do you eah me?"

Caroline laughed at the meaningless threat. Sadie had never even spanked her own son as far as Caroline could recall. "Where's Josh?"

"Josh has his own place," Sadie responded peevishly. "Some things around here *have* changed." Her tone lightened a little and even veered toward pride. "Anyway, you can't have a man running for mayor who's still living with his mama, can you now?"

"No kidding?" Caroline didn't mean to sound so surprised, but Josh hadn't even mentioned it. He'd come a long way from the skinny brat who'd hidden crickets in her bed and let a garden snake under her bathroom door. She snagged a piece of bacon, ripped it in half and tossed a piece to Tango. Tango caught it in midair, gulping without chewing.

"Josh is gonna be The Man!" Augie suggested without a trace of reverence.

Caroline was determined not to rise to Augusta's bait. "Charleston?"

"No, ma'am!" Sadie nodded and smiled. "James Island—if they win the township appeal. He's still with the DA's office for now."

"When does he have to resign? When he announces his intent to run?"

"That's right," Sadie answered pertly.

"That might be a while."

Since about 1993, James Island had been fighting a legal battle for recognition of township—mostly because its residents hated the mayor of Charleston. After winning a suit in 2006, they had gone back and forth and lost again in 2011. The end result was spotty police protection as some areas were still policed by the City of Charleston, while others by the county and others barely at all.

Munching on her piece of stolen bacon, Caroline wandered to the fridge, where her mother's grocery list was posted. *Napkins, dog food, tomatoes . . .* She reached out to snatch the list out from under the Piggly Wiggly magnet and made a mental note to buy more dog food. She'd be here long enough for that, at least, and she might even consider taking Tango back to Dallas—if Sadie didn't want him and if Flo hadn't already made arrangements for him. "I don't suppose she needs this any longer."

They all knew who "she" was.

Sadie glanced over her shoulder, her dark eyes melancholy, and then returned her attention to the eggs without a word.

Both Savannah and Augusta watched as Caroline crumpled the grocery list and tossed it into the trash.

CAROLINE DROVE her mother's vintage Town Car into the city.

Although she'd practically had to force Augie to get in while Savannah kidnapped her cell phone to

keep her from calling a cab, so far Augie hadn't complained even though the Monday morning traffic was
unusually bad. Caroline hadn't taken her foot off the
brakes for at least twenty minutes. Ahead, a battalion
of police cars was slowing everything down.

Seated in the passenger seat, Augusta craned her
neck out the window, trying to get a better perspective
as they wended their way through King Street traffic.
"Jesus! It looks like they're at Daniel's!"

"Why the hell does he keep his office in this part of
town anyway?" Savannah asked from the backseat.

Augie turned to glower at her. "Maybe he feels he
can help folks best by staying put—doesn't he still do
pro bono work?"

"Yes," Sadie interjected, eyeing Augusta with some
exasperation. "But your sister's right. That man's fool-
headed to keep his office up here. Anyway, seems to
me you would fare so much better in life, Augusta, if
you stopped picking up every torch you found layin'
'round, eah!"

Caroline braced herself for the full brunt of
Augie's wrath, but apparently Sadie was still the only
person who could speak to her sister that way and get
away with it. Caroline wasn't brave enough to do it any
longer and Savannah seemed beleaguered enough defending herself.

As they neared Daniel's law firm and could finally
see past the throng of passersby, Caroline spotted Josh
standing outside the doorway, talking with a few of
CPD's finest.

Augusta stared curiously as they drove past while
Caroline searched for a parking space. "They *are* at
Daniel's. . . ."

Sadie sounded worried. "I wonder why."

This part of King Street had yet to benefit completely from the new influx of tax dollars. Not far ahead, beyond Marion Square, the lower streets had been mostly renovated, but this part of town still had some boarded up windows and metal bars on businesses. Although there were a few trendy restaurants making a go of it, the homeless walked around talking to themselves and kids not much older than nine stood smoking on street corners. The closer you got to Marion Square, the better the neighborhood.

They found a parking spot about a block up the street, where a scruffy teenager stood leaning against a telephone pole, sizing up their rims. Caroline tried not to pay him any mind. She took care of the meter and together they walked back to Daniel's office, where Josh was still standing outside the doorway. He motioned them inside, where Daniel's partner, George, greeted them.

Sadie's expression was full of dread. "What on Earth happened eah?"

"Break-in," George replied. "Maybe kids."

Caroline remembered the teenager leaning on the telephone pole.

"Danny came in at four this morning because the alarm went off. Seems they hit him over the head with a bat, nearly cracked his skull. Luckily, they smacked him with the skinny end. They found the broken bat lying next to him on the floor."

"Oh, no!" Sadie exclaimed. "Is he okay? Where is he now?"

"St. Francis. Banged up and lucky as hell, but mostly fine."

Sadie's hand went to her breast. "Thank the Lord!"

"You can visit him later," George suggested with a wink. "He'd like that."

Caroline wasn't sure, but she thought Sadie ducked her head and blushed.

"We can reschedule," Caroline told George. She looked at Augie, raising her brows, telling her without words to say nothing.

"Not necessary," he said. "I'd already offered to walk you girls through your mother's will. It's pretty straightforward. So come on back," he directed. "We're set to go soon as Mr. Childres comes back. Sorry about your mother," he offered to the girls, and added, "The funeral was real nice."

"We appreciate your coming," Caroline offered.

They passed Daniel's office, where papers were scattered all over the floor and bookshelves were toppled.

"Wow, it's trashed!" Savannah remarked.

George nodded and turned to wink at her. "Good thing he left the will nice and neat in my office last night before heading home."

Once in George's office, they lapsed into silence, watching him rifle through and organize heaps of papers sitting on his desk. Every once in a while, he peered over his bifocals at them and offered an awkward smile.

She knew George only in passing, but Daniel Greene was practically a member of their family. He handled legal business for the *Tribune* as well as Flo's personal affairs. Throughout their childhood, he had come by the house nearly every Saturday morning for Sadie's pancakes, and then he and Flo would disappear into her office. Sometimes George would tag along.

"Sorry," Josh said as he came in and leaned against the far wall, ignoring the remaining seat.

"Ready?" George asked, turning to Caroline.

"Ready as we're gonna be."

"Alrighty, then." George cleared his throat and stood. He walked around his desk and sat on the edge of it, facing them, his expression sober. "How long have we known each other?"

When nobody seemed inclined to answer, Caroline said, "Long time."

George nodded. "That's right. Long time and it's been a shitty morning, so if you girls don't mind, let's make this easy on everyone and skip the formalities. We can take care of particulars later."

Augusta was quick to chime in. "I'm all for that!"

Caroline nodded.

So did Savannah.

"Then let's get on with it," he said and began rifling through the stack of papers he held. He cleared his throat again. "'Item four,'" he said, peering over his bifocals at Josh and reciting from rote, "'To Josh Childres, I leave the Legare Street house that once belonged to my husband's family. . . .'"

"Jesus!" Josh exclaimed, sounding surprised.

"She was a generous woman," George acknowledged and then continued. "I'll skip the legalese here. Read it for yourselves later if you're so inclined." He looked toward Sadie. "'Item five: To Sadie Childres, I leave the gatehouse, its immediate surrounding property . . .

"'Item six: Also to Sadie, I leave a three-percent share of the *Tribune* and a seat on the board . . . along with my eternal love and gratitude for all the years she served, not only my family, but me, as my dearest friend.'"

Sadie choked back a sob.

Caroline couldn't look at her. The tears she

couldn't seem to shed at the funeral stung her eyes like angry bees.

"So on, so forth . . . 'Item seven: Also to Sadie, I leave an annual stipend of two hundred fifty thousand dollars to be paid in monthly installments as long as she shall live.'"

George stopped suddenly, stared down at his feet for a moment and then summarized, "There's an item or two in here about charity. Flo left five hundred thousand to The Palmetto House in your brother's name. Another three hundred fifty thousand to The Beacon in North Charleston, again in Sam's name. She also left Sadie as the will's sole executor."

Caroline had the sudden awful gut feeling that a cannonball was about to drop.

"As for the rest, I'm not going to mince words, or confuse you girls with legalese. There's lots of it. The bottom line is that you will split everything remaining equally, with certain stipulations and adjustments . . . under one condition . . . "

In the silence that ensued, Caroline could hear the grating of Augie's teeth. Otherwise, her sisters remained silent. Caroline inhaled a breath. "What condition would that be?"

"All three of you girls must remain in the James Island house . . . together . . . for a period of one year."

Augie leapt to her feet. "What!"

Caroline grabbed her sister's hand and tried to pull her back down into her chair. "Why?" she asked, trying to remain calm.

George met Caroline's gaze squarely, avoiding Augusta's angry scowl. He took off his spectacles. "I can't pretend to know any of your mother's reasons. Caroline, she states that you are to run the *Tribune*, set it straight. It's losing money." He peered at Savannah, who had yet to utter a word. "Savannah, your mama wanted you to write your book, that's all . . . but she wanted you to do it from the house." Finally, he turned to Augusta and looked at her soberly. "Augusta, your mama wanted you to be the one to restore the family home."

Augusta exploded. "I hate that goddamned house!"

Caroline squeezed Augusta's hand and forced a calm voice. "What if we refuse?"

George's gaze returned to Caroline's. "It's certainly within your power to do so," he offered. "But if you don't abide by the terms specified in this will"—he rifled through his papers, drew out three stapled packets and handed one to each of them—"the remaining twenty-seven million dollars will be donated to various charities, all in the name of Samuel Robert Aldridge III and the house will be sold, all profits also to go to charity."

Caroline blinked. "What about the *Tribune*?"

For Caroline's entire life the paper had been a bit like her mother's unwelcome lover—charming from a distance, but up close, jealous, needy and controlling. Now that it might vanish in the blink of an eye, she couldn't bear the thought of losing it. The *Tribune* might not be the lifeblood of the family fortune, but it was their legacy nonetheless.

His gray-brown eyes were steely, unwavering, and she understood in that instant why Daniel had given him the duty of breaking this news. "Should you refuse to abide by the terms of the will, the *Tribune* will close its doors after one hundred and forty-five years of publishing daily news for the City of Charleston, and the *Post* will happily have one less competitor."

"Just like that?" Savannah asked, her voice barely above a whisper.

"Just like that," George affirmed. "Flo was adamant that no one but an Aldridge sit at the paper's helm and she thought it should be Caroline."

A shiver jetted down Caroline's spine. "Can she do this?"

George nodded. "This is your mother's last will and testament," he said. "That's what it dictates. That's what I intend to carry out."

The room fell awkwardly silent.

Caroline glanced back to find that Sadie had made her way out into the hall with Josh's help. She was sobbing quietly, clutching his shoulder.

Augusta turned on Savannah suddenly, her angry blue eyes narrowed. "Did you know about this? You always seem to know everything before we do!"

Savannah's eyes widened. "Of course not!"

"Yeah, I'll bet!" Augusta stood and grabbed her purse. "Well, I don't intend to sit here for another minute. I'm not going to let mother derail my life from the grave! This is the biggest pile of dog shit I have ever heard!" She pushed Caroline's hand away when Caroline reached for her again. "Get off me!"

"Augie! Where are you going?"

Augusta didn't bother turning. "Where do you think?" she said defiantly as she marched straight for the door. "I have a plane to catch!"

4

Augusta talked Josh into taking her back to the house and from there, suitcases packed, went straight to Charleston International Airport.

One of two things would happen now: After Augusta landed in New York, she'd think about her hasty decision, reconsider, maybe dawdle a bit so her capitulation didn't seem quite so easily won, and then she'd turn around and come back to Charleston.

On the other hand, she might mean every word she'd said and nothing anyone could say would change her mind—in which case, they could all kiss everything good-bye—everyone except Sadie and Josh, of course. Realizing it was a distinct possibility, Caroline spent some time contemplating that particular scenario while she unpacked her suitcase and took a hot bath.

Feeling like an interloper in the house she'd grown up in, she sat immersed in her mother's antique porcelain claw-foot tub, with her feet propped on the ironwork fixtures.

When you got right down to it, not much would change. Neither she nor her sisters had ever asked much of Flo—not that Flo wouldn't have given them whatever they needed. It was simply that . . . to *need* their mother somehow seemed unacceptable.

If Augusta decided to return, Caroline would have to go to Dallas to make arrangements and put her own life on hold. She had already taken a leave of absence from her position at Oliver-Heber Books, and she still had to figure out what to do about her apartment, but that wasn't what preoccupied her at the moment. What tied her stomach in knots was the simple fact that, despite all their conflicts, Flo had placed *her* at the helm of the *Tribune*.

How could she ever have guessed her mother's intent? She wasn't a mind reader and Flo had never once encouraged her involvement with the paper. Caroline had finagled a position there all on her own, and for the two years she'd worked on the *Tribune* before leaving for college, Flo had charged through the halls, barely speaking to her—not unlike their life at home. After Caroline had finished her education, her mother had simply pushed her away. Never had she for one second hinted that she'd wanted Caroline to come back to the paper—much less to run it someday—and Caroline had often imagined her mother felt the family's legacy would die with her. Maybe it still would . . . but right now Caroline felt nervous, excited, guilty, elated, and ashamed. Had she misjudged her mother?

Who the hell was Florence Willodean Aldridge?

It was too late to know.

Tears pricked at Caroline's eyes.

Ducking beneath the now tepid water, she rinsed away all evidence of her sorrow, denying her tears, and rose from the tub, grabbing her mother's fluffy peach, monogrammed bathrobe. Shrugging into it, she decided she'd feel much better once she had her own belongings shipped from Dallas, instead of appropriating items she would never have considered borrowing while her mother was alive. It made her feel like a usurper. A pretender.

Instead of searching for Flo's hairdryer in the immaculate master bathroom, she went to retrieve her own from her suitcase, where she'd returned it after using it this morning. For the first time since arriving, she took a moment to explore her mother's bedroom.

Photos of Caroline, Augusta and Savannah occupied nearly every corner of every piece of furniture, from the antique Georgian nightstand to the shell-colored walls. Not surprisingly, there wasn't a single photograph of their father amidst the bunch. There were a few of Sadie and Josh and one of Tango when he was younger. He was standing on the pier as though guarding the house from whatever might emerge from the marsh. Distracted by the photographer, Tango peered back with astute ebony eyes. Flo had had a soft spot for animals. She'd treated the dog as though he were her child . . . her good little boy, she had called him . . . in just the same tone she had reserved for Sammy. Caroline set down the photograph, shoving it back behind a photo of Savannah dressed as the star of Bethlehem for her third-grade Christmas play.

"What are you doing?"

The grown-up Savannah stood in the doorway, watching Caroline with stormy gray eyes, eyes that had an uncanny resemblance to their mother's.

Caroline lifted one corner of her mouth into a tired smile. "Snooping."

"Funny, how that was never a temptation while she was alive."

"Jesus, no!" Caroline exclaimed. "This room was—still is—a freakin' museum."

Savannah reached up, hanging on the doorframe,

a girlish gesture that seemed completely incongruous with her womanly curves. Her tiny waist accentuated full breasts. Caroline's were sadly lacking in comparison.

"Hungry?"

"Not really."

Savannah looked crushed. "I was hoping you might want to head over to the Shack. I haven't had good Lowcountry oysters in a while and I'm craving 'em somethin' awful."

Unlike Caroline and Augusta, Savannah had never lost her Southern drawl, but it seemed thicker today, as though she had already settled in for the long haul. As for the oysters, Caroline had had better than the clumpy, dirty Lowcountry variety, but she didn't say so. "There's more in that fridge than all of us can eat in a year."

Savannah grinned. "Good thing since we're stuck here, huh?"

Caroline shrugged. "That's really up to Augusta, isn't it?"

Savannah brushed the top of the doorframe with her fingertips, feeling for dust. It was the one thing she'd inherited from their parents that Caroline envied—their dad's height—or at least a bit of it. At five-eight, Savannah was the tallest of the three sisters. Caroline was barely five-three and to look like anyone's boss, she had to wear at least two-and-a-half-inch heels.

The disappointment lingered in Savannah's tone. "I guess."

Caroline blinked, realizing suddenly that her baby sister was asking for her attention. She reconsidered. "I suppose we could go."

Savannah's eyes widened hopefully.

"But I didn't bring anything to wear." The humidity of Charleston's summers was unforgettable, but somehow she had forgotten.

Savannah's eyes brightened. "Come on! There'll be a breeze. I'll let you borrow one of my blouses." Her lips curved a little impishly. "I probably owe you one anyway."

Briefly, Caroline considered the chances of running into a certain someone at the Shack. He lived near there, she knew, but was that really how she intended to live the rest of her life? Avoiding Jack Shaw?

No.

"My treat," Savannah persisted.

Caroline lifted a brow. "Sell that book already?"

"No, but something tells me Augie will come home so her broke-ass little sister won't have to live on ramen noodles the rest of her life—anyway, by the looks of you, you're not exactly going to eat me out of my last dime."

Caroline frowned. "What is it with everyone and my weight? All right," she relented. "Let's go get some greasy seafood!"

Savannah clapped joyfully. "Yeah!" she said, and the sight of her honest smile immediately bolstered Caroline's spirits.

ON HIS WAY out of Folly, Jack stopped at the corner of Center Street and East Ashley, ripping one of the homemade posters off the telephone pole. He folded the piece of paper and placed it in his pocket and then fished out a half-mauled pack of gum—his alternative to cigarettes. Unwrapping a piece, he placed it in his mouth, considering the Hutto girl.

First thing Monday, he'd find out when and how she'd disappeared. He'd learned to trust his intuition and something about her disappearance was chafing him like sand in his shoes. Until he looked into it, he knew it wouldn't go away.

There was plenty enough opportunity for a kid to drown in this town. They were surrounded by water—the Folly River on one side, the Atlantic Ocean on the other, with some of the most dangerous currents on the East Coast. A kid without a chaperone could easily find herself in way over her head—literally. In fact, he once saw a grown man get a face full of sand while he stood ankle-deep in the surf.

Still, if the parents were sure she hadn't drowned, maybe they were right.

At the moment, he was on his way downtown to see Kelly—more sand in his shoes he needed to dump —but as he slid into his car and started to shut the door, he noticed the lemon-yellow vintage '78 Town Car parked in front of the Shack. The model was the last of the full-sized editions before Lincoln shrank them in 1980. The pristine, elongated torso had earned the lust of most local auto collectors and was nearly as celebrated as its late owner. He didn't need to see the plates to know whose it was. But the car's usual driver could not be behind the wheel, which meant there was a pretty good chance one of Flo's daughters had driven it here.

It was almost too much to resist.

His brain filled with thoughts—all too tempting— and he pulled the car door shut and turned onto Center Street, searching for open spots around the Shack. He rolled slowly past a vacant parking spot behind the Lincoln, paralyzed by indecision. He pulled the car to a stop for a moment as he chewed fiercely on his gum, contemplating whether to park.

He'd been meaning to quit smoking for ages, but the fact that he was doing so right now irked him more than Kelly's constant calls.

Caroline didn't want to see him. That much was clear.

So why was he skulking around her car? He was acting like a high school kid with a crush and he didn't like it one bit. Was he looking for another argument? Would that make him happy?

Hell, no.

He stepped on the gas, reminding himself there were old people and kids walking the dusky streets. Gritting his teeth almost as hard as he did the steering wheel, he refused to look into the rearview mirror as he put distance between himself and the Shack, but now he was angry, his mood lowering like the sun setting over Folly's wetlands.

A flock of seabirds scattered from a patch of dry land near the roadside, as though fleeing from his mood. He passed the boat Folly's denizens used as a billboard and read the words, "She said yes!" on its hull, painted in electric blue over a whitewashed patch that covered last week's artwork. He clenched his jaw, wondering what silly kid had thought that message worth advertising. Almost weekly the messages changed, each a celebration of new love, a recent engagement, the birth of a child. Jack usually turned a blind eye to them all, preferring not to remember how it felt to love someone that joyfully. Today, he couldn't find his usual detachment.

Maybe this was as good as it was going to get for him?

Maybe he should give Kelly a chance?

Maybe he needed to see a shrink?

Maybe, but all he wanted to do right now was see if Caroline's mouth still tasted as sweet as he remembered.

SEATED ON THE PATIO, with a bucket of crab legs, a pail of oysters, and a plate brimming with boiled shrimp, Caroline and Savannah avoided any and all discussion of the will. Neither had had any opportunity to process the afternoon's proceedings anyway and it seemed pointless to talk about definitive plans without knowing what Augusta intended to do. Whether they liked it or not, the ball was in Augusta's court. So for the time being, Caroline decided she would reacquaint herself with her baby sister over the Shack's Sunday special.

"I'm glad you talked me into this," she admitted. "I'd forgotten how peaceful it is out here."

The sun was close to setting and the entire sky was awash with color. Too bad they were seated inside on the screened porch. At least they had fans blowing quietly over them.

Savannah peeled a massive shrimp. "There's something really special about the smell of the ocean isn't there?"

"I don't think that's the ocean," Caroline contended, scrunching her nose. She couldn't smell much of anything over the scent of cooked shellfish.

Savannah laughed. "You have a point." She sucked in a deep breath and hiked her shoulders, breathing it all in. "Still, I love it!"

Caroline wrestled with her crab leg, snapping it at the joints and burrowing out as much of the meat as she could get to. She tried to snap the thicker middle where the juiciest meat remained, but it wouldn't give. Caroline eyed the stubby crab leg with a bit of annoyance. "There's no way I'm going to be defeated by a dead crustacean!"

Savannah handed her the crab cracker.

She used it to snap the leg and set it down on the table. "You have to wonder why people love these things so much." She lifted her prize after pulling out a healthy chunk of crabmeat. "It's almost too much work."

As Caroline went after another crab leg, her cell phone rang at the bottom of her purse. The old-fashioned and very loud ring drew attention. A crotchety looking old man eyed her with narrowed eyes. "Damn it!" She grimaced at the thought of putting stinky crab juice in her purse.

"You should get that," Savannah suggested when Caroline didn't move fast enough to retrieve it.

Caroline kicked her purse toward Savannah. "My hands are messy. Will you?"

Savannah grabbed a batch of napkins and handed them to her. "It's probably Augusta. I'm not ready to talk to her yet, but you shouldn't leave her wondering."

Caroline took the napkins and eyed her baby sister. No doubt she was right. It probably was Augusta. Somehow, Savannah seemed to have a sense for these things and Caroline had stopped asking how a long time ago. She wiped her hands and reached into her purse. "What makes you think I want to talk to her? She was pretty rude all weekend."

Savannah's gaze met Caroline's as the phone stopped ringing. "She's hurting, the same as we are, Caroline. She just doesn't know how to show it."

Caroline peered down at the number. "Augusta."

She resented having to jump at Augusta's bidding, but Savannah was right—on both accounts—the last thing they wanted to do was make Augusta wonder—especially when they needed something from her. The phone had stopped ringing before she could answer, so she hit the talk button to return the call.

Augusta answered on the first ring. "What are you guys doing?"

Caroline tried not to sound annoyed, but her tone betrayed her. "We're at the Shack, celebrating your birthday."

On the other end of the phone, Augusta sighed heavily. "Sorry about earlier. It just took me by surprise, you know. Pissed me off."

Caroline held her tongue, certain that anything she might say would only make matters worse.

"But I thought about it on the flight," Augusta continued. "It's not like either of you asked for this either."

Savannah dug into the remaining oysters, searching for missed opportunities while she pretended to ignore their conversation.

"No, we didn't."

"Is Sav mad at me?"

Caroline glanced at Savannah, wondering whom she might have inherited her unflappable patience from. "No."

Another belabored sigh sounded in Caroline's ear. "Obviously I'm coming back."

Caroline released the breath she hadn't realized she was holding. "That's good. When?"

"I need maybe a week here."

Caroline felt another surge of relief. Augusta hadn't even taken her "list of rules" with her. She hadn't so much as looked at them and as ridiculous as it seemed, there were stipulations about how long any of them could be away without prior arrangement. As always, their mother had considered every detail.

"Anyway, I just wanted you to know. I'm not happy about it, but I'll be back next week. Tell Sav I said sorry, okay?"

"I will. She says to tell you happy birthday."

Savannah eyed Caroline over the oyster she was inspecting, raising a brow.

"Tell her I said thank you."

"Okay."

"Talk to you soon."

"Bye." Caroline ended the call and took in a deep breath. "Holy shit, so she changed her mind in record time!"

Savannah twisted her oyster knife into one of the hinges in the cluster in her hand and popped open the shell, revealing her withered prize. "Yeah, well I knew she'd come around." She fished out the shriveled oyster and held it up in disgust. "Twenty-seven million dollars can be quite persuasive. Hey, let's order margaritas! We have celebrating to do!"

"If you can call it that."

Savannah shrugged. "If you can call it that."

The waiter came by and cleared their table, took their drink order and after a few moments, brought back two margaritas in thick blue-rimmed cocktail glasses.

Caroline raised her glass and proffered it to Savannah. "To Florence Willodean Aldridge," she said.

Savannah raised her glass, clinking it against Caroline's. "To Mother."

5

The Chinese had a word for souls who were condemned to suffer an insatiable desire for more than they could consume: ègui̇̌, they were called. Hungry ghosts, depicted with protruding bellies and tiny mouths—teardrop-shaped entities with bottomless chasms in place of souls and eternally ravenous appetites that could never be appeased.

Some people were born that way.

That was the only explanation for the endless yearning that seemed to exist before memory.

At times, there was nothing to be done but surrender to it.

Somehow, in the quiet moments after the very first slaughter . . . there had been peace from the yearning . . . but then the hunger resumed—long before the flesh from that first rib melted into the wet, putrefying ground.

Ten years crawled before the next feast, but it too failed to satisfy, and then the next and the next. The hunger came faster, sooner, stronger—the sacrifice always on the verge of being enough, but never quite.

Even now, the hunger was seeking stillness.

A stillness that was discoverable only in glimpses . . . on

*quiet mornings in the salt marsh . . . when the scent of
death hijacked the morning breeze.*

EARLY TUESDAY MORNING, Caroline delivered a bouquet of sunflowers to Daniel's room at St. Francis Hospital. She left Savannah at home staring at a blank page on her computer screen.

Daniel was alert enough to give her a bit of an overview about where the *Tribune* stood financially. While the company managed to pay the bills, it was losing money and distribution and she learned that, although she had inherited her mother's titles, her mother hadn't exactly placed blind faith in Caroline. She was expected to work hand-in-hand with Daniel in all business matters, and in all things editorial with the help of longtime editor in chief Frank Bonneau.

Bonneau had been running the *Tribune*'s editorial department for as long as Caroline could recall. He was a no-nonsense old-school journalist and George had already warned her he was more likely to go around her and take his grievances to Daniel, who, incidentally, also held a seat on the board—another reason George was apparently brought into the mix.

She wasn't sure how yet, but she knew she had to find a way to win Bonneau's respect and she was pretty certain that after her stint at the *Tribune* she hadn't left him with the best impression—if, in fact, she'd left him with any impression at all, aside from the fact that she was the boss's daughter.

Already, Caroline had a few ideas to implement once she settled into her role—something she felt compelled to do sooner rather than later as a show of confidence. It probably wasn't kosher to begin working full time right away as there was a certain propriety that must be adhered to in the Deep South. To run a daily paper she needed not just her employees' respect, but the respect of the people of Charleston. Her mother had understood that well and she'd become their icon—their genteel princess.

The *Post* might be bigger, but the *Tribune*, with its unbroken lineage, was like a last bastion of Old World American journalism—and was becoming about as relevant as the Queen of England. If they continued down the path they were on, the paper was soon to become obsolete and her mother's boast that they had survived even where Benjamin Franklin's *Gazette* had not, would be moot. The newspaper business had come a long way since the eighteenth and nineteenth centuries and Caroline had a lot of changes to make.

Born during the fall of the Confederacy, the *Tribune*'s history was deeply intertwined with that of the *Post.* Both papers could trace their ancestries to the *Charleston Daily News* and each quietly challenged the other, although by most standards, the *Post* had already won. With a distribution and staff that was more than twice the *Tribune*'s, they could afford not to acknowledge their oldest competitor. But the competition was there nevertheless—a nod here and there, reverently done, because both had a reputation for solid reporting and community service. Her mother had worked hard to continue that legacy.

After her visit with Daniel, Caroline spent the remainder of the day looking over ledgers with George at the King Street office. On Wednesday, Daniel was released from the hospital, and joined them, black eyes, bruises, stitches and all.

Neither she nor George brought up "the incident," as Daniel's misfortune was now being referred to, and Daniel didn't bring it up either. Caroline thought maybe he didn't care to hear lectures about where he conducted his business. But that was really none of her concern anyway. If he and George were content to investigate four A.M. break-ins every other week, it was their right to do so. Caroline's only real concern was the *Tribune*.

She stared at the bottom line for the payroll. "Did Mother consider buyouts?"

"No," Daniel responded at once. "We recommended it, but Flo was adamant the paper remain loyal to longtime employees. Some have been with the *Tribune* going on fifty years."

"Like who? That makes them seventy, or near about!"

"Agnes, for one. Used to be a reporter and now she works classifieds. And Lila, who works in payroll."

Caroline lifted a brow. "It *is* possible to take loyalty too far."

Daniel eyed her disapprovingly. "I'm certain I'd not take too kindly to someone telling me I had to stop practicing law once I hit seventy."

"Which is precisely tomorrow," George interjected, and snickered.

Caroline stifled a smile, though she was pretty sure George wasn't much younger than Daniel.

Daniel gave George a withering glance. "Sixty-three," he clarified for Caroline's sake, and he eyed her pointedly. Apparently, he wasn't through with the lecturing. "Some would say thirty-three is too young to be placed in a position of influence to affect the welfare of others."

Caroline refrained from pointing out that at thirty-five—just two years older than she was—one could be elected president of the United States and in a position to influence many more lives than those connected to a small-town newspaper. Lifting up the stack of papers in front of her, she tapped them on the desk to line up the edges and then set them aside. "We wouldn't be forcing anyone to leave," she argued. "A buyout would just be incentive."

Daniel glowered at her. "A carrot for a pack of old mules?"

George chortled again and that seemed to annoy Daniel all the more. His lips thinned angrily.

Caroline frowned. "I didn't say that."

After a moment, George stopped chuckling long enough to come to her defense. "It's smart business," he asserted and peered meaningfully at Caroline. "I hate to say it, but your mother's enduring loyalties weren't helping the bottom line any."

Caroline appreciated the pat on the back. And right now, she needed that more than anything.

Daniel muttered beneath his breath, and she realized he might be too tied up in her mother's philosophies to embrace any changes she would need to make to keep the company afloat. She'd rather work with George, and Daniel might not like it, but she was in charge now.

Funny how everything—even something as inopportune as a random break-in—sometimes led to unintended but fortunate results. It was a sort of providence . . . except that Caroline didn't believe in providence.

Around noon, Sadie interrupted their meeting to deliver lunch—as she had all week. But this time, Caroline kept her mouth shut and didn't chide her for it, and she noticed something she'd missed before: it could be that Sadie was still trying to take care of Florence's children . . . but just maybe she was using this as an excuse to see Daniel Greene. She watched the two flirt like awkward teenagers.

What else had changed during her absence?

Certainly not Jack.

But *that* too was no longer her concern—and why the hell she should even think about him at a time like this was beyond her.

HOURS AFTER SUNDOWN, the pavement was still warm beneath the girl's bare feet.

A low fog swept in from the salt marsh, unfurling like a gossamer carpet over the blacktop. Carrying flip-flops in one hand, she hurried down the road, thickly lined with oak and blackgum trees.

On this part of the Island, many of the houses were ancient, some were new, one dated back to when these wetlands were occupied by rice plantations tilled by gentlemen farmers. At the end of the road, through the wild scrub, you could almost see the burnt carcass of the original house, its brick framework imprinted with a visual memory of long-expired flames.

Oyster Point Plantation was one of James Island's richest and most enduring legacies. Before it burned down, the original estate had served as a Confederate division field hospital, and nearby sat the unmarked graves of nearly three hundred soldiers who'd died at the battle of Secessionville. Local folks claimed the nearby estuaries were littered with the bones of the Confederate and Union dead.

At this hour of the night, she felt like a trespasser on Fort Lamar Road. Like bony, accusing fingers, the trees shook quivering limbs as she passed, their bent forms casting sinister shadows while the wind sighed with exasperation over her intrusion.

Her mind was playing tricks on her.

It was stupid not to tell anyone where she was going. She hadn't even told her realtor friend who'd listed the house on Backcreek Road. She was so certain he wouldn't mind if she just sat on the dock and snapped a few photographs of the Morris Island lighthouse. Now both her car and her cell were dead and she didn't much like the thought of knocking on strange doors to ask to use the phone.

Behind her, a pair of headlights appeared, two blinding high-powered beams that switched to low once the driver spotted her.

Instinctively, she moved to the right side of the road, avoiding the driver's side.

The car—a brand-new, black Acura with a shiny coat of wax—slowed, and her heartbeat quickened. She heard the passenger window begin to whir and she turned to peer into the shadows of the car. The voice was male. "Need help?"

The girl kept walking. "No!"

"You sure? Where ya headed?"

"Gas station," she replied and quickened her pace. As an afterthought, she added, "My car won't start."

He sounded incredulous. "You don't have a cell?"

The girl cast him an annoyed glance and got a better look at his face. White, in his late twenties, sinfully gorgeous. In fact, she had never met a guy so damned cute—not even her roommate's jealous boyfriend who she secretly crushed on was that good looking. She slowed her pace, thinking he couldn't be much older than she was and relaxed a little. "I do have a phone. It's dead. No charger."

He winked at her and gave her a slow smile. "Lotta good that'll do ya."

She returned a lopsided smile and gave him the full brunt of her sarcasm. "Gee, thanks for pointing that out."

He brought the car to a sudden halt and the girl had the briefest inclination to keep walking. She stopped instead and turned to face the car and the driver.

"Well, you see . . . that puts me in a bit of a bind," he said, but he made no attempt to open his car door and so the girl remained where she stood.

"Yeah? How's that? I'm the one walking."

"That's just it," he said. "Now that I know, I can't just leave you here on this dark-ass road all by your lonesome."

The girl shrugged. "I've walked longer distances."

He seemed to think about her answer a moment and she thought he might actually leave as he gently revved his engine.

"Here's the deal," he said. "I could let you use my cell, but then I'd still feel obliged to wait with you until someone shows up to help . . . or I could take you to the station myself."

The girl chewed her lip. "I dunno . . . I don't make it a habit to get into strange cars."

"Never wise," he agreed. "Well, I could also take a look at your car."

She tilted him a glance. "You know something about cars?"

"Something . . . but can't promise I'll be able to fix it." He peered back in the direction they'd both come. "Where is it? I didn't see it."

"Backcreek Road."

"Ah, right. Okay, here, take my phone." He reached over to retrieve it from his passenger seat and then handed it out the passenger window.

The girl ignored the alarms going off in her head and moved tentatively toward the car, ready to bolt if he opened his car door.

He smiled at her as she took the phone from his hand and merely watched as she began dialing numbers. Her roommate answered on the second ring and she hurriedly explained what had happened while the driver waited patiently in his car. With help on the way, she hung up, feeling better. He was just a really cute, nice guy trying to help out. She handed him the phone back. "Thanks. I appreciate it. I'm Amy."

"Nice to meet you, Amy. I'm Ian. So what do you want to do? Should we turn up the radio and sit on the hood until the cavalry arrives? Or do you want me to go take a look at your car?"

Amy chewed her lip again. "I don't know . . . I think it's going to be a while. She's not much of a hurrier."

He considered that, tilting his head as he looked at her. "You're meeting her at the gas station?"

"Yeah . . . "

"Tell you what," he suggested. "Get your friend back on the phone, tell her to meet you at the car. Give her my name and my license plate and I'll give your car a look-see." He handed the phone back to her through the passenger window.

Amy considered the suggestion. The warm pavement had already blistered the bottom of her feet.

Really, any decision seemed stupid at this point,

but sending him on his way and taking her chances alone on a dark, lonely street seemed the least wise of all. The dark road was spooking her. Going straight to the gas station was probably the better choice, but her friend would easily be another hour coming from downtown, especially the way she dawdled. Plus, she'd already used his cell phone. If he'd meant to harm her, he wouldn't have let her use his phone. How stupid would that be?

Anyway, he was too damned cute to be dangerous.

"Are you sure you don't mind taking a look at my car?"

"It's not how I intended to spend my night, but I wouldn't feel right leaving you stranded."

"At least you're honest," Amy said, smiling as she took the proffered phone and opened his passenger door.

"Why don't you walk," he suggested. "I'll follow. It's not far."

Amy slid in. "Nah, that's all right," she said. "We'll have to go to the gas station first anyhow 'cause I know what's wrong: I'm out of gas."

He gave her a look that reminded her of the way her older brother looked at her when she did something stupid. "You're kidding, right?"

"Unfortunately, not. I put my entire paycheck into new camera gear. I thought I had enough gas to make it home."

"Jesus," he said, shaking his head. "Who does this anymore?"

She grinned. "Dirt poor college kids who drive prehistoric clunkers," she replied.

"Jesus," he said again, and sighed. "All right."

Barely twenty-five minutes later, they turned into the long driveway on Backcreek Road. Without a word, Ian Patterson, the cutest man who had ever lived, got out of the car and filled her tank for her and then asked her to try starting it. It started just fine, and he turned away, obviously bored with the entire situation. Amy tried not to be disappointed by the blow-off. "Thanks," Amy said. "You sure I can't pay you back?"

"No need. But you should go home," he suggested as he slid back into his car and slammed the door.

"Well, thanks again. I appreciate your help," she said, and followed his car as he backed out of the driveway.

"Go home, Amy," he said firmly as he rolled up his window. The tinted surface reflected the full moon behind her.

"All right," she said, but then she just stood there, thinking about the image of the moon on his window. With the low-drifting fog creeping across the marsh, she thought maybe a few more high def photos of the lighthouse would turn out spectacular. Once he was gone, she grabbed her camera from her car and made her way out back to the dock. She was already here; a few more photos wouldn't hurt anyone.

Once on the dock, she lit a cigarette and stood staring at the vista, wondering if Mr. Gorgeous had a girlfriend. She didn't have a way to get in touch with him—too bad. The truth was she'd probably never see him again. Anyway, he obviously wasn't interested so she finished her cigarette and tossed it into the water and began snapping pictures, beginning with the flash on.

She never heard the rustling in the grass. Never saw the shadow slip through the night. Never knew what hit her. The last sense she had was of the sweet and acrid scent of something pressed against her face. She gripped the camera in her hand as though it were her lifeline to the world, her fingers pressing desperately into the metal casing as she tried to scream, but the scream never came. The sound of her camera crashing onto the wood dock streamed into her consciousness like a bad dream.

6

Approaching the receptionist's desk, Caroline extended her hand to the young woman seated behind it. "Hello," she said. "I'm Caroline Aldridge."

"Oh, God—I thought so—I'm so sorry!" The receptionist stood, knocking her knees against the keyboard, nearly toppling it off the sliding desk shelf. The color drained from her face. "I was at the funeral. Pam!" She slapped a hand awkwardly to her breast. "I mean, I'm Pam! So sorry for your loss!"

Caroline smiled, liking the girl already. There was something genuine about her. "I do that too when I'm nervous."

Pam's eyes widened a little and she nervously pushed her dark blond bangs out of her eyes. "Oh, God, am I rambling?"

Caroline smiled. "A little, but don't worry. I'm probably way more nervous than you are. My mother's shoes will be hard to fill."

"Don't I know it!" Pam exclaimed without the least bit of guile.

Caroline lifted a brow, surprised by the agreement, though not the least bit offended by it. The truth was the truth, after all.

"Oh, God! I'm such an idiot!" Pam declared, suddenly realizing her gaffe. "Please tell me what I can do to help you—besides shutting my mouth!"

Caroline took a deep breath. "Actually, a lot, but first, if you don't mind, why don't you introduce me to the crew?"

Pam hurried around her desk. "Of course! Let me help get your things into your moth—I mean, *your* office, then I'll show you around."

"Thank you," Caroline said gratefully.

They dumped her satchel and purse in her new office, and made their way methodically through the editorial and sales departments, followed by circulation and accounting. Pam introduced her to a few of the braver souls who came forward to meet the new boss: Brad Bessett, one of their lead reporters—fairly new to the paper, because Caroline didn't remember him; Agnes, a portly older woman with bright blue eyes and a double chin whom Caroline vaguely recalled from the editorial department a decade ago— she now handled classifieds; Doreen Hill, who held the education beat; and Bruce, the obligatory computer guy, who seemed to just follow them around as Pam led her from desk to desk.

Considering the state of the paper's finances, Caroline was surprised to find the offices had been renovated since her last visit—with modern desks and cubbies. The entire reception area now resembled a Victorian parlor, probably to highlight the paper's venerable history. Although Caroline didn't quite share Augusta's extreme prudence where money was concerned, she would never have spent funds on decorating when the company was losing so much money. The price of the chandelier in the reception area alone could cover someone's salary for a year.

They passed a small windowless room and Pam waved to the occupants as they passed, but didn't stop. "What's that?"

She pointed at the room they'd just passed. "That? Oh, Web slash audience development," Pam said a little dismissively.

Caroline didn't hold it against her. She was pretty sure the girl had come by that attitude honestly. Her mother would only have had a skeleton crew on hand for the most rudimentary of Web tasks. Aside from having a presence on the Web as a substitute for the Yellow Pages, Flo had never been too keen on new media. This was something Caroline intended to change. The Web, with all its inroads into social media, was the undeniable future.

"How many work in there?"

Pam held up four fingers. "Four—an audience development specialist, two developers, and a designer, but one of the developers is on vacation and our designer broke his middle finger and, uh . . . can't work."

Caroline smirked. "I won't ask how."

Pam leaned to whisper, "I didn't either, but once you get to know him, it'll make sense."

"Do you know how many people work for the paper now?"

"Not exactly, maybe one hundred and twenty—but Lila, in payroll, can tell you for sure."

Caroline's brows knit. If her guess was accurate, her mother must have already begun to pare down the payroll, despite what Daniel claimed. The last summer she'd interned for the *Tribune,* they had reached nearly one hundred and fifty employees.

In the newsroom Caroline recognized the most faces, but the one person she'd expected to run into— dreaded it, in fact—she didn't. Apparently, the editor in chief had a toothache and was spending the morning at the dentist.

By the time Caroline made it back to her desk, it was lunchtime and she considered stepping out to call Savannah, but Pam had no sooner walked out of her office than she stepped back in, knocking tentatively on the doorframe. "Sorry to interrupt, but there's a woman out here who says she really needs to speak with you."

Caroline stood, her brow furrowing. "She asked for me?"

"Well, she asked to speak with the publisher, not the editor. That would be you, right?"

It sounded strange to hear the title from someone else's lips. The shock of it made her hesitate an instant too long.

"Frank's back, but I thought . . ."

"No . . . go ahead and bring her back," Caroline directed.

Pam left and returned in less than five minutes, leading in a young woman whose eyes were full of torment. At first, Caroline barely noticed anything else about her, so palpable was her distress.

"Thank you," the woman said, stepping meekly into her office. She couldn't be much older than Caroline and looked as though she had been sobbing for days. Her brown eyes were red rimmed, bloodshot, the lids swollen.

Caroline walked around her desk, afraid the woman would collapse she looked so frail. "How can I help you?" she asked.

"My name is Karen Hutto," the woman said, her voice catching on a sob. "I-I need your help to find my little girl."

APPARENTLY AMANDA HUTTO's father was supposed to have picked her up for school the morning she disappeared. Late for work, and in danger of losing her job, Karen Hutto had left her six-year-old standing out on her front lawn, book bag in hand, waiting for her father, who apparently forgot it was his court-appointed day to play dad and just never showed.

Certain it was going to be another late night, Jack ran by the house to shower and clean up, and while he was there, he took a few minutes to speak with a few of the neighbors about Amanda. No one had seen the kid the morning she disappeared—no one saw anything—though a few voiced suspicions about the dad who, apparently, had a bit of a violent streak. From what little digging Jack had done, the mother had filed at least one restraining order that didn't stick and the accusations seemed to fly between them more virulently than between reality-show celebs.

At this point, there was nothing Jack could do. The little girl had disappeared from in front of her own house, so this case belonged to Folly Beach PD. If they needed assistance, it probably wasn't CPD they were likely to call. They'd call in the sheriff's office most likely and in the end, Jack couldn't justify spending more time on a case that wasn't in his jurisdiction—especially now that it seemed there was a murderer to catch.

He'd been up half the night because a college student by the name of Amy Jones had been discovered under the dock of a nearby James Island residence. The inside of her mouth had been painted with a blue dye and her tongue was removed. Whether it was fish bait, or the killer had taken it with him, was yet to be discovered, but one thing was certain, it wasn't in her mouth.

Could her death somehow be connected with Amanda's disappearance?

Logically, Jack didn't think so. Other than the fact that they both were both female and the Islands were generally sleepy, with relatively few crimes, there weren't any common denominators.

At any rate, this case was going to be enough of a pain in his ass without adding unnecessary strife with FBPD. Jack had a feeling his new partner, Garrison, was going to be a thorn in his side. Luckily for Jack, Joshua Childres was assigned to the Jones case. Childres would give him all the space he needed while he worked with his team to solve the murder.

7

At the end of the day, Caroline felt a little like a bastard child who had come to the throne after the death of a king who had no heirs. Clearly, no one had bothered to tell anyone at the *Tribune* the outcome of the will, and Pam had sent the minions into a tailspin simply by bringing Karen Hutto into her office instead of to Bonneau's.

Although it wasn't certain how much of the disorder was due to her mother's death, little more than two weeks without Florence W. Aldridge at the helm, and it was no longer certain who should be running the office. She realized only now how prudent it was that she had connected with Pam because Pam was the gatekeeper, and for all her artlessness, her every action now was decisive—which, unfortunately, only seemed to force Bonneau to draw lines in the sand.

The real test came during the afternoon, with news that literally stopped the presses: sometime last night, the body of a twenty-two-year-old College of Charleston student was discovered under the dock of a James Island home. The property, which actually wasn't far from Oyster Point, was unoccupied and for sale, but the girl's car was found in the driveway, keys still in the ignition. That's all they knew. The police weren't forthcoming with more details.

Finally, Caroline came face to face with Frank Bonneau—over an argument about bumped heads on the front page—two similar headlines he felt certain competed with each other—especially since Amanda Hutto's disappearance was old news in his book. In the end, Caroline made the decision to run both articles, arguing that a still-missing six-year-old was hardly the same story as a not-so-much missing and very dead twenty-two-year-old. She was pretty certain her mother would have made the same call. If there was one thing she knew Flo took to heart, it was her community.

And yet as hideous as news of the murder was, the entire drive home, all Caroline could think about was Karen Hutto and the look of turmoil in the woman's eyes. Her child seemed to have vanished without a trace. They had exhausted every resource and no one had responded to her flyers. Worse, separated and each blaming the other, she and her husband were now the primary suspects in a flagging investigation. The whole thing reminded Caroline of Sammy's disappearance, minus the presumption of guilt. Hands down, her little brother's death was the single most traumatic event of Caroline's life and more than twenty-five years later, there wasn't a day that went by that something—some tiny thing—didn't make her flash back to that awful moment on the beach when Sammy was four and Caroline was eight.

In some ways, Caroline would remain eight forever.

Today, looking into that woman's face, she could

never have found the resolve to turn her away. It was that same look Caroline recalled seeing in her mother's eyes—that look of quiet desperation and fear that had later become hopelessness, melancholy, and finally the emotional void in which her mother had lived until she'd died. But one thing was different: all those years ago, when her brother had disappeared off the same beach, Caroline had been powerless to help. She was in a position now to do *something*, even if it was just to help keep the woman's story before the public so the police wouldn't just close the case and look away.

On her way home, she took the Expressway. Sailboats, big and small, dotted the Ashley River, billowy black silhouettes against a golden sunset. Along the shoreline, the marsh grasses slow-danced in the breeze.

As serene as the vista was, it was difficult to believe that right across the channel, just a stone's throw from her house ... a girl had been brutally murdered.

Despite that gruesome thought, she kept the window down, determined to enjoy the last of the temperate days before summer converged upon them with all the wrath of hell itself.

Pulling the Town Car into the driveway, she found both Sadie and Savannah seated on the front porch. Caroline slid out of the car, leaving her satchel in the backseat for the moment, along with her purse. "I'm glad someone seems to have had a carefree day!" she called out, trying to sound cheerful.

"Yeah, well, think again!" Sav replied. "I think we washed and returned fifty million dishes today. I would've gladly traded places!"

"Did you hear from Augie by chance?"

"Nope," Savannah said, "but apparently Josh did. He came by for lunch."

Caroline made her way up the steps, stopping to snag an azalea bloom from the bush near the stairs. She lifted it to her nostrils. "They don't smell like much, do they?"

"Some do," Sadie offered. "Not those, but they were your mother's favorite color."

Caroline tossed the blossom away. "Oh, crap! I forgot to stop and get dog food."

"No worries," Sadie said. "Got it while we were out."

Caroline gave her a tired but grateful smile. "I wouldn't blame you if you quit, but I'm sure glad you're still around!"

"You look tired," Sadie offered. "Go on in and get some rest, eah. Dinner'll be ready soon—and before you say a thing, don't. All I did was heat up some leftovers. Once that mess is gone, y'all are on your own."

"Now you've gone and done it," Savannah interjected. "When we're starving, remember this is entirely your fault, Caroline. You're the one badgering her into retirement!"

Caroline wasn't worried. Sadie wasn't going anywhere.

All bluster, the housekeeper said, "You girls know where to find me if you forget where the can opener is."

Caroline gave Sadie a thumbs-up and ducked inside, craving silence.

She found Tango lying at the bottom of the stairs with her mother's running shoe and she snagged it wearily. "No, no!" she scolded, and went upstairs, tossing the shoe unceremoniously into her mother's closet. She wasn't quite ready to go in there yet and deal with her mother's stuff. Tango, on the other hand, didn't have the same hesitation. He raced in, retrieved the shoe, and ran to the other side of the bed to hide it out of Caroline's sight.

"Whatever," she relented. "Keep the blasted shoe!"

Too beat to do battle with a dog, she lay on the bed to rest her eyes before dinner. Tango jumped up without invitation, bringing the shoe, settling next to her on the bed and Caroline automatically rolled over and hugged him, wishing the husky presence belonged to a very different male as she drifted off to sleep.

THE SOUND of glass breaking registered somewhere . . . maybe in a dream.

Caroline's eyes fluttered open.

Tango was no longer on the bed beside her, but it took her a full moment to remember where she was and that he had been there in the first place. The shoe was a distinct reminder. It was pressed against her forehead, wafting the unmistakable odor of foot sweat. Groggily, she picked up the shoe, examined it and tossed it onto the floor, then got out of bed, glancing at the clock.

The house was perfectly silent. It was after eight.

Why had no one called her down to dinner?

Rubbing the sleep from her eyes, she walked to the window, peering out, noting the car was no longer parked out front.

Maybe Savannah took Sadie home?

Her laptop was still in the backseat, so work was out of the question until her sister got home—thank

God! She was completely sick of numbers by now. With a sigh, she headed downstairs straight for the kitchen and realized belatedly that she'd skipped lunch entirely. Her stomach rumbled in protest. "Patience is a virtue!" she said.

But the doorbell rang the instant she stepped into the kitchen. Cursing softly, she spun around, heading back to answer it and opening the door without thinking.

Jack lifted a brow as the door opened wide. "Did you know a girl was murdered on Backcreek Road last night?"

"Yes. I heard. What are you doing here, Jack?"

"You really need to be more careful, Caroline."

"What are you—my daddy now?" She hitched her chin. "What can I do to for you, Jack?"

"Are Savannah and Augusta around?"

"Augusta's in New York. She'll be back in a few days. I have no idea where Sav is. What is it?"

"Nothing pressing."

"You often make house calls after eight to talk about nothing pressing?"

He didn't even blink at her cantankerous tone. "You still get up on the wrong side of the bed," he remarked with a slight curve to his lips. He rubbed at his forehead to indicate the spot on her head where the shoe's imprint was still visible, but fading.

She gave him a half smile. "And you are still ever so observant."

"Comes with the job," he claimed. "Anyway, we got the toxicology report on your mom back today and I wanted to share results."

"Okay, well . . ." Caroline threw open the door and then her arms out in exasperation, annoyed with herself for having made Jack's face the last thing she saw before falling asleep. Apparently, she had conjured him here. "By all means, do come in!"

He stepped inside, peering around. "So you're alone?"

Caroline ignored her tripping heart. How many years had it been since she'd been alone in a room with Jack? She told herself she wasn't the least bit affected by his presence, but it was an outright lie. "It would seem so." He closed the door and she started for the kitchen, expecting him to follow. "Since you're interrupting my dinner, are you hungry?"

She caught the humor in his tone. "Any of Rose's greens left?"

Caroline tossed him a wry smile over her shoulder, warming to his presence, despite her resolve not to. "We can look."

"Alrighty then."

He followed into the kitchen and then just stood watching as she opened the fridge and pulled out a number of plastic containers. "Josh has been here, so no telling what's left."

She placed a few of the containers on the counter, grabbed two plates and set them on the counter as well, then retrieved forks from the drawer. "So, spill it, what did you find?"

"Nothing. *Really.*"

Caroline opened up one of the containers, peering inside, cocking her head at him in disbelief. "So let me get this straight. You came all the way out here to tell me you found nothing in my mother's toxicology report?" She set the newly opened container of cow peas on the counter and opened another, searching for the greens.

His eyes were filled with thoughts she couldn't

read. "It was on my way home, and I came by just as much to see how you were doing, Caroline."

She set another opened container—this one with ambrosia salad—on the counter. "It's a little late for social calls, don't you think?"

He looked at her with such a weary expression on his face that she felt immediately contrite. "Do you want to know everything we found, or would you rather rehash old bullshit?"

Caroline exhaled a breath and leaned on the counter. "Okay, tell me . . . what did you find?"

"Very, very little, and that's the thing that bothered me. We found minute traces of benzodiazepines and alcohol, but we expected to find more based on what we discovered in her medicine cabinet."

"Alcohol?"

"Only trace amounts. She was sober when she went down those stairs."

"Sober? Wow."

Caroline couldn't remember a moment from the instant of Sammy's death that Flo had gone without a little *help*. Although she had somehow managed to run the paper better than Caroline seemed to be doing at the moment. "Maybe she'd just woken up . . . she must have been disoriented? Augusta has the board on her list of things to fix. I can definitely see where it would be dangerous for someone who wasn't paying attention in the middle of the night."

He stared at her. "Based on your mother's autopsy report, the time of death was placed at approximately seven-thirty—a little early for bedtime, don't you think?" He averted his gaze. "I know she was depressed."

Caroline sat on the stool and stared at the food in

front of her, suddenly not the least bit hungry. "I don't know what Flo would be like if not depressed."

"You all right?"

Caroline swallowed. "Fine," she lied, and clenched her jaw as she peered into Jack's eyes, trying not to betray the storm of emotions brewing inside her. "This just isn't how I expected things to end . . . for Mom."

Or for her and Jack.

"I'm sorry, Caroline. I thought you would want to know."

Caroline held back tears, feeling much too vulnerable and hating herself for feeling this way even after all these years. "Is there anything else?"

"No."

She stood, facing him, her eyes stinging with tears she refused to shed.

Jack studied her, his blue eyes much too knowing. The last thing she wanted right now was his pity. "Well," she said, "thanks for coming by."

He shoved his hands into his pockets and Caroline wondered why he hadn't sent someone else to update her. It would have been easier.

Thankfully, she didn't have to ask him to leave. He was very intuitive. "Please come lock the door behind me," he directed and Caroline followed him. When they reached the foyer, he stopped and said, "I see you turned the mirror around." He pointed to the massive gold-framed mirror that hung in the foyer. "For some reason, your mother had it facing the wall."

Confused, Caroline stared at the mirror, wondering why it would be facing the wall. In any case, she hadn't touched it. Could have been Sadie and her leftover Geechee hoodoo—but it was just as it was right now when Caroline walked in the door. She made a mental note to ask Sadie about it later.

Caroline let him out, flipping the deadbolt. She moved to the front window to watch as he got into his unmarked car, a silver Ford Mustang. He sat there a moment staring at the house, then started his car and left.

It was only after he was gone that Caroline realized she hadn't even pressed for details about the murder last night. That was her job now, but everything, including Karen Hutto, flew out of her head in his presence.

Suddenly, needing to talk to Savannah, Caroline went in search of her cell phone to call her sister and find out where she was—and realized belatedly that her purse was still in the car along with her laptop. She veered off to her mother's office, where she knew there was still a landline. Her mother had hated phones, and preferred not to be surrounded by incessant ringing at home as well as at the office so she kept two landlines in the house. One in her office and one in the guest bedroom, as a courtesy.

Sequestered at the back of the house, her mother's home office was separated from the rest of the house by arched interior French doors. Matching exterior doors opened to a sweeping view of the marsh. It was a stately throne room fit for the queen of Charleston media.

With a shuddering breath, Caroline stood outside the office door, her hand hesitating on the handle. None of them was invited into Flo's office often and she cracked open the unlocked door with a mixture of reverence and trepidation.

Get over it, she told herself. *Flo isn't going to come around the corner and yell at you for poking your nose into her business. Anyway, this is your business now.*

She peered inside and her heart slammed against her ribs.

On the other side of the room, on the French doors leading to the back veranda, one of the beveled panes was shattered, offering a clear view into the night. One door was left ajar.

8

Jack pulled the phone off the dash and glanced at the caller ID. His fingers fumbled as he rushed to answer. "Caroline?"

For a moment, there was dead silence on the other end. "Jack!" she whispered, "Come back—hurry!"

Words he'd been waiting to hear for a long time, but something in her tone told him that it wasn't for the reason he hoped. Thankfully, he hadn't gone far. Even as he asked, he turned the car around. "Is everything okay, Caroline?"

"No!" The single word exploded into the receiver, and the tightness in Jack's chest intensified.

"What's wrong?"

"I don't know! Someone broke in—hurry!"

Wedging the phone between his face and shoulder, he turned on his blue lights, but not the sirens. "Stay on the phone, Caroline!" he demanded and radioed for backup.

CAROLINE CROUCHED by her mother's desk with the phone clasped to her ear. She had gone straight to it, intending to call the police but her fingers automatically dialed Jack's number, knowing he couldn't have gone far.

She hadn't realized she still remembered the number.

There was no sign of the intruder, but night sky beyond the broken glass and the open door made her feel vulnerable. She heard Jack radio for backup and then wrestle with the phone. "Okay," he said.

"Hurry!" she whispered.

"I'm here, Caroline—coming around now. Stay down!"

She hadn't heard his car pull up, but she did hear him toss down the phone without hanging up and waited for what seemed an eternity while he made his way around the property to the office in back. The front door would be locked. She hadn't bothered to set the alarm because Savannah was still out there.

Somewhere.

Where was she?

A new wave of panic set in. She hadn't even considered that maybe someone had taken her sister while she'd slept. The entire time she'd been sitting in the kitchen talking with Jack, consumed with their past, her sister might have been in danger. But no, she reminded herself, the car was gone. So was Tango. Savannah was fine.

Hurry, Jack.

Her thoughts strayed to last night's murder.

The site where the body had been discovered was near Oyster Point, but she couldn't imagine the killer being stupid enough to still be in the area.

Where are you, Sav?

"Police," Jack said. "Hands up!"

Caroline poked her head up just enough to peer over the desk.

"Thank God!" she said, never happier to see him in her life. At the moment, she didn't care what history there was between them. She could have leapt at him and kissed his face ecstatically, except that his gun was drawn and the sight of it was enough to keep her rooted to the spot.

"It's just me in here."

"We're clear out here, too," he told her, "but stay where you are." He kicked the door open and came in. "Could they have gotten into the house?"

Caroline shook her head. "The inside door was closed, but maybe. I don't know. The office door wasn't locked."

"We'll wait until backup arrives to search the house. Have you touched anything?"

Caroline shook her head. "Just the phone. And the office door." And the desk she was gripping right now, but that was obvious.

"Good."

He flipped on the light and inspected the room. Aside from the broken glass, nothing seemed out of place. Papers were still neatly stacked on the desk, drawers were closed and books on the shelves were all in place. Flo had been a meticulous organizer and her office was no exception. But Caroline's heart wouldn't stop pounding.

"Whoever it was must have gotten spooked, but we might get some prints off the door."

They fell into an awkward silence.

What the hell did you talk about when your house had just been vandalized and your savior was the man you were supposed to marry, but didn't because he cheated on you? Nothing. That was what.

After what felt like the longest ten minutes of Caroline's life, they finally heard the screech of car tires out front. Suddenly, there were men in uniform spilling into the room, three to begin with and a fourth moments later.

"I checked the entire perimeter," the fourth said. "Nothing."

Caroline decided it must be safe to leave her spot behind the desk, but Jack ushered her back, then led a group inside the main part of the house.

A very tense few minutes later, one of them returned. "The house is clear," he said and marched out the back door.

Caroline heard yet another car pull up and a car door open and slam, followed by a deep bark and Savannah's voice.

Abandoning her spot behind the desk, Caroline ran out to reassure her sister. The instant she saw Savannah, she ran to embrace her, hugging her tight.

Tango woofed at her in confusion.

"Caroline! What the hell is going on here?"

Caroline explained briefly what had happened and then demanded, "Where were you?"

"I took Sadie home. We had a glass of wine. When I'd gone upstairs to call you down for dinner, you were so out of it you didn't even stir, so I took Tango with me and let you sleep. When did this happen?"

Caroline shook her head. "That's the crazy part. I have no idea! I woke up from a dream, thought I heard glass breaking, but Tango didn't bark and the house was quiet. I didn't think any more about it. Then the doorbell rang, it was Jack, maybe he scared them off—I have no idea!"

Savannah shuddered and hugged Caroline again. "Thank God you're safe! Now slow down and tell me again what happened."

Caroline took a deep breath and told her the story

once more, without the benefit of theatrics. They walked arm in arm into the house as yet another police cruiser came skidding to a halt in the driveway, lights flashing, spraying oyster shells from under the tires. At this point, she was starting to feel a little foolish, considering that no one had actually gotten into the house, and she had to wonder how much of the police response had to do with Jack, and how much had to do with the simple fact that her mother had been a respected pillar of the community. Thinking of the blow-off Karen Hutto seemed to be receiving, she felt a little guilty.

Tango turned and barked as two more men launched out of the cruiser and Jack walked past them, greeting the newcomers. Caroline met his gaze only briefly and looked quickly away.

Savannah gave her a meaningful look. "You know a girl was murdered just down the road last night?"

Caroline shuddered and gave Savannah's arm a squeeze. "Yeah, we'll lock Mother's office door from the inside tonight and maybe you should call Sadie, let her know—no more ducking out without telling me where you're going!" She turned to call Tango into the house, but Jack was petting him. "And he stays home from now on."

Savannah peered over her shoulder. "Tango or Jack?"

"Funny," Caroline said without Savannah's attempt at good humor. "I meant the one who barks."

"Good thing you didn't say the one who bites," her sister teased. "We both know which one that is."

Caroline gave her baby sister the evil eye, annoyed because she had successfully conjured intimate images of Jack in Caroline's mind—sexy memories she really didn't need or want to deal with at the moment. She wholly regretted telling Savannah anything.

Her sister smiled knowingly.

IT WAS NEARLY one A.M. before the police cleared out.

If there was a fingerprint anywhere in her mother's office, they found it and lifted it. As far as anyone could tell, nothing had been taken and there was no evidence anybody had made it inside, but the incident left Caroline feeling a sense of dread, especially after the break-in at Daniel's office.

Savannah stayed by her side, until she couldn't keep her eyes open any longer, and then excused herself, leaving Caroline to say good-bye to Jack.

Feeling awkward, Caroline stood on the top step of the porch, peering down at him, keeping her distance. "Thanks for coming to my rescue," she offered.

One side of his mouth curved upward, and for a moment, she could almost forget there were years of resentment between them. "I'm surprised you remembered the number."

Caroline smiled ruefully. "I'm more surprised you didn't change it."

He lifted both his brows. "It wasn't me who left."

Caroline nodded. "Fair enough," she said. But they both knew why she'd gone.

He shoved his hands into his pockets, something he did whenever he was feeling a little uncertain and Caroline wished she didn't know that detail about him. "Anyway . . . make sure you set the alarm tonight."

Caroline crossed her arms against the slight breeze in the air. "No way will I forget!"

"You sure you don't want me to stay . . . on the couch?"

"We'll be fine, Jack. Josh is coming over after he checks on Sadie."

For a moment, they just stared at one another. Caroline recognized the regret in his eyes and it only served to confuse her.

"Alrighty, well . . . try to get some sleep." He turned to go.

"Jack?"

He stopped and turned.

For some reason, she was suddenly reluctant to see him go, but couldn't ask him to stay. "There was a break-in at Daniel's last week. Could they be connected?"

"King Street?"

"Yeah. They said it was kids looking for cash for drugs. They trashed the place and put Daniel in the hospital."

"Rough area," he acknowledged, and seemed to think about it a moment, conceding, "Probably not. I'll look into it anyway."

"Thanks."

"Good night, Caroline," he said, opening his car door and sliding in.

"Night, Jack," she said.

He waited for her to go inside before driving away.

9

"*When life hands you lemons, make lemonade.*"

It had been Sadie's favorite saying when Caroline and her sisters were pouting over perceived injustices and that advice might seem to apply right now, Caroline thought, except that, no matter what lens you peered through, complaining about inheriting twenty-seven million dollars fell smack under the rubric of "poor little rich girl."

Pretty much Caroline's entire life, she had been acutely aware that, in the grand scheme of things, complaints from any Aldridge were perceived as ungracious. All three girls attended Ashley Hall until high school, when Augusta had begun her personal crusade against her station in life. Aside from Sammy's disappearance, they had lived relatively sheltered childhoods, chauffeured to and from school and wearing tartan uniforms that made them look a little like Highlander dolls, right down to the varying shades of red in their hair. When Augusta had insisted upon being treated like a "normal person," they had all three switched to public school in order to support her—much to Flo's dismay. It was about that time they all discovered boys, and it was about that time Caroline met Jack.

He was the reluctant heartthrob football player who tended to spend his time off field alone and oblivious to the sideways glances girls threw in his direction. A brooding loner, raised by an alcoholic drug-addicted mother and abandoned by his dipsomaniacal father. Although their mothers couldn't have been more different, or come from more different backgrounds, both had neglected their kids. Caroline's mother had left her for the paper and a mountain of grief while Jack's had abandoned him for drugs and prostitution. Both were products of their circumstances.

A champion for the underdog, Jack was the first and only person to ever see Caroline the way she felt. He saw in her what no one else did—that bottomless well of sadness that was inherent in neglected children, no matter what the price of their clothes.

At the time, some part of Caroline had needed the compassion Jack showed her, but the problem with being someone's project was that, eventually, another project would come along to pull at the heartstrings. It seemed to Caroline that Jack's need to nurture was as much an addiction as drugs or alcohol and Caroline had to face the fact that it didn't take much to eclipse the hardships of being a poor little rich girl.

They were engaged to be married when she learned of Jack's "indiscretion" with her best friend. She had completely rejected his impassioned assurances that nothing had happened—mostly out of fear that it was just a matter of time before he would break her heart anyway. But later, even after she'd finally come to believe him, the one thing that had kept Caroline from picking up the phone and calling him was a nagging sense of doubt that love was never a part of their equation.

Simply put, Jack needed to fix things.

He still needed to fix things.

Apparently, so did Josh. He slept over until the door was repaired, which took far longer than anyone would have anticipated. The beveled Italian glass had to be custom ordered, but even once the repairs were done, Caroline had to assure him repeatedly that they would be fine on their own and she promised to set the alarm every night. If he were going to stay with anyone, Caroline reasoned, it should be his mother. It made no sense to leave Sadie alone while he watched over grown women who were perfectly capable of fending for themselves. Anyway, what was he going to do? Move in indefinitely? That would be ridiculous. Flo had lived here for years alone. They would be fine.

The real reason he wanted to stay, she suspected, was that Augusta was finally on her way home. Caroline took the opportunity of her sister's arrival to book a flight to Dallas. She hadn't accumulated much in life, but enough that it would necessitate making some arrangements, including getting her car back to Charleston. Her mom's Town Car was great if you were a collector, but Caroline didn't really give a damn about cars and she didn't care to be the center of attention every time she got on the road. She'd rather be invisible in her little silver Lexus.

As for Dallas, she didn't feel much regret over leaving the place, but since she couldn't get out of her lease, she decided to use the apartment for storage, which would allow her ample time to make a long-term decision. Whether or not she continued at the helm of the *Tribune* remained to be seen, but she wasn't going to stay in Charleston an entire year without her belongings, so she packed up everything she couldn't live without, and whatever wouldn't fit in the car, she shipped.

After all was said and done, it took her five days to accomplish what Augusta had taken nearly two weeks to complete—or rather, what she claimed took her two weeks, because, in fact, she'd shown up in Charleston without much more than she'd left with. Caroline foresaw many more "trips" to New York for her recalcitrant sister.

Caroline made her escape from Dallas during lunch-hour traffic, and once she was settled on I-20, with gas in her car and a steaming cup of coffee, she called Savannah to let her know she was on her way.

"Everything's quiet here," Savannah reassured.

"Good. How's Augie?"

Savannah gave a little snort. "Augie is . . . well, Augie. She's fine."

Not much more needed to be said. "At least she's predictable," Caroline offered. "Once I get back, you can go do whatever it is you have to do in D.C."

"I'm good for now."

Caroline furrowed her brow. Savannah had already been in Charleston more than three weeks. At some point, she would have to go home to make her own arrangements.

What was she avoiding?

"Are you sure?"

"Positive."

"All right. Well, you know best. So how's everyone else?"

Savannah seemed relieved when Caroline abandoned the topic of D.C. "Fine. Josh is MIA—he and Augie got into a tiff. Sadie's fine. She's here now. Wanna talk to her?"

"Nah, that's okay. I still have to call the office, and then I need to pay attention to the road. I haven't driven this way in years."

"All right," Sav said. "Drive carefully."

"I will. Love you," Caroline offered.

"Love you, too."

They hung up and Caroline tried to recall the last time she had said those words to anyone besides her sisters. The last man she had said them to was Jack. And though she was certain she had, at some point, she couldn't ever recall having said those three little words to her mother. Nor could she remember her mother ever having said them to her—or to anyone else, for that matter. Not even to their father. It was difficult to know conclusively if Flo had truly ever loved anything or anyone. Certainly she didn't hate anyone, but she'd always seemed so emotionally barren. Though if Caroline thought back . . . to a time before that day on the beach, she could vaguely recall her mother's laughter. But it was such a ghost of a memory that she couldn't even be sure it was real. She sighed, staring at the road ahead. A semi passed her and she caught the guy in the cab staring down into her car.

"Jerk," she said aloud.

What about the *Tribune*?

Had Flo loved the paper? She'd guarded it jealously—still did, right from the grave—but to Caroline, that smacked of the need to control, not love. But while Caroline wasn't Augusta—tireless in her rebellion—neither was she Savannah. Her mother had lost the right to control any aspect of her life. The paper was on the path to change and Caroline had already engaged an expanded Web team. As soon as she was able to, she intended to hire someone who was experienced with social media.

What about her father? Together, Flo and he had produced four kids within four years. Was that love? Or simply lust? Pretty much the only thing Caroline remembered about her dad was his absence. He was either coming or going or planning to leave. Before his death, he'd built a very promising political career, but apparently—despite the differences in their politics— he had one critical flaw in common with John F. Kennedy. He had a weakness for women. Caroline knew little else about him—at least nothing that wasn't public knowledge. Flo was closemouthed about him and never welcomed that discussion.

Her father had moved out less than two months after Sammy's death and three months later became one of Hurricane Hugo's fifty-six victims—but not for the reason people were expected to die during a natural disaster. While Hugo's winds whipped through Charleston, yanking up ancient trees and mangling bridges, her father keeled over dead upstairs in his Legare Street home from a massive heart attack at the age of thirty-eight—five years older than Caroline was now. His new girlfriend, a twenty-three-year-old College of Charleston graduate, broke the news to Flo sometime during the chaos of reconstruction. Caroline didn't recall her mother shedding a single tear. She'd thanked the girl politely and then directed Caroline to gather her sisters. Once she had them all in one room, she broke the news as a matter of fact, somewhere between haggling with the roofers and cajoling Sadie into making her famous key lime pie—as though key lime pie would magically be able to cheer them.

Admittedly, Caroline had never felt more than a morbid and very detached fascination over the details of her father's death. She often tried to imagine what it must have been like for the girlfriend—barely out of school, and probably crazy about her older, distinguished senator—to have to face his death alone in that house, without any access to a phone or EMS, with water rising all around her.

Caroline took a sip of her coffee, realizing she'd been clutching the phone in her left hand for nearly thirty minutes. She set it down. She didn't know the office number anyway. For the past few days, Pam had called her every hour on the hour, but the ringer was strangely silent today. In fact, when she realized it was nearly four-thirty, she started to pull over to locate the office number in her call history just as the phone rang.

"Pam here."

"Hi, Pam."

"Frank wants to know if you'll be here for the morning meeting?"

"I don't see why not. I'm on my way back now."

"Oh, good!" She was talking low suddenly, whispering. "He's been super grumpy today and he isn't happy you're proposing a six P.M. bedtime. He says we've been putting the paper to bed at midnight since we rolled out the first edition and it's a desecration of tradition."

"I appreciate your telling me, Pam."

Caroline had already begun to set a few cost-saving decisions in motion, and putting the paper to bed earlier was just one of them. "Anything else?

"Well, yes. You know that lady, Karen Hutto?"

"Yes?"

"She wants to run an ad for her missing daughter."

Caroline didn't even think about the decision. "She doesn't have to. Tell Frank to fill the news hole with a small update."

Pam was whispering again. "You sure? I mean, he's going to split his skull on his desk if I tell him that."

Caroline sighed, probably more for Pam's benefit than because of weariness. Truthfully, everything about the *Tribune* invigorated her as much as it terrified her. "Do you work for Frank, or for me?"

"You."

"Then tell him, please. Get someone to call Mrs. Hutto. Let's get some details out there. If the police aren't making any progress, let's give the public something that might help Karen find her daughter—get everything she's got and print it."

"Okay. Who do you want to cover it?" There was a hopeful note to her voice.

"Tell Frank to decide."

"Okay." She sounded disappointed.

"Don't be afraid of him, Pam. He'll come around."

"Okay. Got it. Fill the news hole with Amanda, get details from Karen, tell Frank to decide who covers the story and don't be afraid of the big bad wolf."

Caroline grinned. "You've got it, girl! Remember, he'll huff and he'll puff, but that's about all he can do because he's one cigarette shy of an oxygen machine."

Pam snickered. "Okay."

Caroline laughed, realizing she hadn't seen Jack smoke even once since she'd come home. "Oh, and before I forget. I glanced at your résumé. You have journalism experience!"

Pam suddenly sounded a little sheepish. "I do."

"Do you want to write, Pam?"

"I do!" she exclaimed. "And I have—a little—but Frank is particular about the newsroom and Ms. Aldridge—I mean your mother—she thought I could win him over by learning the ropes from the ground up. So she started me at the receptionist desk." She paused and said much lower, "I've been there a *long* time."

"Okay, put some of your clips on my desk. Let's see what you've got and I'll see if we can't speed up that process a bit."

Caroline could hear the smile in Pam's tone. "Thank you!"

Caroline's phone beeped. "Call me if you need me," she said. "I'll be there in the morning." She ended the call with Pam and glanced down at the caller ID, her heart jumping a little at the sight of the name on the display.

10

C aroline tossed her phone into the passenger seat without answering. It rang three more times, and she stared at the road ahead, feeling painfully ambivalent.

What are you afraid of?

Her feelings for Jack were the one thing she had never been able to control. She could deal with her mother—and pretty much everything else in her life —without waffling, but she had never been able to take a stand with Jack. That, more than anything, was why she'd left Charleston.

It was past time to face her fears, she told herself— all of them. Not just those having to do with measuring up to her mother's expectations. Except that where he was concerned, she didn't have a clue what it was she was truly afraid of.

Having his love then losing it?

Or was it that she was just afraid she wasn't worthy of love—anyone's—and that Jack might wake up one day and figure that out?

For years, any time she had considered more than drinks and dinner with a guy, Jack's face always popped into her head. She could lie to herself, but the reason was perfectly obvious. What she'd felt for him was real. But loving someone didn't mean that being with him was right. Nor did it mean he reciprocated her feelings. Caroline didn't want to settle.

That's why you're still alone.

But she was going to be living in Charleston, and her position at the paper would put her face to face with Jack more often than she might like. Was she really going to continue to go to incredible lengths to avoid him?

She eyed the phone, annoyed by the dialogue in her head. Reaching out, she picked it up and weighed it in her palm a long moment, staring at the road ahead. And then she took a deep breath, unlocked the phone and tapped the first entry on her call history.

───

IT'S JUST ANOTHER PLACE, Caroline assured herself.

The new building with its meandering wooden ramp reminded her less of the original graffiti-etched edifice and more of something you'd find on the strip in Myrtle Beach. The only thing that was familiar to her now was the enormous mountain of discarded oyster shells out back. The original restaurant had been a Charleston institution until it burned in 2006. It was also where she and Jack had had their first date. Unfortunately, she didn't recall that part until after she'd already hung up. But where in the city could they have gone to be free from the ghosts of their past?

Nowhere.

"Wow," she exclaimed, as she got out of her car. "This is so different!"

Jack waited at the bottom of the ramp, his lips slanted a little ruefully. "Of all places . . . you picked this spot?"

Caroline lifted a brow as she reached his side. "Technically, our first dinner here wasn't a date."

"Just like this isn't?"

He was challenging her.

"That's right," she said with an anxious smile.

Truthfully, she had no idea what *this* was and she hoped he wouldn't ask for further clarification, at least not now. Her attraction for Jack was alive and well, but tonight was more about setting boundaries, forging a tenuous new friendship, and maybe a little fishing— although not the sort generally done with a pole. Caroline hoped to get a little insight about Amanda Hutto's investigation—anything that might give her mother hope. Although Folly Beach had its own small police force, which was handling the case, Caroline knew Jack had friends among them.

Touching a hand to her waist, he urged her up the ramp before him and Caroline jumped at the contact, peering up at him in surprise. The glance they shared was far too revealing, and Caroline averted her gaze. Thankfully, he didn't touch her again, but the air between them was charged with undercurrents.

Inside the restaurant, the atmosphere was no less touristy and Caroline had the overwhelming impression of plasticity. Gone were the mismatched graffiti-covered chairs and rickety, newspaper-covered tables. Although still a hodgepodge of furnishing, the tables and chairs were all now plastic and the shack-like atmosphere was gone. The tables were covered in red-and-white plastic checkered cloths and there were talking fish on the walls. And it was clean.

Jack seemed to sense her disappointment. "Mind sitting on the dock?" he asked. "There's a breeze tonight. Mosquitoes shouldn't be bad."

"I'd like that."

"Let's do it."

Caroline stepped back to let him talk to the hostess, studying the small crowd. It was chic to come here now. A couple sat at the bar with martinis, staring dreamily into each other's eyes. Back in the day when she and Jack had come for the occasional oyster fix, there was no glamour to the experience, and the place was usually empty but for the few locals who knew where to find the hidden entrance on Folly Road. It looked to Caroline as though they were now set up for bigger functions—weddings maybe.

Like the one she'd never had.

The thought sidled through her brain before she could filter it out.

This wasn't about her and Jack.

It was about Amanda Hutto. It was about proving, at least to herself, that she could live up to the expectations her mother had set. There was more at stake here than feelings and the death of romance. The picture was far bigger.

With Jack's natural charm, they didn't have to wait long for a table on the narrow dock, surrounded by Sol Legare Creek. The waitress placed them at a table for two and tried a few times to light their candle. Caroline nearly told her not to bother, except that the sun was setting and there didn't appear to be any other light source on the dock.

A sliver of sunlight on the horizon sent tendrils of pink and peach for miles, casting a supernal light over the creek.

Caroline sat, wholly regretting her choice of restaurants. She had chosen this place because it was the least romantic setting she knew of in the entire city, not realizing until Sadie enlightened her on the way out the door that it had been rebuilt.

Ignoring the other couple at the end of the dock and the too-intimate setting, Caroline compared the images to the ones that lived in her memories. The evening breeze was balmy and the scent of pluff mud, whence the oysters they'd soon eat had been so recently plucked, was pungent and strong. Out here, she could easily imagine that nothing had changed . . . that inside, every inch of the interior—chairs, tables, walls—were covered with the graffiti of ages. Back in the day, there was only one reason anyone came to Bowens Island—for the oysters. She hoped that hadn't changed.

"Don't worry," he said, seeming to read her thoughts—at least the part that didn't have to do with lovers or regrets. "They're still great."

"Oh, good!" Caroline said a little uncomfortably.

Luckily, they didn't have long before the waitress returned. "Drinks?" the girl asked buoyantly.

"Not for me," Caroline announced, setting down her menu. The last thing she needed tonight was impaired judgment.

"Guinness," Jack said easily, scooping up her menu and handing both back to the waitress. "We'll have two all-you-can-eat oysters and one Frogmore stew sans the frogs."

The waitress didn't catch Jack's wink to Caroline. "Oh, there ain't no frogs in the stew," she reassured.

Jack sounded disappointed. "Not even one?"

"No sir. The stew gets its name from . . ."

Despite herself, Caroline hid a smile but Jack didn't hold back his chuckle.

"You're teasing me!" the girl declared in a thick Southern drawl, and laughed, lingering a moment too long, her gaze on Jack while she shuffled the menus nervously.

"Just a little," Jack confessed and his grin was full of good-natured mischief.

He still had the same effect on women—the moment he opened his mouth or smiled, he somehow charmed every last one—except her mother.

"So tell me why we're here," Jack said, not bothering to mince words. He didn't even notice the girl's moony-eyed expression as she walked away. "I was surprised you called back."

"Well," Caroline began, unraveling her napkin, "I'm not sure whether you've heard yet, but I'm home to stay . . ." She glanced up to gauge his expression. "For a while."

He didn't appear all that surprised, but she explained anyway, in detail, not realizing until this instant how much she needed to talk about the changes in her life. She went on to tell him about the stipulations of her mother's will, Augusta's temper tantrums and even her concerns about Savannah's avoidance of her life. She hadn't realized how long she'd been talking until the waitress returned with Jack's Guinness.

"So is this what you want?" he asked, referring to her return to Charleston.

Caroline shrugged, relaxing a little. "As much as I don't like that Mother is calling the shots from the grave, I'd be stupid to walk away from it all. Even Augusta can't do it."

Jack shrugged. "You can do a helluva lot of good

with that kind of money," he acknowledged. "That's for sure."

As though someone kicked up the volume on the background music, the sounds of the marsh rose as the sun set, leaving them bathed in the light that spilled from the windows amidst a chorus of crickets.

Caroline's thoughts drifted to her mother.

Flo had certainly done her share for the community. People loved her for it, but it would have been nice if her charity had begun at home. Their lives, in so many ways, were a mess—all of them. Caroline couldn't commit, or even have a normal relationship. Augusta seemed to feel she had to bleed for the betterment of mankind. As far as Caroline knew, she had no life and devoted all her time to her position as the Director of Volunteer Services and Youth Services for the American Red Cross. And Savannah . . . Caroline had to confess . . . she didn't know her youngest sister any longer. She knew her life history, of course, but she didn't really know what made Savannah tick. Savannah was quiet and distant and intensely private— something Caroline hadn't realized until returning to Charleston.

"How are you holding up?"

The tenderness in his question took her by surprise. Her chest constricted a little and she opened her mouth to answer, but found her voice jammed in her throat. She swallowed and shrugged and for a moment, she could only stare into his knowing blue eyes, confused by the emotions his question roused.

He looked exactly the same, except for a few lines around his eyes and mouth.

Laugh lines?
Was he happy?
She didn't dare ask.

Caroline reminded herself to breathe.

"Your sisters look up to you . . . even if they don't show it," he offered.

Only Jack had ever truly understood her relationship with her sisters . . . even when Caroline didn't. Memories too sweet to be discarded filled her head. Defensively, she pushed them away and clung to the here and now.

It wasn't his job to bolster her any longer.

She changed the subject. "Anyway, thank you again for coming to my rescue the other night. I guess you can say this is my attempt to thank you . . . I thought we could find a way to bury the hatchet."

He grinned. "So long as it's not in my back."

Caroline laughed. "There was a time I might have contemplated that," she admitted, "but we're past that . . . right?"

His smile softened, his lips turning only slightly at the corners, but the smile faded a little from his eyes. "Caroline," he began, and she braced herself for a tense conversation. But then he seemed to think better of whatever he was about to say, and conceded, "I'd like nothing more than for us to start over."

Something fluttered in her belly.

She wanted to ask him what, exactly, he meant by that. Her idea of starting over was trying to find a middle ground where they didn't want to kill each other, but she was afraid she already knew what he was proposing.

The breeze lifted slightly and the candle flickered nervously between them.

Caroline couldn't avert her eyes from his. "So . . . how's Kelly?" she found herself asking without wanting to know. It was impossible not to know about Jack's love life. For all its cachet, Charleston was still a very small town and gossip had reached her clear to Dallas—mostly through "well-meaning friends" who thought she had a "right to know."

Jack picked up his glass, took another hearty swig and then lifted it to show the waitress he was ready for another. He swallowed hard, as though biting back more than just the words he wanted to say. "We're done."

"I'm sorry," Caroline said automatically.

"Don't be. It should have been over a long time ago. What about you? Leave any unfinished business in Dallas?"

"No."

The single word left a thousand unanswered questions hanging in the air. Jack had the courtesy not to ask any of them.

The waitress brought him another pint, and Jack tended to it conscientiously as they talked through a first and second oyster dump on their table. By the time the stew came out of the kitchen, Caroline was too full to eat any of it, but she picked at the sausage and shrimp. She noticed Jack avoided the shrimp, even pushed a few in her direction, remembering that she liked those best.

A lover's gesture.

She preferred to think of it as his peace offering.

"Delicious!" she said. "Thank you!"

He watched her as she ate, his gaze focused on her mouth and Caroline tried not to care what he was thinking.

He leaned forward, and her heart skipped a beat at his nearness. The table was entirely too small, too intimate. Even with the cool breeze, her palms grew damp. Butterflies fluttered in her belly.

"You're beautiful, Caroline," he whispered.

Caroline swallowed the bite of shrimp and then swallowed again, a nervous lump rising into her throat.

His hand slid toward hers on the table and electric pulses shot through her body. She didn't move, couldn't seem to.

"Jack . . ." Caroline protested and tried to pull her hand away—too late. He reached out, snatching it and pinning it to the table.

"Tell me you haven't thought about us," he demanded.

Caroline shook her head, confusion clouding her senses. "I-I can't . . ."

"Can't what?" he asked, his voice husky and low. He pulled her closer and Caroline didn't have the will to resist. He leaned forward, his lips hot and soft. The light touch gave her an instant fever, a longing for more. Her body convulsed and she pressed her legs together, feeling the stirrings of desire. She jerked her hand away and sat back, inhaling a mind-clearing breath.

Jack simply looked at her, his brow furrowing. He didn't sit back, didn't move, simply looked at her with a mixture of disappointment and torment.

"Will you do me a favor?" he ventured.

"Of course."

"I need you to promise me you'll be careful coming and going . . . especially when you're alone."

"Of course," Caroline reassured him. "Because of the break-in?"

His blue eyes pierced her. "Not exactly."

THE COUPLE at the end of the dock, having finished their meal, walked past them on the way out, laughing together . . . in that easy way lovers had with each other.

The way Caroline and Jack used to be.

The alcohol was supposed to numb Jack, but it had the opposite effect. It hurt to sit this close to her and not be able to touch her. He had never stopped loving her and his sense of duty warred with his heart. If she were anybody else, he would never consider saying what he wanted to say . . . what he felt compelled to say, despite years of commitment to his job. Still, he considered his words carefully, knowing he was about to step over the line.

Since the break-in at her house, his nightmares were giving him cold sweats at night. The Aldridge estate was a stone's throw from the site of the Jones murder. There was a rising sense of dread in his bones that he couldn't shake. If anything happened to Caroline— or to her sisters—because he kept what he'd learned from the coroner to himself . . . well, he couldn't live with it.

He sipped at his beer, waiting for the couple to leave before continuing. "It's just a hunch," he said, once they were alone, "but it's a strong one, Caroline . . . it's not safe for anyone to be out alone at night."

She laughed. "Now I suppose you're going to offer to be my bodyguard?"

He didn't smile. "I'm dead serious."

Caroline visibly stiffened. "Why, Jack? Do you think there might be more murders?"

Jack took another long pull of his drink before answering, feeling tortured to the core of his soul. Still, he couldn't quite bring himself to betray his badge. "Not sure," he said. But those two little words held the entire welfare of a city within them and carried the weight of his professional responsibility. He was a police officer. Wasn't that what he was supposed to do? Protect people? If he couldn't even protect the woman he loved—that he had loved nearly his entire life—what the hell good was his badge?

The surrounding marsh took on a far less benign air.

The waitress brought Jack another pint without his having to ask for it and he waited for her to leave.

Caroline sat forward. "Are you saying what I think you're saying, Jack?"

He weighed his words carefully. "Bottom line . . . we don't know what we're dealing with yet."

But Jack did know to trust that feeling in his gut. Only once—ever—had he not listened . . . and the next morning they'd escorted him to the morgue to ID his mother's body.

Judging by the condition of Amy Jones's body, her murder had not been perpetrated impulsively—not fueled by rage or hostility. No matter how he looked at it, he couldn't shake the feeling the murderer had been interrupted . . . preparing the body for something else . . . that this wasn't his first murder . . . nor would it be his last.

He could see the wheels turning behind Caroline's bright hazel eyes. "Are you going to hold a press conference?"

Jack's shoulders tensed. He'd said too much already . . . and yet not enough. He'd rather lose his badge than lose her. Filled with turmoil, he shook his head.

"Don't you believe people have the right to know?"

"There's only one body," he said pointedly, and felt like a hypocrite because that was precisely why he'd warned Caroline—so she could protect herself—but talking to the woman he loved was far different from sending an entire city into a panic.

Her expression suddenly turned to fury. "What about Amanda Hutto?"

"What about her?"

"She's missing, Jack!"

"That's the problem, Caroline. She's missing. You can't make a determination about a person's fate when you have no body."

Her nostrils flared and Jack sensed she wanted to say more.

"Do you believe her disappearance is connected to the Jones case?"

He shook his head. "I don't see what a twenty-two-year-old college girl and a six-year-old kid have in common."

Her shoulders were back and her expression revealed unreserved anger. "Remember Gaskins? His victims had nothing in common!" Caroline sat back in her chair, tossed her napkin on the table and whatever tenuous connection Jack had felt between them vanished. "Do you at least have a lead?" she asked, a little calmer now, but with an edge he'd never noticed in her before this second.

In fact, for the first time since meeting her—at just fifteen—he saw not the sweet susceptible girl he had fallen in love with and nearly married, nor the woman who had practically left him standing at the altar . . . nor the object of his current obsession, but a total stranger. "Maybe," he admitted, clamming up. "I can't say."

A SUDDEN CHILL jetted down Caroline's spine.

Despite the warm breeze, she wished she'd

brought a sweater.

The chirping of crickets and the croaking of frogs were suddenly like death shrieks. The night seemed forbidding, black, and that scent she had become so ambivalent about lately turned foul, like the indissoluble smell of decay.

Her emotions hovered close to the surface.

Her memory flashed to that day on the beach with her brother. What if it were Sammy who was missing right now? She remembered Karen Hutto's face, full of anguish and pain. There was a city full of Karen Huttos out there—all of them ready to protect their children—if provided the right information. She didn't understand a sense of due process that endangered the welfare of others.

Whatever she felt for Jack, it was eclipsed by an overwhelming desire to do the right thing. No, she *needed* to do the right thing.

The waitress returned to ask Jack if he wanted another beer, but before he could respond, Caroline picked up her purse and fished through it for her wallet, retrieving her credit card. She handed it to the waitress, smiling tautly, "Dinner's on me," she announced, turning to Jack. "I'll expense it."

He looked too shell-shocked to protest and the waitress hesitated only a moment before walking away with Caroline's card.

Caroline stood. "Thanks for the conversation, Jack. It was very enlightening."

He sat there, peering up at her, his blue eyes shuttered, and Caroline was too rattled to know what more to say. He seemed somehow cold and removed, and this moment, she felt anything but. Every nerve in her body was screaming and her heart was thumping like a fist against her rib cage. She couldn't just sit there and pretend everything was okay.

She followed the waitress inside to sign the check and left Jack sitting alone, not daring to look back to see if he watched her leave. All she knew was that this time, she wasn't helpless. She didn't have to sit idly by and watch the world go to hell.

11

Only a blind man could have missed the screaming front-page headline in the morning edition of the *Tribune*.

Succession Creek Killer: Authorities Fear More Deaths.

Jack did a double take at the dispenser outside the Lockwood station, and fished money out of his pocket to pay for a single issue. Once he had it in his hand, he went inside and threw the paper unceremoniously onto his desk, then sat down, cursing.

He wasn't at his desk more than twenty seconds before his partner came in to show him a copy of the same paper. Jack threw him out and got up and slammed his door shut. Don Garrison was a good detective, but with his mildly competitive nature it was a little like rubbing salt on a wound right now.

He understood why Caroline felt driven to warn the masses. The Hutto girl. It hit her right where she lived—in the long shadow of her brother's death. She was thinking with her heart, not her head.

He sat down and took a deep breath as he fished his cell phone out of his pocket. Even before he exhaled, he was dialing Caroline's number.

No answer.

He wasn't surprised. He hung up and dialed again, and again, leaving a message only after the third time he heard her short, impersonal greeting.

Maybe he should have expected this—and he would have from her mother—but this was Caroline. Despite her abrupt dismissal last night, her preemptive action blindsided him.

"You aren't qualified to run this paper!"

Frank Bonneau's voice boomed throughout the brick walls of the old building. Beyond the glass doors of her office, Caroline could see that heads were down in the newsroom, staff members hiding in their cubicles as though they were holed up in trenches, bracing for heavy artillery.

Having been dragged in against her will, Pam sat in a corner chair in Caroline's office, head down, not daring to speak a word. Frank had been yelling so long and hard that even her office windows were beginning to fog. To say he was angry was an understatement.

Caroline let him blow off steam, feeling worse for Pam than she did for herself, because she had expected his anger. For better or worse, she believed she was doing the right thing and she was prepared to defend her action.

Red faced, waving a copy of today's *Tribune*, he continued shouting, "Do you have any idea what the *Post* will do with this?"

The "this" he was talking about was the front-page story Caroline had pushed through late last night after leaving Jack. Colluding with Pam on the paper's final twelve P.M. bedtime, she'd given Pam the story and the byline. They had worked together all night, until the last possible minute, verifying information and securing a second source.

From the moment the issue hit the stands, the phones began to ring—the police department, Pam's new source at CPD, wanting to make certain he wouldn't be identified, Jack, random strangers, other reporters wanting more information.

"In all my forty-some years," Frank was yelling, "I have never seen more shoddy journalism! Who in their right mind releases a story like this when there's only one body! Congratulations, Ms. Aldridge," he said. "You're going to scare the shit out of this city based on speculation!" He shook his head in disgust and hurled the paper onto her desk. "I would never have approved that!"

"Then you should have stayed last night."

In protest of the changes forthcoming, Frank had gone home early and Caroline bumped one of his front-page stories—not that she had intended to do anything behind his back. It had just turned out that way, and she didn't call him because, well, she didn't want an argument.

"I am not going to babysit you, and I am not going to spend my last years in the newsroom butting heads with a snot-nosed girl who thinks she knows more than anyone else because she went to an Ivy League school and worked at a handful of sensationalized rags!"

"I have never worked at a rag!" Caroline assured him, trying to keep her voice calm. "Every paper I have ever been associated with has received industry recognition. That's completely unfair to say, Frank." She understood the principles of journalism and she could back her story. "I stumbled on a lead," she said defensively. "I ran with it and my source is one hundred percent reliable."

"Your source is anonymous!" he shouted back, riling himself all over again.

"We checked with a second source at CPD, who verified that the possibility of a serial killer has been discussed."

"Surprise, surprise! A second anonymous source!"

And now, Caroline was getting angry. She'd had about enough of his temper tantrum. "We quoted on background! That's perfectly legitimate! Not the same thing as anonymity!"

"Are you really going to teach me about journalism?" he asked, his eyes bulging and his face florid.

Caroline brought her tone down, realizing how high it had risen in response to his. "We named both sources as detectives and Pam called to verify everything. We even corroborated details with the roommate."

"That's another thing!" he said, his tone rising again. He peered over at Pam. "Did you or Pam do this goddamn interview?"

Pam ducked her head lower.

"I did the initial interview but gave Pam the story."

"You gave her the byline when you brought the key details to this piece of speculative fiction?"

"No! Pam had her own source at CPD. I only gave her the lead! She went after it and wrote the story." Caroline was perfectly willing to accept his anger for her part in this, but she was not going to have him take it out on Pam. "Considering that I am the publisher, I didn't want to set a precedent by writing the story myself."

"Maybe you should have thought about that before you gave a story to an inexperienced journalist!"

"Damn it, Frank! Have you even bothered reading her résumé? She's got plenty of experience and she's damned good. You haven't even given her a chance. She's been waiting two years to move into the newsroom. Even my mother hoped you'd make room for her, but you apparently are such a control freak that even Flo was afraid to step on your toes!"

He came forward and tapped his index finger so hard on the offending paper that Caroline thought he would break his finger. "This is stenographic journalism at its worst! You're going to take heat for this one—no, correction! *We* are going to take heat for this one! The *Post* will hang us with this! We are holding on by the skin of our teeth, here, and the only reason we haven't gone belly up is because people respect us. We've still got a little cachet in this city, but not if we're going to run cowpats like this!"

"This story's no different from a thousand I have read!"

"That's the point, Caroline. We're better than that! This is 'he said, she said' bullshit! If you're going to run a story like this, you need to roll up your sleeves and do some real investigative journalism! Identify your sources, stand by them." He shook his head. "As for your mother . . . she would roll in her grave if she knew what you'd done!"

That was the one thing Caroline couldn't bear to hear.

Caroline dug in her heels, defending her position. "We *did* go after this story. We spoke to the best friend, we corroborated details. I felt it was our responsibility to inform the public of what I'd learned. Don't you think people have a right to make decisions about their lives with all the information available?"

"Goddamn it!" he exploded. "It's not our respon-

sibility to warn the public, Caroline—it's our responsibility to report news responsibly! I would never
have sent this story to the desk. If you want to run
this newspaper like a fish rag, you can do it by
yourself!"

He stormed out of her office suddenly, slamming
the door and shouting obscenities that no office
should ever have to hear.

Caroline turned her attention to Pam. "Sorry
about that."

"He's so angry," Pam said, standing as she stated
the obvious.

Caroline was angry too, but not for the same reasons. "He'll get over it."

Pam looked ashamed, despite Caroline's defense
of her, which only made Caroline feel worse. "I've
honestly never seen him like that."

Caroline felt suddenly confused. She'd reacted in
anger and fear. Had she abused the power her position afforded her? "You can go," she said.

The moment Pam walked out of her office, Caroline's office phone rang again—probably Jack for the
hundredth time. After his first message, she didn't really care to talk to him. He was angry, too. He felt betrayed. She understood that, and she had braced
herself for his anger, believing she was doing the right
thing—but suddenly she was no longer quite so sure.
The vehemence with which everyone seemed to be
reacting to this story took her by surprise. She truly
thought she was doing the right thing. Contrary to
what some might think, it wasn't about selling papers.
It was about doing something that mattered, and
arming a community—her community—to deal with
what was to come.

She had sacrificed Jack for her sense of duty. There

was no way she would have betrayed him for less than moral decency.

Again the phone rang, and she stared at it, tentatively picking up the receiver. She was grateful to hear Josh's voice on the other end. "Caroline?"

"Jesus! Thank God it's you!"

"Taking heat?"

"You wouldn't believe how much!"

There was a moment of silence on the other end of the phone. "I can't say I'm on your side. I actually called to ask where you left your head."

Caroline sat in her chair, feeling utterly defeated. "Not you, too!"

"Damn it, Caroline . . . your sources are two anonymous investigators—you didn't even name them as CPD. You could have at least specified neither was with the county solicitor's office. They could point the finger at me!"

Caroline leaned her head into her hand, a bad feeling settling in her stomach. She had reacted. She had made a decision in the heat of the moment. She wasn't prepared for this. When her mother had drawn up the will, surely she hadn't expected Caroline to assume this role so soon. Maybe Caroline had made a mistake? And, worse, she had dragged Pam into it.

Josh's tone, at least, was gentle, even if his words made her feel sick. "I'm already taking shit over it. You have to reveal your sources," he pressed.

Caroline's gut twisted. "I can't, Josh."

"Can't or won't?"

"Won't. But I will assure you that both my sources are one hundred percent reliable."

"Jesus, you come home for one month and you've already done more damage to my politics than I could have with all my pot-smoking college days."

"You didn't smoke pot in college," Caroline reminded him, her voice hollow.

"You know what I'm sayin', Caroline. If you don't reveal your source, they could assume it's me. I'm the closest to you. You have to make this right."

If she revealed either of her sources, both of them could lose their badges, and Pam had promised her source anonymity. It wouldn't be right to reveal one and not the other. God, it seemed she had made a mess of everything. "I can't, Josh!"

There was a long pause on other end of the phone. "All right, well . . . I've gotta go."

"Are you mad?"

"Not mad. Disappointed. See you tonight."

He hung up, and Caroline held the phone in her hand for the longest time, knowing the instant there was a dial tone, it would only ring again.

How could something she had intended for good turn out to be so very wrong?

THE INSTANT CAROLINE hit the street, blue lights flashed in her rearview mirror.

Dismayed after the day she'd had, she tried to determine what traffic sin she had committed in the fifty or so yards since leaving the garage. A few hard glances channeled her anxiety into anger.

It was Jack.

Navigating her way through rush-hour traffic, she pulled over as soon as she could, but not before finding a decent spot, unwilling to delay others simply because Jack was angry with her. The instant she pulled over, Jack pulled his unmarked car up alongside her, parking at an angle in front of her as though to prevent her from leaving. Nor did he bother turning off his blue lights as he got out of the car.

Jackass.

He was at her door by the time she rolled down the window, his jaw set with a fury that must have escalated with every ignored phone call during the course of the day. At last count, there had been thirteen. She tried to keep the anger from her tone. "Do you mind telling me why you've pulled me over?"

His tone was cold and hard. "License, please."

Caroline rolled her eyes. "You've got to be kidding!"

If his eyes had been daggers, she realized she would be a dead woman sitting behind the wheel of her car. "License!" he demanded.

"Okay, so now what . . . you've been demoted to traffic cop?" Caroline was exasperated, but she complied, taking her license out of her purse and handing it over.

"That's a distinct possibility," he told her, snatching the license from her hand. "Do you understand what you've done, Caroline?"

Now it began.

This was precisely what Caroline had been trying to avoid all day. "Yes, Jack, I know what I've done. I've alerted the public to look after themselves since you guys don't seem to be up to the job." It was unfair to say, she realized, but she didn't appreciate his attitude.

A muscle at his jaw twitched. "Is that right?"

"Yes, for God's sake! We have a missing child and a mother who's traumatized. We have at least one dead body and reason to suspect there will be more—yes, I do believe that's what I'm doing!" Maybe she hadn't gone about it right, but she was trying to help.

Something in his gaze softened. "You took advantage of your position," he countered. "Jesus, Caroline, you put words in my mouth!"

"I'd say you were taking advantage of yours!" Caroline waved a hand in protest over his traffic stop. "What the hell is this?"

"I guess we're even."

"No, we aren't!" Caroline exclaimed. "You still have one hell of a lot to make up for if you were so inclined!"

"Is that what this is about?" His blue eyes glittered with renewed fury. "Because you believe I fucked your best friend ten years ago?"

"God, no!" That he would reduce all this to *that* was intolerable. Caroline was trying desperately to do the right thing, and while she was still angry about that long-ago betrayal, that was *not* what this was about. This was about one dead girl and a missing child and lives that might soon be damaged forever.

"I don't believe you," he said. "I think that's exactly what this is about—tit for tat!"

"Really, Jack? You think I would publish a story that affected the lives of thousands just to get back at you? I got over our bullshit years ago," she lied. "This isn't about us!" At least part of it was true. Caroline would never stoop to revenge and she would never, ever, toy with the lives of others. Her sense of responsibility was too great. She was an oldest child, driven to take care of her sisters, driven to take care of everything and anybody whose lives might be impacted by her decisions.

"Like I said, I don't believe you. I think you're still angry and you might as well admit it."

Caroline felt heat infuse her face.

She wasn't about to admit a damned thing!

His car sat smack in the middle of traffic and one

look in the rearview mirror revealed annoyed expressions on the faces of passing drivers. "Is this the place and time for this discussion?" She smacked her steering wheel with the butt of her hand, losing her temper, losing her mind. "We're in rush-hour traffic, for God's sake!" She couldn't deal with this. Her entire day had gone to shit and ninety-nine percent of it was her own damned fault.

Jack's expression was unrepentant. He looked down at her driver's license. "I don't give a shit where we are. How long have you been in Charleston now?"

Caroline blinked, feeling a little like a deer caught in headlights. Too many things were happening all at once. "You know how long I've been here, Jack. Stop it!"

He studied her Texas driver's license, turning it over; his previous anger appeared to have melted from his features. "Do you intend to remain a permanent resident of the State of South Carolina?"

Caroline simply looked at him, suddenly understanding the direction he was going with this line of questioning.

"Do you?" he persisted.

She resented having to answer. "Reluctantly."

He held out her license. "You have forty-five days from the time of residency to transfer your registration," he said in his most authoritative tone, "ninety days to obtain a new license and surrender your old license to the State of South Carolina."

Caroline gritted her teeth. "Thank you so much for that info. Now do you mind telling me why you pulled me over in the first place?"

"Out-of-state plates," he stated—unlike Caroline, his voice was now completely devoid of emotion. "It's our responsibility to check the status of driver insurance and vehicle plate information, but as you know, there has also been a homicide in the area and it's also my duty to stop suspicious nonnative vehicles."

Caroline felt a pulse tic at her temple. "You are *still* an ass!"

His gaze met hers and whatever emotion he had managed to keep out of his tone was visible right there in the depths of his sapphire blue eyes. "And you're still a spoiled little rich girl who can't quite fill her mommy's shoes and doesn't know any better than to stop trying!"

He knew exactly what to say to hurt her.

Caroline gripped the steering wheel, forcing a breath through her lungs. She turned away, tears pricking her eyes, hiding the telltale burn. "Is that what you think of me?"

He didn't hesitate before answering. "Have you known me to ever say things I don't mean?"

Caroline narrowed her eyes accusingly. "I can think of at least three words!" At this point, drivers were no longer quite so annoyed by the police car blocking traffic. She imagined them all with bags of popcorn in hand, looking on with interest as cop and offender argued like lovers. Even Pam drove slowly by, craning her neck to see what was going on. Caroline was mortified. She pretended not to see her. "Are we done here? I see things much more clearly now."

"No. You don't see. Your head's still crammed too far up your mother's ass to grasp the big picture here! For better or worse, you haven't just betrayed *my* trust. I told you that shit because *I love you* more than I do my fucking badge! But never mind that! You haven't just risked my life's work over a half-baked story; you've scared the shit out of these people. Do you understand that, Caroline?"

Caroline blinked, her brain zeroing in on three little words. "There is a killer out there," she said without quite the same resolve. "I believe people have a right to know to look over their shoulders!"

"You can be damned sure they will, because you've just set the mood for this entire city. Next time you sit in your mother's chair, remember that! You're not just a reporter. Mommy can't fix your mistakes. Everything you do and say makes an impact now! That's something your mother understood clearly and apparently you do not!"

Caroline's head began to ache.

So did her heart.

She couldn't even counter him, because deep down, she was coming to the realization that maybe she had truly made a career-shaking mistake. And the question wasn't whether she would survive it, but would the paper survive it.

Would she and Jack survive it?

Probably not.

"I have news for you," he said, adding insult to injury, "you've got a long way to go before you fill your mother's shoes. I don't care if she was Mommy Dearest behind closed doors. Out here, she did the right thing. Always." He dropped the license back inside the window. "Drive safely," he concluded and walked away, leaving Caroline's head hammering. There was an even bigger ache in the region of her heart, but she couldn't afford to focus on that right now.

She had to fix this awful mess.

12

J ack slid into his car, turned off his blue lights, and pulled into a mob of rush-hour traffic. Like lemmings charging to a precipice, people would follow wherever the media led them. *That*, he told himself, was the true source of his anger—*that*, and not the fact that he had trusted Caroline and she had betrayed his trust too easily.

The truth was that he was angrier with himself than he could ever be with her. He should have told her nothing. Fortunately, he hadn't revealed anything that might endanger the case.

For Christ's sake, he'd admitted to Caroline that he loved her.

Hopefully that little bit of info had gone right over her head, although judging by the disoriented look in her eyes after he'd said it, he didn't think she'd missed a single word. For better or worse, he'd said too much already.

The ball was in her court.

SOMEWHERE OUT THERE Caroline thought her mother must be enjoying the show. Point made! No more stone throwing from her quarter. Everyone was human. Everyone made mistakes. And Caroline seemed to be making way more than her share. But apparently, her bad day wasn't nearly over.

She pulled into the driveway to find a young blond woman in police uniform seated on the back end of an old red Jeep Cherokee. Caroline parked behind her, concerned that something might be wrong. From the minute she had come back to Charleston, it seemed there had been one drama after another. She bolted out of the car, shoving the door closed. "Can I help you?"

"Not really," the woman said calmly, looking Caroline over as she approached. "I just came to get a few things off my chest."

And an ample one it was, Caroline couldn't help but notice. She extended her hand. "I'm Caroline Aldridge."

The woman didn't bother to uncross her arms and all that was missing to complete her belligerent attitude was a wad of chewing gum in her mouth. "I know who you are."

There wasn't much patience left after the ordeal with Jack, but Caroline waited for her to speak—something the woman didn't seem inclined to do until she was good and ready. "How's the back window?" she asked.

Confused, Caroline's brows collided. "You're here about the break-in?"

"No," she said. "Though I hope you got it fixed. Apparently, there's a serial killer on the loose . . . have you heard?"

Annoyance ripped through Caroline. "I told Chief Condon my sources are confidential. I won't reveal them. I don't have anything more to say!"

The woman looked Caroline up and down, sizing her up, eyes smoldering with what Caroline interpreted as anger. "I'm not here to find out who leaked that info. I already know who leaked it and so does every other cop on the force. The only reason he hasn't been suspended at this point is because no one wants to see a good guy get a bum rap, but I can tell you this . . . showing up at his ex-girlfriend's house over a broken window with half the police force didn't help his cause any. But, like I said, I'm not here about the break-in. I'm off duty."

Caroline was through playing games. "*Why* are you here?"

More to the point, who the hell was she?

"Because I needed to see the high and mighty Caroline Aldridge for myself! You never gave a shit about Jack back then. You still don't and he doesn't seem to care that you drag his heart around like an abused puppy on a leash!"

Caroline's hackles rose. "You must be Kelly," she surmised aloud. "I'd say it was nice to meet you but for obvious reasons I'd be lying."

Caroline started toward the house and Kelly shot off the car. "Why did you come back here?" she asked. "Jack and I were doing fine until you showed up!"

"Fine is not the word I would use," Caroline contended. "But if it makes you feel better, Jack and I are not together—haven't been for ten years and I don't see that changing. Whatever is going on between the two of you has nothing to do with me."

"It has everything to do with you! I held on patiently for ten years! Ten years while he pined over you!"

Suddenly, Caroline felt a rush of pity for the other woman. But she didn't trust her. The last thing she needed right now was to get into a catfight with a police officer—off duty or not. She could picture those headlines now. She made her way toward the house, escaping. "If you've been with him that long, it's not my problem—it's yours for hanging on to a man who obviously doesn't love you. And frankly," she added, hurrying toward the steps, "if he was sleeping with you that soon after we broke up, he didn't love me either!"

So much for declarations of love!

Thankfully, Kelly didn't follow and Augusta opened the door abruptly, coming to Caroline's rescue. "What the hell is going on out here?"

"Nothing," Caroline said, hoping Kelly would go now.

A backward glance reassured her that their unwelcome guest was leaving. "Bitch!" Kelly exclaimed, as she opened her door and slid into her Jeep.

Augusta started out the door, but Caroline pushed her back. "What the hell is that all about?" her sister demanded.

"Nothing! Everything!" Caroline said and bolted up the stairs, her eyes stinging with unshed tears. She'd been holding it together for far too long and it took every bit of fortitude she had to make it into her room—her mother's room.

She was nothing but a pretender.

Outside, she heard the sound of the Jeep driving away and she threw herself on the bed, staring at the ceiling as tears streamed silently down her cheeks—every last one that she had denied since the moment she'd gotten the news about her mother's death.

She cried for every second she had missed out on with her mother. Cried for the harsh words and lost opportunities to mend fences. Cried for the memories

that were already gone and those that were fading—
smiles her mother had once bestowed upon them and
laughter that hadn't rung through the house for far
too long. She cried for the years she and her sisters
wasted running away from the pain and sadness—for
all the years they spent running away from each other,
because facing each other was just a reminder of
things that would never be. And most of all, she cried
because she knew that no matter how many times
she'd assured herself that she hated her mother—and
Jack—the opposite was true.

The line between love and hate was so very, very fine.

For about ten minutes, Caroline cried with unre-
strained emotion until Tango jumped up on the bed.
Whining sympathetically, he peered down at her,
dropping her mother's shoe on her face. Caroline
laughed.

And then she cried some more.

There was a tentative knock on the door and Augusta peeked in when Caroline didn't answer. "You
wanna tell me what happened?"

Caroline sat up, swiping at her eyes. She ran a
sleeve across her raw nose. Tango whined and licked
her lashes and she pushed him away. "Not really, but
I'll give you the short version."

Augusta came in and sat on the bed, reaching out
to pull Tango away from Caroline's face. "I'll settle for
that."

Caroline sighed. "It's been a shitty day. Half the
city is pissed off at me. The other half is scared shitless
—thanks to me. Frank is probably going to quit. Jack
hates me. And so does his horrible ex-girlfriend!"

"Wow, and I thought I had it rough taking inventory of this stupid place."

Caroline had a moment of genuine confusion. "Why are you taking inventory?"

It was Augusta's turn to sigh. "Because if we're going to restore this stupid house, I guess we have to keep tabs on everything."

Caroline snorted. "You mean, you want to give the cat burglar you're paying to wipe out the house a to-do list, right?"

Augusta laughed. "That's right. You've found me out."

"Yeah, well now I'm wondering if the break-in wasn't that psycho out there looking for Jack. He was here that night, you know, and she asked about the window tonight. It sounded a little like a threat."

"She threatened you?" Augusta's eyes widened with indignation. "Only I get to do that!"

Caroline choked on laughter.

"I suppose we owe CPD a phone call," Augusta said. "That stupid cow had a lot of nerve coming here!"

Caroline shrugged. "No, I don't want to do that."

"But you will," Augusta demanded. "Or I will. And I will make it sound way worse than it was, so if you want justice to be served, you'll do it yourself."

"Jesus," Caroline said, but grinned. "You've become quite the watchdog, Augusta!"

For the first time since coming home, Augusta smiled a genuine smile. "You're my sister," she said sincerely and reached out to brush a strand of hair away from Caroline's face.

It was the first tender moment Caroline could recall between them since their childhood.

She wanted to hug Augusta, but too many years of separation kept her from reaching out. Still, her tone was softer when she spoke, "All right, I'll call. Are you seriously going to restore this monstrosity?"

Augusta's smile turned up at one corner and her eyes sparkled with mischief. "Unless I find a way to burn it all down and still walk away with the money."

Caroline chuckled. "Well, read the fine print first, or we'll all end up with nada. Seems Mom planned for everything, except the stupidity of her daughters."

She was talking about herself, but Augusta misinterpreted. "Don't worry, Caroline. I won't do anything stupid. I can feed a lot of Haitians for twenty-seven million dollars."

Caroline lifted a brow, attempting a smile. "With your third of it, anyway."

Augusta smirked. "What . . . you don't want to donate your part of the inheritance to earthquake victims?"

Caroline sighed, grabbing the shoe from under Tango's chin and tossing it onto the floor. Not that she cared any longer that it was perpetually on the bed. She had already accepted it was the dog's way of dealing with her mother's absence, but their conversation was wandering into uncertain territory. "We have natural disasters here too, you know."

"I know," Augusta replied, and lapsed into a moment of silence.

Her sister seemed so distant lately, so ready to disappear somewhere far, far away. Caroline wondered how to reach her.

Augusta changed the subject abruptly. "Whattaya say we take that crazy mutt for a walk?"

"Nah . . . not in the mood." Caroline lay back on the bed.

Augusta stood. "But I am," she countered. "And

you're not going to let your little sister go wandering in the woods when there's a killer on the loose."

Caroline's brows collided. "God! Not you, too!"

Augusta's grin returned. "Come on, a walk will do us both good. Look at that poor doggie," she suggested. "If that isn't a hint, I don't know what is."

Tango stood in front of them, the running shoe dangling by its laces from his mouth. He whined pitifully and Caroline forced herself up. "All right, all right," she relented.

13

Two hundred yards before reaching the ruins of the old house, the oyster gravel road forked into a narrow lane that led to Sadie's house. Like the road to the main house, it had never been paved and probably never would be. According to the will, everything from the byroad to Secessionville Creek now belonged to Sadie, and technically the ruins sat in the trees and thick scrub on Sadie's side of the road.

When Caroline was ten, her mother considered donating part of the property to the City of Charleston, including the overseer's house—where Sadie lived—along with the slave quarters and a good portion of the surrounding wetlands. Today, nothing remained of the slave quarters. The rows of white wooden houses had been completely demolished, much to the dismay of the Historical Society. Flo made a public show of their demise, calling it a "gesture of continuing good will." But Caroline thought maybe she'd done it partly to appease Augusta, who had begun to show a passion for civil rights causes. Now all that remained of the original structures was the overseer's house and the burnt remains of the original house.

The sun was setting, and the shadows were growing, like specters squeezing out from every crack and crevice. The wind whispered long-forgotten secrets and the scent of the marsh was strong in the air.

Caroline was pretty sure she was only spooked because of the recent news, but she couldn't help concluding that innocence was an obvious casualty of knowledge. The more she buried herself in headlines, the less she could see of any wholesome goodness in the world. Maybe that was another reason Flo had closed herself off from her daughters? To protect them?

As they passed the gravel road, Augusta peered down it, shuddering. "I don't know how she still lives there."

Caroline glanced down the road, where Sadie's blue porch was barely visible.

Augusta contorted her face into a mask of confusion. "It doesn't seem to bother her that her bed sits right smack in the same room where a man once slept who beat slaves."

Caroline couldn't change the past so she didn't care to rehash it. All she could do was make sure she was a part of change for the better.

Tango sniffed the ground with interest.

Augusta turned to walk backward, staring up at the massive oaks draped with Spanish moss. "I mean, Mother saw our roots here, our history—I see *Roots*—the movie!"

Knowing better than to engage Augusta, Caroline nodded and hoped for a change in subject. She really thought Augusta spent entirely too much time begrudging and running away from the past.

How was that different from Caroline spending years resenting Flo—and Jack—for past wrongs?

If she could be completely honest with herself, she had used Jack's indiscretion as a reason to bail because she had feared ending up like her parents—lonely and bitter—and utterly alone in the end. Jack's words hurt mainly because they were mostly true.

Tango stopped abruptly, barking in the direction of the woods.

Augusta turned and stopped.

They spotted the man hidden in the brush at the same time.

Instinctively, Augusta moved protectively toward Caroline and Caroline tugged a little at Tango's leash. The hair on his back stood on end and a chill raced down Caroline's spine.

"Evening," the man said.

Probably in his mid-thirties, he was easily one of the most attractive men Caroline had ever seen. His blond hair was shoulder length, and looked a bit like spun gold under the glow of the waning sun. He wore a week's worth of stubble that on anyone else might have looked unkempt. On him, with those angelic blue eyes and a smile that seemed genuine and easy, it made him look like Jesus.

For a moment, she thought he might be cradling a football in his hand, but she could see now that it was a shoe.

Tango continued barking.

"Lovely evening," the man said when neither Caroline nor Augusta responded.

He stood about fifty feet away and made no attempt to come closer, but the hair at Caroline's nape prickled faintly—much like Tango's.

Augusta looked at her, confusion in her deep blue eyes.

Tourists sometimes stumbled onto their property,

lured by the historical landmarks and the Confederate gravesites nearby. As children, it had been a common occurrence to run into strangers, but at the moment, everything seemed more sinister. Simply knowing there was a killer out there, somewhere, changed everything, and although Jack might blame her for the shift in the neighborhood's mood, the truth was that keeping the truth quiet didn't change facts: someone had killed a girl just a stone's throw from their house and Amanda Hutto was still missing.

Caroline bent to soothe Tango, petting his haunches. "Did you realize this is private property?"

The stranger tossed the shoe back and forth between his hands. "Yeah," he said, looking a little sheepish. He shrugged his shoulders. "Sorry 'bout that . . . I was checking out the ruins back here."

Augusta leaned to whisper. "Jesus H. Christ, he's fucking beautiful!"

Caroline ignored her. She didn't care how beautiful the guy was. This was no time to blindly trust strangers. "That's all right," she said. "No harm done, but if you don't mind . . ."

"The ruins are private property too?" He shifted the shoe to his hip and held it there as he waited for her reply.

The wind shifted between the trees and another chill raced down Caroline's spine. "Yeah."

"Interesting," he said and he pointed in the direction of Fort Lamar Road. "I'm renting a house down the road, spotted the ruins while I was out running." He shrugged, and lifted the shoe, as though to highlight the coincidence. "Anyway, here you go." He reared back and, without warning, tossed the shoe in their direction.

Augusta held out her hands to catch it, but Caroline never took her eyes off the stranger. The shoe whizzed past her head and she was vaguely aware that Augusta caught it.

Tango turned and whined, sniffing the shoe, then turned back to bark at the intruder. That was all the incentive Caroline needed to get the hell away from him.

"Figure it might belong to one of you," the guy offered. "Expensive shoe . . . and fairly new. Someone must've lost it out here."

"Thanks!" Augusta said with a friendly wave. Caroline glanced briefly at the shoe and another chill jetted down her spine. It was the match to the shoe Tango had been carrying around in his mouth for weeks.

Tango suddenly lunged in the stranger's direction, unrelenting in his barking, and Caroline pulled back at the leash, her heart tripping.

How many innocent women died because they didn't trust their gut?

Right now, hers was screaming.

Caroline looked directly into his eyes, and he seemed to read her thoughts. He knew she recognized the shoe. She could see the acknowledgment in his eyes.

"Well, guess I'll be going now. You two have a good evening," he said, and smiled congenially before turning and sauntering off in the direction of the ruins without looking back.

Caroline watched him go, unwilling to turn her back on him. "Augie . . . do you have your cell phone on you?"

Tango stopped barking as the guy disappeared into the woods, but the hair on his spine was still ruffled and so were Caroline's nerves.

Augusta seemed genuinely confused and oblivious to the significance of what had just happened. "Yeah, I always have it handy, why?"

"Because that's mother's shoe," Caroline told her.

Her sister's confusion bled into her tone. "This shoe?" She turned the shoe over, inspecting it, checking the sole. Just as the guy had said, it was fairly new, and other than a little mud in the tread, it didn't appear as though it had been in the woods long. Augusta peered from the shoe to Caroline, shrugging. "So?"

"It's the match to the shoe Tango's been running around with."

Augusta screwed her face. "You're overreacting, Caroline! You're scaring yourself with your own press. Call it a hunch, but that guy's no killer! And, guess what, he's gone now—without even giving me his number!" Augusta laughed, but Caroline didn't share her amusement.

There was no sign of the stranger, but the shadows were deepening by the second and Caroline was finished with their walk. "Yeah, well, how the hell do you lose a running shoe in the woods?"

Augusta gave her a mischievous grin and lifted her brows. "For starters . . . maybe Mom wasn't running?" She gestured in the direction the stranger had gone. "Make no mistake, if that guy were standing in front of me, I'd happily lose more than my shoes!"

"Someone tried to break into Mom's study," Caroline reminded her.

"But they didn't! Think clearly, Caroline. Even if there is a killer on the loose, why the hell would he break into our house, steal a stupid shoe and then meet us in the woods to offer it back?"

Put like that, it sounded utterly ridiculous, but

Caroline couldn't shake her unease. "To warn us maybe?"

Augusta laughed. "Yeah . . . that's really funny. Since when do murderers warn their victims? Come on . . . let's go run your theory by our future mayor. Josh should be at the house by now and Sadie's been cooking all day."

CAROLINE'S ARTICLE earned Jack a big fat warning.

Chief Condon slammed the door on his theory, warning him to do his job without perpetuating rumors of a possible serial murder—that included within the department. No one doubted the Jones case was a premeditated homicide, but Jack was told to work with what he had: One body. One death. One killer.

At this point, they were batting zero with forensic evidence, but he was still waiting on tests from the lab. If Jones had been sexually violated, at least they would have DNA to work with.

To drown someone suggested a crime of passion— the act of holding the victim under water, the struggle. It was a very intimate way to kill someone. Usually, a strangler's motive was fury and his victim was no stranger. Yet the hyoid bone in Jones's neck was still intact, which meant that no hands or bindings had wrapped around the victim's throat in anger. It was all very cool and calculated.

During the autopsy they found evidence of cyanosis and petechial hemorrhaging in the eyes, and blood staining around the mouth and nose—all signs of asphyxia. They also found water in the lungs, which suggested Amy Jones probably died sometime after entering the water.

While he waited for the lab reports, he checked the ViCAP database, cross-referenced asphyxiation, strangulation, manual, non-manual, blue dye, nudity —nothing. Although not all law enforcement agencies contributed to the FBI's violent crimes database, most did, and it seemed that despite the growing, gnawing feeling in Jack's gut there was no sign of the killer on anyone's radar. Yet the crime felt too methodical for it to be an isolated incident. If there was a clue here somewhere, Jack was bound to find it.

CAROLINE HAD FORGOTTEN Josh was coming to dinner.

In the few short weeks since the girls had returned home, they had already fallen into a routine of sorts. Wednesdays were Sadie's "kitchen visitation day." She'd decided she should get at least one day per week to reacquaint herself with her stainless steel babies, sort of like children lost in a custody battle. With the money Sadie had inherited, Caroline was pretty sure she could afford to pimp out her own kitchen, but she realized it was Sadie's way of trying to keep them all together—at least for one night every week.

Tonight, she'd made red beans and okra, a distinctive Gullah dish that hailed back to Sadie's roots— along with the blue bottle tree that sat outside her house and her blue porch, which she claimed kept evil spirits out of her home. Caroline thought maybe she should have painted her face blue, because Josh was giving her the evil eye. She guessed maybe he was still concerned that he would be accused as her source.

Caroline refused to react. Pushing her red rice around her plate, she thought about her mother's shoe, wondering how the hell it ended up in the woods near Sadie's house.

Of course, Augusta was right; it was ridiculous to assume anyone would break in to steal a stupid shoe and then lie in wait just to give it back . . . but Caroline couldn't shake the feeling that there was more to the shoe. Unfortunately, that wasn't the only tough thing she had to chew on tonight. There was Kelly . . . and Jack . . . and Frank . . . and, oh, she couldn't forget Pam. Caroline had dragged the poor girl in way over her head. Really, at this point, it was easier to list the folks who weren't mad at her.

Everyone laughed at something Josh said, but Caroline didn't hear it, though they were all suddenly staring at her. Her fork froze before her mouth. "Huh?"

With a smile, Savannah explained, "Josh swears Mom must have thrown that shoe at Sadie."

Although she was smiling too, Sadie shook her head and waved the notion away. "Your mama wouldn't throw no damned shoe at me, eah!"

"Not even to shoo you away from a certain somebody on Saturday mornings while they were trying to work?" Josh immediately sidled away from his mother, anticipating the playful slap she threw in his direction.

"That's not even funny!" Sadie contended.

"We know you like him, Mama," Josh persisted. "No use denying it."

Sadie got up from her seat at the head of the table, shoving her chair back in feigned annoyance. She gave Josh a pointed stare. "Who I like or don't like is none of y'all's concern, eah!" She scooped up her plate and whisked Josh's plate out from in front of him, too.

"You are all a bunch of ungrateful brats!" she declared, waving her hand over the entire table. "I don't know why I put up with any of you."

Augusta smirked and handed her plate over. "Because you love us."

Savannah handed her plate over too, her smile as wide as Josh's and Augusta's.

Caroline got up to help.

"Chicken shit," Josh said under his breath as Caroline hurried after Sadie. It was the first thing he had said to her all night, and though he'd said it jokingly, she knew there was an edge to his teasing.

Sadie slapped him lightly upside the head as she passed by. "She's doing the best she can. You do your job and leave her be!"

Josh winced. "Yes, ma'am," he replied, but once Sadie and Caroline were in the kitchen, the dining room exploded with peals of laughter.

At the sink, Sadie grabbed Caroline's plate out of her hand. "Baby girl, don't you let anyone tell you how to do your job, eah!" she advised. "Your mama put you in charge of that paper for a reason."

Sadie couldn't possibly understand the mess she'd made of everything, but until that instant, she hadn't realized how much she needed to hear those words. For the second time today, tears threatened.

Sadie reached out, grabbing Caroline by the hand. "Listen to me, child. Your mama loved you! Maybe she didn't know how to show it while she was alive and breathing, but this is how she's showing you now."

Sadie's big black eyes were full of love and her smile was the same smile she had given them as children whenever they took a spill in the oyster gravel, skinning their knees.

Words caught in Caroline's throat. "But Josh . . ."

"Don't you worry a minute about my son! Right now, he's concerned about nothing but himself and that's not how I raised him! Truth is he's probably already over it, but he's not going to let you off the hook so easily, eah."

Caroline mustered a smile, realizing Sadie was probably right. Josh liked to see people squirm.

Sadie patted her hand. "Listen, I can't pretend to know why you did what you did, Caroline, but I'm sure you had your reasons, and I know in my heart you'll always do what's right. It's in your blood!"

Caroline nodded, choking on her emotion.

Sadie let go of her hand and gave her a much-needed hug.

Caroline wiped her tears on her shoulder as she hugged Sadie back, and deep down she felt a twinge of guilt for being relieved it was her mother who was resting eternally in Magnolia Cemetery and not Sadie.

Sadie peeled away from her abruptly and went to the fridge, chortling softly to herself as she pulled out a key lime pie, unveiling it to Caroline. "Let's see how long that boy keeps his mouth shut when he's got to ask you for a piece of this!" She handed the pie over to Caroline and grabbed a serving knife from the counter, winking conspiratorially.

Caroline laughed. "You're so devious!"

Sadie grabbed a stack of dessert plates. "Child, how the hell do you think I survived in this house so long?"

She and Caroline shared a crooked smile and then returned to the dining room together, where Josh held out approximately thirty seconds before he was all smiles and sweet-talking Caroline into giving him the first fat piece of key lime pie.

Sadie gave Caroline a smile that said simply I-told-you-so.

14

Caroline walked into her office the next morning to find two things on her desk: a copy of the morning edition of the *Post* and Frank's resignation letter.

Today's front-page headline in the *Post* read:

Secessionville Creek Killer: Ex-Priest Questioned.

Caroline focused on the photo of the man the police had taken in for questioning and her heart somersaulted into her throat.

She read the headline a second time with a sense of dawning horror. And then she grabbed her purse, snagged Frank's letter and the newspaper and ran out of her office, stopping by the front desk long enough to give Pam instructions: call Amy Jones's roommate, call CPD, verify the *Post's* facts—even though she knew the *Post's* reporting would be solid.

She had been so preoccupied with her own agenda, with telling a particular story, that she had completely missed the real news. The *Post* had scooped them, but that wasn't the worst of it. She had been so preoccupied with hurt feelings and doling out key lime pie that she had endangered the people she most loved.

Obviously, Frank had already checked out and she would deal with him later, but right now, she had to talk to Jack, because the ex-priest—the one they were holding for questioning—was the same man who had tossed Augusta their mother's shoe last night.

Why he should have had her mother's shoe, she didn't know. The particulars weren't exactly working themselves out in her head, and none of it made a lick of sense, but she should have called the police. The one saving grace was that they had him in custody—no thanks to her or the *Tribune*! But she knew Jack would figure it out. He was good at his job. Unlike her, it seemed.

On her way out to the parking garage, Caroline called Jack first, but he wasn't available, so she called Augusta and read the paper aloud to her sister from the car.

"Jesus, I was completely out to lunch!" she said, her head still reeling after reading it for the second time. "It says the victim called her roommate from Patterson's cell phone! How could I have missed that? All it would have taken was for me to ask the right questions. Why didn't I, Augie?"

"Don't be so hard on yourself," Augusta countered. "I don't believe that gorgeous man is a killer!"

"Lucifer was the most beautiful of God's creations! Focus with me here, Augie—I'm having a serious self-pity moment! I missed everything—my God, that girl's murderer was standing right there, not fifty feet from us last night!"

"Alleged murderer," Augusta corrected. "Use your investigative reporter head, Caroline. He's not guilty until he's proven guilty in a court of law."

"My God—what if I don't have a reporter head? What if I'm a fraud?"

"Caroline," Augusta admonished, "you're being ridiculous. You've got a more solid education than mother ever had and you come from a newspaper family that goes back generations. You're listening with your heart, not your head."

Augusta had a point.

Her mother had been an expert at detaching herself from her emotions. Call it high-functioning multiple personality disorder if you will, but she had been able to step outside of her crippling depression to look at hard, cold facts—at least for the sake of her work. She had, in fact, been able to look beyond her own traumatic losses to be of service to her community. Caroline couldn't even look beyond Karen Hutto's tragedy!

She was letting her emotions color every decision she made, and she wasn't looking at the big picture. "What if I can't think with my head?"

"When did you stop?" Augusta countered, as though it were a perfectly ridiculous notion.

Caroline thought about that a moment and found a new headache spawning. In the corner of the garage, behind a column, she noticed movement, and looked more closely.

Was someone there?

It was just her imagination.

Patterson was in jail, she reminded herself.

She locked the door anyway, and leaned on the window, putting a hand to her forehead, staring at the paper so closely that her myopic view of it settled on two words: EX-PRIEST QUESTIONED. "That man did not look like any priest to me," Caroline said plaintively.

"He doesn't look like a killer either," Augie said with conviction.

"Well, I have to go," Caroline said. "Let me call you in a while. Lock the doors!" she added fervently.

"Stop worrying," Augusta countered. "The doors are already locked, Caroline."

"And please make sure Savannah is home!"

"Really? We're supposed to put our lives on hold and lock ourselves away because there's a freak out there?"

Even here in the shadowy parking garage, people were coming and going, completely oblivious to any danger.

"Take a chill pill, Caroline. We're big girls. We'll be fine."

"You're right," Caroline conceded, and hung up, intending to drive straight to the police department. Instead she found herself detouring and headed to the one place she never thought she'd return.

TUCKED AWAY near the banks of the Cooper River, Magnolia Cemetery was all but forgotten amid the ancient, drooping oaks. The remaining empty patches of earth belonged to those whose families could trace their heritage back to when news of Sherman's March sent women to bed with the vapors. The cemetery now held some thirty-five thousand bodies, including two thousand Confederate soldiers, five governors and four U.S. senators—one being Senator Robert Samuel Aldridge II.

Caroline's father.

Reunited in death, her parents lay beside one another beneath the shade of an old live oak . . . peaceful . . . as they had never been in life.

The tree, which had certainly seen better days, was humpbacked now, with tired limbs that sank toward the ground as though yearning to rest alongside Magnolia's inhabitants. On the south side, its branches were a little sparser. No doubt before there were laws in place to protect these deciduous mammoths, some of the vast network of roots had been mangled during the digging of nearby graves. Now, like scars that refused to heal, there were ligneous scabs where immense limbs had lived, withered, and died. On the north side, Spanish moss clung to the thicker mass of boughs like hoary curtains, weighing the tree down much like a bent old woman straining under the weight of her striplings. It was on this side her mother had been laid to rest.

Caroline's gaze dropped to the grave on the other side of her mother's plot . . . an empty piece of land reserved for their baby brother.

It would never be filled.

Even after the authorities stopped searching for Sammy . . . long after there was even a remote chance he might be found alive . . . her mother had paid to have the shoreline dredged for miles.

His body was never found.

Caroline noticed there were flowers on his grave— baby's breath and sun-bleached peach roses—recent enough that she could still tell what color the petals had been in life. Flo had never once mentioned her visits to Magnolia. Apparently, she had grieved here all alone until her dying day, sharing secrets with no one. Knowing that didn't make Caroline feel any better.

Bright morning sun penetrated the thick mass of

limbs above, shedding dappled light over the graves at her feet.

Already, the soil over her mother's plot was beginning to settle, the rich color of freshly turned dirt fading into the surrounding earth. She looked around, inspecting the rows of graves. Her brother's and her mother's were the only ones in plain sight that had fresh flowers. Other urns held washed-out plastic roses, but most had none at all. Even the next of kin of those buried here were likely dead, buried and forgotten. And once the flowers in her mother's urn were gone, reduced to dust . . . along with those on Sammy's grave, they would lie as bare and forgotten as her father's plot.

She and her sisters weren't the type to stroll in cemeteries.

Caroline didn't believe in making appointments to visit regret and despair. She believed in moving forward, forging a better tomorrow . . . but here she was.

Why?

Did she think somehow she might forge a connection with her dead mother simply by standing at her grave? Find answers that eluded her by staring at a plot of earth? Why the hell would she hope for that when she and Flo had never even had a minuscule connection while Flo was still alive?

And yet, she admitted, she had never needed her mother more than she did at this moment . . . when it seemed she was most lost to her.

Taking a deep, shuddering breath, Caroline turned to walk back to the car, feeling a little foolish and a lot reckless. She'd come here completely on a whim, and even though Patterson was being held and questioned for the murder of Amy Jones, Augusta was right, until he was proven guilty beyond a shadow of doubt, an isolated graveyard where few people ventured was not the place to be alone.

She slid into her car, stabbed the key into the ignition and drove away, this time heading straight to the police station to report last night's visit from a certain ex-priest. At some point, she intended to tell Jack about his ex-girlfriend's visit, too, but at the moment, it was completely overshadowed by Patterson's.

She made her way out of the cemetery, peering one last time into the rearview mirror . . . but she never saw the figure watching behind a nearby crypt.

15

Ian Patterson didn't behave like a man who was concerned about a homicide conviction. He sat quietly in the interview room, answering questions without breaking a sweat. Nor did he lose his temper even with the most leading questions. In fact, he seemed, as far as Jack could tell, like a man who was genuinely willing to cooperate. His face practically turned green when Jack revealed the detailed photos of Amy Jones, postmortem lividity transforming her milky skin to bluish- and reddish-purple splotches where gravity pooled her blood into the lowest regions. Unless he was a damned good actor, he wasn't their guy.

On the other hand, he didn't look like a straitlaced priest either. Tall and lean, with scruffy hair, a Vandyke, dark Lennon sunglasses and a small hoop earring, he reminded Jack more of a pot-smoking drummer—a heartthrob in a star band.

Without blinking, he agreed to a polygraph, and in the end, they weren't able to hold him, nor did they have probable cause to legally search his house since he had an alibi for the time of the Jones death. Apparently, he was watching a girlfriend's band play a gig at the Windjammer.

They had phone records to tie him to the victim, witnesses who placed him at a nearby gas station with the victim at about eight P.M.—two and a half hours before the actual murder—and fingerprints on the back end of her car—near her gas tank, all consistent with his story. The evidence was purely circumstantial and the guy had zero motive as far as Jack could tell— if they were dealing with a single homicide.

Patterson claimed Jones had run out of gas. Apparently, he lived in the area and he was on his way out for the evening and found her walking down Fort Lamar Road in the dark so he gave her a ride to the station, bought her a can of gas and took her back to her car to empty the contents into her tank—pretty straightforward. The guy's Good Samaritan story checked out one hundred percent. He even had receipts and credit card records to wrap up a nice little paper trail.

None of it added up.

After they released him, Jack put a tail on him and returned to the crime scene to do another walk-through. The crime scene team had already been over the dock and surrounding area with a fine-toothed comb, but he could think more clearly without an army of people underfoot.

His gut told him that no one who was about to cut the tongue out of a girl's mouth and strangle the life out of her would lend her his cell phone—not once, but twice—with a follow-up call to the girl's roommate, giving both girls his real name. In fact, it was the roommate who had given them Patterson's number to begin with. Only an arrogant prick would take that sort of chance, and ultimately, arrogance was stupidity. Patterson didn't strike Jack as stupid or arrogant.

No calls were made from the victim's phone after seven o-five P.M., which gave credence to the fact that her phone was dead. They found it sitting in the passenger floorboard of her abandoned car.

At nine-seventeen P.M., Amy's roommate called Jones, lost and searching for the address she'd been given, then again at nine-nineteen, ten twenty-four, and again at ten twenty-seven. All four calls had gone unanswered. Annoyed, the roommate went back to the station to wait, hoping Jones would call back. For about thirty minutes, she said she sat at the station, in her car, on the phone, arguing with her boyfriend, until their conversation ended at approximately eleven o-three P.M.— all verified by phone records— after which the roommate made one more attempt to find the house. This time, she spotted Amy's car in a driveway, and about eleven-thirty P.M., she ventured around back, but didn't see Amy, so she returned to her car and called the police.

The initial responding officer showed at twelve-thirty P.M.—a full hour after the roommate called for assistance—not surprising considering some of the politics going on in James Island. Amy's body was discovered at twelve forty-three A.M. The time of death placed at roughly ten-forty P.M.—very likely while the roommate had been busy arguing with her boyfriend at the station, which meant she'd barely missed the killer.

Lying in the temperate, shallow water, her body was still warm when Jack arrived on the scene around one-thirty in the morning. Rigor mortis had only begun to set in.

Now he stood on the deck, studying the scene critically, staring at the bright yellow police tape that was still intact, except for a small piece that flapped in the breeze near the established point of entry.

He stared down at the area beside the dock.

When Amy's body was discovered, it was lying next to the dock, half concealed by the spartina grass and wrapped around a dock post. With her car parked out front, it was pretty certain she didn't float to shore, but they found no body fluids on the dock and no signs of a scuffle above deck, which meant that any struggle would have taken place in the creek.

He made a mental note to check the tide charts and got down on his knees to peer under the dock, just to make sure they hadn't missed anything—no scraps of clothing or snags of hair in the splintered wood.

He stared down at the water and stinking pluff mud.

The odor, he knew, was a ripe brew—a result of warm water conditions, bacteria, and decomposing organic matter in the muggy climate, but despite the life that teemed within the dark, dank, soft soil, it stank of death and decay. No matter that the crime scene team had taken care not to disturb anything, the gray muck never dried between tide changes and traces of the girl's form had already eroded away. All that was left at this point was a slight depression where tiny shrimp waltzed. The only remaining footprints near the body were theirs. It had been impossible to get the body out without creating a few impressions, but the water was just deep enough that the constant movement had already eroded the impressions anyway. A little deeper in, the muck was so wet and boggy that it had been known to suck the boots off a man's feet. Walking in it wasn't easy and necessitated special gear or tight-fitting boots. It was a bit like quicksand . . . if you sank to your ankles and struggled, you might sink to your knees. . . .

It seemed the killer had just laid her down gently . . . without too much of a fight . . . probably with the aid of the chloroform they'd found in her system. He'd stripped her naked, tied her feet and hands and positioned her precisely for a macabre show, and thanks to the techniques publicized by prime-time crime drama, he'd known enough to minimize the likelihood of evidence.

There were traces of blood on her body and hair, some in the creek bed and in her stomach. But not nearly enough, it seemed. The tongue was full of blood vessels so she would have bled profusely—if cut while she was still alive. Maybe not so much if he'd cut her tongue out after death. But the tape over her mouth didn't seem like something he would do after death, and Jack couldn't see him removing the tape and replacing it again. Her clothes might have soaked up some of the blood, but since they were missing, it was impossible to assess how much exactly. Anything that didn't end up in her clothes could have ended up in the creek, washed away by the tide.

Had the killer cut the tongue out before or after she was drugged? Before or after he killed her? Why cut it out at all? Why the dye?

The guy needed to see her die, Jack realized— every stage of the process, from the instant she came to, realizing she couldn't breathe, to the panic and pain she must have felt—he needed to experience everything . . . right up until the instant the blood vessels burst in her eyes.

Did he wait for her eyes to flutter open before pushing her down into the shallow water?

For some reason, the act reminded him of a sort of baptism.

Underwater, the killer wouldn't be able to see her as clearly—especially at night. Even with a full moon, he would have needed to be close to see . . . maybe he was straddling her . . . hovering a breath away so he could feel her heartbeat flatline?

He rubbed his eyes. Some day, he needed to sleep.

He stood, brushing himself off, needing a smoke— was it any wonder? He was no longer trying to quit for Caroline, he told himself as he reached into his pocket, pulling out his last stick of gum. He was doing it for himself, because he hated the habit. He un- wrapped the stick and popped it into his mouth, chewing thoughtfully.

In the distance, Morris Island Lighthouse stood stranded . . . a lonesome sentinel, guarding the channel . . . like an unarmed soldier. Long ago decom- missioned, it was slowly being devoured by the Atlantic.

The channel could be hairy. The inlet creeks were like spidery veins, both siphoning the life from the marshes and washing it back in. Even at low tide, the middle of the creek was deep enough to accommodate a good-sized boat . . . one that could easily handle Clark Sound or the winding rivers and estuaries around Morris Island. But you wouldn't need a big boat to maneuver the salt marsh . . . if you knew where to go.

Supposedly, the victim was here taking pho- tographs, but no camera was found. The only indica- tion she had, in fact, been taking pictures was the camera bag in her backseat, filled with lenses and ac- tual film. He didn't even realize people still used that stuff in this digital age, but apparently, she was a talented film and photography student with art work on display somewhere downtown. They'd scoured the entire area, hoping to find her camera but it was gone.

Jack studied the landscape.

The houses around here were surrounded by woodlands—high-dollar properties—not too close together. Backcreek Road, aptly named, was surrounded by water with a single entrance from Fort Lamar Road. Just behind Backcreek Road sat Fort Lamar—three acres of sequestered grounds owned by the city that included earthworks dating back to 1862 . . . lots of places to hide. And the streets . . . lined with massive, tangled trees, went pitch black after dark, smothering the moon from view.

The roommate didn't recall seeing any boat docked behind the house that night . . . no cars came through on the isolated road.

The house itself had been searched, even though there was no sign of forced entry and nothing inside hinted at the violence that took place out back.

Could it be that Amy Jones's murderer hadn't meant to leave her body as he had, quite possibly interrupted by a twenty-year-old college student looking for her AWOL roommate? If so, how and where had he intended to move the body?

They sent choppers up to do an aerial of the salt marsh . . . but the surrounding landscape was undisturbed. For now, the salt marsh was keeping its secrets.

He stared at the boathouse in the distance with its tin steepled roof. Bright sunlight glinted off its surface.

The Aldridge dock was easily one of the longest in the area. It meandered across fifteen hundred feet of salt marsh. He could throw a stone in the direction of

Caroline's house and hit it. Its proximity to the crime scene made his stomach turn.

The attempted break-in at Oyster Point had occurred the following night—not much of a chance the killer was still in the area, but it left Jack a little desperate for answers. . . .

As far as anyone else was concerned, this was not a race against time. Jack didn't agree. He felt it down in his gut.

The attention to detail—the complete lack of evidence—told Jack this wasn't the guy's first kill, and the fact that there were no other bodies was merely a testament to the fact that the killer knew what he was doing.

But he was on his own with this one. Not even Garrison, his partner, was pursuing the same leads.

The closest he'd come to a case like this was a spree killing a couple of years ago—nothing like Amy Jones's murder. A true serial killer didn't just hit three different gas stations and pop the attendants, he needed downtime . . . time to plan . . . time to make sure every move was orchestrated to perfection . . . so he wouldn't get caught. But maybe after a while some of them thought they couldn't be caught . . . maybe if this guy had been doing this a while, he was getting arrogant. Arrogant people took shortcuts, and people who took shortcuts made mistakes.

Who else would die before his mistakes revealed him?

Caroline was right about one thing: playing by the rules was a luxury you didn't have when lives were at stake.

Two could play at that game. . . .

"I'm surprised you're still here," Caroline joked, though the minute it came out of her mouth, she realized how stupid the remark was. Frank Bonneau was the sort of man who did everything by the book. If he gave a two-week notice, he did his time, even if he had to swallow antacids every hour on the hour to do it.

He eyed her over bifocals that had been put on and removed so many times they were crooked beyond repair. Clearly unhappy with her awkward attempt at conversation, he went back to looking over the dummy, trying to determine where to place stories, ignoring her.

Caroline had had a full day—none of it spent at the office. She could only have done that with someone like Frank in place—someone who knew what he was doing—someone she trusted. "Can we talk?"

"I'm happy to listen," he said. "I think I've said more than enough at this point."

Clearly, he wasn't happy with his outburst yesterday, justified though it may have been. While Caroline still believed she had acted in good faith, she had to admit she had behaved more like the boss's daughter rather than the boss. "Have you talked to Daniel?"

"No," he said, sounding nonplussed. "Why would I do that?"

That he hadn't run to complain to their attorney both surprised and impressed her. It gave her all the more resolve to keep him onboard. "Good, because I don't want you to resign."

"You should have thought about that before you undermined me."

"I'm sorry, Frank."

"You should be."

He wasn't going to show her any mercy, Caroline

realized, but she was ready to prostrate herself at his feet, and she meant every word. "I've learned a valuable lesson and I hope we can repair this, because I realized today how much I need you. I'm not ready to run this paper on my own."

His attention perked and he set his pen down, looking up at her, listening now.

"I realize how my mother was able to be the face and voice of the *Tribune* . . . it's because she had you, Frank."

"She didn't exactly twiddle her thumbs on the sidelines," he protested, clearly uncomfortable with the compliment. "Your mother was involved with every aspect," he told her. "She just didn't micromanage her people—especially not me—and she didn't try to do everything on her own. You can't be the publisher, writer, salesperson, media contact and community servant, Caroline. You hire good people and trust them to do their jobs so you can focus on yours."

As lectures went, it was pretty basic, but Caroline took heart that he was talking to her at all—and clearly she did need the reminders. All these things she knew, but somehow when it came down to doing them, she had promptly forgotten every one. Encouraged, she ventured into his office and sat down in the seat facing his desk. "I want you to teach me to be as good a newspaperwoman as my mother was."

"Your mother wasn't good, she was great!" He picked up his pen and tapped it lightly on his desk, seeming to consider her appeal. "Do you know that even when we were fighting our worst circulation battle, and it was suggested that we should go after the *Post*, your mother refused to engage in yellow journalism? She took her lessons from the mistakes of men like Joseph Pulitzer and William Randolph Hearst.

Your mother knew this business inside out and upside down. If you want to be anything like her, it's gonna take serious dedication," he said, "without any ego. Can you manage that?"

Caroline blinked. If anything, she thought she was much too unsure of herself, but she would say anything to make him stay at this point.

"I need you to trust in what you know," he continued, "and trust me to know when to step in and help."

"Sounds easy enough."

He lifted a white shaggy brow as though he didn't quite believe her. "And I need you to trust that I'm in this for the good of the paper, and if I speak up, you'll listen—not necessarily do as I say," he clarified, "just listen. That's all your mother ever promised."

"If I agree . . . will you stay?"

He grunted. "I should ask for a raise."

"Frank, I didn't know how to come in here and fill Mom's shoes," Caroline confessed. "I thought I needed to command respect, but I understand now you were ready to give it—that I made this about us, when it should have been about the paper. I'm sorry for that. Please stay?"

He cracked a crooked smile. "I expect you to *never* write another story during my tenure at this paper. I don't care how talented a journalist you are. You can't look at the big picture if you're knee-deep in the trenches!"

"Okay, so tell me . . . what's the first thing you think I need to change in my role as publisher?"

He waved the pen at her. "Simple. I understand you want to take this paper in a whole new direction, but before you go barreling out that gate at full speed, learn how to do it all the old-fashioned way." He studied her a moment. "Do you understand what

makes most current news nothing more than stenographic journalism?"

Caroline wanted to roll her eyes, but dealing with
a little bluster and the occasional lecture about basic
journalism was a small price to pay in order to keep
him happy, she decided. "Reporters are just taking
notes?"

"Damn straight!" he boomed. "That's the problem
with citizen journalism."

Some little part of her actually felt relieved she'd
gotten the answer right. As basic as any of Frank's
lessons seemed, it couldn't hurt her to drill them into
her skull. As Jack had already pointed out, this wasn't
a trial run. There were no rehearsals.

"It's all a bunch of 'he said, she said' namby-pamby
bullshit!" he railed. "One idiot writes a thing on
Twitter and another idiot repeats it on *HuffPo*. When
your mother and I came up in this business, you had
to roll up your sleeves and go after your story. That's
why they called it investigative journalism."

Caroline tried to suppress the tiny smile tugging at
the corners of her mouth. "So you'll stay?"

He eyed her speculatively. "You'll let me worry
about filling my own news hole?"

Caroline didn't want to lose complete control. "Do
I have any say at all?"

"Do you trust me?"

Caroline blinked.

There was that word again. Trust. It wasn't something she had in great abundance. She was accustomed to looking after herself, and she'd never
allowed even the tiniest fragment of her life out of her
control. "Yes," she said, and meant it. But it was going
to take a serious daily talk in the mirror.

"All right," he conceded, "but no more anonymous

sources unless it's the only way they can contribute—
and only if we're both agreed. All we have left is respect and we have to preserve it at all costs."

"It's a deal. Teach me how to go after a story the
old-fashioned way—and Pam. She wants to learn."

"She's not half bad," he admitted. "I read her
clips." He cocked his head a little as he considered the
request. "Not bad at all—just had a shitty teacher." He
grinned suddenly, his face splitting from ear to ear.

He was teasing her, she realized. She smiled back.

"All right, so let me tell you how we start." He got
up suddenly, and walked out of the office. A few minutes later, he walked back in with Pam and Brad on his
heels.

Caroline stood, offering the chair to Pam, letting
Frank take center stage.

Frank stood behind his desk. "The first thing we
do," he said to everyone present, "is find out a little
more about this Patterson guy. He's an ex-priest," he
said, pointing at Brad. "Find out where, and why he's
an ex. I want to know whether he's local—if not, I
want to know where he's from. I want to know what he
does for a living now and I want to know what color
his shit was the last time he took one."

Pam giggled and his gaze snapped to her. "You
think I'm being funny?"

Startled, Pam shook her head.

"Good," he continued, pointing to Pam. "You've got
a source at CPD, so you go that route, find out why
they released Patterson. Also talk to the roommate
again—find out every last detail she knows—see if
there's anything the *Post* might have missed!"

Caroline had to admit, there was an air of excitement just listening to the urgency in his voice. "Then
what?"

He tapped his desk with his index finger. "Then we all meet right here and we discuss the angle we are going to take. *Together*."

"All right," Caroline said.

He slapped his hands together. "Let's go!"

Both Brad and Pam scurried out of his office at once—like roaches scattering at the stomp of a foot—but Caroline hung back.

"You too!" he said with false reproach.

"Thank you," she said, and turned to go, but not before spotting the telltale gleam of moisture in his eyes. She didn't dare turn back, somehow knowing he wouldn't want her to.

16

"How about a truce?"

After a week of not hearing from Jack—even after she'd filed her report about Patterson—Caroline had to admit it was a relief to hear his smart-assed tone of voice on the other end of the line. But she had too much pride to just lay down her arms. "You don't see me wavin' any white flag!"

"No," Jack countered, "I am."

Caroline sat quietly on her end of the phone. She'd been looking over the financial reports Daniel had brought her to review, but her eyes were glazing over and now that Jack had called, her brain officially threw in the towel and quit for the day.

"But I'm all out of Get Out of Jail Free cards after this."

She knew her tone sounded incensed, but she couldn't help it. "*You're* all out?"

"Didn't we just agree to a cease-fire?"

Caroline rolled her eyes. "I don't think we got that far."

"Of course we did," he assured her. "I smell the conciliatory feast and you've got to be hungry—it's six-thirty."

Were they really going to do this after nearly ten years?

There was quite a lot Caroline wanted—needed—to talk to him about, but she wasn't about to sit here and try to convince herself that her interest in seeing him was purely professional. It wasn't. She wanted to see him. This past week had been horrible, thinking he would never forgive her. "A little," Caroline admitted, setting her reports down and shoving them aside.

"Good," he said, "Because you really are much too thin."

"What is it with my weight? I'm starting to think you, Sadie and Rose Simmons all got together to conspire about how to fatten me up so no one will ever look at me again. Is that your idea of revenge?"

"Trust me," Jack said. "People are looking."

A tired smile curved Caroline's lips. "People?"

"Well, I only know about one people."

He was flirting with her . . . and it felt good.

"Person," she corrected, falling for the bait, even though she knew he was goading the writer within. "People is plural."

His tone took on a sober timbre, like a lawyer on the courtroom floor. "I wholeheartedly disagree, Ms. Aldridge. People can be singular as well. What about when they say, 'hey, she's good people.'"

Caroline lifted a brow. "Who is they?"

"Did I say they? I meant me."

Caroline laughed. God, she missed his easy banter. She missed him—even more than she dared to admit. "I never heard you say that before!"

"Of course I do—I say it all the time," he assured. "Come to dinner with me tonight, and I'll prove it. We'll discuss the new publisher of the *Tribune* and I'll be sure to tell you how she's good people."

No matter how confused Caroline might be over ninety percent of her life, there was nothing uncertain about this connection she and Jack shared. Despite the tension between them, it was as strong now as it had ever been—minus the trust issue. Could they survive without trust? "You still think so?"

"I know so."

"What about Kelly?"

"What about her?"

"Well . . . I've been meaning to tell you, she stopped by the house."

He answered her with silence. When he spoke again, she could tell by his tone that she had thrown him for a loop.

"Really."

It wasn't a question. Clearly, he hadn't known, but either he wasn't entirely surprised, or he was trying to keep his annoyance from ruining the uncharacteristically light banter between them—or both. "Your treat tonight?"

"I don't know . . . depends on whether you're going to consider this business or pleasure?"

Caroline smiled. "Jack, you can't ask a girl out on a date and then ask her to expense it."

"Oh," he said, "then I guess I'm paying."

"Then yes to dinner, and I'll tell you all about Kelly's visit," she promised. "I was actually going to file a report, but wanted to talk to you before I did that, and it seems you've been avoiding me."

"Not avoiding exactly."

Caroline shuffled the papers in front of her, pushing them to another spot on her desk. "What else would you call it when I've been calling you for days and talking to your voice mail with no response."

"That depends on whether you actually expected a response from a machine."

"You know what I mean, Jack."

"I had a little development on the case . . . I'll tell you about that at dinner too . . . after you tell me about Kelly's psycho visit."

"Deal," Caroline said. "How fast can you be there?"

"Five seconds. I'm parked outside."

Caroline snorted. "Someone was very sure of himself!"

"No," he countered. "I just don't know a single Aldridge who can resist a newsworthy carrot. If I couldn't appeal to your stomach or your heart, I knew I had an ace in my pocket."

Caroline ignored the little jolt of joy she felt over his interest in her heart—and the thrill of excitement over his dangled carrot. "You're incorrigible!"

"Come on down," he directed, ignoring the accusation. "I'll drive."

THERE WERE cicadas and there were cicadas.

The average green-bodied variety, which emerged in the dog days of summer, generally went unnoticed. But there was another genus—the Magicicada. Emerging from the ground in biblical numbers every thirteen years, they formed a black, roaring cloud that devoured all green in its path, leaving the landscape ravaged and the frailest of striplings lifeless in its wake.

They climbed and attached themselves to nearby branches, shimmying out of their exoskeletons with fresh new skins and bulging red eyes, before launching into the air to sing for their mates.

The drone was maddening.

Once fertilized, the female returned to the trees to lay her eggs, and the newest generation of cicadas burrowed deep into the ground where they remained another thirteen years, feeding off a network of tangled roots . . . while they waited for the cycle to repeat.

In their wake, you found fragile carcasses attached to trees, inexplicably clinging to life in death, their gossamer wings looking like stained-glass windows, but with the glass shattered and plucked out—the temple of their bodies abandoned.

This was the same.

His body was an abandoned temple; all feelings of humanity had escaped through a crack in his physical form. Only the bloodlust remained in the deepest confines of his soul, like a thousand dark whispers smothered by layers of derma. And sometimes, like a plague of locusts, the endless buzz resurfaced, undeniable and psychotic in its influence.

Those were the times he feared the hunger most, when the voices rose to such a deafening roar that all reason was confounded by the sound.

It was rising now.

He had to unzip his skull and let out a little crazy— enough to function without suspicion. He didn't know what would happen if he didn't.

He had never let it go that far.

17

J ack took Caroline to a little Mediterranean café
on South Market Street. Quaint mosaic and ironwork tables spilled onto the sidewalk and soft
background music accompanied a delicious shared
plate of Mediterranean fare. They sat in a corner surrounded by short potted palms—cozy and quiet. But
the coziness was short lived. Whatever warmth Caroline had been feeling toward Jack didn't survive
dinner.

She told him about Kelly, and he listened quietly,
reassuring her that she wouldn't have to deal with
Kelly again. Jack was pretty sure that, while she was
temporarily angry about the entire situation, she was
a good person and wouldn't hurt a fly. Caroline wasn't
sure about that. In fact, she was pretty damned sure if
Kelly were holding a fly swatter and Caroline were a
fly in front of her face, she'd be as flat as the pita bread
sitting on the table right now. Still, he said he would
look into it and that satisfied her.

Kelly wasn't what sent her over the edge.

Jack wanted her to retract her story. He wanted her
to print the "official police story." "Just say you made a
mistake."

"Let me get this straight. You still don't believe this is an isolated homicide, but you want me to report that it is anyway?"

He sat forward, leaning into the table, leaning into the pitch. "I'm just asking you to report the official story, Caroline. If you call the Public Information Officer, that's exactly what he'll tell you. No matter who this guy is—he's likely to be following the story in the paper. If this isn't an isolated incident, maybe the guy's already gotten a taste for media attention. . . ."

The atmosphere at the paper was only now beginning to normalize, and Caroline was unwilling to compromise her relationship with Frank any more. "Can we quote you saying that you believe this is an isolated case?"

"No."

"Because you don't believe it?"

"Caroline, you owe me. . . ."

Caroline looked at him in that instant—really looked at him. His eyes were sunken and bloodshot, probably from lack of sleep. And while his clothes were neat, he obviously hadn't shaved in days. He ran a hand through his hair, looking weary, but he was persistent.

"Look, I'm hoping that if we deny his existence, this guy will make a move to show everyone he's out there."

"No, Jack! I won't play with the truth that way!"

He sat back in his chair, his blue eyes darkening as he studied her. "Seems you're pretty choosy about your ethics," he said after a moment.

Caroline tossed down the piece of pita bread she'd been munching on, her appetite vanishing. "That's not even fair to suggest! I published the initial story because I believed I was doing the right thing. If you're sitting here telling me you don't believe it's over, and yet you want me to say it is—I don't care what the Public Information Officer has to say or what the official story is—you're asking me to mislead the public and I won't do it!"

They were like oil and water, Caroline decided in that moment. The feelings she had for him were undeniable, but she didn't like him very much at this instant.

Thankfully, he didn't ask her again, but the rest of the evening passed in a blur of quick, angry bites and accusatory looks. It was all Caroline could do to shove her food down without throwing it at him. She wasn't sure which galled her most—that he was asking her to do this at all, or that he was asking her to do it under the guise of a stupid date.

She had foolishly gotten it into her head that he was trying to make it up to her and that he actually *wanted* her company—that maybe he still wanted to see if there was something left between them.

She tried to tell herself that he had essentially done to her no more than she had done to him—but something had changed for her—maybe because she wholly regretted having used him and she realized she still had strong feelings for him. Maybe she'd hoped he realized the same.

But this was nothing more than tit for tat. And it pissed her off.

By the time they got back to her car, Caroline had worked herself into a furious state that was only exacerbated by what she found on her return to the garage. Someone had written the word "BITCH" in capital letters through the thick yellow pollen coating her driver's-side door.

The exit booth was unmanned, the lights out, and the garage was mostly empty.

Jack got out, took a look around, then took her keys from her hand and opened her door to check inside her car. When he was sure it was safe, he started it for her. "I guess it's time to visit the car wash," he said, but his attempt at humor fell on deaf ears. Caroline didn't find any of this funny at all. She hadn't asked to be thrust into the middle of mayhem.

Although deep down she knew the thought was ridiculous, at the moment her life felt like a cruel joke —her mother's way of saying with her last dying breath, "And you thought you were good enough. See, I told you so—you'll never measure up!"

Tears stung the back of her lids. She swallowed hard.

Right about now, she desperately missed life in Dallas—free from serial killers and jealous girlfriends —free from crushing responsibility, decisions and expectations—and most of all, free from Jack!

He got out of her car and she slid in without saying a word. The last thing she heard him say before she slammed her car door and drove away was, "I'll talk to her, Caroline."

She squealed out of the parking garage.

JACK HAD to stop himself from pulling out onto the road after her. She wouldn't welcome his attention right now, but he wasn't comfortable just letting her go without some reassurance that someone would be there to see her safe inside her house—which was ludicrous. He couldn't be there to protect her every second of every day. Still, he couldn't let her leave like this after finding something like that on her car.

Maybe they should have called a report of the graffiti in to have it on record—though there was no property damage, and if every person who had a nasty note left on their car reported it as a crime, there wouldn't be enough manpower in the city to log all the complaints.

The truth was that if Caroline weren't the daughter of Florence Aldridge, if they weren't in the middle of looking for a killer, if she weren't the woman he was still in love with, he wouldn't even second-guess himself right now.

He would just let her go.

Caroline was so angry, she didn't even wipe the smear off her car door.

Had Kelly done that?

He sure as hell intended to find out.

He called Josh first to see where he was, to see if he was heading to the Aldridge estate tonight. He was relieved to know that he was at his mother's, just down the road, and he promised to go wait for Caroline to arrive. Jack explained what had happened, and thanked him, then he hung up and called Kelly.

She answered on the first ring, as though she had been expecting his call, so he asked her straight out.

"I didn't do it," she replied.

Jack couldn't imagine who else would have done it, especially in light of her recent visit with Caroline. She was feeling needy and unhappy and maybe even a little angry at him for wasting her time. He couldn't blame her.

"I said I didn't do it!" she offered a second time, and her tone grew more furious.

Jack was so worked up he couldn't take her at her word—not tonight. He wanted her to understand beyond any shadow of doubt that he was through. It was over between them. Finito.

Not that he had a chance in hell with Caroline at this point, because he'd managed to fuck that up too, but he felt for the first time in years that he was doing the right thing where his personal life was concerned.

And more to the point, he was feeling.

God was he feeling.

Like complete and total shit.

He'd been going through the motions for too long now, just doing the job—whatever that meant. Even fucking had grown to be a perfunctory task, and he hated to admit that Kelly was just a vessel—not that he hadn't tried to make a go of it. He had desperately wanted to love her. Just as he had desperately wanted not to love Caroline.

People couldn't help the way they felt.

But they could damned well control how they behaved. Kelly had every right to be angry with him. She didn't have a right to defile Caroline's car. He told her as much.

"For the last time," Kelly screamed, "I didn't do it!"

She hung up on him.

A lightning rod of anger shot up Jack's spine and he nearly hurled his phone out the window. He tossed it onto the passenger seat, staring furiously out at the road ahead.

The moon was new, and the night dark. Crossing over the Ashley River, he left the glow of the city behind him, and drove into blackness.

He was angry.

Anger clouded judgment.

He wasn't thinking straight and he needed to start. Right now.

Whoever had written that note on Caroline's car was angry too, or they wouldn't have gone into a public garage to leave a message like that for a public figure.

Not a smart move.

Clearing the fog from his brain, he allowed himself to ask, "If not Kelly, who else would leave a message like that?

Could it be connected to the attempted break-in at her house?

If that were the case, it would be personal. The murder of Amy Jones, by contrast, was *not* an act of anger. They were two separate things, he reassured himself. Completely unconnected. But who the hell had she pissed off?

Just about everyone, he realized.

On the heels of that thought came the realization that he hadn't even had enough wits about him to check to see if there were surveillance cameras installed in the garage.

He turned the car around. If they were lucky, their artist's moment of stupidity would be caught on tape.

As soon as Caroline pulled into the drive, she got out of the car and wiped her hand over every inch of her driver's-side door, erasing the offending letters.

She felt as though she was nearing a breaking point; something had to turn around—fast.

What if it was true that she couldn't measure up? No matter how much Frank worked with her, the shoes she had to fill were massive. What if she could never be the community darling her mother had been?

She certainly wasn't off to a great start, inciting

anger and contempt in the people she was trying to protect.

They were dedicating a garden for her mother. What would be her legacy? A great, big empty building on Meeting Street where people would point and say, "That used to be the eighth oldest paper in the country, but some dipshit bankrupted it."

She dusted the pollen from her hands onto her skirt and stood there, staring at her car, and for the second time in two days started to cry. Tears were becoming an everyday occurrence for the girl who didn't know how to cry!

A movement caught her eye on the porch and her tears stopped abruptly.

From the windows, a soft glow emanated. Not enough to shed light on the figure standing in the shadows, watching . . .

Caroline stiffened, and the tiny hairs at the back of her neck tingled. "Who's there?"

Josh stepped out of the shadows, onto the top step, and started down the steps toward her. "Rough day?"

Caroline let out a breath of relief. "You scared the hell out of me!" She swiped at her eyes. "You don't know the half of it."

"Actually, I do. Jack called."

Caroline glowered at him, without really meaning to.

"He just wanted to make sure you got home all right, but he told me what happened."

Her gaze narrowed. "All of it?"

"No, just about the car. I'm assuming you two fought?"

Caroline didn't want to admit to Josh what Jack had asked her to do—the things he had said to her.

The thought of it alone was enough to bring another swell of tears to her eyes.

Josh held out his arms and she went into them automatically. He patted her gently on the back. "I can't seem to do anything right," she said plaintively.

Josh squeezed her. "You're doing the best you can, right?"

Caroline nodded, wiping tears from her cheeks with her shoulder.

He pushed her away and peered into her face, his dark skin even darker under the moonlight. "That's all you can do, Caroline. Come on over here." He took her by the hand, dragging her to the stairs. "Sit down," he commanded.

Caroline did as he asked, feeling as wretched as a little girl whose feelings had been hurt by the mean boy in school. Except that Jack had always been her protector—not her tormentor.

She sat next to Josh and he squeezed her hand, but didn't let it go. "We've come a long way," he told her. "Who'd have thunk you'd be running the *Tribune* all by your lonesome . . . and look at me. I'm gonna run for mayor if James Island ever gets its shit together. Together, we'll own this city, Caroline. They don't know how lucky they are to have us . . . but they will."

Caroline appreciated the pep talk. This was why family was important, she reminded herself. Her family was her anchor. Without them—without Josh right now—she would be lying in a quivering heap on the oyster shell driveway.

She squeezed Josh's hand. "I wonder if Mother had this much trouble in the beginning. I wish now I could ask her more about her early days. My grandfather died young and she inherited the job not much older than I am now."

He let go of her hand and slid an arm around her shoulder, drawing her close. "I'm sure Flo had her own troubles, but you Aldridge ladies come from a long line of strong, solitary females."

He might as well have said "alone," because that's where it felt like she was headed. Caroline peered up at him. "Do you think Mother ever dated?"

"Oh, hell yeah!" he exclaimed, and looked down at her, his perfect white teeth flashing a grin that she knew made most girls' knees weak.

Caroline laughed and shoved him a little. "What do you know?"

"Girl!" he said, "You're mother was a MILF if I ever saw one! Trust me, she wasn't near ready to go to her grave."

Caroline swiped at her eyes again and they sat there on the porch, quiet for a moment. She looked up at the stars. "I hear the cicadas out there. They're starting to emerge."

Josh shuddered. "Ugly bastards! Sometimes I can actually hear them snapping out of their skins." He shuddered again, an over-exaggerated gesture.

Caroline grimaced, but laughed.

"It's going to be all right," he said, changing the subject. "I promise. You'll get it together, Caroline."

Caroline looked up at him. "So does that mean you're not mad anymore?"

He took his arm from around her shoulder and joined his hands in front of his knees. "For now . . . but I'm going to be one pissed-off muthafucker if I miss my shot at the mayor's desk because of you."

Caroline frowned, but said, "Look at the bright side . . ."

He eyed her uncertainly. "Yeah, what's that?"

"James Island might not ever get another mayor."

He lifted a brow. "That's not a bright side, Caroline."

"Well, at least then you wouldn't have to worry about messing things up."

"That's where you have it dead wrong, girl. I'd rather get in there and fuck everything to hell and back than never get the chance." He stood, brushing himself off. "You should go in. I want to check on Mama before I head home."

Caroline stood too, wishing she were more like him. Nothing seemed to bother him for long. "All right. Thanks for checking in on me. Tell Sadie I love her and I'll see her soon."

He winked at her. "Night, Cici."

Caroline's heart jolted at the unexpected endearment. "G'night, Josh."

"Get the hell inside and lock up," he demanded.

Without another word, Caroline smiled, went to pick up the bags she'd abandoned beside the car and hurried inside.

18

There were no surveillance cameras in the garage. Jack also poked around for witnesses, but nobody had seen anything. He wasn't surprised. It probably would have taken all of three seconds to write a five-letter word in pollen dust on a dirty car. Telling himself that Caroline had just angered one of the *Tribune*'s readers, he refocused his energy.

At the moment, he had more urgent business to attend to. He sat in his office, staring at his computer screen with an unlit cigarette dangling from his mouth, poring over what he knew so far—which was precious little.

It was quiet.

Too quiet.

Like the moments during a hurricane, when the eye passed over, and it seemed the worst was over, but you knew down in your gut that despite the eerie silence, the worst was still to come.

He had a dull headache—probably lack of sleep—and he craved a smoke.

Right now, he could use the resources the FBI had at their disposal—resources CPD wouldn't have access to. But at this point, he couldn't even request FBI assistance because the case didn't meet the criteria, and locally, the higher-ups didn't want to call it a serial homicide—despite the implications—and despite Caroline's suggestive article. At the moment, they were way more concerned with doing damage control than they were with profiling a killer—particularly since there was only one body.

He had to give the higher-ups this much: serial homicides were rare, making up less than one percent of all murders committed during any given year. The odds were against this being the work of a serial killer . . . and still somehow he knew it was. Still he didn't need a bunch of talking heads telling him what to look for in a suspect—half that shit was a bunch of TV mythology anyway. He rubbed his eyes.

Focus, Jack.

So this was what he had: a handful of facts that might, or might not, be relevant to a solid profiling. But A) the investigation was his until they took it away or they fired him—which was becoming a distinct possibility. And B) until someone gave him a reason to think otherwise, he was going to listen to his gut.

Data indicated most known serial killers were white males between twenty-five and thirty-five and since the victim was Caucasian, the killer most likely was Caucasian, too. Also assuming their killer was male, male serial killers had a consistent pattern of killing strangers, so he probably didn't know his victim either. If one surmised he had killed before, it would stand to reason he was also an extremely organized killer since there were no bodies to be found.

According to the Holmes typology, they were probably dealing with an organized, nonsocial offender—

someone who had an above-average IQ, a college graduate maybe. He was someone who probably attacked using seduction into restraints—possibly a father figure—someone people trusted . . . someone people *wanted* to trust. Sometimes, serial killers even had jobs that put them close to the action, so they could keep tabs on the investigation and stay ahead of the game. He would likely be socially functional— probably even drove a flashy car and wore Italian shoes, and didn't need to work at night, because he wasn't hiding . . . he left his crime scene whistle clean, killing one place, dumping the body at another . . . except that this time their guy had been interrupted.

The typology for male serial killers also divided them into four groups: visionaries, missionaries, hedonists and power seekers. Visionaries responded to voices telling them to kill. Missionaries felt they had a duty to clean up the dregs of society. Hedonists were further subdivided into three groups—lust, thrill and gain. Lust killers got off on it, thrill killers simply liked the game, and gain killers believed they would profit. Then there were the power seekers who were busy playing God. But this was the problem he had with the experts from Quantico: any and all of these attributes combined could be their killer's profile.

Studying the screen, Jack plucked the offensive cigarette from his lips and tossed it onto his desk. Then, just for good measure, he picked it up again and tore it in half, tossing it back down, thoroughly annoyed by his own ambivalence.

The results were back on most of the forensics. Apparently, the victim's tongue was cut while she was still alive. No semen was detected on or in her body, nor was there any other sexually relevant evidence.

Still, they couldn't rule out lust as a motivation. It was entirely possible that since the guy was interrupted, he just hadn't had time to violate her. Plus, not all rapists penetrated their victims while still alive. Then again, just because he didn't get off inside her, didn't mean he didn't get off.

On the spreadsheet, he had written: power seeker: check; thrill seeker: question mark; missionary: question mark; visionary: question mark; rape: not evident; souvenirs and trophies: question mark. Under each of these, he had written the available evidence placing the killer into each of these categories.

A blinking cursor sat by the last category. If it had been written on a chalkboard, the space beneath it would have been milky from multiple erases, but the cursor sat there blinking insistently, beckoning him to find the answer. His gut told him the tongue was probably a trophy, but he couldn't be sure—again, just the one body.

Thrill seekers loved sending messages and wanted the world to know the authorities were too stupid to catch them. Jack had a hunch that wasn't their guy. He jotted a note on his pad to check the national missing persons database, although he didn't have a clue where to start. As far as types went, it was all guesswork at this point. Unfortunately, until another body turned up—something he was trying to prevent—they couldn't begin to put two and two together.

As for the blue dye . . . apparently, it was just your common grocery-store-variety food coloring, a purchase that wasn't easily flagged.

He scribbled a few more notes onto his pad. Some things he still had to do the old fashioned way—but he knew lots of folks used their smart phones for everything now. Unfortunately, the victim's phone had been dead and produced no helpful history. Patterson's hadn't yielded anything more than they already knew.

They looked into Jones's romantic interests—at least two guys were talking to her, though according to the roommate she wasn't sleeping with either of them. There were a handful of friends she talked to daily— including the realtor who had listed the house on Backcreek Road. Jack met him at the house and did a walk-through, watching the guy's demeanor. He seemed appropriately disturbed and entirely too curious about the details.

Tossing his notepad onto his desk, he considered Patterson.

Why would the guy show up over at the Aldridge estate? And why the hell would he have Florence Aldridge's shoe? He felt the guy was innocent . . . but what was he missing?

Something.

His door opened, and Kelly's head popped in. "Hey," she said a little meekly. "Are you avoiding me?"

Jack stood, grabbing his jacket off the back of his chair.

"Leaving?"

"Yes."

She came in anyway, closing the door and Jack cringed, certain no good could come of yet another discussion about their failed relationship.

"I just wanted to apologize."

"You've already done that," he said. "Let's drop it."

"Consider it dropped." Her expression looked about as forlorn as that of a sad puppy. "I'm sorry, Jack. I don't know what got into me. I was just so mad."

He shut off his computer. "I understand why you

did it, Kelly." He turned to face her. "I'm not mad. Just don't do it again."

They both had to keep a certain decorum for work, and he was sure Kelly needed all the help she could get. Assuring her again that he wasn't angry, that he was just busy and didn't think it was a good idea for them to keep focusing on the past, he walked out.

KELLY STOOD there a moment after he left. Her gaze fell to the sleeping computer screen. She didn't dare touch it, but his notebook was sitting right there on the desk in plain sight. In the middle of the page, she spotted a note in his handwriting that caught her attention: Check national missing persons database. Start south. White females.

Kelly touched the notebook, rubbing her finger over Jack's familiar handwriting. It wasn't within the scope of her job, but if she could find a way to help him do his job and stay under the radar, maybe he would soften a little toward her.

She picked up his pen and turned a page on his notebook, scribbling his notes word for word, then tore out the page and left.

WHILE BONNEAU LED the troops in the war room, Caroline sat back and listened.

He reminded her a little of a short, stout, whiskey-drinking Confederate captain, strategizing for battle—not that he acted like a drunk by any means, but he was definitely high on excitement and he had that florid face and veiny nose Caroline associated with good-old-boy drinkers. All that was missing was a uniform. She smiled privately at the images she conjured in her mind and watched him work, pointing enthusiastically at his whiteboard.

Since their talk a week ago, she'd noticed a monumental change in the atmosphere at the paper. There was an underlying ease to the entire operation that wasn't marred in any way by a lack of excitement. This was how she had imagined it to be when she was a little girl picturing her mother at work.

There was something very exciting going on here, in this last-of-its-breed newspaper—something she had never experienced as a writer for bigger dailies.

"So he left of his own accord," Brad said, speaking of Patterson. "Though it looks like he pretty much had to. The climate wasn't exactly friendly after the indictment."

Caroline depressed the end of her pen on the conference table. "Weird though . . . you usually hear of them shifting dirty old priests to some other parish after an accusation like this. You almost never hear of them leaving the church."

Brad shrugged, the gleam in his eyes almost feverish. Like Bonneau, he lived for this. "Judging by his appearance—long hair, earring— I don't think he was ever a by-the-book priest. My guess is he just didn't have enough years in the church to earn much love up high. He probably lost whatever loyalty he had from his parish after the charges."

"But he was acquitted," Caroline reiterated.

"Of a pedophilia charge," Brad said. "Any doubt about his innocence would surely make his flock think twice about sending their babies to catechism. I wouldn't trust my daughter with him."

"But the girl was sixteen," Caroline argued. "Way past puberty, so it wasn't exactly pedophilia."

The entire room turned to look at her.

Caroline realized how it must sound only after she said it. "I'm not saying that makes it okay. What I am saying is that he was found innocent of molesting a sixteen-year-old—almost an adult—and the girl admitted she lied."

Brad shrugged. "Risk of the trade, I guess."

Caroline was beginning to notice an edge to Brad that didn't set well with her. Maybe it was that competitive gleam in his eye that bugged her for Pam's sake.

"Doesn't seem fair," Pam interjected, and went back to chewing on her pencil eraser.

Bonneau patted Brad's shoulder. "Have you talked to the girl's parents?"

"Yep. The mother. The girl's father died a few years ago of pancreatic cancer. The mom blames herself for not paying more attention to the daughter. I guess she realized her daughter was looking for a strong male figure in her life. She apparently chose Patterson."

"Poor guy," Pam interjected.

Bonneau glared at Pam. "Have you made your mind up about this case, Pam?"

Pam's eyes widened. "Oh, no—sir!"

"Good, and when you do, I don't want to see your opinion bleeding through your words."

Pam sank down into her chair. "Yes sir!"

"So ready for the clincher?" Brad asked, grinning slightly. He gave the moment a weighty pause, obviously enjoying the anticipation. "The girl who accused Patterson of molesting her is missing, too."

Bonneau's attention was piqued now.

Caroline sat up straighter and nodded for him to go on.

"That's all I have," he said. "There's not much

more. She ran away about a year ago, the mother went to Patterson to ask him to help find her daughter and bring her home. Apparently, she left a 'good-bye apology' for Patterson."

Caroline could almost see a progression of thoughts ticking behind Bonneau's eyes. "Where's she from again?"

"Murrells Inlet, north of Charleston."

"I know where Murrells Inlet is!" Bonneau exclaimed, his face turning a little deeper red. Caroline was pretty sure it wasn't anger. His eyes were animated.

She started to read through her notes aloud. "So we have a guy who was arrested for suspicion of murder, but released. This same guy was also tried and acquitted on a sexual abuse charge."

"But it never went to trial," Brad corrected. "The girl confessed, told her mother and all charges were dropped."

"Wow. Okay, so no trial, but he was accused of sexual abuse, and the girl who accused him of molesting her is now missing, right?"

"Right."

"So we have three girls, two missing—"

"One," Frank corrected.

"No, two. They still haven't found Amanda Hutto," Caroline reminded him. "And frankly, this really begins to make sense when you add Amanda to the equation."

Frank's bushy brows collided. "Why?"

"Because she's a child and Amy Jones was barely an adult. Jennifer Williams is sixteen. It connects them a little more . . . don't you think?" After she said it, she realized maybe she was reaching. She just so badly wanted to get answers about Amanda Hutto.

Frank seemed to consider the angle, and while he continued to mull it over, he turned to Pam. "What about you? What did you find?"

Pam immediately looked flustered. She nervously flipped through her notebook. When she got to the page she was searching for, she smoothed it with her palm, looked quickly at Caroline for support and said softly, "Patterson has an alibi for the time of the murder. Supposedly, he was sitting in the Windjammer watching a girlfriend perform for a CD release party."

Bonneau looked at her sternly. "A girlfriend?"

Pam took a deep breath and said in a rush, "Maybe. I think so."

He lifted a brow.

"I'll ask!" she said quickly.

"What else?"

"I think that's it. His entire defense is based on the fact that he has witnesses placing him somewhere else —on the other side of the city—at the time of the Jones murder."

"Witnesses?"

"Sorry, one," Pam amended.

"An 's' can make all the difference in the world," Bonneau told her. "Be specific."

"Yeah, but let's face it, Isle of Palms isn't exactly Timbuktu," Brad pointed out. "I mean, how long would it take to get there from James Island—especially now that we've got the Expressway?"

Everyone turned to look at Pam. She shrugged. "Maybe thirty minutes?" she said uncertainly.

"In bad traffic," Brad scoffed.

"Well, if she is a girlfriend, she could be lying for him," Bonneau suggested. "Find her and talk to her, Pam."

"The witness?"

"Yes."

"Okay."

Caroline placed her notebook on the table and her pen on top of it. "So where do we go from here?"

Frank considered her question a long moment, then said, "Let's focus our story on Patterson and the new missing girl—what's her name?"

Brad interjected at once, "Jennifer Williams."

"I want to know everything about this Willams girl —when did she go missing? Has anyone heard from her? Did Patterson track her here from Murrells Inlet?"

Did he kill her?

The question hung in the air, though no one asked it.

"Just the facts," Bonneau stressed. "No embellishment, no melodrama. I want to know every detail about his relationship with that girl and the details surrounding his leaving the church. Dig up everything. If it's dirt, great. If it clears him, great. We just want the truth."

"Who gets to write the story?" Brad asked. Caroline could almost feel the glee of his anticipation.

Frank looked at Caroline and she gave him a nod, hoping he was asking what she thought he was asking.

He gave her a nod back. "Pam," he said definitively. "But I need you to help her."

Brad sounded surprised, and maybe a little cross. "Do I get a byline?"

"We'll talk about it," Bonneau said, but didn't promise, Caroline noted. "Let's do it," he directed and clapped his hands in a booming gesture Caroline was growing familiar with.

The man certainly loved his job and despite the nature of their story, she had to admit, sitting there, listening to Frank and surrounded by the commotion of building not just a story but a daily paper, she had never felt closer to her mother. At least now she understood Flo in a way she had never understood her before.

19

In the distance, a small boat motored by, a black speck moving against a blacker sky. The ripples in its wake swept toward the bank, flatlining as it moved toward the shore. It died slapping feebly at the inside of a disintegrating boat hull nearby.

For a moment, he stood staring at the rotten landmark, wondering how long it would remain there before the city decided to remove it.

Maybe forever.

Still . . . the thought of someone unearthing it . . . stumbling across his sacred burial ground . . . made his heart beat a little stronger. He had never cared if anyone knew . . . then again . . . he had never experienced such a thrill as he did knowing people feared him.

He was the boogeyman. The chupacabra. Michael Myers.

A legend.

But deadly real.

No one could stop him.

They hadn't yet.

They hadn't even known.

He flicked the sharp tip of his knife beneath his fingernails and smiled at the thought of what lay beneath the *earth . . . where no one would ever think to look . . . so deep in the mire that not even the pluffmudders, who plucked their precious Lowcountry oysters from the prolific beds, dared to tread there.*

Special soil for special people.

Hallowed ground.

He could almost feel the energy they channeled.

The remembered taste, the feeling of power, excited him and he unwittingly pressed the blade into the tender skin beneath his nail.

Blinking, he peered down at the knife in his hand, automatically bringing the fingertip to his lips, sucking the tinny taste of his own blood, and feeling the immediate stirring in his groin.

The blade was eight inches of forged Solingen steel, polished until it gleamed. Some people called it an Arkansas toothpick . . . he thought the name was derogatory. It was a sacred tool that, so far, had only been employed to slice the tender muscle from inside their mouths . . . but last night . . . in his dreams he saw the Hutto girl rise up from the bog and vomit putrid black bile. So he'd come here to make certain they were undisturbed.

Not so much as a breeze stirred the sticky night air . . . and now that the boat had passed, the water was a sheet of ebony glass.

Maybe the demons were still inside them?

Maybe if he slid his knife inside them and sliced them in two, helping them peel off and discard their carcasses like dirty cicadas, he could leave them with the certainty of peace.

But he couldn't be sure.

He was still learning.

Still seeking the source of peace . . . a tranquility that eluded him except in these moments of communion. Only now did the voices leave him in peace . . . in the waning seconds of the witching hour.

Some folks claimed the veil between the spiritual and physical world was thinnest between the hours of three and four A.M. *. . . so that's when he buried them.*

And sometimes when he stood here after, surrounded by a mantle of fog, watching the pluff mud mold itself around his offering, like a snake's mouth enveloping a rat, he could feel a connection with every one of them.

And he was God.

———

THE CLOCK on the bedside table read three-o-seven A.M.

Caroline awoke to the sound of Savannah's voice as she crawled into the bed next to her. "Everything's fine," Savannah whispered as she slid under the covers. "Just a bad dream." Drawing the covers up, she snuggled close.

Caroline was too exhausted to acknowledge her with much more than a weary groan. She hadn't even closed her eyes until almost one o'clock because she'd been poring over financials on her laptop until she couldn't keep her eyes open any longer.

Shivering, Savannah scooted closer, burying her face into the back of Caroline's hair . . . just like she used to do when she was a little girl.

"You okay?" Caroline asked sleepily.

"Just a bad dream," Savannah repeated, shivering again.

The blinds were three-quarters of the way down and moonlight slid in beneath them, spilling across the knotted wood floor. Tango lay facing the bed, his muzzle bookended by both of her mother's shoes.

Because Caroline wouldn't allow the shoes on the bed, he'd taken to sleeping on the floor beside them, but she could see by the moonlight that he wasn't asleep right now. Savannah had awakened him. But he remained quiet and mostly still, his tail swishing softly when Caroline met his gaze.

Caroline had nearly forgotten her sister had the night terrors.

As a child, she'd had them nearly every night, dreams so real she had been completely inconsolable at times. She had spent many a dark night shivering in Caroline's bed, strangling the breath out of Caroline with a death grip around her ribs that shouldn't have been possible coming from the arms of such a skinny little girl.

"Are they still the same? The dreams?"

"Not so bad anymore," Savannah whispered, but she shivered again.

"Want to tell me about it?"

"Not really."

"Was it scary?"

"Yes."

"Wouldn't it help?"

"No," she entreated. "I just want to sleep."

Caroline turned over onto her back to stare at the unlit ceiling, suddenly awake and left with a feeling she wasn't quite certain how to interpret.

On the one hand, she was glad Savannah had instinctively come to her. It was familiar, made her feel connected to her sister in a way she hadn't felt in a long, long time. But Savannah's silence only highlighted the fact that their closeness was an illusion.

Too many years were wedged between them.

At five, Savannah would ramble on about her dreams, reliving every terrifying second through colorful details, drawing Caroline into her stories as though she had been there to witness it all. Together, they had learned to revise her dreams while she was awake, so that she could go back to sleep with a happy ending.

Like Caroline, Savannah had always had a knack for words and it had been no surprise to anyone that she had become a writer—exchanging real-life tales for the safer world of fiction. Caroline imagined it was Savannah's way of trying to control her world. In a way, they were the same—both of them shutting their windows and doors to the outside world. Except that Caroline did it by shutting out people and Savannah accomplished the same by creating fantasy.

What a mess they were—all of them!

As though she sensed Caroline's troubled thoughts, Savannah slid an arm around her, hugging her. "Good night," she whispered, and Caroline thought she felt moisture from Savannah's lashes on her bare shoulder, but couldn't find her voice to ask.

She didn't move.

And despite the fact that she had never been able to sleep easily lying on her back, she didn't turn over either. Not for a long time, and then she turned to face her sister, throwing her arm protectively over her shoulders.

They fell asleep huddled like they were telling secrets beneath the blankets . . . just as they had when Savannah was five and Caroline was eight.

20

"I'm so bored!" Augusta announced at breakfast.

Except for Wednesdays, Sadie had somehow managed to keep herself out of the Aldridge kitchen for most of the first month of their return home, but gradually, she began showing up more and more, and now it seemed she was flipping French toast or eggs more mornings than not.

Caroline stopped making any pretense at complaining. She actually liked it, and if Sadie wasn't inclined to stop, then Caroline decided maybe she liked it too much to make her.

This morning, Sadie brought over a dozen pasture-raised chicken eggs to highlight the difference in taste over the grocery-store variety and she painstakingly produced plates for taste tests that included one of each kind—without revealing which was which.

All three of them sat at the kitchen island, with Tango at their feet, and one by one, Sadie shoved plates of Southern goodness in front of them—grits, bacon and eggs, sunny-side up, with fat slices of sourdough toast topped with apple butter.

"Bored and getting fat," Augusta added, when Sadie produced her plate.

Caroline laughed at her sister's wide-eyed expression. "You could just not eat," Caroline suggested.

"Are you kidding? And turn this away? I have absolutely no willpower!" she exclaimed as she tore a piece of bacon off.

It seemed to Caroline that Augusta had been born with more than enough willpower for all three of them, but she didn't say so. "How's the inventory coming along?"

"Fine, but B.O.R.I.N.G.—boring!"

Savannah kept eating, without addressing Augusta's complaint, making a quiet production of dipping her thick slices of toast into the egg yolk.

How had she eaten breakfast alone every day of her life for the last ten years? That was what was boring, Caroline decided.

Augusta and Savannah were both working out of the house. Caroline wondered if there was tension between them. She felt a bit of it, but if they were fighting, neither shared that information with her.

"You are bored because you're focusing on *things* rather than *actions*, eah," Sadie interjected, grabbing her own plate and bringing it over to join them at the kitchen island.

Caroline eyed Sadie's plate, noticing she had two very bright yellow eggs sitting prettily on it.

"Those look like Caroline's boobs," Augusta said dryly.

Caroline furrowed her brow, uncertain whether that was a compliment or an insult. "Did you get two of the pasture-raised instead of one?" she asked Sadie.

"Of course!" Sadie said, with a tiny smile. "I don't need convincing!"

Caroline laughed. "Honestly, if you brought us a plate of Tango's pooh and told us it was good for us, we'd probably eat it, Sadie. That's how much we trust you."

Sadie lifted a brow. "That so?" she asked, then went about the task of piling her entire meal onto her toast.

"Yep, definitely true," Savannah chimed in.

"So wait a minute," Augusta interjected. "I think Sadie's onto something and you guys are changing the subject." She waived her fork in the air. "I want to talk more about me!"

Even Savannah laughed at that.

"Okay, so you're bored," Caroline said. "What can we do to help Augusta Marie Aldridge no longer be bored?"

"Give the girl a damned cause," Sadie suggested. "Something public spirited so she can appease her social conscience."

Caroline shoveled a bite of food into her mouth. "Good point. Augie hasn't bled enough since she's been here."

And bleeding was what Augie did best. If it demanded self-sacrifice, Augie was all in; if there was an earthquake, a flood or a hurricane, she was right there to pitch in and help—she would, in fact, go anywhere and do anything that would make her feel like a "better person." Caroline understood that about her sister better than Augie seemed to realize it herself.

"I don't need to bleed," Augusta countered, denying the accusation, "but Sadie does have a point. I can't sit here all day counting the eggs in my basket without feeling really shitty about the people who don't even have baskets to put eggs in. Do you realize that Mom probably has a million bucks worth of furniture in storage alone? Original antiques and ridiculously expensive paintings."

"Would you feel better if you just gave it all away?"

The kitchen went silent.

Caroline was being flippant, but she realized almost as soon as she said it that Augusta was considering the question seriously.

"Well . . . we wouldn't have to give it all away, but how would you guys feel about selling some of it and maybe starting a foundation in honor of Sammy?"

Sadie's attention perked at that. "Oh! I like that idea, and I think your mama would too, Augusta!"

Augie turned to consider Sadie, surprised by the show of support from unexpected quarters. She and Sadie had a long history of strife—mostly Augusta's doing. Like Josh, Augusta felt, in this day and age, that Sadie's continued employment at Oyster Point perpetuated or somehow condoned the injustices of the past, but Sadie had insisted that no one could understand their bond but her and Flo. As far as Caroline was concerned, it was Sadie's decision, just as it was her decision to continue caring for them despite the fact that Flo was no longer around. Good thing too, because her apple butter was to die for.

"Caroline?"

She noticed everyone was staring at her, waiting for a response, and she realized she'd tuned them out.

"What do you think?" Augie persisted.

"I'm not attached to anything here. I haven't even seen most of these things for almost a decade, so I'm good with selling stuff if you guys are. But we should make sure we're not breaching the will somehow."

"I will talk to Daniel!" Sadie said excitedly and wiggled a little in her chair.

Caroline smiled to herself, realizing that Sadie probably would love any excuse to see Daniel, particularly since his Saturday visits to the house had come to a halt since Flo's death. Maybe for Sadie's sake, she would reinstate them. Besides, it couldn't hurt to touch base weekly. She had so much to learn.

"There are things I'd like to get rid of at the office too," Caroline admitted. "Can we all agree to make decisions together?"

"Absolutely!" Augie agreed. She elbowed Savannah, who was still eating and Savannah dropped her bacon on the floor.

Caroline had forgotten Tango was even there. He leapt up so fast to snap up the bacon that he shoved Savannah's stool out from under her with his massive rear end. She went flying backward, landing with a thud, attempting to break her fall with her left arm. They heard the crack of her bone as it bent beneath her.

"Jesus!" I'm so sorry," Augusta said yet again.

Augusta, Savannah, Caroline and Sadie all sat patiently in the ER, waiting for the doctor to call Savannah back. If their mother had been alive, there would be no way they would have endured this long wait. Flo would have moved heaven and Earth and gotten immediate treatment, but today, accompanied by Sadie, they got a little taste of what it meant to be just another patient in a busy hospital.

For the tenth time, Savannah reassured her. "Don't worry about it. It's not like you planned it or anything."

Augusta wasn't appeased. Even after Savannah was called back for X rays, she continued to beat herself over the head with guilt.

"She's going to be fine," Sadie assured, patting Augusta's leg. "Eah me?"

Caroline had to admit that, for the first time in so long, despite Savannah's black-and-blue swollen wrist, they all seemed as healthy as they had ever been—open and forgiving. Barriers were down, and she hoped they would remain that way—in fact, she would do everything in her power to bring them down further. It felt great to be reconnected.

Finally, after about two hours, Savannah was called back and while they waited for her to return, they hashed out a plan for the event Augusta would oversee—an auction, maybe.

Sadie was still executor of the will and as long as the final stipulations had yet to be met, she would, ultimately, be in charge of any final decisions—although she assured them fervently that as long as they were "loving each other," she didn't give a damn what they did with their material possessions.

So Augusta planned to continue her inventory, but with the intention of setting aside anything she deemed to be "disposable." Then the four of them, together, would decide what from her original list they would sell.

Augusta agreed, without prompting, not to put items of obvious sentimental value in the to-be-sold column. And just like that, Augusta's mood lifted, albeit still guilt-ridden over Savannah's broken wrist.

When there was a lull in conversation, Caroline told them about her visit to the cemetery . . . about the roses on Sam's grave.

Sadie remained quiet, listening.

"Wow," Augusta said. "I don't remember Mom ever once taking me there after Dad died."

"Me either," Caroline said.

Sadie nodded soberly. "Your mama wasn't the sort to talk about things that made her heart sore, but she missed Sammy desperately."

Both Augusta and Caroline shared a look and probably the same thought, but neither of them voiced it. Flo had been so busy missing her son that she had never realized how much her daughters were missing her, too. But that was water under the proverbial bridge.

Savannah emerged another two hours later with a small cast on her left arm. The intra-articular fracture was minor enough that they were able to treat it without resetting it, but she would be wearing her new wrist jewelry for about six to eight weeks.

They gathered their belongings, and it wasn't until they got into the car that Savannah admitted, "Thank God I don't have to try to write for a while!"

21

The lemon-yellow vintage Town Car was the first thing they all agreed must go. In pristine condition, the 1978 edition car their mother had cherished had already caught the eye of nearly every local auto collector in town, but as beautiful as the car's condition might be, none of the sisters could picture herself behind the wheel. Better to let someone have it who might actually appreciate it.

Pulling the auction together was becoming primarily an effort for Augusta and Savannah, because Caroline had her hands full with the paper.

They ran the first story about Patterson a few days after his release, and continued with periodic updates as new material emerged. Right now, with the intense spotlight on his life, Caroline would hate to be standing in his shoes. She almost felt sorry for him—almost, but not quite. It was difficult to find any sympathy for a man surrounded by so much suspicion and she was a firm believer that "where there's smoke, there's fire."

Sitting at her desk, she picked up the morning's edition to read over Pam's handiwork. With Brad as a tutor, and Frank overseeing both, Pam was quickly learning to be an ace reporter.

This morning's article was completely unbiased—although Caroline noticed Frank had allowed her to slip in a pat on the back for the *Tribune*.

The article read:

Ian Patterson, the defrocked priest identified as a person of interest in the death of twenty-two-year-old College of Charleston student Amy Jones, is now facing possible new charges in light of recent information brought to the attention of the Charleston Police Department by the Tribune's *ongoing investigation.*

Patterson, who was originally charged April fifth, 2011, with three counts of sexual abuse committed upon a minor, was forced to leave St. Luke's Parish in November of 2011, despite all charges being dismissed against him, or face excommunication.

At least one child sex abuse civil suit was also filed against the Murrells Inlet diocese, where Patterson taught religious education classes, but was later dropped after the alleged victim came forward to repudiate accusations. Patterson, a Charleston native, denies any inappropriate behavior with the alleged victim.

The victim, Jennifer Williams, could not be reached for questioning and is presumed missing.

The Archdiocese intends to make a stand and continue with excommunication proceedings for Patterson. "Next to murder," said Archbishop James McMillain of the Murrells Inlet diocese, "this is the most heinous crime a human being can commit."

The disappearance of Jennifer Williams has now allegedly been connected to the ex-priest and the chief of police, along with the county solicitor's office, are working in tandem with Murrells Inlet police to pursue new charges.

"If he's found responsible for Williams's disappearance," said Assistant Solicitor Joshua Childres, "we're going after him. It's that simple."

At the time of press, Williams's mother was unable to be reached for questioning regarding Patterson's excommunication.

Authorities are still searching for six-year-old Amanda Hutto. To date, the two disappearances have not been connected.

The article didn't say the two missing persons were connected. In fact, Pam pointed out they were not . . . yet, it left one wondering. She was doing well, Caroline thought.

Bonneau had also talked Caroline into moving the paper's bedtime back to midnight, despite the extra cost in man-hours. He insisted it was the only way to remain relevant, and having their editors break away from brushing their teeth to tweet sound bites wasn't going to get them the increased distribution they needed to stay afloat. The *Tribune* needed to get and publish news first. Caroline realized that now more than ever.

Although the mellow competition with the *Post* continued, winning took on a new meaning. Winning was all about persevering. And although Caroline still wanted to bring the *Tribune* into the new millennium, she didn't intend to do it by sacrificing trust. There was something very noble about reporting the news the old-fashioned way.

It was four fifteen. She had about an hour and a half before the City Market closed.

Setting down her copy of the day's paper, she

packed up her laptop and gathered a few documents. She had begun to work from home in the evenings, where Bonneau could reach her if necessary. Today, she was beyond tired after spending half the day at the hospital with Savannah and she wanted to run by the City Market to see if she could pick up a gift for Sadie —as a thank you for the constant care she provided. She stopped by Frank's desk to tell him she was leaving, and then headed out the door, dropping her briefcase off at her car in the garage. The City Market was a few blocks away, and it was too beautiful not to walk. Besides, the streets were always crowded with tourists at this time of the year.

Charleston's City Market sat on a strip of land between Meeting and East Bay Streets. She began shopping at the Meeting Street end, walking past the Greek Revival Market Hall that housed the Daughters of the Confederacy Museum, skipping the indoor market. She worked her way down the vendor sheds, where descendents of West African slaves gathered with their expensive sweetgrass baskets alongside T-shirt salesmen and Lowcountry photographers. Charles Pinckney had ceded this land to the City of Charleston back in the 1700s with the stipulation that a public market be built on the site. In those days, vendors sold meat, vegetables and fish, along with another more lucrative Southern commodity—slaves. These days, no one liked to think of it in terms of its original name, but locals sometimes still referred to it as the slave market.

On the streets parallel to the market, horse-drawn carriages trotted by. Tourists flashed photos of daughters and mothers and wives along the arched brick ways and the weavers sat weaving their baskets at the end of each walkway while tourists watched. Caroline wove in and out of the vendor sheds, searching for something Sadie might appreciate. She had no idea what to get her, but there was nowhere else in the city to find more creative gifts, all lovingly made by local artisans.

She stopped at a table with pie tins. Right next to the tins sat beautiful, hand-painted porcelain cake pedestals and Caroline fingered one with sweetgrass blooms, admiring the artwork. She didn't mean to eavesdrop, but she caught snippets of the conversation between the two women standing next to her.

"It *is* him. I think he's looking at us!"

"That man is beautiful!"

Beautiful wasn't a description attributed to many men and Caroline was reminded of Augusta's fervent declaration about Patterson.

"Do you think he's guilty?"

Caroline's attention perked. Peering up, she looked around to see who it was they were speaking about.

"Don't you think if they had something on him, they would have arrested him by now?" one woman asked.

"Well, he's guilty if you believe the *Tribune!*"

Caroline's breath caught as she spotted the figure standing on the other side of South Market Street, watching through the wide brick arches. Her heart tripped. She backed away from the table, automatically slipping into the crowd. She made her way quickly out of the pavilion, peering through passersby to see if he was following. He was. He kept pace with her, walking along the street, watching her. Caroline walked faster, her skin prickling with fear.

He can't hurt you here, Caroline.

There are too many people.

Those assurances didn't stop her heart from pounding frantically.

Suddenly realizing she was going the wrong way—away from Meeting Street and away from her car—she doubled back, ducking through the mass of shoppers, peering over the shoulders of people she passed.

He wasn't there. She didn't see him any longer. Now was the time to make a run for it. She took off her heels, placing one in each hand. She raced toward Meeting Street.

Almost there. Almost there.

The sound of idle chatter was a roar in her ears and the echo of a thousand footsteps was magnified in the pavilion. Just before reaching the last section, the indoor market, she slipped out onto North Market Street, shrieking as she ran directly into Patterson.

"Ms. Aldridge," he said in greeting.

Caroline swallowed convulsively. They were surrounded by people, she reminded herself. He wouldn't dare hurt her here. Still, she backed away, keeping a safe distance. "Why are you following me?"

His brows drew together as though he were genuinely confused, but he was mocking her, she realized by the gleam in his eye. "Oh, I'm sorry, you don't like being singled out and hassled?" he asked easily. He placed his hands into his pockets and leaned backward in a non-confrontational stance, but Caroline felt anything but reassured.

Their proximity to so many people gave her more bravado than she felt. "If you have nothing to hide, you have nothing to worry about."

"You are making it very difficult for me to do my job," he complained.

"And what exactly is your job, Mr. Patterson?"

He eyed her shrewdly, blue eyes piercing. "You have no idea what you're getting into, *Ms. Aldridge.*"

Caroline straightened her spine, automatically turning the shoe in her right hand so she could use the heel as a weapon if it came down to it. "Is that a threat?"

He shook his head. "No, ma'am. You have nothing to fear from me, but I'd say it is a warning. There is a difference, you know?"

"I don't need a lesson in the meaning of words, Mr. Patterson! Though apparently, you do. This is harassment!"

"No, ma'am. This is a simple conversation," he argued. "*One conversation.* But I can see how you might have trouble with the concept of one. However, if you think this is harassment, I guess we're even because I would say your paper is harassing me." He smiled thinly. "I'm just here asking you nicely to stop."

"Is that all you have to say?"

He nodded. "Pretty much."

"Then I guess we're done," Caroline said, and walked away.

He didn't move to follow and Caroline hurried toward the corner of Meeting Street, where she turned again to see that he was still standing exactly where she'd left him. She fished her phone out of her purse, but even as she crossed the street he made no move to follow, just watched her go. Caroline resisted the urge to dial Jack's number, remembering the women's conversation in the market. Anyway, Jack hadn't called her. What was she going to do? Go running to him every time she had a problem? He wasn't her husband, or her boyfriend, and right now, she wondered if he were even a friend. The problem was that she couldn't shake the desire—or the need—to hear his voice.

Even more than her sisters, he was the one she instinctively turned to.

Still, all Patterson had done was scare the shit out of her. He wasn't following her any longer; he had simply taken advantage of their proximity. In his position, Caroline might have done the same. In fact, he was a hell of a lot less angry about the whole ordeal than Caroline might have been in his shoes. She dropped her phone back into her purse and resolved to—what? Stay away from everyone she managed to piss off?

It comes with the territory, Caroline. Get over it.

Or better yet, stop pissing people off.

22

Whatever Caroline's personal feelings about Patterson, the conversation between the two women in the market struck a chord. She urged Frank to back off on the stories—or at least give the topic of Patterson a break. There was more than enough fear permeating the city already. You could smell it in the air—a muggy, lung-filled breath of reeking sweat and humidity.

That was the thing about serial murders and rapists: everyone became a victim. While the physical victims were no doubt the ones to suffer the worst, the psychological effects of the crime were perpetrated upon thousands. Every alley held threatening shadows and every dark corner hid gruesome possibilities. Caroline doubted there was a female in the city right now who wasn't looking over her shoulder— if there was, she was stupid.

On the other hand, through Augusta's auction, Caroline also witnessed some of the best efforts of the city at work. Many of the local charities had already offered to assist and the Aquarium was going to donate its facilities for the actual event. Sometime this week, her sister planned to come into the office to start an inventory there as well; Caroline had never seen her in such good spirits.

Caroline purposely didn't intend to bring up her encounter with Patterson to Augusta, because she sensed Augusta would just champion him.

She left work a little later than usual because yesterday she'd spent her entire morning at the hospital and then left early to go the market—where she didn't even accomplish her task. Trying to think of another place she might find something suitable for Sadie, she noticed the bulbs in the garage's overhead lights were brighter than usual—that was good. Still, she felt compelled to hold her keys in her hand the way Jack had taught her to hold them long ago—with the sharp nose of the key nudged out between her fingers while she made a fist—an unlikely weapon to be used in the unlikely event she was attacked. The idea of carrying mace or pepper spray had never appealed to her, but right now, she wished she had some.

Most of the cars had already cleared out. She'd parked within sight of the attendant's booth, which was now being manned in the evenings since her ordeal with the obscenity on her car door. She noticed, however, that the girl who took their tokens was not in the booth. The light was on, but the booth appeared empty.

Caroline picked up her pace, keenly aware of her surroundings, every creak of the garage's foundation, every whiz of cars passing on the street. One of the halogen lights flickered, and she held her breath, repeatedly pushing the button to unlock her car door. Lately, it had begun to stick, and she needed to get that fixed.

She thought she heard footsteps, and grabbed the car door handle, lifting it quickly and jerking open the door. Her heart thumped wildly as she slid into the driver's seat, slamming the door shut and hitting the lock button immediately. She couldn't wait to get out of here and on the road home.

Putting the car in reverse, she started to back out, then noticed the folded slip under her wiper and stopped abruptly.

A parking ticket in the garage?

She sure as hell wasn't getting out to snatch it off the window. Right now, she just wanted to go home. She drove to the booth and a head popped up from below, scaring the crap out of her. She rolled down the window.

The girl grinned sheepishly. "Sorry 'bout that! I was talking to my boyfriend—didn't want anyone to see me on the phone."

At least she was honest, if stupid—on multiple counts. Caroline guessed the girl didn't care much about her job or her life. "You ought to pay attention," Caroline advised her, and suddenly felt guilty for insisting the booth be manned at this hour of the night. The girl was just a kid. Caroline was going to have to talk to the building managers again and work out a better solution. It seemed you couldn't make one simple decision without considering all the consequences. No wonder her mother had shut down emotionally.

"Oh, look!" the girl exclaimed, completely ignoring Caroline's rebuke. "You have a love note under your wiper!"

Caroline sighed. Oh to be young and in love, she thought and gave the girl a wry smile. "I was going to grab it when I got home."

"Oh, no!" the girl exclaimed. "You'll lose it when you get on the road. Let me get it for you!" She stretched out across the booth's window and plucked it out from under the wiper, reading it first—rather rudely, Caroline thought—before handing it to Caroline with furrowed brows. "It's just church people," she said, sounding thoroughly disappointed.

Caroline took the piece of paper from her, straightened it and squinted to read the computer-generated type in the dim interior of her car.

Death and life are in the power of the tongue; those who love it will eat its fruit. Proverbs 18:21.

Caroline automatically looked around the garage, her gaze skidding to a halt at a shadowy corner, where Brad Bessett stood smoking a cigarette in the dim light. The look he gave her—a half smirk—sent a chill down her spine, but then . . . she was starting to see everything as nefarious. He hitched his chin at her, acknowledging her and then tossed down his cigarette, tamped it out, and got into the little smoke gray Honda S2000 that was parked in the corner where he stood.

———

JACK'S CELL phone rang as he was tugging off his T-shirt. He struggled out of it, glancing at the clock. It was nine-thirty. Who the hell would be calling at this hour?

He hoped to hell it wasn't Kelly, and, at the moment, he was on the fence about Caroline. Every time they talked, it seemed there was another battle.

Maybe that was never going to change, and the idea dismayed him. If he were a praying man, he would have predicted all his prayers would be answered by her return to Charleston. But that was not the way it had turned out; he was on the verge of wishing she would just go back to Dallas.

His mood soured with his thoughts. It took him a minute to muster up the will to go after the phone, but it stopped ringing so he sat back on the bed, trying to figure out where the muffled ring had come from. More to the point, was there anyone he wanted to talk to badly enough to expend the effort to find it?

The answer was no.

But he was in the middle of an investigation that wasn't exactly yielding results so he supposed he was obligated.

It rang again.

Was persistence a virtue?

He couldn't remember.

He got up, staring at the pile of dirty laundry near his bed, resolved to find the phone. He bent, scattering a week's worth of dirty clothes, but it stopped ringing for a second time.

Now he was annoyed. Mostly at himself. But he was determined to find the goddamned phone, even if he told himself he didn't give a damn who was calling. It was a matter of principle now. His house was a pit stop. The dishes stank. His clothes weren't laundered. His face wasn't shaved. His life was a wreck. And he really needed to find a killer before anyone else got hurt. The thing was . . . as determined as Caroline seemed to be to pin Amy Jones's murder on Patterson, Jack was equally sure the guy was innocent.

But he was starting to wonder about a connection to Amanda Hutto's disappearance. After weeks of searching for the little girl without any leads, she was presumed dead, even if that wasn't the official story. No body had been recovered. And that was the point . . .

When his phone rang for a third time, he dove into the pile of clothes, locating the phone in the pocket of a pair of jeans he didn't remember wearing. He dug it out, using words that would have made his mother proud, and finally answered.

"Bad mood?"

It was Caroline.

"Slightly."

"Sorry to bother you at this hour . . . are you dressed?"

Jack cracked a wry smile, his mood somewhere just south of reckless. "You're either fishing for phone sex, or you're on the way over. I'm guessing you're on the way over."

"I have something to show you," she said. "It's probably nothing, though I called Josh because I thought it was odd . . . he thought I should show you."

"All right." Jack ignored the little victory dance his heart did between his ribs. It was tackled immediately by his concern. "Come at your own risk," he warned.

"Funny."

He wasn't remotely kidding. "You know how to get here?"

"East Ashley, right?"

"Past the Washout. Look for the naked yard with the unused kayak hanging out of the bushes and the half-built motorcycle in the carport."

She laughed. "I'll be there in a sec. I'm just around the corner."

"See you then."

Jack hung up, and despite the warning he'd issued, he scurried to straighten up, shoving laundry into his closet and throwing away PowerBar wrappers.

. . .

CAROLINE FOUND the house easily enough, but as always, she thought Jack was too hard on himself. Many of the houses on this street were summer rentals. Mottled with beach scrub, it wasn't as though any of them were Yard of the Month candidates. The residents here were mostly low key, preferring bare feet over designer shoes—except in the intensity of summer, when the sand was so blistering hot that even sandpipers hopped about nervously along the white-hot sand.

The lights were on inside his house, but the blinds were down, offering just the faintest glow. Along the beachfront, lights burned behind the heavy blinds of a long row of houses—like a train of luminaries.

Caroline wondered which house was Karen Hutto's, and felt a twinge of guilt for not calling to check on the woman. The longer her daughter remained missing, the deeper the despair she was bound to fall into, and Caroline could scarcely bear the thought of looking into her eyes. It was like watching her mother all over again—her inner fire burning a little colder every day, until it finally sputtered out.

She parked her car next to Jack's kayak-sprouting bush and made her way up the rail-tie path. He opened the door before she got the chance to knock and stood there, silhouetted by the soft amber light inside, his shirt buttoned haphazardly and one side tucked into his jeans.

A shiver swept through her.

She told herself it was the damp night air, but it was too hot for shivers.

"Come on in."

She wasn't ready for the memories that accosted her at the sight of Jack half dressed. He no longer had the lanky body of his youth. His arms were well defined and his chest sculpted—not like the muscle-heads she often saw in the gyms in Dallas, just well defined, like a guy who wasn't afraid of work or sunshine.

Caroline stepped in around him, careful not to touch him, and peered around his humble house, catching sight of familiar items—the soft doe-colored leather couch he had bought for his first apartment— their first apartment—a red paisley sixties-era lamp he had pilfered from his mother's house before she was locked up and the rent had gone unpaid long enough for the landlord to padlock the house and seize her belongings. Jack had realized it was inevitable. He had bailed her out too many times, so he'd let them box up his baby photos and auction off the valuables before tossing out the trash—the mementos of his life. Later, after his mother was released, her body had been discovered in an alley downtown, in a condition no son should ever have to bear witness to—even if he was her only next of kin. He had refused any help from Caroline and he had never really talked about it much afterward.

Caroline felt a twinge of regret for the way she'd treated him when she'd first come home. Dissing his mother was a low blow, and she had only done so because she was hurting. She realized that now.

Jack was right. She was still mad at him for waking up in another woman's bed thirteen days before their wedding—even though he had sworn he hadn't had sex with her. It hadn't mattered. She'd been furious at her mother for sending him home with Claire—angry at Jack for taking her in the first place—and even angrier at him for not calling to tell her that her best friend had nearly O.D.'d on her mother's pills. To make matters worse, some part of Caroline suspected her mother had set the entire thing up to keep Caroline from marrying Jack.

Well, it worked.

She tamped down a sense of indignation over the memory.

He was staring at her, eyes gleaming slightly, studying her reaction to his home. "Want something to drink?"

Caroline lifted her brows, taking in the glasses strewn about—all bar steins. "Are there any clean glasses left?"

He shrugged.

Caroline smiled wanly. "Really, I only came to show you this." She opened her purse and fished around for the slip. "At first, I thought it was a parking ticket. . . ." She handed the piece of paper to him.

Jack took it and moved closer to the lamp, unfolding it.

His eyes grew wide, and she saw something register there—for just an instant; then he shuttered his gaze, and looked up with a tight smile. "Where did you get this?"

He was hiding something.

"On my car. Under the wiper."

Even the single word sounded strained. "When?"

"Tonight. When I was leaving work."

"In the garage?"

"Yeah."

He nodded, his eyes shifting back and forth between Caroline and the piece of paper, and he suddenly seemed on edge in a way he wasn't previously. Caroline knew instinctively that whatever he was keeping from her was something important, but she also realized that he wasn't going to tell her anything after she'd broadcast his last disclosure to the entire city.

Do you really blame him?

"Was it there during lunch?"

Caroline shrugged. "I don't know."

She could see the wheels turning behind his ocean-blue eyes. "Do you mind if I keep it?"

She met his eyes, unblinking, trying to read him. "Do you think it means something?"

He shrugged, setting the pious declaration down on his coffee table.

She noticed he couldn't discard it fast enough, but he chose a spot on the table that to someone else might seem unintentional—out of range of potential spills and away from all other articles. He even moved a glass out of the way that had no more than a swallow left in it.

"Dunno," he said. "Maybe. Could be just a Bible-thumper leaving his calling card. Was there a similar slip on anyone else's vehicle?"

"There were a few cars in the garage, but I didn't see it until I was already in my car and I wasn't about to get out to check." She wondered if she should tell him about Brad, but decided not to. Brad had to have walked out after her, because she'd spied him talking to Frank moments before she'd left the office. The note was already on her car.

He stared at the note on the table.

"Good girl," he said, and finally focused his stark blue gaze on her. The tension from his body permeated the room.

Caroline felt nervous merely standing near him.

"There's something else . . ."

He tensed, the muscles in his biceps flexing.

"I ran into Patterson in the market yesterday."

His brow furrowed. "Did you talk to him?"

"Briefly. He asked me, in his words, 'nicely' to stop harassing him."

"Did he threaten you?"

"Not really."

He moved toward her, the look in his eyes anguished.

Caroline sucked in a breath, startled by the advance.

"Caroline, promise me from now on you'll go home when the rest of the world goes home . . . you don't need to prove anything to your mother." He reached out to touch her face. "Promise me," he pleaded.

Her hand automatically moved toward his, intending to pull it away. "Jack . . ."

"I warned you to come here at your own risk," he reminded her, his eyes swirling with emotion.

Caroline didn't pull away.

She didn't want to.

She held her breath as he cupped her chin and leaned into the caress.

That was all it took.

Ten years of yawning, unsatisfied hunger was unleashed with a simple touch. Jack took her into his arms, his hands sweeping over her body, his mouth lowering to hers. He kissed her, and Caroline dropped her purse on the floor and threw her arms around him, her body responding in a way it hadn't ever responded to anyone, ever. She groaned, kissing him back, pressing into the firm contours of his body, craving the warmth of his skin against her bare flesh.

The next thing she knew, his hands were lifting up her skirt and she let him. He reached between her legs, beneath her panties, found her wet and growled deep in his throat.

Tiny orgasmic spasms wracked Caroline's body with that simple touch and the next thing she knew, her clothes were on the floor . . . and so were she and Jack.

23

Jack wasn't sure what got into him—something primitive and possessive.

They fucked once on the living room carpet, like animals. The sight of her naked was a little like taking a starving man straight out of the desert, ribs sunken with hunger, and standing him before a table overflowing with all the sustenance he could possibly want.

Afterward, he brought her into the bedroom to love her with his heart, making love to every inch of her body the way he had imagined doing for ten long years.

He spread her legs, found the precious button he loved and feasted on the rich nectar of her body, drinking it in when she came on his tongue. He traced the outlines of her breasts, remembering the contour with his lips, the valley between and the pert nipples that pebbled against the warmth of his tongue.

Every time he had ever been with Kelly—anyone for that matter—he had been thinking of Caroline. Every time he satisfied his body, he wished the communion were with Caroline. He didn't want to make love to anyone else—ever.

Only Caroline.

Jack came three times through the night, but he was pretty sure Caroline did at least twice as often. Like fireworks in July, each culmination of her desire came in rapid succession, one after another, making her toes curl and filling his heart with warmth.

They made love, gently, one last time and when they were done, she purred happily and he rolled to her side, thrusting his hands into her hair, caressing her cheek with his thumb. "I love you," he whispered. "I have always loved you."

She remained silent. But that was all right by him. He'd let her go slowly, knowing she needed to do this on her own terms. If he pushed her, she'd shut down and he didn't want to take any more backward steps. As Neanderthal as it might sound, she was his, always would be—proof of that was in the way she'd responded to him—but he could afford to wait until she realized it all on her own. They had waited ten years already.

She peered up at the clock and Jack's arm snaked around her waist, reading her mind, locking her into his embrace.

It was two twenty-two A.M.

"I should go home," she said, smiling.

"But you're staying right where you are," he told her with certainty. "Unless I'm coming with you, you are not leaving my house at this hour of the night—even if I have to tie your ass to my bed."

She giggled, and gave him a sultry look that heated his blood all over again. He didn't think he had anything left in him. "Yeah? And what will you do to me then?"

Jack hardened fully at the question and repositioned himself on his knees, lifting a brow as he peered down at her suggestively.

There was one condom left in the drawer.

Her wide-eyed expression when she realized how fully she affected him brought a wicked smile to his lips. "Let's find out," he suggested with a roguish grin.

As an invitation, she tossed off the covers, gloriously naked, offering him her wrists to bind.

He didn't need further encouragement.

———

MAKE a left-hand turn instead of a right . . . and later you hear you missed a three-car pile-up. But you listened . . . and you're safe at home, pouring a glass of wine and flipping through news channels . . . feeling superior because . . . you knew.

Instincts.

Everyone had them. Most people ignored them. Even in absolute innocence, a child knows when to be wary—they feel it down in their little pile of twisting guts—an "uh oh" feeling that sends them wailing after Mommy's skirts.

The Hutto girl knew better.

She'd followed him anyway, wanting to see the turtle nest he promised to show her.

At some point, most people stopped listening to that inner voice.

Then one day, you're thirty-five, you've got kids at home and gray hair peeking through a dye job, and you're alone in a parking garage when a guy approaches asking for directions.

Maybe you think he's cute, despite the scruffy, three-day beard and the hand buried in his hoodie . . . or maybe the color of his skin makes you feel guilty because your first instinct—your most primitive instinct—is to roll up the window and drive away.

Or maybe you're just stupid.

That's what predators like Donald Pee Wee Gaskins counted on: stupid people. Gaskins grew so bold he even purchased an old hearse, telling folks at a local bar he needed it to haul victims to his private cemetery.

No one believed him.

They thought the short little man with the gimp leg was perfectly harmless.

If they couldn't find an idiot like Gaskins until he slipped up and tried to off a man for fifteen hundred bucks, they would never catch him.

You're too smart.

Prove it.

IN TOTAL, Caroline got maybe three hours of sleep.

If she stopped to think about what she had done, she might be mortified, but she'd sworn off thinking this morning as a matter of self-preservation.

As soon as the sun crept in under the window shades, she got up and hurried to dress, gathering her belongings. She checked her cell phone. Sixteen missed calls and five texts—all from Savannah and Augusta. She felt instantly contrite for not having let them know where she was. If either of her sisters had done the same thing to her, she would kill them. But it had been a long time since she'd felt obligated to check in with anyone—or, for that matter, since she'd hooked up with a guy—so she just didn't think—but she should have, considering the climate of fear in Charleston.

Then again, this wasn't just any guy, and deep

down, she knew it wasn't a hookup. That both terrified her and thrilled her at once.

She woke Jack to say good-bye.

"It's Saturday," he complained groggily, grasping her by the hand and tugging her down so he could kiss her. One hand grabbed her buttocks, pulling her close.

"I have to go," Caroline protested with a smile. "Augie and Sav are probably angry at me as it is for not calling."

"As well they should be," he offered, but released her. He lay there completely naked, looking unrepentant and very fit.

"So do we . . ." She gestured between them awkwardly. "Should I . . . call . . . maybe later?"

It seemed not much could derail his good mood, Caroline decided as his grin widened. "Later. Five minutes from now. Anytime works for me," he assured, laying a hand over his very defined left pec and scratching his chest absently. That hand—those fingers—had been places she had never imagined.

Caroline's brows collided. She wasn't comfortable with expectations, but the lackadaisical answer somehow displeased her. "Right. Okay, I'll call you later."

"Be careful," he demanded. "Wear your seatbelt and be sure to look both ways before you cross the street."

Caroline laughed, despite her unease. "You're still a dork," she declared.

"And you're still fucking beautiful in the morning!" he said emphatically.

Caroline's face split into a grin over his flattery. "Bye," she said, and as she turned to leave, she found her own smile broadened.

24

The instant Caroline walked out the door, Jack got up and hurried to the kitchen. He grabbed a plastic bag and a pair of spaghetti tongs—the only clean utensil he could find—and walked bare-assed into the living room, carefully picking up the slip from the coffee table with the tongs and placing it inside the bag, zipping it tightly.

In his gut, he felt it was a message.

So their guy was a bit of a thrill seeker, after all. That was both good and bad, because while he was communicating, Jack realized he was also ramping up for another grisly show.

At this point, he couldn't do a damned thing about Caroline's or his fingerprints on the paper, but he didn't want to take any chances with the first possible piece of evidence in the case—even though so far their guy had left them zero evidence and Jack was pretty certain he wouldn't send a message like this without taking similar precautions. Later, he would have the lab take a look at it—but first, he planned to make a few inquiries.

THE ASHLEY WAS a thirty-mile blackwater river fed by the Wassamassaw and Great Cypress swamps. Sister to the Cooper, the waterway was as mercurial as the tides that governed it. Like twin, black moccasins, the rivers' murky depths slithered toward the sea, spitting their daily flotsam into the Charleston Harbor, where the tides fluctuated like backwash into a cup.

On the other side of Folly, the Stono River cut its way through more swampy terrain—land that was deceptively beautiful and uncorrupted even after centuries—except for a few scabs left upon the land by fleeing humanity—the ruins, the earthworks and the bulwarks.

You could literally throw a stone at one such scab from Brittlebank Park, a quiet little public green nestled on the Ashley River. Across the street from the park sat the police station, making it an ideal location for a family outing, complete with a playground and dock for incoming boats.

Certainly, no one working inside the two-story brick building would have any concerns over working on a Saturday. Inside, Kelly Banks sat poring over her computer screen.

She had begun the missing persons exercise as a means to earn Jack's pardon, but found it fascinating. First, she spoke to John Sever, the detective in charge of the Missing Person's Unit, to get a little insight. Luckily, she found him working on a few derelict reports. At any given time, there seemed to be a stack on his desk—growing more than receding—and instead of playing ball with his son at home, he sat at the office tagging and filing the missing and the dead.

Missing person files were retained indefinitely, until the individual was located or the record canceled. The number was always high, Sever told her—

up six times since the eighties—the increased number primarily due to the simple fact that law enforcement took the reports more seriously. But while the number of missing reported nationally in any given year could reach seven hundred thousand and more, the active missing persons report was a fraction of that. At the end of 2010, for example, NCIC's active report contained roughly eighty-five thousand, and only a fraction of those were related to abductions or kidnappings.

Once Kelly was ready, she borrowed an empty desk in the criminal identification unit. There were several databases available, including NCIC and NamUs, a relatively new public repository for missing persons sometimes used by medical examiners' and coroners' offices. The last list was public, which might give her access to cases that, for whatever reason, had not been properly reported. She started with NCIC, made her notes, printed copies of the list and then moved to the NamUs database, which revealed a total of two hundred and twenty-four cases for South Carolina—one hundred and forty still open . . . dating as far back as 1972.

That didn't make her head spin, but it didn't tell her anything either, so she narrowed the search to currently missing adults only, which reduced the numbers to a one-page printable list, but when she pulled up a map, the concentration revealed nothing. The virtual pinpoints were all over the state. Clicking on the dots revealed people of all ages and types—a twenty-seven-year-old white female from Gaston, a fifty-year-old black female missing from Greenville, an eighty-six-year old white male from Greer.

She saved that search and tried another approach, removing missing persons who were older than sixty-five and cross-referenced that list with NCIC's list of EMDs—persons of any age missing under proven mental disability and senility. She removed those from her list.

If she discovered anything significant, they would have to get someone else to do a more professional analysis. There was no way anyone was going to accept her search officially, but then again, she was only doing this to help Jack.

The list narrowed to maybe twenty for the entire state—but the concentration again revealed nothing. So she ran the report, not by the area in which they resided when they were reported missing, but the location they were last known alive.

Her map shifted slightly, but not enough for her to make any correlation. The numbers were just too low to reveal anything. There were still lots of representational dots all over the state, but a pattern seemed to be emerging near the coastal areas, and particularly in places known for high drowning rates.

It seemed crazy, but despite enormous signs posted anywhere there were dangerous currents, the number of drownings each year never declined. It was almost as though it were a challenge some people just couldn't pass up; the bodies recovered were usually those of healthy young men—often military guys who thought they were in exceptional physical shape and who believed somehow the laws of nature didn't pertain to them. During spring and summer months, it was not uncommon to hear Coast Guard choppers circling above.

Following that logic, she filtered out males between the ages of sixteen and thirty-five and cross-referenced that list with NCIC's list of EMVs—persons missing after a catastrophe. A thin jagged line of virtual pinpoints stared back at her from the computer screen.

She clicked through the pins surrounding Charleston, revealing mostly women—girls—from the ages of sixteen to thirty-seven. One of them happened to be Jennifer Williams from Murrells Inlet. There were a few young girls—including six-year-old Amanda Hutto—a handful of males, and a four-year-old boy, missing since 1989 . . . Robert Samuel Aldridge III. She knew the name—who didn't?

Staring at the kid's last published photo, she tried to make out a resemblance to Caroline. She could barely see it. The boy was too young and the photo too blurry. Maybe he looked more like his dad? She wondered what it must have been like for the Aldridges to lose a child so young. She didn't know much about the circumstances, except that Caroline's dad had briefly been in the news, accusing his estranged wife of substance addiction and avoiding all blame for his son's drowning death. Kelly remembered her parents talking about it. Afterward, her mother had refused to let her go to the beach with her aunt, citing the missing Aldridge kid as her favorite cautionary tale. It became an urban legend, like Jaws . . . or the little four-year-old girl in Florida who was snatched by a gator out of her own backyard.

She sat there, trying to find empathy for Caroline and even as a small kernel of emotion appeared, she tamped it down, telling herself she didn't need to feel sorry for the girl who had everything, including Jack.

As she studied the mass of dots on the screen, she was aware that behind her, some of the men in the unit were chattering with a newcomer. Distracted, she turned to see who had come in.

Josh Childres flashed her a warm smile, his unnaturally blue eyes brightening at the sight of her. They had worked together for a while before he'd gone to work for the county solicitor's office and if she hadn't been so nuts about Jack, she might have actually gone for Josh. He was an ambitious up-and-comer, with a charming personality and smooth tongue that somehow managed to win you over despite the overkill of sugar behind his words. Now, it seemed ridiculous to have dated two men who were intricately connected to Caroline Aldridge. So that was ruined for her, too.

"Hi, beautiful," Josh said, winking.

Kelly blushed. "Hi you."

"Whatcha doing locked up here on a Saturday morning?"

The heat in her cheeks intensified, aware that the attention of the room turned in her direction. "Checking the missing persons database." There was a question in his eyes, and though she didn't really want anyone to know exactly what she was doing, she couldn't seem to not answer it. "Trying to help Jack."

"I see," he said. "Well, whatever you're doing for him, I don't want to know about it." He turned to go. "Get yourself some sunshine, sunshine. It's a lovely day!" To the guys he tossed out a final, "Don't work too hard."

"Hey, Josh."

He turned to face her. "Do you have a sec?"

His brows twitched. "Sure."

She waved him over, not wanting to ask out loud. Although he wasn't related by blood, he was bound to have feelings about Sam Aldridge's disappearance and she didn't want an audience.

He knelt at her side. "What's up, sugar?"

She whispered. "You're such a flirt! I just wanted to ask about Sam Aldridge . . . he's still in the database."

The brilliant smile vanished from his face and his expression sobered. He peered down at his shiny Versace shoes, leaning on the chair suddenly for support. "That's because they never found his body."

"I guess I was just surprised for some reason. Everyone seemed so sure he drowned."

He glanced up at the computer screen. "Those your results?"

Kelly glanced at the screen, too. "Yeah, there are only a handful of unexplained disappearances in the area . . . until ninety six. Then we have a few. I was thinking about removing everything before then, but I wanted to see what you thought. I mean, the last thing I want to be accused of is leaving Sam Aldridge out because he's Caroline's brother. If it's relevant, I'll leave it. Can you tell me what you know about his disappearance?"

Josh ran a hand over his jaw. "I don't know. I was pretty young. He disappeared in eighty-eight so I was —what—seven? That was some rough shit," he admitted.

"Well . . . what do you think?"

"I think you're safe removing it if you want to. They were pretty sure Sammy drowned. He set out in a little inflatable raft and that's the last anyone saw of him."

"Okay, well, thanks anyway."

He shrugged. "My advice to you: let Jack worry about it. That's his job. And I'd better get to the evidence unit and do mine or I'm not going to have one to get back to." He stood and patted Kelly's shoulder. "Good luck with that list."

"Yeah, thanks."

"Catch y'all later," he said to the guys.

They responded in unison, waving him off.

"You working on a missing persons list for Jack?" one of the detectives asked.

Kelly winced. "Yeah." At all costs, she wanted to avoid a conversation about this so she didn't turn around to address him. She knew the last thing Jack would want was for the entire department to know she was trying to help him, especially after Condon had warned him to focus on the single victim and solve the crime without scaring the hell out of people.

"Find anything interesting?"

"Not really."

Kelly studiously ignored him, staring at the map a moment longer, and then she hit the print key, concluding that, at this point, it might all be relevant. She wanted to get out of this office and away from prying eyes and rude eavesdroppers. As Josh suggested, she would let Jack decide. Pulling all her documents together, she found a yellow envelope and wrote Jack's name on the back, then sealed the envelope and took it with her.

25

Augusta had waited until Saturday to go to the *Tribune's* offices.

The fewer people who were present the better. She didn't want to do any explaining and the last thing she wanted to do was to scare folks into worrying about their jobs. The plan was to go in, take a quick look around and then touch base with Caroline later to see what she thought might be sellable versus what she wanted to keep.

Caroline had already warned her what to expect when she went through the offices. She drove the Town Car into the city, far less offended by it now that she knew it was soon to be sold off for charity. But she couldn't say the same for the *Tribune's* offices. The entire reception area now looked like a giant sorbet, complete with berry-colored carpet and peach walls. The colors alone made her want to put an ice cream scoop down her throat and gag.

Her jaw dropped when she spotted the chandelier, and she would have stood there gaping, except that she was afraid the ten-ton contraption might drop from the ceiling and crush her where she stood. Jesus, if her mother's ghost was still hanging around somewhere, she might actually find a way to cut the iron chains from which it hung—especially if she caught wind of the fact that her daughters were going to gut the place and sell off all her overpriced crap. It galled her that Flo had probably spent more on that one lighting fixture than she had for all their birthdays combined throughout the years.

It wasn't easy for Augusta to think of her mother sympathetically. She would never say it out loud for Sav's and Caroline's sakes, but the world was better off without Florence W. Aldridge.

Fishing a tin of Altoids out of her purse—her one remaining vice—she opened the box and popped one into her mouth. She'd traded the vice for both her smoking and drinking habits about five years ago, after she'd realized she was turning into her mother—running around permanently anesthetized and sucking on cancer sticks as though she had a death wish.

Keeping to herself, Augusta wandered the maze of cubicles, avoiding eye contact with the occupants. If she pretended not to see them, maybe they would leave her alone—or better yet, go away.

She found Caroline's office easily enough—mainly because it was in the same spot her mother's office had been.

Tossing the tin of Altoids back into her handbag, she went in and poked around the office, opening drawers and file cabinets. Unlike the uptight Confederate sitting room that doubled as a lobby, Caroline's office was stark in comparison—nothing on the walls, except for a fine line of dirt where old paintings must have hung. Further evidence of museum-grade framing: a big, fat hole in the wall that probably used to accommodate a nail the size of a redwood trunk—

perfect for hanging massive, gaudy, gold-framed paintings of the sort their mother would have displayed.
Augusta hadn't been around the offices in far too long
to say what had actually hung there, but she wouldn't
be surprised to learn it was a portrait of the lovely and
accomplished Florence W. Aldridge herself, righteous
daughter of the fallen I-can't-seem-to-forget-the-past
Confederacy and an icon for the women's league of
America.

She was glad her mother had given the responsibility of the paper to Caroline. Augusta didn't want a
damned thing to do with it.

Then again, she didn't want anything to do with
the house, either, but here she was buried in lists of
items that included antique bed warmers, pee-pee
pots and handmade quilts that were probably lovingly
hand-stitched by Betsy Ross herself.

At least the lion's share of the inventory would
make someone with a hole in their pocket very, very
happy. Getting rid of it made Augusta ecstatic.

She sat down at Caroline's desk, watching the paper's employees mill about under the intense overhead lights of the editorial department—which also
meant they were probably watching her back. From
here, she could spy on everyone, except the farty old
man who had been running the editorial desk since
dinosaurs roamed the planet. She thought his office
was right next door and he probably had his ear to the
door, making sure Augusta didn't overstep her boundaries. Crotchety old codger.

Setting her handbag on the desk, along with her
notebook, she sat down in Caroline's chair, rifling
through the papers on Caroline's desk—past editions
—front-page stories about that guy Patterson, who
had pitched her a line drive with her mother's shoe.

Poor gorgeous scapegoat. For some reason, she just couldn't picture him as guilty. He had the face of an angel. And the body of a Greek god.

She sat there, trying hard to picture him strangling the Jones girl, but it just didn't materialize in her head.

As far as Augusta was concerned, a man was innocent until proven guilty and possession of a stupid shoe and a few fingerprints on the victim's car weren't proof enough. Supposedly, he was getting her gas, right? Of course his prints would be on her car.

But what was he doing hanging around Oyster Point? That much Augusta was curious about, but the difference between her and Caroline was that she wasn't afraid to come right out and ask him instead of publishing his entire life.

She stared at his picture in the paper—that sinfully gorgeous face—and set the paper aside, nosing around a little more. She found notes from a meeting —lots of shorthand references to Patterson—all questions that, as far as Augusta was concerned, presumed his guilt.

Why was Caroline so hell-bent on getting the guy arrested and convicted?

Augusta poked through the papers she held in her hand. At least three of them sported front-page stories about Patterson. Harassment. That's what it felt like, and his ordeal struck a chord deep down in her soul. Admittedly, she had a thing for underdogs . . . as far as she was concerned he was about as much of an underdog right now as anyone had ever been.

Was there a single person out there asking whether this man was innocent? Anyone? Anywhere?

She glanced at her notebook. She had one item written down—the chandelier in the lobby—but suddenly she had no impetus to go through the rest of the office—at least not today. She could always come back later.

Ian Patterson might not have later.

On a mission now, she pored through all of Caroline's notes until she found what she was searching for —phone numbers, addresses—anything that would help her ferret out Patterson. Then she got up, shoved her notebook and pen into her purse and left.

WHO KILLED AMY JONES?

After more than six weeks, the police weren't any closer to answers.

The initial media attention had kept the ongoing investigation under sharp focus, but now it was drifting off the front page. Pam's chance to make a name for herself was slipping away.

She felt weird about violating a crime scene—even after all this time and despite the fact that the yellow tape had long been removed—but Caroline had gone to bat for her and she didn't want to let her down. She had to find something—anything—to revive the story without harassing Patterson.

Even Frank had begun to listen to her, giving her appreciative nods and including her in their morning planning meetings. This was what she had been waiting for her entire career. This was the reason she had spent two years in a crappy admin position, despite her well-received résumé. And now, instead of envying the rest of the reporters, they were envying her, because she was working on the biggest potential story of the year—maybe the decade.

But she had to dig. She wasn't about to wait around for hearsay to end up on her Twitter stream at two A.M. She wanted to be the one breaking news on this story. She really wanted that old coot Frank to be proud of her. And maybe there was a little I-told-you-so wrapped up in there, because Frank hadn't believed in her to begin with. Still, she was genuinely proud that he thought her work was good enough to print on the front page. Frank reminded her a lot of her grandfather and made her want to live up to the standards he set and kept for himself. One of the things Frank kept drilling into all their heads was that if you wanted a story—a real story—you had to go out and find it.

So that's what she was doing.

She knew Patterson lived nearby, but she was trying to figure out exactly what he had been doing out near the Aldridge estate. Caroline had told her about the shoe and she'd been doing a lot of reading. There were studies suggesting that a serial killer's home base could be calculated using the disposal locations of his bodies. In this case, there was only one, but the study implied they didn't travel far from a home location to commit their crimes—something they referred to as distance decay. In fact, most started their killing careers in their own neighborhoods—a fact that gave her a shiver.

What if she uncovered clues that led investigators to unearth a gruesome graveyard to rival Pee Wee Gaskins' private cemetery?

If she found something like that, she could blow this investigation out of the water in a hard-nosed investigative report that would certainly put her name in the same bracket as solid *New York Times* reporters. Imagine where she could go from there: she could write her own ticket maybe—move to New York, make a real name for herself.

Figuring nobody was going to mind if she parked in the driveway of an empty house, she got out of the car and walked toward the back, scrutinizing the surrounding property. Even during the day, the house was shielded from prying eyes, surrounded by gnarly live oaks festooned with beautiful, draping Spanish moss and bloomed out azalea bushes. The scent of blooming magnolias reminded her of her grandmother's perfume. The truth was that if you didn't already know what had happened here, it would seem like a Garden of Eden: serene and lovely.

It was funny how deceiving beauty could be. . . .

26

Caroline walked in the door at Oyster Point a little after ten A.M. The scent of Sadie's breakfast lingered, but Sadie was gone. Her kitchen sparkled in her absence.

She made her way through nearly every room downstairs, but Tango was the only sign of life. The house was too big, she thought, wondering how her mother could have managed all alone for so long. It gave her the willies—especially since the death of the Jones girl, and the break-in afterward, connected or not, didn't much help. Really, the only reason this house felt like home was the presence of family—her sisters and Sadie. When they were gone, it was a cold museum and the only thing that kept her from feeling downright unnerved at the moment was the simple fact that Tango had been lying on his back, sleeping peacefully until Caroline walked through the door. Now he was following at her heels, tail wagging happily.

With Tango as her shadow, she made her way upstairs and found the attic stairs pulled down and the light in the attic on. She called out both Savannah's and Augusta's names.

"She just left!" Savannah shouted back.

Caroline expelled a breath she hadn't realized she was holding and started to climb the stairs. She found Savannah in the attic hovering over half a dozen open boxes. "What the hell are you doing up here?"

Savannah smiled at the sight of her, eyes twinkling mischievously. "Helping Augie."

Caroline had the immediate sense her sister's good humor had nothing to do with Augusta's inventory. "Sorry, for not calling," she offered a little sheepishly, before Savannah had a chance to say anything.

Savannah's smile remained, but she continued rummaging through the box she had in front of her. "No problem. I wasn't worried."

Caroline's brows drew together. "Really? 'Cause I would have been really upset—and scared—if you had done the same to me."

Savannah's tiny smile lifted the right side of her mouth. "I know."

But she continued rummaging through the box, looking as unconcerned as she claimed to be and Caroline admitted, "I can't figure you out, Sav. You crawl into my bed, terrified over a nightmare, but you don't worry at all when you don't hear from your sister all night long?"

Savannah looked up again with a patient smile. "I wasn't worried because I sent Jack a text last night asking if he knew where you were."

"And?"

She smirked. "He said yes, of course."

Caroline's cheeks heated. When the hell had Jack had any time to stop and send anyone a text? "Is that all? What else did he say?"

Savannah's grin persevered, but she fell silent,

going through her box with a knowing smile that made Caroline's face burn a little hotter.

"Well! Are you going to just sit there looking smug or are you going to tell me what he said?"

"Depends."

"On what?"

Savannah's face split into a wide grin. "On whether you plan to get down here and help me go through this ancient crap or whether you're going to stand there and let me choke on dust alone."

Caroline blinked. "Oh . . . well . . . okay," she said, and got down on her knees.

Savannah tilted her a glance without the least bit of judgment. "He said you were in his bed."

Caroline grunted. "Jesus! He told you that?"

"Yep. I just asked if he knew where you were, and he answered with three words: 'In my bed.' Want to see the text?"

"No! That shithead!" Caroline said, but without any real heat.

For some reason, it was okay that Savannah knew, and truth be told, it actually relieved her a little. Augie was another story entirely. "Does the rest of the universe know I spent last night with him?"

"No. I just told Augie I was able to reach you and she went to bed satisfied with that answer."

"What about Sadie? She must have wondered where I was this morning?"

Savannah shook her head. "Nope."

Caroline wondered what that was supposed to mean. Had Jack texted everyone last night? "You mean she didn't wonder or she didn't ask?"

Savannah eyed her with a twinkle of amusement. "She didn't ask."

"It's just that I find it hard to believe Augie didn't have one smart-assed thing to say when I didn't show up for breakfast this morning!"

Savannah studied her a minute. "She probably thought you were still sleeping. Having regrets?"

Last night had been . . . wonderful . . . every sensational moment, but Caroline didn't know how to file any of it yet. "Not regrets exactly."

"You're just not ready for anyone to know?"

Caroline shook her head. "Especially not Augie. Do you think that's wrong?"

Savannah shrugged. "Everyone has their own life to live, Caroline, so no. You have to do what you think is right—whatever that may be."

She went back to her task and Caroline watched her sister work—her face so much like their mother's, her hands steady and sure as she methodically worked through the box—and she felt a little unyoked. It was as though everything she thought she knew—her role in life, especially in regard to her sisters—was not at all what she'd thought. Certainly she was the eldest, but at the moment, she didn't feel the most mature.

Savannah was an old soul, Caroline realized. But the fact that she was only now discovering that left her feeling self-centered and shallow.

From the moment she had returned to Charleston, her thoughts had been focused around how this all affected her. Augusta didn't leave much room for anyone to wonder how she felt, but Caroline hadn't even considered how it might be affecting Savannah. She realized she didn't just want to know her baby sister better. She *needed* to.

"So is this all for the auction?"

Savannah stopped and looked up—her mother's

face, with one major difference. None of the hard lines were present—nor was that vacant look visible behind her gray eyes. Savannah's eyes were kind and gentle. "Some. Not all," she admitted. "I found a few things I didn't realize were up here." She stretched to reach into another box and pulled out a dirty pink bear. "Like this."

For an instant, Caroline forgot about Jack, forgot about the paper, forgot about regrets. In a flash, the bear served up a fresh memory of the distant past. "Shit!" she exclaimed. "I remember those! Are they all in there?"

Savannah nodded, then rolled her eyes, as though not quite believing it herself.

There were five all together—Easter presents, one for each of them the year Sam died. Caroline remembered because after Sammy disappeared, Caroline had put her bear away with his, at the top of her closet, declaring she was too old for teddy bears.

Sensing Caroline's interest in the box, Savannah shoved it toward her and let her look inside.

There they were—all of them huddled together in the bottom of the box, like scared dirty orphans. Caroline simply stared at them, studying their positions at the bottom of the box, all lying politely together side by side, lovingly placed. As she stared at them, all she could think was that five little bears were the last things she would have ever suspected her mother would keep, and she felt a tug at her heart that threatened to bring tears. She swallowed the knot that rose in her throat.

"I guess Mom was way more sentimental than any of us realized," Savannah said, pulling the box away, saving Caroline from another emotional outburst.

"Yeah," Caroline agreed, settling in beside Savannah on the attic floor.

Together, she and her sister went through box after box as the light filtering in through the tiny attic windows waned.

Some of the boxes contained items Caroline was sure she would be afraid to touch if only she knew their worth—authentic Tiffany lamps and fine silver. Hand-painted porcelain. An ancient handmade violin that looked like it must be two hundred years old. Three Civil War–era muskets and a Union soldier's hat. Neither she nor Savannah had any explanation for that one, and to tell the truth, Caroline didn't want to know the story behind it. They shared a puzzled look and Savannah tossed the artifact into the keepers box.

Box after box of antique treasures sat amidst dusty old commodes and porcelain washbasins. But none of the items received any more special treatment than the boxes containing those things Caroline would never have perceived to be on her mother's radar—her old Spirograph set. A ruined Etch A Sketch, with the magnetic screen gone black from the heat of the attic. A full box of her writings from grade school. Their school uniforms. And Augusta's piccolo flute.

Caroline tried to play a tune, but could barely remember where to place her fingers.

Savannah looked at her and said, "Please stop."

Caroline laughed.

They went through items for hours, moving boxes and rummaging through them. Then Caroline spotted a vintage 1915 Hammond typewriter and her heart did a little summersault. She stared at it lustfully, admiring the ancient gold keys and the dusty but unmarred wooden base. She tested the carriage and it moved freely, as though it had been oiled only yesterday. It looked like it needed a good cleaning, but otherwise it was in pristine condition.

There weren't many material things she valued, but this would doubtless be at the top of her list. In fact, if she had known it was up here, collecting dust, it would have been down a long time ago and occupying a place of honor.

She realized Savannah was staring at the typewriter too, her eyes wide, like an awe-filled child on Christmas morning.

It had been such a long time since Caroline had seen that look on her sister's face. Pure joy, without the least bit of envy, and she knew that if she wanted to keep it for herself, Savannah would let her have it without complaint.

In so many ways, Savannah was the forgotten child. Caroline had been the prodigy, she realized only now. Augusta the rebellious middle child. After Sammy came along, he was the baby. And Savannah .. . well, she was mostly overlooked. There were no hand-me-downs in the Aldridge home, but if it was true that squeaky wheels got the grease, Savannah never made a peep.

Caroline shoved the typewriter toward Savannah. "Needs too much work," she said. "All yours."

Savannah blinked, peering up at her. "Really?"

"Yeah," Caroline said. "Maybe you'll get busy writing that blockbuster and stop texting about my love life."

"Really?"

Caroline nodded.

Savannah squealed. "Oh my God! This is so awesome!"

Caroline laughed, and that little spot in her soul

that previously had felt like a gaping, yawning hole somehow seemed a little less empty.

27

Caroline and Savannah spent the entire day going through boxes, until the last of the light outside faded and the single overhead bulb wasn't enough to keep the shadows at bay.

Savannah scratched her arm above her cast. "It's getting creepy up here."

"Yeah, let's finish up and get down before Augie comes home. I have half a mind to put all five bears in her bed tonight."

Savannah snickered.

Caroline wondered if Jack had called. She felt a little guilty ignoring her work and her cell phone, but it had been much too long since she'd spent any quality time with her sister. She only wished Augusta had been around. They missed her caustic sense of humor, and Caroline was sure she would have found plenty to say about the box of big-shouldered eighties-era business suits that had belonged to their mother. She and Savannah had plenty of laughs about it on their own, particularly when Sav decided to model the wrinkled, dusty jackets. She looked like a business-minded Lady Gaga, especially after she snagged a gold-fringed lampshade and put it on her head.

The most surprising thing they discovered after all the boxes were opened was that the business suits were the only personal items Flo had stored.

From Caroline's current perspective, it was easy to see what her mother valued. Everything else in the attic was either a valuable antique or something belonging to one of the kids. As far as personal items went, she was much more apt to throw away something she was tired of than to save it. Not surprisingly, there was an entire section devoted to Sammy. Every last item from his bedroom had been carted up here and lovingly stowed.

They closed up and stacked the boxes, arranging them so they could easily haul them down later. Right now, Caroline wasn't up to taking them down by herself, and there was no way Savannah could help with her broken arm.

By dinnertime, when Augusta didn't show, they started to get worried. Caroline tried her cell phone to no avail. Savannah tried too, just in case she might be mad at Caroline for some reason—because you never knew with Augusta. About an hour later, they tried Sadie and Josh. Caroline also tried Frank at the office.

No one knew where Augusta was.

CAROLINE'S NOTE appeared to be part of a purchase order.

If there was an address imprinted in the top left corner, it had been snipped off, leaving the accounting portion, along with the P.O. number in the top right corner. Jack didn't believe it was an accident that the number had been left on the slip. Someone wanted him to find the pad it was torn from.

A challenge maybe?

As a precaution, he ran the slip by the station to put it under a forensic light source. Unwilling to part with it just yet, he looked it over himself instead of checking it into the evidence unit. Alternate lights might reveal some prints. It worked a lot like the fluorescent blue-green light from a laser or incandescent source used over a bedspread to reveal evidence of semen in the fibers. If there were organic materials in the paper, it would fluoresce yellow without the addition or powders or dyes. But the kind of fingerprinting really needed in order to expose hidden evidence—prints that were invisible to the naked eye—was a little more involved and necessitated involving the forensic unit. But those type of prints could last up to forty years, so it could wait another twenty-four hours while he made a few rounds. Besides, no one would be able to look at it until Monday—especially since the overall feeling was that they had all the time in the world. Without another body, the prevailing attitude was that this was an isolated homicide. And there was no way Jack could get the go-ahead to bring people in on a Saturday when the average officer's caseload was already bloated and time off was at a premium.

He was nearly finished with a quick examination when Josh Childres sauntered in. "Speak of the devil," he said.

"Well, if it ain't the dude!" Jack teased. "Working for the county solicitor's office must be good for you. It's certainly done wonders for your wardrobe."

Josh made a mock half turn. "Like it? Armani—gotta look good, you know. These days, the White House doesn't seem like such a long shot."

Jack had to admit, Josh looked like a real politician in his gray suit and satiny black shoes. He gave him a half smile. "I guess you're busy putting that inheritance to good use."

"Oh, hell yeah!"

"You'll be right ready if James Island can ever wrestle its way out from under the City."

"Damn right." Josh winked. "In the meantime, I'm here to do my job as the DA's flunky and bring back evidence nabbed during a robbery at Greene's place."

"Did they finally pin it on someone?"

"Maybe. They've got a kid's prints on the grip of a bat that was found in a dumpster not far from Daniel's office. I wanted to see if it's a fit for the piece we've got in evidence. What are you doing? I know you somehow sweet-talked Kelly into giving up her Saturday morning to check the boring-ass missing persons database for you."

Jack blinked, surprised. "No." He shook his head. "I didn't. I have no idea why she would be doing that. I didn't ask her to."

"Whatever," Josh said. "So what brings you in to the office today? I thought you might be too busy trying to hump Caroline's leg."

Jack sat back in his chair, crossing his arms. "You know the piece of paper she called you about? The one you told her to bring to me?"

Josh crossed his arms, leaning back on the doorframe. "Man, I only told her that because I thought it might give you two a reason to put your knives away and get busy. You think it belongs to the killer?"

"No idea," Jack admitted. "But there's one detail we didn't make public that would explain the message."

"Really?"

"Yep. Though it could just as easily be nothing. I'm checking the slip for prints now."

Josh shook his head. "Why are *you* doing it? That's why we have a forensic unit, Jack,"

"Because I'm going to take it with me to knock on a few doors."

Josh stood, throwing his hands up, indicating that he should stop. "Okay, I've heard enough. Don't go making my job harder on me, man. If you think it's relevant and you're not checking it in as evidence, make damn sure you don't let it out of your sight!"

Jack gave him a grin. Too late, he thought. He'd let it out of his sight for about seven hours, while he and Caroline had become intimately reacquainted, but he wasn't about to admit that to Josh. Nor was it relevant anyway. It wasn't like he could have hauled the note in to the station at that hour of the night, and no one had touched it.

"Don't tell me any more," Josh demanded, turning to walk away. "I need these ears to remain pris-tine!"

"Of course. Can't risk your rep," he joked. "How else would you win Augie over?"

Josh laughed. "I gave up on that shit a long time ago! But if you don't want Kelly, I have a thing for blondes," he revealed, "especially a hot one who'll give up a Saturday to please her man."

Jack wholeheartedly rejected the idea of an intimate connection with anyone but Caroline—like a body rejected foreign organs of different blood types—but he didn't bother correcting him. Anyway, telling Josh and the rest of her family was Caroline's prerogative—if in fact, she intended to tell them at all.

"Okay, well, see ya," Josh said, and walked into the hall, his black shoes gleaming like one-way mirrors.

"Don't go gettin' those fancy shoes dirty!"

Josh's laughter trailed in his wake, echoing along the hall. "Don't you worry 'bout it, detective," he called from the hall. "I know a damned good shoe-shine boy!"

Shaking his head, Jack turned around and finished examining the document under the lights. Legally, he didn't have to check the evidence in yet. Like baggage at an airport, as long as it never left his possession, they wouldn't run into issues with the county solicitor's office. All they wanted to be sure of was that it remained untainted—at least from a legal perspective. They didn't want anything standing in the way of a conviction.

After he was finished, he literally walked into every mom-and-pop shop within five miles of Patterson's home address.

According to the data, serial killers lived and worked in the areas they were stalking—they got jobs as school teachers or priests—positions people trusted—positions where vulnerable people turned. They also often left a trail of sexual misconduct, either suspicion or actual charges. Patterson wasn't working right now, but he had two strikes against him: he was a priest, and he lived in the area.

By late afternoon, Jack hadn't found the pad the slip had been torn from, but he hadn't expected to find so few people who even used such pads. Technology made it more likely for people to use computer-generated slips. For all he knew, his guy could have bought a brand new pad at an office supply store, but he didn't think so. The P.O. number was significant. You didn't just tear off a corner of a piece of paper. . . .

He sat in his car, staring at the sealed baggie.

Jesus, maybe it *was* just a random note.

Maybe he was chasing shadows.

And maybe it was as he had told Caroline . . . just some Bible-thumper leaving his calling card. Maybe . .

. but that feeling in his gut said no, and it had served him unwaveringly through fourteen years of police work. Still at this point, he had absolutely nothing to go on except for a hunch.

His phone vibrated in his hand and he jumped. It was Caroline.

He forced a smile before answering, hoping the smile, coupled with the simple pleasure of hearing her voice, would filter the edge out of his tone.

"YOU'RE GOING to get sick of hearing my voice."

"Never. What's wrong, Caroline?"

Caroline sat on the top step of the porch, pressing the phone to her ear, taking comfort in the familiar sound of Jack's voice. "Probably nothing . . ."

"But?"

"It's Augusta . . . she's been gone all day. Nobody's heard from her."

"Not even Josh?"

Caroline kicked at the remains of oyster shells. "No. Josh is right here."

"At the house?"

"Yeah—Jesus, she pisses me off! She said she was going to go to the office to do inventory. Frank verified she was there about eleven, but she left almost as soon as she got there and no one has seen her since. *Nobody.*"

Jack remained silent, and Caroline's heart skipped a beat as she jumped to conclusions. Unlike the numbness she had felt over her mother's death, the very thought of anything happening to either of her two sisters made her scream inside. They were all she had left.

"I probably wouldn't be worried except—"

A pair of headlights suddenly flashed into view in the drive, cutting her off and Caroline stood, terrified it might be a police car pulling up with bad news.

"Caroline?"

As the car neared, she saw that it was their mother's Town Car, with Augusta at the wheel. Completely oblivious to the fact that she'd left them all to worry themselves sick over her, her sister waved, grinning broadly as she put the car into park.

"Caroline?"

"Sorry, Jack. False alarm," she said. "She's back, though you might want to call this one in because I'm going to kill her in two minutes!"

She sensed Jack's grin even through the phone. "Take it easy on her, Caroline. Remember, you did the same thing to her last night. She's back in one piece, that's what matters. Right?"

"Right," Caroline said, not really listening. "I'll call you back," she promised, and hung up as Augusta got out of the car. Her hands went to her hips. "Where the hell have you been?"

Augusta sauntered up, all smiles, and replied saucily, "None of your business, sissy dearest!"

Caroline thought maybe she had been drinking.

Both Savannah and Josh came out of the front door and behind them Sadie sauntered out.

Augusta stopped in her tracks, staring up at the porch. "Really?" she asked, incensed. "Did you guys find it necessary to hold a convention while I was out?"

"We were worried," Caroline reasoned.

"You could have called," Josh chastened, siding with Caroline.

Augusta's hands went to her hips defensively. "Jesus H. Christ! Did I climb out of a time machine?

Since when do I need to check in with any of y'all?" She pointed an accusing look in Josh's direction. "Especially you!"

"Since there's a killer out there," Caroline argued.

Her voice was rising. "Really, Caroline? And where the hell were you last night?"

Caroline's face heated, but she wasn't about to let Augusta turn this around. One mistake didn't absolve another. "That's none of your concern!"

"Well, *my* itinerary isn't *your* concern!" she countered. "And I *know* where you were, but at least I have the good taste not to grill you about it. You might be the oldest Aldridge now, but you are *not* my mother! In fact, I have never had a mother who gave a shit where I was, so I'm certainly not going to start checking in now!"

"Seriously, Augusta? Why so defensive?"

The look in Augusta's eyes was bright and angry. "Because you're offensive!" she said, poking at the air as she passed Caroline. She stopped momentarily. "You're so busy out there incriminating people that you don't even know when to press the stop button!"

She moved past Caroline, leaving Caroline confused in the wake of her accusation.

Caroline had no clue where any of this had even come from or why Augusta would impugn her. She followed her sister up the front porch stairs and everyone moved out of their way, parting like the Red Sea.

"Just in case you've forgotten, you're the one who wanted to do this fundraiser, Augie! Savannah and I have been slaving over boxes all day, waiting for you to come home. We weren't upset you haven't been around to do shit, we were just worried, for God's sake!"

Augusta marched into the house, releasing the screen door without looking back, nearly smacking Caroline in the face.

Caroline threw her hand out to stop it and followed her in. "Stop running away!"

Augusta spun to face her like a human tornado, shrieking with indignation. "You're kidding, right!"

Even Tango, who had been sleeping by the front door, whined and scurried away, tail between his legs.

"No, damn it! We were worried!"

"You're such a hypocrite, Caroline! For years, you've been running from everything! You left this godforsaken piece of shit ten years ago without ever looking back. You rarely called me—and I'm sure you rarely called Savannah, but she's too much of a martyr to ever complain! You thumbed your nose at everything about that stupid paper and everything Mother stood for and then you come back here and act like she was your hero or something! You step into her ruby red pumps, click your heels three times and suddenly she's the good witch! At least I'm standing by what I've always said!"

Caroline took a step backward at the vehemence of her speech. "Seriously? All this because I was worried about you?"

Augusta's eyes shot daggers through her. "No! All this because things don't just change when you suddenly want them to," she said, and with that, she turned and bolted up the stairs.

28

W hile Tango stretched peacefully beside her on the bed, Caroline tossed and turned, remembering the look on Augusta's face. Not even the memory of Jack's loving could soothe the ulcer Augusta's tirade had left on her soul.

Caroline had always felt closest to Augusta. Just eleven months apart, the two of them had always had so much in common, including their powerful discontent with their mother. Augie's was just infinitely closer to the surface, while Caroline worked hard to bury hers beneath a mountain of apathy.

By the time she and Augusta had outgrown their dolls, Savannah had still been planning tea parties, inviting their mother who attended only by proxy—too busy even on a Saturday morning to linger over Sadie's pancakes. Caroline and Augusta had accepted it, feeling sorry for Savannah who, with her perpetual optimism, kept an eternally empty place setting.

As they grew older, the chasm between them had widened, until even Savannah's optimism had become a source of irritation—not just because Caroline couldn't stand seeing her baby sister disappointed time after time, but because her sister's wellspring of hope and goodwill only put a harsh spotlight on her own buried feelings.

When Caroline first heard the song "Cat's in the Cradle," she had easily placed Flo into the role of "Dad." She didn't know who Little Boy Blue was, or the Man on the Moon, but she knew intrinsically how they felt. What the song didn't say could be read between the lines . . . the disappointment turned to anger—the "take-that-how-does-it-feel-Mom" attitude that Augusta promenaded instead of Dolce & Gabbana.

She tried to see things from her sister's perspective, but couldn't seem to get beyond the hurt inflicted by her anger and incrimination.

It seemed to Caroline that there was a volcanic buildup of emotion simmering just below the surface of Augusta's skin, probably building since they were children. Caroline had just never realized that part of it was directed at her.

Take a cold, hard look in the mirror.

Augusta was right. Caroline had walked away and never looked back—until their mother's death had jerked her home like a rubber band that had stretched too far. And then, her thoughts had been completely self-absorbed.

Was she so much like her mother?

She had let both of her sisters down. Coupled with the look of surprise on Savannah's face when she had relinquished the typewriter, Augusta's indictment of her character left her feeling about as cold and selfish as a person could feel.

Her mother at least had the defense of mental illness. Flo had been clinically depressed ever since Sammy's disappearance.

Listening to Tango's easy breathing, Caroline wished she were a dog. Only a dog could sleep that peacefully, even in the face of loss.

He'd snuck the shoe into the bed again, she noticed, but she didn't have the heart to take it away, though the sight of it creeped her out. She hoped, at least, that it was the left shoe, not the right. Something about it made her feel uneasy—even if Patterson had in fact come by it as innocently as he claimed.

Augusta certainly seemed willing enough to believe him, but Caroline couldn't picture her mother simply losing a shoe out there in the woods . . . nor would she have let Tango run off with it.

Caroline was only glad Augusta was distracted with the fundraiser. The last thing they needed was something else to argue about . . . or another cause for Augie to champion.

KAREN HUTTO's house sat at the far end of East Ashley Avenue in one of the last remaining homes before the road leading to the abandoned Coast Guard station. During the peak of summer, people used the access to the beach, but during the off-season, the location might feel a little desolate, surrounded by older houses and acres of beach scrub. The sun-bleached yellow cottage, built on weathered stilts, with its faded gray roof and peeling trim paint, reminded Augusta of the woman who opened the door.

Petite, with slightly greasy, naturally wavy brown hair and blond highlights that hadn't been touched up in months, Karen Hutto looked like a poster child for hopelessness. Dark circles ringed haunted eyes, and she wore a long T-shirt that had apparently seen its share of nervous worrying. The left corner was wrinkled and twisted, as though she had been sitting for hours, diligently working wrinkles into the material. The question in her eyes was mostly unconscious.

"Mrs. Hutto . . . I'm Augusta Aldridge."

Karen Hutto's eyes brightened slightly and she gave a little nod of recognition. "Caroline's sister?"

Augusta nodded.

She opened her door wider. "Please come in," she said. "I was. . ." She shrugged. "Well, reading."

Uncertain whether this was the right thing to do, Augusta hesitated at the door, but here she was, so she might as well continue.

"What can I do for you?" Karen Hutto asked.

Augusta stepped into the house. "I just wanted to talk to you," she said, a little hesitantly. "I thought maybe . . . I could . . . help . . . somehow." But the word "help" suddenly felt completely disingenuous. She had come because Caroline believed Amanda Hutto's disappearance was connected to Ian Patterson, and she hoped to get at the truth, so that if there wasn't a connection, Caroline maybe wouldn't feel so hell-bent on getting an innocent man prosecuted. However, faced with Karen Hutto's obvious grief and pain, she wanted to apologize and turn around and leave.

But, ultimately, Augusta needed to pursue the truth. The only problem was . . . how to get at it without upsetting the fragile woman standing before her.

"I think I know how you must feel," she began, and for once, the lame condolence at least had a backbone. "Not exactly . . . but I'm not sure if Caroline told you . . . our little brother disappeared the same way your daughter did. He was four."

Karen Hutto's eyes grew big and round and glassy. "Oh no! She didn't tell me!"

"It's okay . . . it was a long time ago," Augusta said, and Karen ushered her into the living room, where she spilled her story and her guts.

"You're never going to retire, are you?" Caroline asked Sadie.

Sadie stood over her stove, humming "In the Sweet By and By" as she lovingly wiped prints from the stainless steel. "Mornin'!" she declared, answering Caroline's question with a backhanded admonishment. "This is not a kitchen that should be neglected and I don't foresee you or your sisters ever giving it the care it deserves. Anyway, I went to the farmers' market yesterday, picked up fresh fruit. I cut some oranges and pears and threw in a few blackberries for you." She gestured toward the island.

After yet another restless night, Caroline couldn't quite share Sadie's morning bliss, but she was grateful for the company and the breakfast. If she felt empty inside, at least her stomach would be full.

Venturing into the kitchen, she sat down at the island. "So I guess you've added Sundays to your list of days to donate to the Aldridge cause?"

Sadie's answer was full of exasperation. "Child, how many times have I told you I am here because I want to be—maybe one of these days you're going to believe me!"

Caroline understood the concept of caring about people. What she didn't understand was why Sadie would continue to perform duties she had been paid to do her entire life when she no longer had to. "Have you at least eaten?"

Sadie smiled. "Long before you even thought about wiping the sleep from those mile-long lashes. Did you know people are tattooing their eyelids now? Can you imagine having needles that close to your eyes?"

She was changing the subject of course, but it made Caroline smile. "You always seem to know exactly what to say to make me feel better."

Sadie walked over to the island to continue her cleanup there. "I helped raise your bony little behind, eah me, so I know what's bothering you even before you realize something is bothering you." She crooked a finger at her. "Just you remember that."

Caroline studied Sadie's face. Time didn't appear to have aged her at all, despite the blood and sweat she put into their household. In fact, she seemed to endure, even when no one else did. Hers was the loving hand that persistently stitched and re-stitched the frazzled threads of their family tapestry together.

"I love you, Sadie."

The words came out before she even realized she was thinking them. But it was the first time in memory Caroline had ever said those three words to Sadie and Sadie's eyes grew suspiciously moist. "I know, child."

Caroline pulled the bowl of fruit near and stared at the medley of oranges, greens and deep purples. For a moment, she couldn't talk, knowing Sadie was watching her much too closely. A lump the size of an orange wedged in her throat. Tears came before she could stop them. She brushed them away. "I can't seem to find my way, Sadie," she said, her voice catching on a sob.

"But you will." Sadie's black eyes sparkled. "You've got your mama's tenacious spirit."

More tears came.

Sadie put down her sponge, but didn't run to Caroline's side, knowing Caroline's instinct would be to push her away. "You don't need to listen to your sister, eah me? Augusta is battling her own demons—as we all do. She's doing the best she can. Just as you are doing the best you can. Sometimes we figure it out and sometimes we don't, but we're all just human, baby girl. We're all just putting one foot in front of the other, eah."

Caroline dried her eyes. "I feel like she hates everything about me!"

Sadie shook her head. "No, ma'am, she does not. She loves you—just like somewhere deep down she loves your mama, too. Augusta is just a scared little girl. She shows her fear—and her love—through anger. I know that's why she gets so mad at me, too!" She crooked a finger at Caroline, as though she wanted to say something more and then shook her head. "Look, don't you worry about Augusta, eah . . . she's going to figure everything out . . . just like you."

Caroline nodded. "I guess this is why you came by this morning?"

Sadie hitched her chin, her hands going to her hips in a gesture of challenge. "Why?"

Caroline picked up her fork and stabbed a piece of fruit. "To make me feel better after last night?"

Sadie sighed. "I came here because you couldn't be more my child if they had dragged you kicking and screaming out of me, eah! Yes, I knew you were gonna be upset."

Caroline opened her mouth to respond, but Sadie wasn't quite finished.

"*And* I'm here for the same damned reason my great-grandmother didn't run screaming out of this place when they gave her her freedom—and the same damned reason her daughter and my mother didn't find themselves another job when they had every right to. For more than one hundred eighty damned years we Childreses and Aldridges have been tighter than ticks, and just because the color of my skin isn't the same as yours doesn't make me any less kin to you, Caroline."

Caroline opened her mouth to speak again, but Sadie raised a finger, shushing her.

"What's more, I loved that stubborn fool mama of yours! She was my friend, not just my boss—though I assure you we had our years of strife."

"You and Mama?" Caroline would never have guessed. Flo had never once said a cross word to or about Sadie.

"Yes, me and your mama! Like I said, we are all only human, eah—all of us have our faults. Some of us keep ours a little closer to the surface and some bury them deep down."

Caroline chewed over that bit of info, along with her fruit. Curiosity got the best of her. "What would you and Mama have to fight about? Us?"

"Now that is none of your concern!" Sadie declared. "And while we're at it, you might as well know that your mama tried to give me half this property ten years ago, along with a share of the *Tribune,* but I told her no."

Caroline shrugged. "What was the point in holding her off? She ended up giving it to you anyway after she died, right? You could have been enjoying it ten years sooner."

"Because I wanted her to think real hard about

giving a piece of the land to the city like we talked about. My life isn't going to change much either way— what's an old woman like me gonna do with a bunch of burnt up bricks and way too many acres of stinkin' pluff mud?"

29

"So you're here because you *don't* believe Patterson is connected to Amanda's disappearance?" There was a heartbreaking mix of fear and hope in Karen Hutto's eyes.

Augusta was careful responding, reminding herself that truth was what she was after. She wasn't here to prove Patterson innocent—unless, of course, he was. "No. I'm not. But I'm afraid my sister is so obsessed with finding answers that maybe she's too willing to stop asking the right questions. My sister cares an awful lot, Ms. Hutto, but I believe she's too close to this. It's entirely possible that Patterson is innocent and if we're so quick to pin it on him, we might miss . . . the truth."

Karen Hutto's eyes gleamed with sudden anger. "What makes you think that man is innocent?"

If coming to Patterson's defense was the impression she was giving, then she was no better than Caroline, she realized. "I'm not saying that either. It's just that a man's entire life hangs in the balance—if he is innocent . . ."

Augusta let that possibility hang between them, hoping Karen Hutto would see the injustice.

"But he's not innocent! It takes a monster to molest a child and that man has already had charges filed against him for that. I can't even stand the thought of him touching . . ." She choked suddenly.

Augusta took a deep breath. "But that's my point, Ms. Hutto. Those charges were dropped nearly two years ago. That girl in Murrells Inlet admitted she lied. But it doesn't seem to matter to anyone. No matter what he does now, he's guilty. Your daughter could still be out there . . . somewhere . . . all I'm saying is that I want to help you find her. I think if we can find out what happened to her, my sister will begin to see the bigger picture a little more clearly."

Karen Hutto shook her head. "It's been nearly three months already. We put out flyers. The police searched everywhere. They even had the river dragged. We've searched and searched and searched!" She started to cry, burying her face in her hands. "I don't know what else to do!"

Augusta felt tears well up in her eyes. Moved by the depth of the woman's sorrow, she found her own long-forgotten pain trickling in. "Ms. Hutto . . . I want to put some of my own personal resources into this," Augusta said. "I want to offer ten thousand dollars to anyone who can lead us to Amanda . . . or the arrest of the person responsible for her disappearance."

If someone was responsible.

There was always the chance Amanda had wandered near the water, but Augusta didn't remind her mother of that. The woman probably already suffered a mountain of guilt.

Karen Hutto's head came up in surprise. She blinked, squeezing tears from her eyes. They rolled down her cheeks. "You would do that?"

Augusta picked nervously at her thumbnail with

her index finger. "I want to help you find her," she said.

Ms. Hutto's hand went to her mouth. Her tears came freely now. Augusta let her weep without disturbing her. It was clear she had been through too much already.

She didn't remember her mother losing it like this, but she couldn't help wondering if Flo had cried this way when there was no one else around . . . in her room . . . into her pillow.

"What about Amanda's dad?" she asked once the woman's sobs had subsided. "Do we need his permission?"

Karen Hutto shook her head, her eyes darkening considerably. "He's not in the picture anymore."

"What do you mean?"

"He and I were in the middle of a custody battle when Amanda disappeared."

Augusta nodded, surprised.

Ms. Hutto's eyes glittered with animosity. "Last year, I pressed charges for endangerment because he fell asleep drunk with a lit cigarette in his mouth while Amanda was sleeping in his house. Now this— he was supposed to pick her up for school that day . . . I went to work—but I had to go!"

She started to cry again and Augusta grimaced.

But while she sat there listening to Karen Hutto spill a gutful of vitriol about her husband, she knew with certainty that this was the right thing to do. There had never been any mention of a bitter custody battle in any of the papers—not even in the *Post*, and she had made it a point to read everything she could get her hands on before reaching out to Patterson. If all these events could be explained separately, the case against Ian might be nothing more than a heaping pile of circumstantial evidence.

AT SIX O'CLOCK, the July heat clotted the air.

It was difficult to believe the fourth would mark two months since their mother's death.

The fine sheen of sweat at the back of Caroline's neck dampened her hair so she pulled the long auburn strands into a ponytail, twisted it absently, and fanned herself twice before releasing it—an old habit.

She had forgotten how muggy summers could be in Charleston, but this was somehow worse, because while the mercury was rising, so was the humidity. There was a front passing over the Gulf Stream, bringing moist air inland from the ocean, along with a summer storm with predicted flooding. At the moment, however, the spartina grass lay undisturbed across the salt marsh. The scent of brackish water permeated the stagnant breeze, and in the utter stillness of the afternoon, it was difficult to believe someone was out there hurting people.

Maybe Jack was wrong?

Maybe Amy Jones's death was an isolated incident?

Six weeks had passed since her body was discovered . . . and all was quiet. If Ian Patterson was guilty, maybe keeping him under a spotlight had kept him on his best behavior? Or maybe the killer was gone?

In any case, the creeping sense of dread that had permeated the city after Amy Jones's death was fading now and it was hard to see the ugliness in a world surrounded by beauty.

From where she sat, the salt marsh seemed to

stretch for miles. Sitting on the pier, with her back to the house, she could easily imagine herself in another place and time.

A brown pelican landed on the end of the dock a few feet away. She watched it nose around, looking for food, but their dock hadn't seen gutted fish in far too long to remain of any interest and the bird took flight again, looking for richer bounty.

As far as the eye could see, the surrounding wetlands had once been planted in cotton and rice fields, tended by the hands of slaves, but these lands had never really belonged to anyone, Caroline mused. Her family might hold documents giving them the right to build here, but if the land and sea weren't amenable, even the sturdiest bricks would come tumbling down.

The ruins on their property were a perfect example. The instant the flames had cooled, the land had begun to swallow the remnants, enfolding the structure brick by brick, taking it back into the earth from which it was built. Now, all that was left of the old Georgian house was a pile of scorched bricks hugged by vines and painted with moss.

No matter what men built here, eventually, it all returned to the wild. The best you could hope for was a temporary alliance. But even that was tentative.

Right where she sat some claimed one of South Carolina's most pivotal battles had taken place. Cloaked in twilight, thirty-five hundred Union soldiers had descended on Fort Lamar, treading though swamps that sucked them down to their thighs. Had that battle been lost, the Union might have forced the Confederates out of Charleston two years earlier, but a victory bought Charleston two more years of free human labor. After the war, the pluff mud had been too soft to support machinery and the rice and cotton industries ended—for all but those whose slaves remained despite their newly won freedom. Caroline hated to admit her family was one of those, so she pretended their dysfunction didn't have roots as deep as the Angel Oak Tree's. Like Augusta, she didn't know how Sadie could look out into these wetlands and not feel the overwhelming need to go someplace where there was no memory of the past and the scent of magnolias didn't linger like old-lady perfume.

God only knew, she had felt that way for most of her life.

Ironically, she was finding her peace with it now only after the woman who had brought her into this world was no longer in it.

The sad truth was . . . the only real chance to know her mother now was literally through this house . . . and her role at the paper. Too late, she realized her mother had been just a human being doing the best she could on any given day.

Although Caroline's grandmother had outlived her grandfather, she'd died shortly after Caroline was born, so essentially Flo had weathered every life storm alone—the loss of her son, her husband, the estrangement of her daughters—except for loyal Sadie, who remained steadfast at her side through it all. Those two had had a depth of friendship Caroline was only now beginning to understand. But no one had ever handed Florence Willodean Aldridge a guidebook. She'd learned to be a mother, an heiress and a newspaperwoman all on her own. That knowledge filled Caroline with an intense feeling of sorrow and regret.

The sun was setting, painting the marsh with a warm blush that gave at least the impression of serenity, but Caroline didn't feel any of it in her soul.

She'd made a real mess of everything.

Especially with her sisters.

Luckily, her eyes were open in time that maybe she could begin repairing her relationships. That was the one real gift her mother had given her, she realized—the dead certainty that she never wanted to feel this much regret again.

One by one, she intended to make things right—with Augusta, Jack, Frank, Savannah—with every life she had the chance to touch.

And with those she couldn't help—like the Karen Huttos of the world—she would have to find a way to be okay with it. Or she would go crazy. No one could carry such a burden and not lose something of herself. In retrospect, it was easy to see why her mother had withdrawn to deal with her losses.

What would Caroline lose?

"What the hell are you doing out here?"

Caroline started at the unexpected interruption, but recognizing the voice as Jack's, she didn't bother getting up. She peered back to find him walking purposefully down the dock toward her, as handsome as ever, even when he was unkempt. The man really needed a woman's touch so he didn't look like he'd crawled out of a laundry basket.

"Trying to keep up with the Joneses?"

Caroline caught his reference, and shivered, despite the heat. "Where'd you pick up that morbid sense of humor, Mr. Shaw?"

He winked at her, but didn't answer.

Apparently, that was Jack's price to pay—the loss of his innocence—what little he'd held on to after his mother's death. "The real question is . . . what are you doing here?"

"Apparently, I couldn't wait around like a good

little boy for you to call me." He bent behind her, nipping her playfully on the shoulder.

Caroline shivered again, drawing her knees up, hugging them defensively—a last bulwark against the ambush he waged on her body and heart.

He sat down beside her. "Seriously, this is not the place for a beautiful woman to be alone."

Caroline laughed. "Beautiful?"

"Quite!"

Even through his joking, she picked up the note of concern in his tone. "I'm within plain sight of the house," she reasoned.

"So was the late Ms. Jones."

Except *that* house was empty, with no guardian eyes peering out from inside; still, Caroline didn't bother pointing that fact out. She didn't want to talk about Amy Jones right now, and she knew Jack better than to believe he couldn't wait for a phone call from her. He was the most stubborn man she had ever known and he had gone an entire ten years without calling her even once, despite the fact that he claimed to love her. His patience was not always a virtue. But he was genuinely worried, she realized. "It's still light out. I would have gone in," she reassured. "Eventually."

"Eventually could get you killed," he persisted.

"Jack . . . there haven't been any more murders."

He brought up one knee and linked his hands before him, looking down at the dock. "I know."

"Jesus! Don't sound disappointed!"

"It's not that, Caroline. I know what I know. It's not over."

Caroline bit the inside of her lip. "What if you're wrong, Jack?"

He squinted against the setting sun. "I hope I am."

"But you don't believe you are?"

He shook his head.

"I'm just throwing this out there . . . and it's not a personal indictment, because I am just as guilty . . ."

He threw a hand up to stop her. "I know what you're going to say even before you say it."

"Listen, Jack . . . I ran that story because I believed in your intuition, but at some point, we have to concede that maybe Jack Shaw's infallible gut is not really all that infallible."

He remained silent, listening.

"I'm just thinking out loud here, but so far, we have nothing but circumstantial evidence—not one thing. . . ."

He was still listening, so she kept talking.

"You can't even get CPD to publicly acknowledge the possibility of a serial homicide, because no matter how you look at it, there is *still* only one body. And everything both of us have done since the discovery of that body has hinged on one thing: the fact that you believe there's a killer out there."

He tilted her a questioning look. "Look, all I'm saying is that maybe we are wrong, Jack . . . maybe we should start thinking about that."

"I can't," he said darkly.

"Can't or won't?"

He grinned suddenly, unexpectedly. "Can't—because my feeble, male brain has been hijacked." He winked at her when she cast a questioning look his way.

He was staring at her, Caroline realized, specifically her mouth, and the realization that she still had that sort of power over him gave her a heady feeling. Her voice softened and she smiled. "So what are you really doing here?"

He gave her a lopsided grin. "You think I lied about not being able to wait for your phone call? Apparently, I'm about as disciplined as a junkie in a meth lab where you're concerned."

Caroline laughed. "Now you're comparing me to meth?"

He reached out, grasping her chin. "No way . . . you have something *way* more addictive!"

Caroline's grin turned suddenly mischievous. "Yeah, what?"

Her breath caught as he reached over and brushed the vee between her thighs, burrowing softly, teasing her. "This," he whispered.

"Jack," she protested, even as she let him drag her down to the dock and lifted her hips into his hand. "It's still light out."

"Not for long," he whispered.

30

T he rain began Monday afternoon, swept in by bloated, gray clouds that drained the color from the landscape.

In a way, it felt like it was storming indoors, as well. Caroline longed to barricade her office door against the deluge—not the least of which included Augusta's announcement: her sister wanted to offer a reward for information leading to the safe return of Amanda Hutto.

She sat in the facing chair, her chin lifted in challenge.

"That's not a good idea, Augusta!"

Augusta straightened in her chair. "Why not? You think you've got some exclusive right to go after the truth?"

Caroline didn't know what to say.

"Mom may have put you in charge of the *Tribune*," Augusta persisted, "but technically, we all own a share —whatever, if you don't break this story, you'll just have to publish it second-—or third-—or fourthhand! Because, like it or not, I will take it to the *Post* and every news channel in this city!"

Caroline was only beginning to understand that

every decision she made in regard to Amanda's disappearance would have an impact on how the Huttos ultimately dealt with their grief. After so long without a word, maybe it was best that Karen Hutto begin accepting the fact that her daughter might not come home. "You're giving her false hope."

"And that's somehow worse than implying her daughter was strangled and murdered by some ex-priest?"

"We have never published those words!"

"No, but you've suggested it at least a dozen times in a dozen different articles, Caroline. This entire city —including Karen Hutto—believes Patterson is guilty of murdering her child. You're ruining the man's entire life!"

"We're trying to get at the truth!" Caroline argued, throwing Augusta's own words back at her. "We didn't fabricate the charges he has on record."

Augusta glared at her. "Well, I'm doing this whether you like it or not. You are not talking me out of it. I came to you first so you can publish it first. You can either do that, or be the last to report it—it's that simple. In fact," she added, "if you're smart, you'll use it as a public service opportunity and donate money in the name of the paper. At least then, it shows you're trying to be objective and that you haven't already decided Amanda's fate and Patterson's guilt."

Whatever she was going to say to counter Augusta's declaration, that simple truth stopped her. Caroline had to admit that Augusta had a point. She had, in fact, started out with an agenda, and offering the reward would at least interject some measure of objectivity and do some damage control.

Augusta sensed she was caving, because she

quickly added, "Never mind the money—I'm offering the reward—I don't need any credit."

She had that determined look in her eyes Caroline knew only too well. "Will you at least hold off long enough to let me check in with Daniel to make sure there aren't legal implications?"

Augusta sat back, considering it a moment before nodding. "Fair enough."

Feeling a little as though she'd negotiated a cease-fire with an unfriendly nation, Caroline said, "Jesus, Augie! When did we end up on opposite sides?"

Augusta stood, her eyes glittering fiercely. "Clearly, you don't know me very well, sister dear, because I've only ever been on one side," she said. "The right side!" And with that, she made her exit.

Caroline watched her go, thinking the line between right and wrong had never seemed so thin.

———

THE ELABORATE FOURTH of July celebration planned for Brittlebank Park was canceled. Provided they could find high enough ground to set up a fireworks stage, a small-scale fireworks exhibit was still in the works so people could celebrate from the safety of their homes. But the city was inundated. Flood-producing tides had been predicted, but two days of summer storms put half the downtown streets under water.

By Tuesday morning, the City Market area was deluged, along with Calhoun Street, Ashley and Lock-wood Avenues. The headlines shifted to topics of a more aqueous nature. The morning edition of the *Tribune* read: RAIN, TIDE FLOOD CITY accompanied by a shot of resourceful citizens navigating floodwaters in their kayaks. One woman was spotted out searching for her dog, who'd lost his way home but took refuge on one of the historic porches, under a joggling board. She was pictured holding the little schnauzer to her bosom. Yet another article showed people in their waders—one holding up a copy of the *Tribune*—not that anyone was actually going out for newspapers. However, not even Mother Nature could stop the presses.

A skeleton crew manned the *Tribune* office, while most of the reporters worked from home. Caroline hijacked her mother's home office, but neither Savannah nor Augusta complained. Savannah, who still could do little more than peck with her right hand, embraced any excuse not to work, even with the antique typewriter. Augusta took her laptop into the kitchen where she could easily persuade Sadie to give her a taste of the goodies she was busy baking.

During their childhood, rainy days in the Aldridge house were typically filled with incredible scents—everything from cobbler to brownies and pineapple upside down cake. The great thing about Sadie was that she had a philosophy that too much was never enough and Caroline noticed no one was all that focused on her weight any longer.

She and Augusta forged a temporary truce—wholly necessary when three grown women were stuck for any length of time under the same roof. For the most part, they kept out of each other's way, but Augusta poked her head into the office late in the afternoon. "How's it going?"

Caroline peered up from her laptop. "Okay . . . but this is the sort of day I wish we had a better Web presence. It would be great to be able to give people better updates—street openings, closings—that sort of thing.

Plus I'm sure they are cancelling fireworks shows all over town."

"In due time," Augusta said, venturing into the office. "I have no doubt you'll manage everything phenomenally—that's why Mom put you in charge, you know."

Caroline blinked at the unexpected compliment.

"Sorry about everything," Augusta said. "I guess I'm just a little unnerved about being here, and I probably took some of my frustration out on you."

Caroline shrugged. "Actually, you made me think a lot about the things you said. You were right."

Augusta came in and sat down in one of the two brown paisley-upholstered armchairs facing Caroline's desk. Leaning across the polished mahogany wood, she tested the surface for dust. There was none. For a moment, they were both silent.

Outside, the rain continued to pelt the leaded glass windows. More than nine inches had fallen during the last twenty hours, and they were nearing the all-time record high since 1988.

"What if I fail at my task, Caroline . . . what if I can't fix this house . . . or even stay under this roof? On days like this, I feel like I'm going clean out of my skull!" Augusta confessed.

Caroline pushed her laptop away and looked soberly at her sister. "There's a lot at stake here, Augusta. But you can only do what you can do. If you can't stay . . . no one is going to make you. We're not going to starve and we're not going to hate you. Some charity will just get an awful lot of money."

In that moment, Augusta's face lost all of its hard lines, softening to that gentle, compassionate gaze she'd had as a child—the little girl who had started a cricket hospital to save all the "one-legged" insects.

The one who was heartbroken when Josh took them out to use as fishing bait. She didn't forgive him for weeks.

"Mom isn't around to make you do anything, Augie. Whatever you decide to do, you do of your own accord."

She blinked and Caroline spied the telltale gleam of unshed tears. "But I don't even know where or how to start!"

Caroline shook her head. "Of course you do! You already have. That auction is the first step, Augie. You're doing a great thing there. You're uncluttering this house before diving into the real work and you're getting rid of stuff none of us will ever put on our mantles. Mom's gone, and none of us are all that attached to anything in this house."

Augusta laid her head back down. "Some of us would like to see it all burn," she said without any real passion.

Caroline couldn't help but laugh, despite the low-grade threat. She knew Augusta wasn't serious. "They already did that once, right? Didn't work. They rebuilt the house and bought more shit. Besides, while this crap would make an awesome bonfire, it's too damned hot out there to burn anything —and ashes won't put food in a homeless child's belly."

They sat there looking at each other, and Caroline felt compelled suddenly to bring up the topic of Ian Patterson. Something about Augie's defense of him gave her an odd feeling . . . like maybe her interest was hovering on advocacy. The last thing Augusta needed to do was get involved with a suspect. Maybe he wasn't a murderer, but he sure wasn't "safe." But Caroline knew her sister well enough to realize that bringing it up would only push her in the very direction she was afraid she'd go.

"Good point," Augusta said, and got up. "Thanks for talking me off the ledge . . . for now." She started to walk away. "More to the point, thanks for not pushing me off."

Caroline's lips curved into a half smile. "Thanks for not tempting me," she countered. Augie laughed and walked out, leaving Caroline to gnash her teeth over murderous financials. These were not fun, and she hadn't realized just how much they were integral to her job. She was not a journalist any longer, she was a damned strategist.

31

The girl wasn't his type.

Lucky for her, she had been in the right place at the right time to help him prove a point. That's what he had to remind himself, because with the impending celebration, it felt more like he was accompanying the wrong date to the prom.

The only satisfaction he would glean from this one was the simple joy of watching them scramble to find clues, watching them beat their little heads against the walls while they tried to figure out how something like this could happen right under their noses. But that was a hollow triumph.

This game was not fulfilling.

Nothing about the girl excited him.

He positioned her with as much love as could be mustered for the wrong prom date, making sure she was ready to flash her tits for the world.

He started to leave, but something beckoned him back . . . that prickling sense of intuition that always seemed to lead him to the special ones.

Right there, when he least expected it, he felt the stirrings . . . that hot pulse through his veins and the quickening beat of his heart.

The boy was perfect.

From the water, he watched the man onstage continue to work on his fireworks display, oblivious to the world outside the periphery of his spotlights. His four- or five-year-old son sat a short distance away, looking longingly over his shoulder at the father, who, during the short time he was watching, had already yelled at his kid twice to stay put.

Sitting beyond the radiance of the spotlight in the shadows of the night, the boy was scared. You could read it clearly on his face. He watched the kid, desire spreading through his groin.

Or maybe it was just piss in his wetsuit.

The kid turned, and his heart somersaulted. The boy's eyes slanted as he squinted, peering into the night, placing a little hand to his forehead to shield his face from the manufactured lights.

Brave boy.

Facing his demons.

There was innocence left in that face, but the resentment was growing like a cancer, bubbling up from the depths of his soul like a cauldron of putrid blackness. There was nothing so potentially dangerous as an unloved child.

The boy was seated on a bench facing the water, his lips contorted into an ambivalent twist. Despite the warm night, he crossed his little arms over his chest, an attempt to bolster himself.

His father remained committed to his work, never once looking back.

He was within reach. Like a gator with its prey, he could snatch the kid before the father realized there was danger. . . .

Gently, silently, he treaded water, feeling powerful, primitive, invulnerable, eternal.

He recognized the instant the boy's eyes focused on the spot in the water where he quietly waited. His little brows collided, though it took him another moment to feel the threat from the darkness. Once he did, he leapt up from the bench and ran screaming to his father, who was stubbornly committed to his fireworks stage.

"Daddy!" the child shrieked. "I see a frogman!"

"Tommy! Sit down, godammnit! You're going to get us both electrocuted!" He picked the kid up, hauling him unceremoniously back to the bench and sat him down so hard the wooden slats reverberated in their steel frame.

The dad walked away, and the kid jumped up to follow. "No, Daddy! I see a frogman with giant yellow eyes!"

The dad spun about, grabbing the kid and backhanding him across his bare thigh, not once, but three times, the crack of his hand sounding a little like tiny firecrackers as his fingers impacted against skin.

"Daddy!" the boy squealed. "Please Daddy! Please, no!"

Only after he spanked the kid a third time did he finally turn to look out into the black river, squinting hard to see what had spooked his child.

He stilled, except for the tick at his temple he couldn't quite control.

The dad's sight was compromised, having stared too long into the bright work lights. Satisfied that he was in the right, and his son was in the wrong, he turned and shook a finger at his frightened boy. "Stay right here! Don't make me tell you again! You're going to get us both killed!"

No, just one of them.

He wanted the boy.

Desperately.

He could almost taste his purity.

He waded closer as the father sauntered back to his stage without looking back. The little boy peered out into the river, his face frozen in a cry that wanted desperately to escape.

"Daddy," he whined.

"No, Tommy!" the dad said firmly without looking back. And then, feeling guilty maybe, added, "I just have to get this done, then I'll take you to get an ice cream, okay?"

The child was frozen, those big round eyes staring directly into his . . . the little chest hiccupping with emotion, and in that moment, he sensed a kindred spirit.

They were the same.

That's where he had begun . . . staring straight into the eyes of the beast.

"Da-d-dy," the boy whimpered—too softly to be heard, but the dad peered up just as the first of his rockets exploded into the damp night sky.

The sound of the rocket's ascent stopped him cold in the water and he paddled backward, further back to watch from a safe distance as the rocket burst into a thousand bright pinpoints of light, illuminating a park that was half submerged.

He retreated far enough back that you could no longer hear the child's sniffles, and he watched the scene unfold under a brilliant explosion of color. One by one the rockets launched after the first one, and the sky flashed from light to dark and back again.

On the stage, the father turned and froze at a glimpse of the night's handiwork. He slowly turned his spotlight.

The girl's body lay not twenty feet from the stage, on a slip of higher ground where the water had begun to recede. She lay with her hands bound together prayerfully . . . much the way she had died . . . begging for her life through bulging, terror-filled eyes because her mouth could no longer plead.

Beyond the stage, beyond the park, the police station glowed across the street.

The frogman smiled, inhaled a breath of watery air and dove soundlessly down into the black water.

CAROLINE PEERED out of her bedroom window, watching the raindrops slide down the outside windowpane. The property was puddled, otherwise undamaged, and she wondered how Sadie's house had fared with water up to nine feet higher than flood level.

Finally, the rain was subsiding and she was glad, because Augusta—stubborn hellion that she was— was out there in it . . . somewhere.

Tango watched as she moved away from the window, his tail wagging halfheartedly when she made eye contact with him. Caroline grabbed her cell phone from the dresser and dialed Frank's number, hoping to get some information before Augusta returned home. She had already tried calling Pam to no avail.

Knowing her sister, she would hold off just so long before impatience set her on a forward trajectory, and then she would become an irresistible force. It was in everyone's best interest not to wait it out, hoping she'd just go away. That wouldn't happen.

Caroline and Bonneau had already agreed that if

Daniel gave them the go-ahead, Pam should write up the reward story. Because she'd written the majority of the articles about Patterson, Frank thought her reporting could use a little more balance.

Despite the flooded streets, Frank was still at the office and Caroline was beginning to wonder if the man had any life at all outside of the *Tribune*. "Any word?"

"No," he said. "Daniel doesn't seem to be returning phone calls. For that matter, neither is Pam."

"I was hoping to be able to give Augusta a thumbs-up today."

"I haven't heard from Pam at all—neither yesterday nor today. In all the confusion, I assumed you told her not to come in. She hasn't checked in with me."

"No. I didn't," Caroline assured him. "When was the last you talked to her?"

"Friday."

"Damn," Caroline said, and she had a sudden, icy feeling in the pit of her stomach. "Do you have her number on you?"

"In my office, but if you hang on, I'll grab it for you."

"Thank you, Frank. I'll talk to her first thing tomorrow morning—everyone in fact. I'll make it clear that if they aren't coming in for whatever reason, they are to discuss it with you. You're their boss."

There was silence on the other end of the phone, and then he said, "I appreciate that."

But Caroline thought she sensed a smile.

"No problem.

"Okay, ready?"

"Shoot . . ."

Caroline snagged a pen from inside the drawer of

her mother's nightstand and he rattled off Pam's number. "Thank you, Frank," she said, and hung up, realizing only as she dialed the number and it began to ring that she already had Pam's number in her contacts.

The call went straight to voice mail.

32

J ack waited to leave the station, just in case there were folks willing to brave the receding floodwaters to come see fireworks. Thankfully, people used their brains and stayed home.

For the first time in a long time, he was feeling frisky.

Maybe it was because of the slightly cooler air, or maybe it was the fact that, after all this time, the crushing sense of dread he'd been feeling was beginning to lighten up.

Or maybe it was the simple fact that he'd enjoyed at least a dozen hard-ons during the day, just thinking about Caroline's ass in his hands.

Whatever it was that was responsible for his mood, he didn't fight it.

When his phone rang, he hoped it would be Caroline, so he could play hard to get for all of two full seconds before veering his car in the direction of the Aldridge estate. If nothing else, he could talk her into making out on their porch like they had when they were teenagers. His partner's voice on the other end of the line had the effect of a finger-thump to his dick. "Hey, Jack."

"What's up, Don?"

Garrison seemed to trip over his words, uncertain how to say whatever it was he was trying to spit out of his mouth. Finally, he said, "Jack, listen . . . I know you just left, man . . . but you've gotta come back . . . now."

A bad feeling settled in Jack's gut at the bleak sound of his voice. "What is it, Don?"

"There's . . . another body," he said, but there was something about the way he partitioned the words that made Jack's stomach wrench a little tighter.

He turned the car around immediately.

SHE FELT LIKE A CRIMINAL, hiding and checking over her shoulder repeatedly to see if anyone was following her. That annoyed Augusta, because she didn't feel as though she was doing anything wrong.

She just had this feeling about Patterson.

However, she wasn't stupid enough to meet him at his house. She chose a public place, the only place she really felt at home here—the Windjammer on the Isle of Palms. Although the new construction was nothing like the one-story building that had been there originally, with the volleyball nets tangled out back, it was still the one place she knew where she could escape the scent of mothball-permeated Confederate uniforms and the sweating crush of tourists, even if the one thing the 'Jammer saw in plenty during the summer was people.

Parking was ridiculous, especially in her mother's boat of a car, but once she made it inside, she went straight for the bar, grabbed herself a beer, and walked outside to watch the volleyballers and wait.

ONCE BACK AT THE STATION, nobody seemed inclined to tell him anything.

Apparently, they had already called in SLED—the South Carolina Law Enforcement Division—along with the sheriff's office, and now they were waiting for the chief to return from across the street, where it seemed he was hijacking Jack's investigation. At this point, all Jack knew was that it was a woman they'd discovered and he knew the M.O. was similar to the Jones case, but that's all they seemed inclined to reveal.

Finally, tired of the hemming and hawing, he grabbed Garrison and pulled him out the door, urging him toward the street, toward the park. "Who found her?" Jack demanded.

Garrison wouldn't look at him. "Some kid and his dad."

"Where are they now?"

"Inside. Waiting for an interview." And then he added, "I'm real sorry, Jack."

The knot in Jack's stomach grew.

Caroline was the first person who popped into his mind. He hadn't talked to her at all today and his stomach threatened to empty its contents right there in the street. They crossed into the park, where uniforms were already scouring the perimeter.

The fireworks stage sat on higher ground and the spotlights were still on, but no longer aimed at the equipment itself. Harsh light spilled across the half-submerged park, toward a twisted form by the water's edge.

As Jack neared, he could begin to make her out, and the pit of his stomach turned violently.

The girl's long wet blond locks pooled onto the ground around her face. Her body was completely bare, her naked breasts pointed skyward, feet and hands bound. Her body was draped, like a sacrifice over a boulder. He recognized the bags on her water-logged hands as their own. They lay positioned on her chest in prayerful repose . . . like Amy Jones.

It wasn't Caroline.

He felt vomit rise up into his throat.

He forced himself not to look away, to go straight to the body and look down on that face he had looked at a hundred times before. Only now her skin would be cold to the touch. She was pale and waterlogged and if he turned her over, postmortem lividity would have begun to stain her perfect white skin. Her mouth was covered with tape, but it was, beyond a shadow of doubt, Kelly Banks.

Her blue eyes stared up at him, unseeing. The whites of her eyes stained with broken vessels spinning veiny webs into her sockets.

He stared down at her a long moment and then walked away and did something he hadn't done since the early days of his career. He puked in the bushes.

33

Knowing Gormley Sr. was waiting in the interview room with his son, Jack returned to the station and took a moment to get his head straight.

He'd seen a lot of dead bodies during his years as a cop—though some of them might not even qualify for the term because they were in such a state—but this was the first time since his mother's death that he had looked into a face he'd wanted desperately to love and found nothing but vacant space staring back.

How the hell did one interview a four-year-old who might possibly be the sole witness in the entire case?

He thought about Kelly's mother and groaned, burying his face in his hands. Out of everyone he knew, Kelly had had the most loving, healthy relationship with her parents. Jack would have to be the one to tell them, but what would he say? How did you tell a mother who still brought her daughter bagged lunches to work that her baby girl was dead?

Murdered.

Tortured.

The last time he'd talked to her, he had been cold and distant. He was trying to be kind by yanking off the Band-Aid, but now that dejected look in her eyes would haunt him forever.

Josh had said she was working on something for him. Was she dead because of that? Or was she just unlucky enough to be in the wrong place at the wrong time? Could this be aimed at Jack . . . as the investigator in charge? The police in general? Or was Jack just the lucky dude picked to play the game?

Now Kelly was dead.

Was it a coincidence she was connected to Jack? A warning? A challenge? How many more innocent women would die? How many missing persons were already notches on this killer's belt? Had Kelly figured that out?

Chief Condon came in while Jack was mentally preparing himself for the interview. Leaving the crime unit to finish up the scene investigation and wait for SLED, he sat down in the seat facing Jack, his expression sober. "Jack," he began.

Jack knew where he was going before he said another word.

"I can't let you keep the case," he said.

"I can handle it!"

Condon shook his head. "I looked the other way with the whole media leak bullshit, because I trust you to do what it takes to get the job done, but this is different. I can't let you work this case now that Kelly is involved. We can't risk it, Jack. "

Jack's jaw worked. He stared down at the floor, his eyes burning.

"As it is, I heard from the DA's office that you may have compromised evidence—"

Jack's gaze shot up, fury surging through his veins. "Childres told you that?"

Condon shook his head. "It doesn't matter who

told me what. I defended your actions and reminded them as long as you had that piece of evidence in your sight at all times before checking it in, it's all good. You're a good enough cop to know when not to break the rules."

"But?"

"This is Kelly, man."

"I know who the hell is out there!" Jack assured him. "Please, Bill, at least let me do the interview with the kid."

Condon shook his head, his mind made up.

"But he's our *only* witness!"

"Listen to me, Jack. Anything you do on this case at this point could damage the county solicitor's case. I can't risk it."

Jack wanted a cigarette. He wanted to get up and grab his chair and smash the entire room to shreds. He wanted to catch the son of a bitch and strangle him with his bare hands. That would be justice, right?

"You can watch," Condon conceded.

Somewhere in the rational part of Jack's brain, he understood that Condon was doing the only thing he could do, but the idea of losing control of this case made him potentially violent.

On top of that, now that he was taking Jack off the case, he was giving the go-ahead to pursue it as a serial homicide. With two bodies that might or might not be connected, they still couldn't technically classify it as a serial killing, but Condon was willing to trust Jack's intuition, if not his police work—even if it meant taking a stand publicly. Kelly was one of their own and her murder was clearly a gauntlet tossed down.

"I'm just supposed to stand by and just let someone else work this?"

"I'll leave Garrison on it."

"He doesn't have the experience!"

"Listen to me, Jack. It doesn't matter. I can't leave you on this case. They'll say I did it out of friendship and neither of us can afford that. You can consult so long as you stay out of sight."

Jack shook his head, unwilling to accept that he was expected to walk away now—especially with so much of his life at stake. He had the awful feeling that they had a narrow window to nab the guy.

Jack was the best DT on the force—no hubris there—his record spoke for itself—especially since his arrests never ended up going free on a mere technicality. That's what galled him most about Childres's accusation.

He knew it was Childres who'd blabbed. Who wouldn't that asshole throw under the bus for political gain?

He tried to see it from Childres's perspective—knew the guy wanted to land the mayor's desk, and Jack understood that anything that threatened his reputation or any case he was working on undermined his political ambitions. He understood all that, but it angered him that Josh would take unfounded complaints to Condon.

He felt as tightly wound as a Swiss watch. What if they missed something?

Condon sensed his thoughts. "Our crime scene unit is as good as it gets, Jack. They'll look at every inch of that park under a magnifying glass and every wrinkle on Kelly's body. If there's a pube on her that isn't hers, we'll know about it."

Jack was forced to concede.

After Condon left, he purposely didn't call Caroline, uncertain how to tell her the news and dreading the wedge it was bound to put between them.

At all costs, they had to find this guy—as much for Caroline's sake as anyone else's—but she wasn't going to deal well with the fact that he would rather have his nuts placed in a crab cracker than compromise the investigation further. Trusting her had probably cost him the case. From now on, he couldn't treat her any differently than he would treat someone from the *Post*. She would find out soon enough.

THIRTY MINUTES into the interview the Gormley kid hit the wall. He was tired and wanted to go home and answered every question posed with a firm shake of his head.

The father grew agitated. "I gave a statement earlier. Can we please come back tomorrow?"

Jack held his breath.

Garrison acknowledged the request, but didn't give him a verbal answer. He asked the kid yet another question that the boy stonewalled.

The father was about two minutes away from taking his kid home and refusing further cooperation, but if he went home now, a night of bad dreams could wipe away any and all important details from his memory.

Jack paced the observation room, watching Garrison lose his only witness until he tried a different tack. "Dude . . . I heard you saw a frogman tonight?"

Watching through the glass, Jack held his breath while the kid thought about it. He didn't deny it, but he didn't respond either, except to kick angrily at the air beneath the table.

Progress . . . maybe.

"I saw Spiderman once, but no one believed me."

Tommy glanced up at Garrison, probably wondering if he was telling the truth.

"Was your frogman dressed in a superhero costume, Tommy?"

Tommy gave him a narrow-eyed scowl but shook his head slowly.

"Was he wearing a mask?"

The kid looked down at his lap, picking at his pant leg, and shrugged.

"Do you know what kind of mask I'm talking about?" Garrison persisted.

Tommy didn't look up, but he shook his head.

"I'm talkin' 'bout the sort people use when they go swimming. Do you ever go swimming, Tommy?"

The boy looked up, shaking his head again in an exaggerated slow motion.

"Why not?"

He gave his dad a beleaguered glance, rolling his eyes and said plaintively, "On 'count . . . I'm not 'lowed in G-ma's pool, 'cause she prolly pees in it."

Any other day, Jack might have been amused.

Not today.

"That so?"

The little boy nodded soberly and his father turned red. "The ex's mom . . . and me," he said by way of explanation, "we don't get along."

Garrison turned back to Tommy. "You're sure it was a frogman, Tommy?"

Tommy nodded a little more enthusiastically.

"Was he green?"

He made a scared face. "No! He was black with yellow eyes!"

Jack wondered if the guy had been wearing a wet suit and mask. It would explain the lack of fibers on the bodies.

"Think you'll have bad dreams tonight?"

Jack had to admit Garrison's patience was far more evident than Jack's at the moment. The boy hesitated, thinking about the question, then replied, "No, 'cause I'm already big."

"How old are you, Tommy?"

He held up three fingers and a crooked thumb and said, "Four." He looked up at his dad, looking for confirmation.

"When will you be five?"

"On my birsday."

Garrison looked at the father.

"September."

"So, Tommy, do you want to play detective tonight . . . tell me what happened?"

"What's a tective?"

"It's where you help catch bad guys and put them away so they can't hurt anyone."

Tommy nodded, even gave a hint of a smile before going through as detailed an account as a tired four-year-old could muster.

"The frogman looked straight at you?"

Tommy rubbed his eyes and nodded again.

"Was he close enough for you to tell his eyes were seeing you back?"

Tommy nodded. "For a long time," he said sullenly. "I was scared."

"But he didn't hurt you and he went away, right?"

He put his hands together and gestured like he was going to dive. "Down and then he swam away!" He kicked his little feet frantically as though he were swimming.

"That's great. Thank you, Tommy. You're good at being a detective," Garrison said. "Next time you see something like that, promise to tell your dad right away?"

Tommy peered up at his father, his little brows colliding fiercely, and that quickly, his temper was back. "I want to go home!" he screamed.

Jack noticed the dad couldn't meet Garrison's gaze afterward, and he hoped the guy realized how close he had come to losing his child tonight.

Jack stared at the exhausted little boy with the green rain jacket and little yellow waders and thought about Amanda Hutto.

The number of the missing and dead were adding up. But not a one of them had anything in common except for the fact that they were female. A six-year-old girl. A seventeen-year-old runaway. A twenty-two-year-old college kid and a thirty-year-old police dispatcher.

The whole thing felt disjointed to Jack somehow.

Once the interview was over, he headed back across the street, hoping Garrison's patience extended to coworkers because Jack intended to be certain they missed nothing.

The body was still unmoved while a team of medical examiners finished their initial exam. Jack stared down into Kelly's face, knowing she was the only one who really knew what they were dealing with. The best chance they had to catch this guy was to figure out where he would strike next.

"Who did this to you, Kelly?"

Her mouth remained still behind the sheets of tape. They had yet to remove it and wouldn't until they got her into the lab.

Her mouth and hands had been left just like Amy Jones's, but something felt different, and he couldn't get past the idea that this one seemed personal.

His phone rang, and he walked away from the scene, reaching into his pocket and fishing his cell out without looking at the caller ID.

Caroline's voice had that razor-sharp edge that used to make him dive for cover. "Did you ever plan to tell me?"

From where he stood, Kelly's face momentarily morphed into Caroline's, and he couldn't find his voice to speak. His answer came out sounding more like an unintelligible grunt.

Whatever anger Caroline might have felt seemed to soften when she sensed his distress. "I heard there was another body."

He swallowed. "Yeah."

"They haven't revealed who yet. Can you say?"

He considered his next words carefully. "Are you asking because you give a shit about who we've got lying cold on a stone . . . or are you asking as Florence Aldridge's daughter?"

Dead silence was the answer he got, and Jack remained silent, waiting.

"I can't believe you would ask me that," she said finally, sounding defeated, and maybe a little defensive and hurt.

The image of Kelly's mother flashed across Jack's brain.

Despite the circus of newspeople already gathering outside the station, no one had disclosed the name of the deceased—and they wouldn't—not before they were able to notify her next of kin. He took a deep breath and gave her the standard line, "The identity of the victim isn't being released at this time pending notification of next of kin."

"Okay," she said. "I'll let you get back to work."

"Bye, Caroline," he said, and ended the call.

34

Caroline paced the den, waiting with her sisters to watch the breaking news. The TV was on channel eleven, and both Augusta and Savannah were hugging their knees on the couch.

Savannah's eyes were glued to the screen. "I wonder who it was."

So did Caroline. But she was thankful both her sisters were present and accounted for. She hugged herself, the knots in her stomach tightening with every second that passed.

She wondered who Frank had sent to cover the press conference, but trusting others to do the job came with the territory, she was learning. Frank had been handling this sort of situation as long as she had been on Earth. Right now, she belonged with her sisters.

Augusta craned her neck back, peering at Caroline. "I can't believe Jack wouldn't tell you."

Caroline frowned. She didn't want to talk about Jack. As a matter of fact, she didn't even want to think about him!

After multiple teases by the anchor team, they were waiting for Chief Condon to appear in front of the Lockwood building. The anchorwoman cut to reporter Sandra Rivers on location outside the station. The reporter's bright red suit and lipstick were probably a bad choice under the circumstances, but at least she looked appropriately sober. Finally, Billy Condon, a burly man in his early fifties with a shaved head and mole above his left eye, emerged from the building and an entire mob of reporters accosted him at once. Caroline spotted Brad on the sidelines, ready and eager to scribble down anything that came out of the chief's mouth. Pam was conspicuously absent from the crowd.

The look in Condon's eyes was clearly emotional. "Earlier this evening," he began, "at approximately ten thirty P.M. . . . the body of Officer Kelly Banks was discovered in Brittlebank Park."

Caroline felt as though a bowling ball dropped inside her belly. The breath left her all at once.

Savannah gasped aloud. "Jesus!"

"Isn't she—" Whatever Augusta was going to ask froze on her lips when she turned and saw Caroline's ashen face.

On the screen, camera flashes set off a miniature light show.

Looking sober behind the microphone, Condon continued. "Officer Banks was a valuable asset to our force . . . we offer our deepest sympathies to her family and we honor her service to the City of Charleston. I'm sorry, that's it. We're all a little shocked, but we would like to answer your questions if possible."

"Chief Condon," someone shouted. "Is it official? Do we have a serial killer?"

Condon's jaw worked. "We are not currently using that term in connection with the deaths of Ms. Banks and Ms. Jones."

"Currently?" Sandra Rivers asked, catching the distinction immediately and going after it with all the finesse of a cougar. "Does that mean you believe the status will change?"

Condon avoided the camera directly. "At this point, there have been two similar homicides, which suggests only that everyone should take certain precautions in their everyday lives, but as yet, it has not been established that both were committed by the same person."

"Will you call in the FBI?" Brad shouted across the crowd.

Caroline chewed her cuticle.

"No," Condon said without hesitation. "We have every faith in our local forces to solve these murders. However, we have formed a task force and will now work together with SLED and the sheriff's office."

"Was Officer Banks strangled too?"

"Asphyxiated," he corrected.

"Chief Condon! We heard there was a witness tonight! Can you elaborate?"

"I'm sorry, that is all we have at the moment. As more news becomes available, the Public Information Officer will keep you informed. Thank you!" He started to walk away.

"Chief Condon—wait! Is it known whether the killer is targeting victims or do you believe the women were chosen at random?"

Condon stopped and turned to answer the question. "All we know conclusively is that the victims were both outside alone at night. Again, please take necessary precautions."

Brad edged his way in. "Chief Condon," he shouted. "Doesn't strangulation suggest this is a personal crime? Wouldn't that indicate the victims knew their attacker?"

"Officer Banks died of asphyxia associated with drowning," Condon clarified again. "We believe it would be a mistake to assume the victims were acquainted with the murderer."

Brad followed his question with another. "Was there a struggle? Can you clarify, please?"

Condon held up a hand. "I'm sorry. That's all—I am not at liberty to discuss the details of the case. The ongoing investigation will now be led by Detective Donald Garrison."

"Will Detective Garrison be available for comment?"

"Negative."

"What about Detective Shaw?"

He shook his head. "Detective Shaw is at this moment with the Banks family."

Sandra Rivers edged her way in, holding out her microphone, and said in a practiced old Charleston accent, "Chief Condon, can you tell us if Detective Shaw was removed from the case because of his—"

Condon cut her off. "Shaw is a dedicated professional. His personal life is not at issue here. This press conference is over, Ms. Rivers," he said and started toward the building.

The mob followed. "Chief Condon! Chief Condon! Chief Condon! Do you believe we'll have a third murder?"

"Let's hope not," he replied without turning, and with those final words, he dove into the safety of the building, barricaded by his men.

Augusta muted the sound of the television, and you could have sliced the silence in the room with a knife. "Holy shit," she exclaimed.

CAROLINE WOKE AROUND THREE-FIFTEEN, the numerals on her mother's clock glowing red, staining the room with the color of blood. She tossed and turned the rest of the night. About six, she gave up trying to sleep and got up and went straight down to the kitchen, hoping to find Sadie. She wanted to gather everyone together under one roof, lock the doors and let no one ever leave again—which was entirely ridiculous, she realized. Still, she would feel better if they were all together. Savannah she trusted to do the right thing, and she intended to take every precaution herself, but she wasn't so sure about Sadie or Augusta. Augusta was entirely too reckless and Sadie was too accustomed to being alone. She thought maybe she could talk Sadie into staying with them for a little while, but the vehemence with which the housekeeper responded completely took her by surprise.

"No! I'm not gonna pack my bags and move into this damned house, eah me—not even temporarily!"

Caroline would probably feel the same about abandoning her privacy, but it seemed to her that it was a small price to pay to ensure that everyone was safe. "You barely leave the kitchen anyway, Sadie! You might as well drag in a cot and sleep here, for God's sake. Come on! I bet Josh would support this. There's more than enough room!"

Sadie gave her a quelling glance, as only Sadie could, and warned, "Don't you dare talk to my son about any of this, eah! I am not going to do it and that's all there is to it! I've been living in that house my entire life and I ain't gonna leave it now!"

"Jesus Christ!" Caroline said. "You're like those

stubborn folks who drown in their homes during hurricanes because they refuse to evacuate!"

Clearly upset now, in a way Caroline had never witnessed, Sadie began tossing pans into the sink. "Now you listen to me good, young lady! Josh bought me a new alarm system last year. I'll be fine in my own house! You three are way more apt to burn yourselves up alive in this museum than I am to end up some pervert white man's sexual deviance!"

"These things are not always about sex," Caroline pointed out. "I had no idea this house offended you so much."

Sadie tossed more pans into the sink, making an ungodly racket. Caroline wondered if it were for effect. "This house does not offend me! I have managed it longer than any of y'all have been alive, but this is not my house! And I'm not staying in it no matter what you say! You worry about your own self!" she said, and walked out of the kitchen, conversation over.

Savannah appeared in the kitchen doorway, looking completely bewildered. "How in the hell did you manage to piss her off?"

"Seems lately I could start an argument in an empty house."

Her youngest sister came in the kitchen and stood on the other side of the island where Caroline had taken refuge. "This hasn't been easy for any of us," she said. "I can't pretend to know how it feels to have a mother's responsibility for three grown women who aren't your flesh and blood, but I imagine Sadie feels guilty enough over the resentment she must feel at being left with such a huge burden without adding a sense of forced gratitude as well."

Caroline screwed her face. "Good Lord! She's our

family! Why in God's name would she feel any of that?"

"She is, but think about it for a minute. No matter how we may feel about her, Sadie earned her living taking care of us. Mom *paid* her to do the things she couldn't—or wouldn't—do."

"Not any longer! And I actually seem to recall telling her not to! She's not being paid to take care of us! She's doing what she's doing because she chooses to!"

"Is she?"

"Yes! She never has to work another day in her life if she doesn't want to."

Savannah raised her brows contentiously. "Think about it from Sadie's perspective. Mom didn't give her a lump sum so she could retire on some tropical island and sip Mai Tais the rest of her life. She's still earning probably exactly what she was earning before Mom died . . . except that now she owns her house outright and doesn't have to put in notice for days off."

Caroline thought about it.

Savannah continued. "I have no doubt that Sadie loves us and that she wants to help, but there's still a fine line that must be painfully visible from her perspective. Essentially, she's still getting paid to take care of us—business as usual. She doesn't know how to deal with you changing the rules at this stage in the game."

Augusta had said something similar and the bit of wisdom struck a chord. "But she and Mom must have been friends."

Savannah shrugged. "I think they were. But what does that have to do with this?"

"Do you think Josh feels the same way?"

Savannah shook her head, then followed it with a

shrug. "Different generations. It probably wasn't the same for them as it is for us and Josh."

Caroline considered her younger sister and the wisdom that seemed to come out of her mouth as easily as turning on a tap. Even hers and Augusta's leg up in years didn't seem to make up for Savannah's innate sense of intuition. "Why does it feel you sometimes know everything and that you're just patiently waiting for everyone else to figure it all out?"

Savannah laughed. "That's so not true!" Then she sobered suddenly and pointed out, "If I knew everything I'd be able to lead you straight to the monster who's killing these poor girls."

"Yeah about that . . . somehow I feel I made everything worse."

Savannah narrowed her eyes, giving her that look that always made Caroline feel a little spooky, and said, "Every action has a consequence, Caroline . . . all you can do is start out with the best intentions . . . then come what may."

Caroline was still mulling over that bit of advice when Savannah interjected, "You'll figure it out." And she left Caroline alone in the kitchen, wondering what she could do to help Sadie feel more a part of their family.

She appreciated Sadie's help, but she truly loved her—in some ways more than she loved her own mother. No matter how much regret she might feel over her dysfunctional relationship with Flo, it didn't change the truth. She stared at the pile of pots and pans in the sink and tried to remember the last time any of them had picked up a sponge while living under this roof.

The answer was never.

Walking over to the sink, Caroline peered at the

mess inside and turned on the tap, grabbing a sponge. The office could wait ten minutes longer. Nothing was going to fall apart before she got there—nothing that wasn't already unraveling. Frank knew what to do, and she could use a little empty space in her head to consider next steps.

———

WHILE JACK WAITED for information to filter down, he went through Kelly's effects for her parents. He found no documents bearing his name. Nothing. Whatever she had been working on, she had taken it with her, maybe to the grave.

He put her belongings into a box and hauled it back to his office, running into Garrison on his way. Thankfully, they weren't shutting him out cold. Technically, Garrison was still his partner. He could still have the information; he just couldn't handle evidence, ride shotgun on the investigation or talk to anyone connected to the case.

"We got the initial word back from the lab," Garrison said. "Like the first victim, her tongue was missing and her mouth was painted with the same blue dye."

Jack nodded, and couldn't keep himself from wondering whether she had been alive for the dismemberment. "Any word on her car?"

Garrison shook his head. "They're pretty sure he must have dragged her into Brittlebank from the Ashley because she had water in her lungs and stomach consistent with prolonged submersion so the choppers are flying the river line."

Jack held back a floodtide of emotion. "Did we send the crime scene team to her house yet?"

"Done," Garrison said.

He wanted to put someone on Caroline, but knew they would question his motives. Instead, he focused on their one suspect. "Can we put the tail back on Patterson?"

"Already on it," Garrison said, and Jack was relieved that all the bases were being covered, even though it galled him to lose the investigation.

The box in his hand suddenly felt as though it held the weight of the world. "Thanks for letting me know."

Garrison gave him a nod, and his normally competitive nature was absent. He reached out, patting Jack's shoulder. "Don't worry, we'll get this guy, Jack."

Jack nodded, and walked away, taking the box to his office, resigning himself to the fact that at this point, there was really only one thing he could do that wouldn't jeopardize the investigation: he had to find out what Kelly had known.

He logged onto his computer to check the NCIC and NamUs databases, contemplating which database Kelly had used and whether he could hack her sign-on. Maybe she had saved search results he could access? Maybe she'd discovered something that could help them find her murderer? Maybe whatever she had learned had sent her straight to the killer?

One of the dispatchers poked his head in the door before he could begin. "The *Tribune's* on hold for you."

"Tell Ms. Aldridge I'm not available."

"Uh, it's not a she. It's a Frank Bonneau, says you're the only one he'll talk to."

CAROLINE BARELY HELD BACK her hysteria.

The face she gave to others—she hoped—was solemn and composed—her best poker face. Inside, however, she was quivering like a frightened child.

When Pam didn't return to work, didn't call, or answer persistent phone calls, Frank finally sent someone to her apartment to check on her. No one answered her door and the guy came back to work and discovered her car in the garage. That was when they called the police.

Tucked under Pam's windshield wiper was a piece of paper, in exactly the same spot Caroline had found her slip of paper, folded in just the same way. Except this one was pink. Instinctively, she knew there was more to her note than Jack had led her to believe. Obviously, he didn't trust her.

Was there anything salvageable between them?

On the driver's-side window, the number three was written in the same white crayon that drive-through car washes often used to mark windshields for the attendant managing the wash line. In fact, the car was spotless, despite the week of rain they had endured. Pam's oversized purse was still sitting on the passenger's seat on top of the laptop she had checked out from the office, as though she had just stepped out of the car momentarily or simply forgotten it.

No one touched the note on the window, but Caroline already knew what it would say: *Death and life are in the power of the tongue; those who love it will eat its fruit. Proverbs 18:21.* The words were imprinted on her brain.

She heard the sirens wailing down the street and knew Frank had finally reached him. Not only was Jack not answering her phone calls, he obviously hadn't bothered to listen to any of her messages.

Was he blaming her?

She didn't understand anything that was going on.

Right now the only thing that really matters is Pam.

Caroline had gotten her involved in things she oughtn't to have been involved in maybe. And because of her, Pam was possibly—God, she couldn't think about that!

Pam's family lived in Athens, Georgia. Who would make that phone call? The police? Or would Caroline, as her employer, be expected to be the bearer of bad news?

Don't think that way.

They would find her.

Jack would find her.

Like Amanda?

Or the way they'd found Kelly and Amy?

Caroline shuddered.

At least three police vehicles squealed into the garage, one of them a crime scene unit. Another two cars came in silently, both unmarked—one of them Jack's. He gave her a simple nod as he got out of his car but went straight to Frank, talking to him while someone else—another cop—barked orders to the men.

Caroline stood there, hugging herself, watching them work, feeling the ten or so feet between her and Jack acutely. They might as well have been standing in different cities.

The men worked quickly, but not quickly enough. A local news van pulled into the garage, conveniently blocking the exit in a pretense of unloading the vehicle. The rest of the local news teams were sure to descend soon.

Caroline recognized Sandra Rivers, wearing a red suit similar to the one she'd worn last night. Clearly, her radar was on high reception. She spotted Jack and brushed nonexistent wrinkles from her skirt, heading straight toward him, her red high heels clicking loudly in the nearly empty garage. Even as she made her way toward him, two more news channels converged on the scene.

"Detective Shaw!" Rivers called out, hurrying toward him.

Jack threw out a hand to stop her. "This is a crime scene, Ms. Rivers! Back off!"

She looked for a moment like she considered balking, but Jack's words rang like a God voice in the garage. "Everyone out now!" he demanded. "Move the van!"

Frowning prettily, Sandra Rivers waved her camera guys away—not that the gesture was necessary. They had already leapt back five paces merely at the sound of Jack's voice. He might not be leading this investigation, but he commanded enough respect that they didn't question his authority.

Rivers spun around, her radar settling on Caroline, and her expression perked. She made a beeline in Caroline's direction, walking with renewed purpose. "Ms. Aldridge! I understand Ms. Baker has been missing since Monday, possibly longer?"

Caroline's stomach sank. Her mother wouldn't have run from this, she told herself. She blinked at the camera. "No comment, Ms. Rivers. I hope you understand."

Sandra Rivers nodded, surprised maybe. "Of course," she said, with a forced smile, but she persisted with the microphone. "On a related note, can you confirm that the *Tribune* is offering a reward for any information leading to Amanda Hutto's whereabouts?"

"I wouldn't say that is related at all," Caroline

countered. "No one has established any connection between any of these cases, but yes, the *Tribune* is offering a reward."

Rivers smiled thinly, her eyes gleaming. "Your late mother would be so proud, God rest her soul," she said, in her thick Southern drawl. "As for your investigations, are you stepping in now because you've lost faith in our boys in blue? And will you continue the more hardcore stories or do you plan to abandon them now that it seems too risky for your employees?" She pushed the microphone in Caroline's direction.

Caroline blinked again, startled by the mouthful of words Rivers had just attributed to her. Not only was she implying the *Tribune* was generally fluff and couldn't handle mainstream news, but the answer to either of those questions was potentially explosive. She weighed her words carefully. "Do you tweet, Ms. Rivers?"

"Well, yes! Who doesn't?" Rivers replied, but looked suddenly confused. She turned to smile nervously for her camera and then turned back to Caroline.

Caroline smiled benignly. "We don't," she said. "And we will continue to report the news to our community in a manner the City of Charleston has grown to trust. However, we feel it is best, given the nature of what's at stake here, to leave the criminal investigations to the capable hands of the CPD." Caroline forced a gracious smile.

"Well, yes," was all Rivers said. "Thank you, Ms. Aldridge." And she smiled brilliantly, turning to her camera and signing off. Only once the camera was down did her smile vanish. She muttered something low, snapping at her men to get everything back into the van. Fellow media cohorts or not, Caroline was pretty sure she hadn't made a new friend today, and the look Rivers gave her as she walked away only validated her suspicion.

Leaving Jack standing alone, Frank moseyed up beside her, his thick arms crossed. He eyed her with equal measures of pride and censure.

"What?" Caroline asked, staring hard at Jack's back. He hadn't even bothered to turn once to look at her.

Frank scolded her. "What's the matter with you? Don't you know better than to go talkin' to the press?"

Caroline's cheeks heated. "I wasn't going to run away like a scared puppy!" she said defensively.

Frank shook his head, but smiled. "Just like your mama."

"Anyway," Caroline remarked. "Whatever happened to professional courtesy?"

"That only applies if you're not a greedy bitch," Frank stated matter of factly. "Sandra Rivers is a greedy bitch. No matter how you look at it, even without these murders, you're big news right now too. So next time, stick to 'no comment.' It actually works."

Caroline knew he was right, of course, but she wasn't in the mood to be chastised. She stood a moment, watching Jack go after Rivers again, ordering her off the premises. He glanced briefly in her direction. She didn't bother lingering to see if she would be his next target. She left Frank to deal with questions and went back to the office.

35

"Can't wait to see the farmer's tan you're gonna get!" Augusta said, as she made her way down the long dock.

Savannah stopped in the middle of trying to push one of the smaller boats back into the boathouse. Wearing a white wife-beater to match her cast, she was already getting sunburned in areas not covered by material. She was sweaty, sticky and her arm itched.

"What are you doing out here?"

"Going through the boathouse."

"Obviously." Augusta pointed at the boat. "If you keep at it, you're going to end up with a cast on your other arm. Why didn't you ask for help?"

Savannah shoved at the boat one more time, then tugged to no avail. It was good and stuck. "Because I obviously overestimated my coordination and strength." She grinned.

The smallest of their boats, the dory, sat wedged in the door, caught on something just inside the boathouse. Savannah couldn't drop it, because it wouldn't quite rest on the dock. She didn't want to damage the wood.

"Here, let me help you." Augusta poked her head

inside, kicked something out of the way, and then pushed the dory out onto the dock. "How the hell did you get it off the hooks?"

They both eyed the small craft. Though their mother had probably never set foot in one of these boats after Sammy's death, all of them were in pristine condition. "I bet she had Josh look after the boathouse," Augusta mused out loud.

Savannah shrugged. "Probably should have sold them all a long time ago, but good for us, because it's more for the auction. In fact, there's a twenty-five-foot Chris-Craft in there that's probably worth at least a hundred grand."

Augusta glanced inside. "I think it was Granddad's."

"Yeah, I was going to ask Josh about it."

"Maybe we should just give them to him?"

Savannah placed her good hand on her hip and wiped the moisture beading over her brow with her cast. "Instead of selling them?"

"Maybe." Augusta poked her head back in the boathouse. "If he's put this much work into it, I'd say his feelings would be hurt if we didn't at least ask, but hopefully, he'll just let us sell them."

"Yeah, okay. That's fine."

Augusta stood there, studying her, and Savannah knew she was about to get personal. She could see it in her expression.

"So you've been working on everything but your book since you got the cast on your arm and if you can move boxes and boats, you can't tell me it's preventing you from writing. What's going on with you?"

Savannah shrugged. "Writer's block, I guess."

"If I've got to deal with this bullshit, and all you have to do is a write a book, you'd better get something down on paper, even if it's total shit, Savannah . . . or we'll all end up with nothing after all this is done."

Savannah recognized the accusation in her sister's tone. She knew exactly what Augusta was thinking. Beyond the fact that everyone seemed to believe it was so easy to write a book. Augusta thought their mother had played favorites one last time, giving Savannah the easiest of the three tasks. She sighed. "I tried using the old typewriter, but it's not helping."

Augusta frowned at her. "Has this sort of thing happened before? You got one book out and published—why can't you write another?"

"Writer's block. It happens all the time," Savannah admitted, skirting the actual issue, "but never this bad."

She'd been having night terrors again lately, and even tried writing some of them down, but whenever she attempted it, her fingers sat paralyzed on the keyboard.

In fact, she hadn't been able to write much of anything for about a year, and she was terrified to try. The last time she had spilled her words on paper, thinking they were nothing more than a construct of her own imagination, she had experienced a macabre sense of déjà vu one day after a fruitful day at the keyboards. Seated on her couch, watching the news, suddenly detail for detail of her story began to unfold on the screen, narrated by a busty anchorwoman with shiny pink lips. It freaked Savannah out.

"Anyway," Savannah said, steering the conversation away from uncomfortable territory. "I just wanted to see what was in the boathouse; then I got a sudden urge to take the dory out."

"Out on the water? You can't steer that thing one-handed, Savannah!"

Savannah raised a brow and offered a little grin. "I bet I could, but I got it out here and then decided a boat ride on the marsh alone, while great for my muse, might not be so great for my overall health."

"Jesus . . . no kidding!"

Savannah scratched her arm above her cast. "Yeah . . . I was putting it back when you came out."

They both peered down at the boat, lying upside down on the dock, with its recently polished wood surface gleaming under the midday sun, and started to giggle. It was the first time Savannah remembered laughing with Augusta since they were children. It felt good.

Obviously, Augusta felt the same. "You wouldn't still be in the mood for that boat ride?" she asked.

Together they peered around at the peaceful setting, at the spartina grass ruffling gently in the breeze. The rains had left the water levels high. But with just the slightest breeze and the sun peeking out from behind paper-thin stratus clouds, it was about as idyllic as it could get. Add one boat with a female passenger—or two—and maybe funky hats—and you had the makings of a Renoir painting. But it wasn't what you could see out there that gave Savannah a sense of ambivalence. She shook her head, scrunching her nose.

"Yeah, me neither," Augusta admitted.

So they worked together to get the boat back in the boathouse and on the hangar where it should have remained.

"Has Sadie come back?" Savannah asked.

"Nope. I was going to call her, but I figured I'd give her some space."

"Yeah, I talked to her this morning—walked by her house. She says she reckons we ought to figure out how to fend for ourselves and that she's not doing us any favors by hovering."

Augusta seemed to take offense at Sadie's innuendo. "I can't speak for you and Caroline, but at home, I do everything for myself and what I don't do doesn't get done."

"Yeah, but, we're home just a few months and suddenly we're counting on her for everything. I guess it's too easy to fall back into old habits."

"True, but Sadie's an enabler," Augusta countered. "I mean, how many years did she do everything for Mom—right down to refilling her meds and stocking her liquor cabinet, even though she knew Mom's weaknesses better than anybody?"

Savannah cocked her head. "What would you have had her do? Tell her employer to go shove it?"

"Right. Well, I guess nothing is really black and white, is it?"

They fell into silence as they pored through the boathouse, looking for things to throw out, things to sell. It had the smells and the aura of a well-loved workspace—not a musty, moldy forgotten old storage unit. In some ways, Savannah felt like an intruder in her own home. Sadie and Josh were far more deserving of the place.

Savannah watched Augusta poke through sailing paraphernalia, noting her vacillating mood, and decided it was as good a time as any to talk about the dreams she'd been having. Sometimes they had a frightening link to reality, and Savannah had come to recognize the ones that shouldn't be ignored by the knot of apprehension they left in the pit of her gut.

"So you've been seeing Ian Patterson on the sly, haven't you?"

The expression on Augusta's face was almost comical. Her eyes widened incredulously, and she looked momentarily chastened, before her brows collided. "How . . . did you know?"

Savannah didn't feel comfortable explaining, not even to her sister, so she used the same line she always used. She shrugged. "I just guessed."

In fact, Augusta was keeping her secret about as quiet as humanly possible. She hadn't said a word about anything, but Savannah *knew*.

"Are you gonna tell Caroline?"

Savannah bit the inside of her lip. "I really think you should."

"Are you kidding? She'll go out of her mind! You saw how she reacted when I told her I wanted to offer the reward for Amanda Hutto!"

"Augusta, that man is a suspect in two murders."

"Yeah, well *I* believe he's innocent!"

Savannah looked at her meaningfully. "Are you willing to stake your life on it?" The question wasn't meant to be hyperbole. The risk was about as real as the sweat trickling between Savannah's breasts, down her arm and into her cast.

Augusta gave her a beleaguered look, full of confusion, and that didn't do much to reassure Savannah. "I just have this feeling, Sav. Please don't tell Caroline."

"I can't promise and it's not fair for you to expect it."

Augusta frowned.

"Come on . . . what would you say if the situation were reversed? Would you let me carry on with some guy who was being investigated for multiple charges?"

Augusta didn't answer, because both of them knew the answer. Augusta wouldn't balk at telling Caroline —or for that matter walking straight into police headquarters and demanding police protection whether Savannah wanted it or not.

"Okay, this is important, Augusta, so listen to what I'm about to say...."

Augusta glared at her. "Are you taking lessons from Caroline about how to be Mommy in absentia?"

Savannah wouldn't allow Augusta to bait her. "There might come a moment when you will ask your-self, 'what should I do?' Do what Augusta Aldridge would never do."

Augusta screwed her face. "What the hell is that? A commentary on my life? You think I need to second-guess my actions because they aren't the ones you and Caroline would take?" She tossed down a brush she had picked up. "Boy am I sorry as hell I came out to commune with my baby sister!" She stalked out of the boathouse.

Savannah followed her out, yelling after her. "It's not a commentary, Augusta! You're just too damned predictable!"

Augusta turned, walking backward, her face a mask of indignation. "Yeah, well, doing the right thing *is* predictable, Savannah!"

"That's my point, exactly!"

Augusta spun on her heel and Savannah watched her go, knowing it was time to talk to Caroline. There was no way she could keep what she knew to herself, especially now that Augusta had confirmed it.

CAROLINE WOULD HAVE CLOSED the office early except that news didn't stop for anyone. Life went on; so did the headlines.

She couldn't imagine how her mother had weathered the disappearance of their brother, making decisions, smiling bravely for the cameras. For Caroline's part, she felt as though her life was coming unglued and she couldn't even afford to focus two minutes of her own time to piece it back together. There were so many other things that took precedence.

When she got home, she found Augusta sitting on the porch, sipping a glass of lemonade, jeans rolled halfway up her calves and her strawberry-blond hair twisted haphazardly on her head. Augie regarded her with cool blue eyes, watching her walk wearily up the drive. "Long day?"

Caroline nodded, but couldn't quite find the energy to speak.

She stood there a moment, looking at her sister, and wondered how long it had been since they'd all been back under the same roof. It felt like an eternity, but the days were passing in a blur and she had barely spent any time with either of her sisters. At this rate, the year would be over . . . and then what? Would they each go their own way? The thought of that made Caroline glum. Dropping her briefcase on the bottom step, she sat down next to Augusta on the porch step. "What about you?"

"Me?"

"Yeah, how are you holding up?"

Augie sighed. "Okay, I guess." She took another sip of her lemonade and offered the glass to Caroline.

Caroline took a tentative sip and nearly gagged on the unexpected taste of vodka.

Augusta laughed. "I got into Mom's stash."

"That's not like you."

Augusta narrowed her eyes at Caroline and asked, "Yeah? How the hell would you know?"

Even in the growing twilight, the air was thick and

hot after the heavy rains. The sun had beaten down mercilessly all day, baking everything it touched. Whatever moisture the rains had infused into the landscape was quickly evaporating. Caroline noticed the fine sheen of sweat on Augie's arms and the slight sunburn on her shoulders, and meant to ask if she'd been out in the sun, but the barb stung. "Touché," she said.

So they sat there, cocooned in the silence that followed.

"Where's Savannah?"

"Inside."

"Sadie?"

"Still angry."

"No dinner?"

Augusta turned to look at her, her eyes gleaming. Caroline thought they held a trace of challenge. "Nope."

"So what are you doing out here?"

"Waiting for the sun to set."

"Why?"

"I don't know. Felt like it."

Caroline wanted to remind her that there was a psycho out there somewhere, but something about Augusta's expression made her hold her tongue. Her blue eyes were a little glassy, and she looked a bit like she had been crying at some point during the day.

After a moment, Augusta continued, "You know . . . I read an article in the *Tribune* that said researchers were concerned the fireflies are vanishing. Apparently, Clemson is doing a study, asking folks to sit out in their yards from eight to ten and count fireflies, then go online and record the numbers on their site."

As much as she wanted to say she read every single

article every day, Caroline couldn't possibly. "You read that in the *Tribune*?"

Augusta nodded and swirled the drink in her cup. "Somewhere in there between all that death . . . maybe page five. I had to look hard to find a story that didn't make me want to stuff myself in a sack of stones and jump off that dock out there." She gestured in the direction of the boathouse.

Caroline thought maybe she understood how Augie felt.

Life here had never quite seemed like a fairytale, but since they'd come home, everything was stained a pale shade of death.

"There's something so magical about fireflies," Augusta said wistfully, peering at Caroline with one eye closed. "Remember when we used to catch 'em and put 'em in jars and pretend they were fairies?"

Caroline nodded and Augusta drained her lemonade and set the glass down next to her on the other side of the step. "It would be sad if they vanished."

"I know what you mean," Caroline admitted. "You know, I'm starting to understand what's keeping me here this time and it has nothing to do with money. . . ."

Augusta lifted a brow in challenge. "Liar . . . it has something to do with the money."

Caroline couldn't stifle a chuckle at Augusta's glittery-eyed expression. "Okay, maybe a little, but seriously. I think the real magic we were feeling way back when wasn't about what we thought we were putting in those jars," she explained. "It was about the fact that we were trying to catch those bugs together."

"So they could live out their short miserable existences in our stinky peanut butter jars instead of out here where they belong," Augusta added with false wonderment, waving a hand at the expansive great outdoors.

Caroline grimaced, but laughed.

"Jesus!" Augusta exclaimed suddenly. "*We* are responsible for killing off the fireflies!"

Caroline laughed again. "Well . . . if we are, the least we can do is sit out here and take a survivor count together. I'm in if you want the company?"

Augusta smiled a nostalgic smile and shook her head. She sighed loudly. "There's got to be something more to this place than bad shit and good people dying, doesn't there? I still feel a little magic out there . . . *somewhere.*"

"So do I," Caroline agreed, and leaned unexpectedly to kiss her sister on the cheek . . . and they sat together, waiting for nightfall . . . and the reassurance of a single firefly.

JACK COULDN'T STAND the thought of going home.

He couldn't get the image of Kelly's sightless eyes out of his head.

He stopped by the Dive Inn—ironically still avoiding Kelly, though now he was avoiding the confusing emotions her death left him with—particularly the gut-wrenching guilt. He sat at the bar, and thankfully even the bartender avoided him, probably responding to the dark look on Jack's face. Without a word, he poured Jack a Guinness and slid it over the bar toward him along with the remote, eyeing the television.

Jack blinked at the screen, grabbing the remote

and turning it up in time to listen to the last minute of the clip of Caroline with Sandra Rivers.

"Are you stepping in now because you've lost faith in our boys in blue?" the bitch said. "And will you continue the more hardcore stories or do you plan to abandon them now that it seems too risky for your employees?" She pushed the microphone in Caroline's direction.

Although he knew she was in distress, Caroline's expression reminded him of her mother's—she had the same grace under fire—the same cool gaze—but if he said as much to Caroline, she would think he meant it as an insult. The truth was that he admired the way her spine straightened in the face of challenge, the way her chin hitched high against adversity.

"I was sorry to hear," the bartender offered. "She was . . . er . . . a sweet girl." He only knew Kelly at all because she had tracked Jack to the bar one night. He'd been annoyed, and he'd given her a bit of the cold shoulder, earning questions from the bartender later.

Jack nodded, staring at Caroline's face, needing her. He focused on her lips, watching them move and even in his grief, his body responded as it always did.

Now was not the time for distractions.

Caroline tilted Rivers a sly glance. "Do you tweet, Ms. Rivers?"

His lips twitched.

"Who doesn't?" the blond reporter replied, looking a little like a mouse facing a cat.

Caroline smiled confidently. "We don't."

Jack broke into a smile for the first time all day.

"She don't look much like her mama, but she sure acts like her," the bartender remarked, grabbing a hand rag and starting on the mugs still in the sink. He waved at a customer walking out the door. Jack heard the door close, then the small barroom was empty.

"Mind if I turn this off while I finish my beer?" Jack asked.

"Take your time," the guy said, moving out from behind the bar, going to the door to lock up. That's what Jack liked most about him. He wasn't a huge talker and he didn't mind a little silence.

Jack clicked off the TV, bathing the dimly lit barroom in easy silence.

He wanted to call Caroline, but didn't know what to say. He stared at the blank screen, replaying the events of the last two days over in his head.

The game seemed to have changed. Once again, he thought that Kelly's murder felt personal. And Pam Baker's disappearance was too close for comfort. However, without a body, there was no murder. She was just another missing person.

What if they weren't meant to find more bodies? What if the sole purpose of planting Kelly's was meant to confirm their worst fears and remove Jack from the case in one fell swoop?

Where was their guy stashing the bodies?

Did they have another Dahmer on their hands? Were they stuffed in someone's deep freeze? Was he burying them somewhere? Where?

There was another aerial search planned for the morning.

Not often, but whenever a gator took prey—mostly dogs—they found some underwater burrow to stash the meal until the meat was soft and ripe enough to eat. Could that be what the killer was doing? Burying them somewhere in the swamp where the tide couldn't carry them to the surface? If that were the case, the state of South Carolina had more than four million acres of wetlands, and even if they concentrated a search on the greater Charleston area, it was impossible to comb every inch of that boggy land. Over much of that wet terrain, even dogs wouldn't be able to track a scent.

To top it off, Caroline's note was clean—not a single print to be found—but that didn't surprise Jack. Why should the slip be different from the rest of the forensic evidence? The guy was meticulous. What it did affirm, however, was that it wasn't a calling card for some church salesman. There was no way the slip would be so clean if it had been handled by some Holy Roller.

The guys in the lab had made one connection Jack didn't—not until he saw the pink slip on Pam's car. They were carbon copies. Without another piece of carbon-laden paper, a single sheet wouldn't look or behave any differently from a normal sheet, but combined with another piece of carbon-laden paper, they made copying possible. Not that it mattered—because there were no prints—but if they had used conventional fuming techniques, it would have turned the paper black and any retrievable prints would have been irrevocably lost.

But unlike carbon copies of the past, there would be no black residue on the hands of someone using it, though there might be chemical residue. There were a slew of chemicals used to make the sheets—enough that their safety in everyday use was being questioned. Some of the chemicals included phenol-formaldehyde resins, Bisphenol A, AZO dyes and others. How long would traces of these chemicals remain on the skin?

It was a moot point if he couldn't find probable cause to connect Patterson to the slip.

It seemed impossible to commit two crimes so close together and not leave loose ends . . . somewhere. At some point, the guy must have made a mistake and Jack was going to find it and nail him.

He squeezed his eyes shut, piecing everything together. Today was Wednesday. Kelly's body had been discovered Tuesday evening. Provided the killer had, in fact, been the one to nab Baker, when would he have taken her? Over the weekend or sometime Monday . . . but the streets were mostly flooded Monday and Tuesday. If he didn't nab her straight from work, he would have had trouble getting the car back into the garage . . . which meant he must have snatched her sometime before the rain began . . . with enough time to get the car back into the garage.

Baker's laptop was being scrubbed, along with her Honda, but the car was spotless—not a watermark on it so it probably hadn't been driven through the rain and probably wouldn't yield any prints. But he doubted the killer would leave a laptop if it might contain evidence . . . which told Jack there probably hadn't been any previous contact between them. Baker's cell phone was missing among her belongings. Jack had already contacted her provider to ask about GPS tracking. He had also subpoenaed her phone records.

What were the chances both girls had been in the wrong place at the wrong time? More importantly, where was the wrong place?

Everything had happened so quickly, they hadn't even had time to wonder about Kelly's Jeep. After the discovery of Baker's car in the Meeting Street parking garage, they'd sent a patrol car out and found the Jeep missing from her house so they sent out an immediate bulletin. If her Jeep were a newer model, they might have had the benefit of GPS tracking, but no such luck. First thing in the morning, with fresh new light, he was going to see if they'd let him go up in one of the choppers.

Unless...

A thought occurred to him, and he jumped up. "Hey Kyle, can you unlock the door please?"

Almost as though he had forgotten Jack's presence, the bartender stopped in the middle of cleaning his mug, blinking, but, seeing the look on Jack's face, he didn't say another word. He hurried out from the bar to unlock the door. Jack slapped a twenty on the countertop and grabbed his keys and cell phone.

No cop wanted to assume something so shitty could happen on his own doorstep—and because the kid had witnessed a swimmer, they'd all surmised the body was transported and dropped at Brittlebank Park, but what if Kelly was taken straight from work? No one had even considered checking the Lockwood parking lot for Kelly's car.

36

All you can do is start out with the best intentions. . . .
Caroline spent the entire night hearing Savannah's words bounce around her head. She tossed and turned, trying to figure out what she might have done differently.

She was missing something. Brad had been the one to talk to Jennifer Williams's mother, but what if Brad had handed Pam the baton, knowing he wasn't going to get the limelight for the story, and what if Pam were pursuing some lead they didn't know about?

She probably could have called, but rather than take the chance of being turned away, Caroline got in her car the next morning and instead of driving into the office, she made the hour-and-a-half trek to Murrells Inlet to talk to Jennifer Williams's mother. Some interviews were better done in person. Although she had promised Frank she wouldn't write another story, this wasn't about seeing her name in a byline, or about needing to control the paper, it was about locating a young woman Caroline felt responsible for.

Amanda Hutto had never been found. Jennifer Williams was still missing. Was Pam still alive?

If there was something—anything—Ms. Williams

might tell her about her daughter's disappearance or about Ian Patterson, it was worth the drive. She called Frank to let him know where she was going. He surprised her by not offering a single objection.

The trip, however, yielded nothing, except to highlight the ambivalence of the woman's faith in Patterson's innocence. It seemed to Caroline that the woman's guilt over the falsified charges was keeping Ms. Williams from looking at circumstances clearly.

In her late forties, the woman lived alone in a small house along Creek Drive. She welcomed Caroline warmly, made her tea and brought out her most recent picture of Jennifer. She printed it out on her color printer and brought it to Caroline, her hands shaking slightly.

Caroline stared at the photograph of the teenager with strawberry blond hair. She looked a little like Augusta, not just her coloration or features, but that defiant look in her eyes.

The photo was taken at the ruins, there was no doubt.

Caroline felt a little pinprick in her chest when she recognized the spot she and her sisters had played so often as children. The image was faded, the colors all blending together, making it hard to distinguish boundaries. But no matter what the quality of the photo, she would have recognized the location regardless. Behind Jennifer, one of the crumbling chimneys soared into the trees, the top covered by limbs that were dripping with Spanish moss.

Was Patterson there covering his tracks?

Caroline waved the photograph. "Do you know who took this photo?"

Ms. Williams shook her head, uncertainty peeking through her dark brown eyes.

Was Jennifer there checking out the ruins . . . or

was there something more sinister at work? Who took the photo?

"How did you get this photo?" Caroline asked.

"Ian Patterson e-mailed it to me."

The little hairs on Caroline's nape prickled. She stood at once. Suddenly, she felt the need to get back to Charleston. She had to call Jack. Had to talk to Frank. Ian Patterson had questions to answer, but Caroline realized that anything she said now would only distress Ms. Williams all the more. "Thank you," she said, standing. She waved the photograph again. "May I keep this?"

"Of course."

Caroline said her good-byes and left, folding and tucking the photo into her purse. Once she was in the car, she called Jack three times. He didn't answer. Then she called Frank and left a message, telling him what she'd discovered. Afterward, she tried both her sisters. Neither answered, so she just drove.

———

AUGUSTA MET WITH DANIEL. She'd spoken to him only briefly to get the OK for the reward money and the reward notice was supposed to have been published in this morning's edition. But he'd been difficult to pin down lately, so when he offered to see her to help her iron out details for the auction, she took him up on it, literally running out the door.

She was glad to see that he seemed completely recovered, bruises healed, and had a skip to his step that she attributed to something other than work, but she didn't pry. She really didn't want to know—especially if the explanation included Sadie.

When they were finished with their meeting, he apologized for the need to lock up and rush off, but he didn't want to leave the office open and he had a court case that had reached its final continuance and couldn't be missed. Ushering Augusta out the front door, he locked up and exited through the back of his building, where his car was parked, leaving Augusta standing on the street, annoyed that he hadn't offered her a ride to her car. She hadn't been able to scoop a parking spot anywhere near his office, nor on King Street and now she had to walk down a pretty iffy street.

Since when are you afraid to walk down a stupid street?

She lived in New York, for God's sake. She had been down a million iffy streets.

The difference being, in a city with more than eight million people, it was difficult to find one with no one on it.

But it was still light out, she told herself, even if the street was strangely empty and the lamps were off despite a new set of dark clouds rolling in overhead. They needed the summer rain to take the edge off the heat, she thought, but it would sure suck to get stuck in it.

The ambient light was fading, shadows falling like a gray curtain over the city. In the historic district, there was always the added glow of gas lamps burning day and night. But here, the city was only beginning to correct the shortage of lights and a few were broken— not because they were being neglected, but probably because they hadn't been reported. If you preferred to do your business in the dark, why would you want lamps?

About thirty paces down the road, Augusta re-

gretted the decision to park so far away and she regretted wearing heels—even short ones.

What time was it? It *felt* late.

Cool air blew in, and steam rose from the blacktop.
She passed a pothole that had recently been filled and
her heel sank down into the hot asphalt. Suddenly,
she felt rather than heard a presence behind her.

The footfalls were quick and lithe, rushing past
her. The kid had her purse even before she could turn
around to see who was coming. He was no older than
twelve, his sneakered feet too big for his skinny body.
He made away with the only designer purse Augusta
had ever bought in her entire life. Instinctively she
bolted after him, incensed.

If she caught him, she was going to turn him over
her knee like a baby and paddle the daylights out of
him in front of everyone watching—if anyone was
watching—and then she was going to march him to
his house and make him tell his mama what he'd
done.

But he was too fast and turned into an alley before
she could catch up. By the time Augusta reached the
alley, she was winded, and even angrier, realizing he
had her car keys.

At this point, she could give a damn about the
purse. She just wanted her keys. In fact, if he would
only come back, she would happily donate the Town
Car to him for the price of a ride home. He probably
needed it way more than she did anyway.

The sky was darkening fast. Shadows crept up the
buildings along the alley. A Piggly Wiggly bag dragged
itself over the brick pavement, the wind teasing it with
a promised sail.

He was just a kid.

Should she go in the alley after him?

Suddenly, Savannah's words echoed in her head.

Do what Augusta Aldridge would never do.

Augusta hesitated—something she rarely did.

She stood at the entrance of the alleyway considering what to do as the wind kicked up leaves and trash. Daylight was fading fast. Her eyes skimmed the second-story windows. Some of them were boarded up. Others were simply empty black holes in decrepit wooden facades. Inside one of them, she thought she saw a face peering out from the shadows.

Sometimes Savannah knew things.

Although it usually took a lot more than a darkening alley, a few shadows and a windy afternoon to daunt her, Augusta turned away from the alley and hurried back toward King Street.

To hell with it! She could get a new purse and phone and change the locks. As for the Town Car, if it was still there in the morning, she'd have a locksmith come out and let her in. In the meantime, she wasn't about to stick around and wait for one.

Hurrying toward King Street, she wondered if she even remembered either of her sisters' phone numbers—something she was going to have to remedy going forward.

———

THEY GAVE up the choppers by late afternoon.

Kelly's car was not in the Lockwood parking lot, nor was there any sign of it abandoned along the Ashley River.

While he waited to hear from Garrison, Jack pored through the contents of Baker's laptop. Officially, she wasn't a murder victim so the cases weren't linked, which only meant that, for the moment, the laptop was flying under the radar of the county solicitor's office. The cases had nothing in common—not even the note, which had been found in the same parking lot where Caroline's note had appeared and could have been placed there on her windshield by virtually anyone. But Caroline wasn't a victim, and until Kelly's car was found and they knew for sure whether it had a similar note attached to it, there was no way to connect Caroline's and Pam's notes to Kelly's murder. It was purely conjecture. In fact, if someone were to look at these cases from a high level, there was nothing to connect them, except coincidence . . . yet . . . Jack somehow knew they were connected.

He had three dead girls . . . another missing . . . what was the connection?

He tried to clear his mind to think clearly.

One of the girls had a direct connection to Caroline. The other to Jack. In his gut, Jack sensed that the game had turned personal. Were the notes a message, not for the police, but for Jack?

He thought about the message itself . . . *Death and life are in the power of the tongue; those who love it will eat its fruit.*

What did it mean? Had the victims been targeted because of something they'd said? Something that was said about them? Something they didn't say? Was the psycho eating their tongues because he believed they held some sort of power?

In Greek mythology Tereus raped his wife's sister and cut out her tongue to keep her from telling anyone about the crime. For Andrei Chikatilo, a Ukrainian serial killer, biting off the tongue was an extension of his lovemaking. Natives in the southernmost part of New Guinea supposedly ate the tongues of slain enemies to take their bravery. Serial killer and cannibal Joachim Kroll killed and ate his victims to save on his grocery bill. And Dennis Rader considered his victims projects and likened killing them to putting down animals. He strangled them multiple times, reviving them, getting off on their struggles, until he finally killed them and ejaculated into one of their personal items.

Questions raced through Jack's mind, but none of the answers were cohesive, none gelled and he was still poring through the laptop when Garrison walked into his office around four P.M.

"You know that tail we put on Patterson . . . you'll never guess where he went today."

Jack was skimming through Baker's e-mails. "Where?"

"Apparently, his girlfriend has a part-time job at the Wash 'N' Shine, a car wash owned by her step-brother out in Mt. Pleasant."

"Girlfriend?"

"The chick who gave him his alibi."

Jack's head shot up. "Anyone been out yet to ask questions and take a look at their invoices?"

He and Garrison locked gazes. He knew Garrison had already discarded the messages as evidence, or at least put them at the bottom of his priority list, and he was unconvinced Pam's disappearance was connected to the case. As far as everyone was concerned, the reference to the tongue was nothing but a coincidence. The white copy, like the pink copy, had been whistle clean, but both were found in the same parking garage on cars belonging to employees of the *Tribune*.

"I'm going now," he said. "I just wanted to let you know."

Jack stood, grabbing his keys, ready to ride with

him. If Garrison wasn't going to ask the right questions, someone had to.

Garrison shook his head. "Sorry. Can't," he said. "Condon wants you to sit this out. Just wanted you to know," he said again, sounding apologetic, if just a little superior. This was his chance to outshine Jack and become the star detective—Condon's pet. At least that's how Jack thought Garrison perceived it. He sat back down, feeling impotent and angry.

"What about the computer?" Garrison asked, probably as a consolation. "Find anything yet?"

"Nothing."

37

Caroline was nearly home when her phone rang. In the few minutes since she'd turned down Fort Lamar Road, the sky had grown black. She answered without checking the number, hoping it was Jack.

"Calling . . . reward."

It was a male voice, although barely a whisper and Caroline could only make out the single word: reward. Her heart skipped a beat and she turned down the radio. "Can you repeat that, please," she requested, "My battery is dying. You're breaking up."

"Calling . . . claim . . . the reward," the man whispered, so low she almost couldn't hear him again. Caroline pulled the phone away from her ear to check the caller ID and gasped at the sight of Pam's number. Her foot slammed the break in reaction, jerking the car and nearly spinning her back end off the road. She put the phone back to her ear, but words caught in her throat.

It seemed an interminable moment before he spoke again. "I know where she is," the voice whispered.

He hung up suddenly and Caroline pulled the car

over to the side of the road, unnerved, her hands shaking too hard to drive even the mile or so left before home.

Call Jack.

She picked up the phone and started to dial when a text came through.

The hair on the back of her neck prickled.

The text was coming from Augusta's number. Caroline clicked on it and waited with bated breath, heart hammering against her ribs, for a picture message to download. The battery was red and blinking. The saliva dried in her mouth as she waited for the image to fully materialize, fear clutching at her heart. She blinked as a close-up of charred bricks crystallized in the photo and she barely made out the initials next to a dark stain that looked like . . . blood. Her chest constricted.

Blood.

The initials were hers and Jack's.

The photo text had come from Augusta's number.

I know where she is.

The battery finally died. Her screen went black.

Caroline didn't think, only reacted. Spinning the car out onto the pavement, she gunned it toward the road's end, toward the ruins.

JACK HIT MORE DEAD ENDS.

Was it possible he was manufacturing a connection where there was none? Could it be these were two completely separate cases, with simple coincidences seeming to connect them?

He raked a hand through his hair, frustrated. Pam's e-mails were clean. Every file on her desktop seemed work-related. There was not one single personal e-mail in her trash bin. He checked her history, and one by one visited the sites she had browsed and bookmarked.

There were a few Internet articles about Ian Patterson, a few articles from the *Tribune*, one from the *Post*. She also visited quite a few sites on serial killer pathology and theory—one that outlined applications of geographical offender profiling for rapists in particular. Through geographic profiling for rapists, they had learned that perpetrators seldom committed crimes outside a circle that was determinable by the rapist's two furthermost offenses. Was she researching an article on the site of Amy Jones's murder? Could that be his missing link?

On a whim, he pulled up another browser. The default was set to her Google account and she was still logged in. Feeling hopeful, he clicked through her e-mail. Evidently, she didn't use the service—nothing in it but spam. Gritting his teeth, he clicked on the link that took him to her photos, and the hairs on the back of his neck stood on end and prickled as one by one Pam Baker's pictures materialized.

Apparently, her smartphone automatically pushed her photos online. The last update was Saturday, July first. At a glance, the photos all looked like mistakes, misshots, and then he realized they were close-ups and he clicked through them one by one, swallowing hard when he realized what he was looking at. A bad feeling twisted in his stomach as he continued examining the photos. More than a dozen, all taken at different angles. All photos of bricks—and particularly a dark stain. He noted the initials carved in the stone and that sinking feeling in the pit of his stomach turned into a black hole.

His cell phone rang.

"Bingo, Jack!" Garrison shouted on the other end of the line. "The invoice matches the pad they use at the car wash. The window crayon, too. We'll get the lab to confirm it, but I'm pretty sure it's the same. Get this . . . the biggest news is that we found Kelly's Jeep, sitting all nice 'n shiny up in one of the parking spaces with a big ole number two written on the driver's-side window—and you'll never guess . . ."

More prickles jetted down Jack's spine. "There was a note on her windshield?"

"Bingo again! You were right!" Garrison said. "Yellow—says exactly the same thing as the other two."

Jack had never wanted to be wrong more in his life. "Where is Patterson?" he asked, his chest squeezing the breath from his lungs.

Now there was dead silence.

"We sent the guys home at four," Garrison said, his tone a mix of self-defense and regret. "Nothing was happening, Jack. Those guys have been working round the clock. Keith's wife was threatening to divorce him if he didn't get home in time to watch his kid's ball game."

Ice cold fear swept down Jack's spine. "Where was Patterson when you last saw him?"

"Home, but . . ."

Jack tensed. "Garrison?"

"Well, we got an anonymous tip he is on Fort Lamar Road, headed toward Oyster Point. But don't worry, Jack, we've got men on the way out there right now."

He was counting down.

Jack blinked as comprehension dawned. The first copy—the white copy—was on Caroline's windshield.

He must have left his head between Caroline's thighs because he saw with crystal clarity the one thing he'd been denying to himself. The mystery in the message wasn't *why* or *what* he was doing with the tongues. Straight up, he was telling Jack who his third victim would be.

Caroline.

He hung up and dialed Caroline's cell phone. It went straight to voice mail. He seized his car keys.

CAROLINE PLOWED her car into the brush and bolted out of the driver's seat, leaving the door open. The sky was darkening to black, but her car's headlights lit her path as she ran toward the ruins, her heartbeat thundering in her ears.

"Augie!" she shouted. "Augie!"

Winded and confused, she reached the remains of the old Georgian house, with its jagged vine-covered walls, but there was no one there.

No one . . . except . . . she recognized that smell . . . not the pungent odor of the marsh, but fumes . . . like gasoline.

It was all around her. She was standing in it. Instinctively, she peered down at her feet, searching for the stain in the picture. There it was, a dark sprawling black shadow next to the initials she and Jack had carved into the bricks the summer before she'd gone off to college. He'd carved those initials the day he'd asked her to marry him and he'd promised he would always be there for her. . . .

That was the last coherent thought she had, and then something sweet and acrid pressed against her nose and mouth—something like the smell of rotting magnolias.

And there was black.

HE SENT one more text from Augusta Aldridge's cell phone to ensure his players would all be present. He worked quickly, deftly, feeling like a master conductor. This was perfectly orchestrated, but if a single note was out of place . . . but no, no it wouldn't be.

Dousing the bricks with more gas, until it covered the bloodstain in its entirety, he heard the sirens in the distance. Distracted for an instant, he took a deep breath, searching for the scent of the marsh, taking comfort and energy from it, and just for good measure, he doused the branches overhead and the surrounding brush until the scent of gas overpowered even the scent of the marsh. When he was done, he lit a single match and smiled.

"THANK God you were actually working for once or you might not have heard the phone ring!"

Savannah cast her sister an exasperated glance, trying not to be annoyed by the backhanded gratitude.

"Actually, you're lucky Sadie was at the house, because without a car or any money, you'd still be sitting on a street corner waiting for rain."

"Yeah, remind me never to give her a hard time again—Jesus! That shit spooked the hell out of me!" Augusta slid her bare feet up on the car dash. She'd taken off her offending heels and tossed them onto the floorboard, vowing to wear only flat shoes for the rest of her God-given days. "Think the car will be okay overnight?"

Savannah shrugged. "Who knows. There probably won't be anything left of it to sell come morning, but I don't think it would have been smart to stand out there and wait for a locksmith either." Savannah kept her eyes on the unbroken yellow line, unnerved by the premature darkness. She hated driving at night, and thought maybe she had a touch of night blindness. It put her on edge—but maybe something else was bothering her, too. She'd had an awful premonition all day long . . . like a black, hovering cloud that just wouldn't go away.

With the trees arching overhead, Fort Lamar Road somehow seemed darker than the rest of the world. Savannah eyed her sister. "Good thing you didn't follow him into that alley, right?"

"Yeah . . . about that," Augusta countered, turning to look at her as though she were some odd curiosity. "How the hell do you seem to know this shit? You're—"

From somewhere down the road came a sudden fireball and Savannah stiffened behind the wheel. "Did you see that?"

Augusta sat up, peering down the road, where there was a rising glow. "Jesus . . . is Sadie's house on fire?"

Flames shot up distant trees like giant peat torches, lighting up the darkening sky like a medieval torch in the bowels of a dungeon.

Suddenly, they heard sirens—police sirens, not fire. Blue lights whizzed past them, coming out of nowhere, shrieking down the road.

"Holy shit!" Augusta said as they neared. "I think the old house is burning again!"

DESPITE THE RECENT RAINS, after a scorching spring
and summer, the trees and scrub were ready to burn.
The flames were already streaking up the trees, incin-
erating moss and crackling dead branches in their
path. A burning limb cracked and plummeted to the
ground. Aided by the rising wind, the fire was
spreading fast.

Jack wasn't the first to arrive, but no one could
have held him back.

Patterson's car was parked precariously by the
roadside. Caroline's car was in the brush, as though
she had driven in too fast to stop—as though she had
been run off the road in pursuit.

Jack raced past his men toward the ruins, weapon
drawn.

The brick façade and the brush surrounding it
were completely engulfed . . . and then he saw the
figure emerge from a portal in the flames—Patterson,
holding Caroline in his arms.

"Put her down!" Jack commanded. "Put her down!"

The look in Patterson's eyes was that of a caged an-
imal, angry and wild, but he moved forward with his
burden, unfazed by Jack's demand.

Jack's hand shook as he aimed.

Caroline lay completely lifeless. He could see her
mouth was taped and his heart sank. She didn't move.

"Back off, Jack!" Garrison's voice yelled at his back.

"Put her the fuck down!" Jack demanded once
more. He aimed at Patterson's head, ready to put a
bullet right between his eyes.

Behind him, more squad cars screeched to a halt.
Doors opened and slammed.

He didn't take his eyes off Patterson for a second.

Eyes blazing almost as hot as the flames at his back, Patterson stopped suddenly, stooping, spilling Caroline's body onto the ground, then slowly rose and lifted his hands in surrender.

Armed men moved in, bringing him down. Jack ran to Caroline's side, ripping the tape from her mouth.

"Jack, don't!" Garrison shouted.

Fuck the evidence! Fuck the investigation! Let them suspend him! This was the only thing that mattered in his life. This was Caroline! He wanted her alive! "Christ!" he begged. He pried her mouth open, gasping out loud to find her tongue intact and no blue dye. He shoved his fingers inside her mouth looking for blockage—anything—tears streaming down his cheeks. She let out a shuddering breath and he pulled her into his arms. "Thank God!" he cried.

He peered up at Patterson, and realized how deadly wrong his gut had been. The instincts he normally trusted had steered him completely adrift. Caroline had been so sure Patterson was guilty and Jack had fought her every step of the way. He was through fighting.

"I'll make sure you fry," he swore, as they cuffed Patterson and read him his rights.

He heard shrill female screams, and was vaguely aware of the frenzied shouts at his back. Then Augusta was suddenly at his side, looking down at Caroline, tears spilling over her cheeks. Augusta gave an audible gasp when she saw Caroline blink. "Oh, Thank God!" she said. "Caroline!"

They led Patterson away as two officers came and tried to pull Augusta off. She reared back and smacked one of them upside the head with her palm.

"Get the hell away from me," she spat. "This is my sister!"

Caroline blinked again, her eyes fluttering open. "Are we having a bonfire?" she asked weakly, peering up at Augusta in a heavy stupor.

"Looks like you tried to have one without us!" Augusta exclaimed, choking on a sob. "But you set the wrong damned house on fire!"

Caroline gave her a feeble smile and Jack choked on his own relief and laughter. He glanced back to see that they were still restraining Savannah, her eyes wide and fearful. He gave the man holding her a nod and he let her go.

Savannah rushed to their side, falling to her knees beside Caroline. "Oh my God, Caroline!"

Augusta turned to stare at Patterson's back, watching as they pushed him into a squad car. He turned to look at her only once before getting in, piercing her with a clear blue glare, and she swallowed hard. "I was so wrong," she said softly, as she stared into the wrathful eyes that peered back at her from inside the car.

In that instant, though she didn't believe in angels or demons, Augusta thought she understood what it must have been like the moment when Lucifer became Satan.

38

It was over.

They found a wetsuit in Patterson's trunk, along with a "hit bag" containing a roll of the same tape used to cover the victims' mouths, rope, a vial of blue food coloring and a bloody knife and rag. The rag would be tested to see if it matched Kelly's or Amy Jones's blood type and DNA. Although none of the evidence at the scene was linkable through DNA, they had discovered a twisted clump of plastic that at one time had been a cell phone. According to forensics, some SIM cards had been known to survive extreme temperatures and although the data couldn't be accessed simply, it was still retrievable. They believed the phone belonged to Augusta and that Patterson had used it to lure Caroline to the scene.

A search of Patterson's house produced Jones's missing camera. It was full of the photos she had been snapping the night she died—mostly the lighthouse and marsh, but there were a few photos that had been taken during the time he was preparing Jones, and a few close-ups of her face while she died—a gruesome sequence of shots that highlighted her terror and finally the instant of her death.

They also found a small box with a tongue piercing in it, and they learned belatedly that Amy Jones had had a tongue piercing—something they had missed during the investigation—something Amy's roommate couldn't have known to tell them because they'd never fully disclosed the details of her friend's mutilation and death. It was just a matter of time before they matched the DNA.

They discovered a number of other paraphernalia, including a little girl's notebook full of drawings of crying flowers and houses on fire. Scribbled on the inside cover in black was a parent's clear print of the word Amanda, along with a page full of a child's attempt to copy it in red crayon.

The area around the ruins had been searched thoroughly, but except for the recent fire, the landscape appeared untouched. Pam's body was not recovered. Neither was Amanda Hutto's. But with so much evidence, there was no question of Patterson's guilt. Caroline never saw her attacker. But it didn't matter. They had Patterson dead to rights and it didn't make any difference whether he refused to talk or that the anger in his eyes could have started a new blaze to rival the one they'd put out.

Right now, there was only one thing Jack's gut was telling him. He had the chance to build a life with Caroline, and whatever it took to make that happen, he was in for the long haul. After fourteen years on the force, he was considering retiring. His instincts had been all wrong and he had broken too many rules, undermined his own sense of self, and nearly lost Caroline in the process.

Patterson was behind bars. No thanks to Jack. Even if he died without revealing the whereabouts of the other bodies, at least he would never hurt another innocent girl. That was enough for now. And sooner or later, the truth would out . . . if anyone was listening.

Jack walked into the little mom-and-pop jewelry shop a friend of his had opened and recently sold, and went straight for the counter, where a young girl stood staring at him expectantly.

"What can I help you with, sir?"

"I need an engagement ring," he said simply, pulling out an antique, hand-carved platinum setting with three missing stones and placing it reverently on the counter. It had once belonged to his grandmother. Caroline had given it back ten years ago and Jack had pried the diamonds out and pawned them, though he kept the ring itself, unable to part with the only heirloom he had from his family. He barely recalled his grandmother after all these years, but she was the only positive thing he remembered about his childhood. He hadn't connected with another living soul to that degree until Caroline. It was only fitting Caroline should have it, but there was no way he give it to her as it was. "It needs something different," he said, "something that shows how much I've waited for this each of the last ten years of my life . . . but something that says we're on a new path."

The girl smiled. "What color are her eyes?"

"Hazel, with bright flecks of green."

"How about an emerald?" she suggested. "With diamonds for the heart motifs?"

"Perfect," he said.

JACK HAD *INSISTED* Caroline meet him at the Dive Inn.

It made absolutely no sense to her—not after he'd

hovered over her for more than a week, treating her like an invalid, and insisting she stay home and recover properly. In fact, he had remained with her at Oyster Point to make sure of it, barely leaving her side. She'd had to argue vehemently that she was ready to return to work this morning and now he suddenly seemed to have forgotten all of his solicitousness, making her go out of her way after a long day at the office to meet him in a public place.

She tried without any luck to call Savannah and Augusta to let them know she would be missing dinner, but neither answered her phone.

Not that she was annoyed or anything.

She really wanted to see Jack—in fact, she really wanted him all to herself, but maybe he needed to do something normal after the chaos of the past few months. He just seemed so adamant she *had* to come before dark and he had hounded her to leave work *right now,* hanging up only after she jangled her keys into the receiver—and now, like her sisters, he wasn't even answering his phone.

She drove toward Folly Beach, trying not to speed, windows down, reveling in the cool evening breeze. It would do her good to get out and relax for the evening, she told herself.

A flash of bright, neon red caught her attention and her gaze skidded toward the beached boat that sat on the side of Folly Beach Road. It had been there for decades, painted and repainted with graffiti. It was impossible to miss the current message. It utilized every inch of possible space. In enormous bright red letters, it said: MARRY ME, CAROLINE.

Caroline blinked as she passed the sign, her heart leaping into her throat. Butterflies took flight in her belly. She was already at the corner of East Ashley before she remembered to breathe.

Marry me, Caroline.

Could it be?

As long as she could recall, the defunct boat had been used to herald birth announcements, graduation notices and shout engagement declarations—or pretty much anything else people wished to proclaim.

Her head spun with thoughts of their first engagement and she frowned over the memory of their breakup—all the wasted years. If he asked her again, she would hold on to what they had until her dying breath and never take it for granted again.

She loved him. How she had lived without him for ten long years Caroline had no idea.

She turned the corner to find Jack standing outside the Dive Inn. He was grinning broadly, waiting for her, and Caroline found herself smiling too, euphoria building inside her.

Marry me, Caroline.

She pulled in, swung into a parking space, parking haphazardly, and bolted out of her car. "Jack!" she exclaimed.

He was still grinning. There was a distinct twinkle in his bright blue eyes.

She stopped and turned toward the direction she'd come, feeling awkward suddenly, second-guessing herself. She pointed. "Did you?"

"Will you?" he interrupted and fell to one knee, producing a small red box from behind his back.

Tears sprang to Caroline's eyes and she lurched toward him, scarcely aware that her feet were moving. She fell to her knees in front of him. "Oh, Jack!"

"Marry me, Caroline," he whispered.

They knelt there in the gravel together, pebbles digging into their knees, facing each other, and Caroline could care less that suddenly it seemed the parking lot was filling with an audience. Folks spilled from the tiny pub out into the graveled parking lot. She didn't bother to look up. At the moment, she only saw Jack—the love in his eyes, the hope and genuine sincerity etched on his handsome face—that face she wanted to wake up to every morning for the rest of her life.

"I love you," he swore. "I want every last person in this town to know it!"

Caroline couldn't find her voice to speak.

"Caroline . . . I promise never to leave you wondering—never to let you down. I swear to God I will always put you first in my heart and in my life!"

Caroline threw her arms around his neck, kissing his lobe. "Yes, Jack!" she whispered fervently. Tears squeezed past her closed lids and her heart felt as though it would explode in her chest.

Jack pulled away long enough to open the box in his hand and Caroline opened her eyes to spy the loveliest ring she had ever laid eyes upon. Set in his grandmother's filigreed silver was an enormous emerald flanked by two heart motifs filled with diamonds.

Caroline's hands shook as he removed the ring from the box. He held her hand and slid the ring onto her finger. Suddenly the parking lot exploded with cheers.

Caroline belatedly looked up, swiping tears from her eyes to spy both her sisters standing arm in arm at the front of the crowd. That would explain why they weren't answering the phone. Frank was there too— the sneak!—along with Daniel and George. Sadie was weeping inconsolably as she clutched her son's arm for support.

"Yes," she said again, and smiled.

For the first time in her life she felt connected, not just to the love of her life, but to her family as well—to this place. This time, she knew she was home to stay.

EPILOGUE

It was impossible not to admire the old typewriter, with its shiny gold keys and polished walnut base. Savannah literally stared at it for hours without even touching it, trying to figure out how to start.

Apparently, their mother had used it until shortly before her death. That's why it was still in pristine condition and explained the perfectly oiled carriage and the recently inked spool. How it ended up in the attic, Sadie claimed not to know. Spotting it on her mother's desk, Sadie remarked on it, wondering why Savannah had brought it down from the attic if she wasn't going to actually use it.

Savannah's cast was off and there was no use avoiding the typewriter forever. Augusta was right: she had to get something down on paper—anything, even if it was crap.

Augusta was mired in preparations for the up-coming auction while Caroline was mired in prepara-tions for an upcoming wedding—her own. After ten long years, she and Jack were finally going to say I do and it was a long overdue happily ever after for both of them.

Funny how sometimes it took loss or coming close

to losing something precious to highlight what mattered most in life.

Rummaging through her mother's desk in search of paper, Savannah discovered a ream of sheets in the bottom drawer, next to a pewter letter opener shaped like a Confederate bayonet. Lucky day, she thought, but once the paper was loaded, she simply stared at the white sheet rolled into the typewriter.

Maybe if she hit a single key and made an impression . . . like the first note of a song, it might propel her into writing more. Frustrated, she hit the F key, and then stared at the heavy impression it made. Crisp. Black. Beautiful.

The sight of the single letter made her inordinately happy, but as she stared at the sheet of paper, she realized there was another impression etched on it. She rolled it out of the typewriter and turned it under the desk light, trying to read the ghost of her mother's scribble.

She could make out a few words, like "will" and "codicil."

Curious, she set the paper down and went searching for a pencil, determined to find out what secrets the paper held. Maybe a little third-grade sleuthing would reveal her mother's words. Finally, she found a pencil buried in the middle drawer—not an old-fashioned number two—the mechanical type. But it would work fine, she thought. The impression on the paper was deep enough.

Positioning the paper on the desk, she began to rub the pencil lightly over the indentations on the page, and slowly, the words began to appear. . . .

I, Florence W. Aldridge, of James Island, declare this to be

*a first codicil to my Last Will and Testament dated May
first two-thousand-fourteen.*

Blinking, Savannah stared at the words behind the
careful shading of pencil, hesitating, her heart beating
a little faster. Whatever this was . . . it had been written
only a few days before Flo's death. These were truly
her mother's last words. With trembling hands, she
continued, . . .

*Item I: I will and direct that item V of my said Last Will
and Testament be cancelled in its entirety.*

What was cancelled? She didn't remember what
item V was. She would have to go look at her copy of
the original will. Heart beating erratically, she continued running the fine lead over the page.

*Item II: I will and direct that the following shall be item
V of my Last Will and Testament.*

Savannah took a deep breath, wondering if she really wanted to know what it said. Had her mother
changed her mind about sequestering her daughters
under the same roof? Had she disowned them? No
matter how difficult it had been in the beginning, Savannah needed this communion with her sisters. Even
Caroline and Augusta seemed better off for it. She
didn't want to go back to D.C. She needed this year
with her sisters . . . the money itself didn't matter.

With a little trepidation, she continued. . . .

*I will and direct that the property bordered by
Secessionville Creek from the byroad to Fort Lamar
Road, and consisting of the original living quarters of*

Oyster Point Plantation, as well as the bordering marshlands, shall hereby be donated to the County of Charleston.

Mouth open, she continued scribbling down to the bottom of the page where her mother's strong signature appeared finally through the pencil shading.

Her breath caught as she realized what she was holding. Florence had changed her mind. She meant to hand the landmark over to the city. Augusta would be thrilled. Sadie would be ousted, although Flo had apparently added a generous stipend to make up for the loss of her home.

Why hadn't the new codicil turned up in the will?

Jesus, she might not ever have discovered this if she hadn't brought the typewriter down from the attic.

. . .

Savannah held the paper in her hands, staring at it.

Was this really what her mother had intended? If she handed this over to Daniel, a signed ghost of a document, would Sadie legally still own the land?

In the end, Savannah was obligated by her mother's wishes. She had to hand it over. *All you can do,* she told herself, *is start out with the best intentions. . . .*

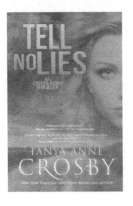

Augusta met every exploration of his hands with her own hungry inspection of his body. She had lived thirty-two years and never experienced this aching need to be filled so deeply by a man's body.

"Is this why you came to see me, Augusta?" he whispered, his voice raw against her cheek. He pressed his groin against her so she could feel the full evidence of his arousal, and her breath caught. She tasted the sweat from his upper lip and lapped it greedily from her lips. She was vaguely aware that one breast had escaped the confines of her T-shirt and her bare flesh was being caressed by cool night air. She wanted his mouth to warm her skin.

His eyes impaled her, those clear blue eyes that made her want to say anything to keep him right here in her arms. "Yes," she said with a shivery sigh, and reached up to nip his lip.

"You sure?"

Would a killer ask permission to make love to her? *She didn't think so.*

Get Tell No Lies

ACKNOWLEDGMENTS

With thanks to Michelle Boubel and William Tisdale. A very special thanks to the cities of Charleston, James Island, and Folly Beach for providing an endless well-spring of inspiration . . . along with a pardon for having taken slight liberties with the immediate history and landscape of Secessionville Creek. The area has its own very rich past and though I spent the majority of my life in Charleston, I stumbled upon that pinpoint on the map after a game of eeny meeny miny mo . . . or just maybe, if you believe in providence . . . it chose me.

ALSO BY TANYA ANNE CROSBY

DAUGHTERS OF AVALON

The King's Favorite

The Holly & the Ivy

A Winter's Rose

Fire Song

Lord of Shadows

THE PRINCE & THE IMPOSTOR

Seduced by a Prince

A Crown for a Lady

The Art of Kissing Beneath the Mistletoe

THE HIGHLAND BRIDES

The MacKinnon's Bride

Lyon's Gift

On Bended Knee

Lion Heart

Highland Song

MacKinnon's Hope

GUARDIANS OF THE STONE

Once Upon a Highland Legend

Highland Fire

Highland Steel

Highland Storm

Maiden of the Mist

ABOUT THE AUTHOR

Tanya Anne Crosby is the New York Times and USA Today bestselling author of thirty novels. She has been featured in magazines, such as People, Romantic Times and Publisher's Weekly, and her books have been translated into eight languages. Her first novel was published in 1992 by Avon Books, where Tanya was hailed as "one of Avon's fastest rising stars." Her fourth book was chosen to launch the company's Avon Romantic Treasure imprint.

Known for stories charged with emotion and humor and filled with flawed characters Tanya is an award-winning author, journalist, and editor, and her novels have garnered reader praise and glowing critical reviews. She and her writer husband split their time between Charleston, SC, where she was raised, and northern Michigan, where the couple make their home.

For more information
Website
Email
Newsletter

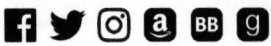

Lightning Source UK Ltd.
Milton Keynes UK
UKHW052343040521
383106UK00005BA/213